BEYOND *Love*

BARBARA J. DUELL

Love is always the answer

Barbara

ACKNOWLEDGMENTS

When stumbling, you remember those who reached out to help you stay upright.

The talented gals who make up the Scottsdale Society of Women Writers are among those who helped guide me, keeping me out of the muck.

I want to thank my editor, Samantha Gordon of Invisible Ink. Her insight and laughter helped me cross over the road avoiding pesky potholes I failed to see.

Special thanks to Cassie McCown of Gathering Leaves, who somehow found the time to proofread my book although her schedule was full.

Thank you, Tabatha and Glendon Haddix of Streetlight Graphics. Your patience and expertise helped transform this book from my whimsical thoughts into a reality.

There is no substitute for knowledge or the generosity to share. So many times during the last few months I actually thought I knew what I was doing, but I was wrong. I sincerely thank Joel Friedlander for guiding me away from the edge of the cliff.

DEDICATION

To Mom
She read every page,
and helped me get it right.

CHAPTER ONE

ICHAEL STUMBLED ON THE LOOSE gravel and almost fell. Regaining her balance, she ran on, toward downtown Sausalito and the lamppost across from the park, her finish line. Without breaking stride, she wiped the moisture from her face and guided unruly curls behind her ears. *One block to go.* She could see the corner now. *Keep running. Run. Only six more steps.* Stealing a peek at her watch, Michael grinned with smug delight. She'd done it!

Drenched in sweat, leg muscles screaming and lungs grasping for air, she pushed her sunglasses on top of her head and leaned against the lamppost, thankful for the breeze rolling in off the bay. Michael raised her face to the sun and savored its warmth, happier than she had been in years. She'd run the mile, from her cottage to the bay, in twelve minutes. A month ago, she could barely walk that distance without stopping to rest. But then a month ago, when her best friend Sarah Clark had bundled her up, checked her out of the hospital, and brought her here to recuperate and get her life back, she hadn't cared about running, hadn't care about anything, even getting out of bed. Like the poet said, life was sweet and God was good.

The sudden sound of screeching brakes jolted her out of her reverie. Her eyes locked on the wrenching scene in front of her. Before she realized what she was doing, Michael lunged for the young boy who had stepped off the curb in front of the speeding car, snatching the child by a handful of his shirt before stumbling back to the curb. Michael held him against her pounding heart and exhaled the backed-up air in her lungs.

"Lady, you're smushing me." The child's words were soft, muffled into her chest, as his hand patted her back. Wondering who was comforting whom, she relaxed her grip.

1

The driver yelled out his window. "Son of a bitch, lady, teach your kid to look out for cars!"

"Don't yell at me, you jerk. You were speeding and almost killed this boy. Slow down."

She looked down at the boy. "Are you okay?"

"Yeah, I think so. I didn't see the car. I guess I was thinking about something else."

"That was close, too close, but like the guy said, didn't your parents teach you to watch out for cars? Where are your parents?"

"I only have a dad, and he's at work. But see, well, I want to go to Los Angeles, but I don't know how. Do you know how to get to Los Angeles?"

"What?" His question caught her off guard. "Sure, I know, but why? Look, let's find a place to sit down and talk about this." Deciding the street corner was no place to confront his worried face and her still-racing heart, Michael took his hand and crossed the street.

She dropped onto the low stone wall at the entrance to the Plaza Vina del Mar, guarded by two massive stone elephants salvaged years ago from the 1915 San Francisco Panama Pacific Exposition. He sat beside her, his lips pursed, his eyebrows drawn.

She watched his nervous fingers twisting his baseball cap and was about to ask about his parents again when he stood up.

"See, well, do you know if the ferry is gonna come back soon? And can I catch a bus to Los Angeles? I mean, over there in San Francisco?"

Michael gazed at the boy, realizing for the first time how handsome he was. He pulled his tall, slim body up straight, but as a light breeze ruffled his blond hair, his blue eyes sought answers to his questions.

"I don't know... about the bus, I mean, but I'm sure we can find out. You aren't thinking of traveling alone. Or are you?"

"My dad's at work, so I'm gonna spend the day with my grandma. She lives in Los Angeles. Do you know how much it costs to go to Los Angeles?"

As his fidgety hands continued to twist his cap, Michael realized he wasn't as old as she had first thought, much too young to be wandering around town by himself, let alone trying to catch a bus to L.A. Something was wrong here, but as a buzzer went off inside her head, telling her not to get involved, another alarm, a mechanism ingrained in all mothers, told Michael she could not let this boy get on any boat or bus. *Just find out where he lives and get in touch with the father*, she told herself. It should be easy enough to do, except she didn't have any money with her to use a pay phone.

"I don't think the ferry will be back for a while. I was just about to go home and have some lunch. Are you hungry? It's a long way to Los Angeles, and I don't think they serve lunch on the bus. My name is Michael. What's yours?"

"David Marc Hampton and I'm eight years old," he said proudly. "Do you think it will cost more than three dollars and eighty-five cents to go to Los Angeles?"

He was so serious, dead-set on getting to L. A. She stood and held out her hand, not surprised when his fingers locked around hers. "Let's have some lunch, and we can call about the bus." They crossed the street and started up the steps leading to the short cut to Michael's cottage.

"Michael sure is a funny name for a girl," he said.

"I know. People tell me that all the time, but that's my name." She couldn't help but smile at him, and he returned her smile with a look of complete trust. It frightened Michael to think how innocent he was, reinforcing the fact that he had no business wandering around town alone. They climbed the narrow path that curved its way to a stand of tall pines and twisted oaks that protected the cottage from the bay, and even though they walked single-file, he held her outstretched hand firmly.

"Wow! What a great tree!" David stopped on the path, pulling her to a halt as his eyes traveled to the top of the giant oak. "Tommy Walker says you're really lucky if you ever find the perfect one for a tree house. I always wanted a tree house, a place to keep all your stuff and a secret password so only special people can come in."

David continued to stare up into the canopy of branches, a palette of spring-colored leaves dancing in the breeze that drifted up from the bay. His finger rose to his lips, silently telling her to be quiet as he pointed to a branch half way up the center of the tree. Michael tried to focus where he pointed as he held his breath and squeezed her arm, directing her gaze to a couple of squirrels looking down at them. Time seemed suspended until the little gray animals scurried out of sight. David's smile spread ear to ear. "Wow," he whispered again, his eyes still glued to the tree.

"You know it's real important to protect the animals," David said as he continued to stare at the top of the tree. "Tommy Walker says you gotta honor Mother Nature. Most grownups don't do that, you know. That's why this earth is such a mess. But this is 1996, and we have to be concerned. Tommy Walker says it will probably have to be our generation that cleans things up."

"Who's Tommy Walker?"

"He's my friend Joey's cousin. Tommy is older than me and Joey, and he knows everything."

"Come on, we were going to have lunch, remember?" David grabbed her hand again and followed her into the house.

Shaded by the large trees, the cottage was dark and cool. Michael turned on the lights in the kitchen. "You can wash up in the sink. Would you like some milk?"

"Sure."

She pulled a carton of milk and a plate of roast beef, cheese, and the mayo out of the fridge and reached for the fresh sourdough bread. She filled a glass with milk. He emptied it in two gulps and then asked for more.

David pulled a stool close to the counter. "When you call, don't forget to ask about how much it costs to take the bus." He twirled the glass in his hands. "I was gonna get some more money, but Allen was busy, and Mary said my dad would give me some when he got home, but I decided to go today. See, today was good 'cause I didn't have to go to school. I just hope I got enough money."

She placed his sandwich in front of him and pondered who Allen and Mary might be. Michael also wondered if David's father had any idea his son was trying to skip town. "Why do you want to go to Los Angeles? Have you been there before?"

"Yeah, a couple of times, when I was little; my grandmother lives there. She usually comes to see us, but Tommy Walker says that grandmas want to have their grandkids visit them. They let you do lots of neat things, and they hug you all the time. So I decided I'd surprise her and go to her house."

"Does your father know you planned to do this, go to Los Angeles today?"

"Well, see, he's really busy, and I don't want to bother him. I thought if I went to see my grandma, maybe she would let me stay with her for a while and then my dad wouldn't feel so bad 'cause he doesn't have time to do things with me. He gets home real late sometimes. Tommy Walker says parents just don't have time to play with their kids. But grandmas do, so that's why I decided to go."

Michael put a plate of cookies in front of David. "Finish your lunch. I'll call about the bus." She left the kitchen and slumped against the wall in the hall, quickly changing her mind. God was not good. How could he let this child think he could get on a bus and go visit his grandma who lived hundreds of miles away? Michael took a deep breath, knowing with a pulse-pounding certainty that the past two years of pain and denial were there, just below the surface, waiting to reappear and take control. She had worked so hard to come to grips with her shattered life and move on. She simply wasn't strong enough to take on someone else's troubles. "Just stay calm. Just call the father. This is not your problem," she kept repeating as she flipped through the phone book.

She found two families named Hampton and dialed the numbers, asking if they knew a boy named David. The first said no. Michael dialed the next number. It rang three times. She was about to hang up when she finally heard, "Hello, Hampton residence."

"Yes, I'm calling to see if you know a boy named David Hampton?" Michael heard a sudden intake of breath. "Hello, did you hear me? Do you know a child named—?"

"Yes, yes I heard you. Have you seen him? Who is this? Have you seen David?"

"My name is Mrs. McCall. Is Mr. Hampton there?"

"Dr. Hampton isn't here. He is at the hospital. I didn't get your name. Where is David?"

"McCall, my name is Mrs. McCall. May I have the doctor's phone number at the hospital? I need to talk to him. David is with me; he's okay. He's eating lunch right now and doesn't know I'm calling."

"Thank God he is all right. He left early this morning, and I've looked everywhere. Tell me where you live and I'll come get him."

The voice on the other end of the line seemed on the verge of hysteria. Michael again asked for the doctor's number at the hospital. So David's father was a doctor, probably one of those guys who never had any time for his family, but where was his mother? David had told her he only had a dad.

"Please, I don't want to disturb the doctor with this. Just tell me where you live and I'll come get him."

Michael couldn't believe what she just heard. "Who am I talking to? Is this Mary?" Again, she heard the intake of breath.

"How do you know my name?"

"David told me. Are you telling me you've been looking for David all day and you haven't told his father that the boy was gone? Lady, do you have any idea how serious this is? I don't think you do, but I am not going to let you just come and get him. You call Dr. Hampton, right now. You tell him to call me, and I will tell him where to come and get his son. Mary? Did you hear me?"

Michael waited for Mary to answer, expecting her to refuse. "Yes, yes, I heard you."

"Good. Now write down my number. You call Dr. Hampton and tell him I will be waiting for his call."

Why did she do that? *Why didn't I just tell Mary where I live?* But as she walked into the kitchen, Michael knew she had done the right thing. David was almost asleep, his head resting on his arms next to the empty milk carton printed with the face of a runaway child. Michael lifted David to his feet. "Come on, David. Take a short rest and let your lunch settle, and then we'll talk some more."

She guided him to the bedroom and onto the bed. She took off his shoes and pulled a coverlet over him and then went into the closet and shut the door. She took off her running shoes and her shirt and shorts, replacing them with jeans and a sweater. She slipped out of the bedroom and went into the small living room to wait for the call from doctor dad. She did not wait long. Michael picked up the receiver on the first ring.

"Mrs. McCall, please. This is Dr. Richard Hampton." His voice was cold and precise.

6

"This is Mrs. McCall."

"I've just been told you have my son. Just what in the hell is going on here? Who are you and why is David with you?"

"Don't you yell at me, Dr. Hampton. Your first question might be to ask if David is all right."

"What do you mean? Is David hurt?"

"No, David is fine. He's—"

"What's your game, lady? How did you get your hands on my son?"

Michael slammed down the phone, her hand shaking so badly she missed and hit the table as she threw the receiver back into place. He was just what she had pictured, a rude, neglectful father, with a short fuse. The phone rang again. She let it ring three times before picking up the receiver.

"Did you hang up on me?"

"You're damn right I did, and if you don't stop yelling at me, I'll hang up again." She took a deep breath and then continued. "Your son is okay. He's sleeping now. Did you know he planned to go to Los Angeles today, and that his itinerary included catching the ferry to San Francisco and then a bus to Los Angeles? By himself?"

Again, she didn't wait for an answer. "But he needed help. He walked to Sausalito to save money, but then he wandered around town most of the morning because he didn't know what to do next. That was before he almost got hit by a car, before he finally got up enough courage to ask me for directions to Los Angeles. Do you understand what I just said? David was leaving town, to spend the day at his grandma's house, although he doesn't have the slightest idea where she lives, only someplace in L.A., and that grandmas like to have their grandkids visit, that they love to hug them. Those are your son's exact words, Doctor." Michael stopped talking and waited for his response, but there wasn't one, and his silence was more unnerving than the shouting as she waited for him to say something, anything.

Dr. Hampton tried to comprehend what she was saying about David running away. He didn't understand. This was crazy. Why would he want to do something like that? Everything was fine this morning. At least he'd thought so.

He was using the phone in the hall outside the OR, and it was impossible to hear. He shouted into the phone and said, "Please don't hang up on me. I am not shouting at you. I just can't hear very well."

"I'm not going to hang up. I just need you to come get your son."

After giving him her address, she replaced the receiver, gently this time. Michael went into the bedroom and gazed at the sleeping child. He had turned onto his side and pulled the coverlet around his shoulders, safely tucked away as the sun hid behind rolling clouds that promised rain.

Twenty minutes later, Michael heard the car pull into the drive. She waited for a pounding on the door, but the knock was light. Had she actually thought he would break down the door and demand his son?

Michael opened the door, again surprised. She had expected a larger image of David, but Dr. Richard Hampton was as dark as David was fair, tall and distinguished, well-dressed but not overdone, just stiff and starched as if he had been forty-something since birth. His hand rested midair, ready to knock again, his broad shoulders square, feet slightly apart. She couldn't help but stare at his strong chin, full mouth, now tight and grim, and piercing eyes the color of midnight. Michael had thought David handsome, but his father's features were almost perfect.

The hair on the back of her neck stood up as his eyes held hers for an instant. He searched her face, as though reaching for her thoughts, then moved on, down to her bare feet, before lifting his eyes to study her again with an accusing look, a look she recognized as a declaration of war.

Michael stood back and lifted her chin, a subtle invitation for him to come in. It had started to rain, and as she closed the door, the room came alive with shadows, quiet spectators that circled around them as they continued their silence. She turned on the light, filling the room with a glow that removed the shadows but not the tension.

His voice was steady, uncompromising yet calm. "Where is my son?"

Michael pointed to the bedroom door. "He's still asleep. Dr. Hampton, you probably think this is none of my business, but when I think of David trying to do this again—"

His hawk-like eyes narrowed, cutting her off. His voice was soft, yet held an undertone just short of polite dismissal. "You're right, Mrs.

McCall. This is none of your business. Now, if you will show me where you have my son, I'd like to take David home."

"Of course," she said, surprised although pleased at how nonchalant she sounded. *Bastard*, she said to herself. She was furious. What right did he have to talk to her like that? Her only concern was for the boy.

She opened the bedroom door, walked to the table by the side of the bed and turned on the lamp. Dr. Hampton followed, and as the light outlined his son, the change in his expression astonished Michael. His dark eyes softened, and a tender smile replaced the grim set of his mouth as he gently gathered the sleeping boy into his arms. Holding his son close to his chest, the doctor buried his head in the hollow of David's neck.

Feeling like an intruder, Michael left the room and realized she had made a mistake. The doctor was not what she had first thought. She had assumed his relationship with his son was anything but strong and had placed all the blame on the father. Rather than seeking a rational explanation, she had simply passed judgment on a man she knew nothing about, but the scene she had just witnessed proved her wrong.

Michael sat on the sofa and wondered again why she had not let Mary come and get the boy. Why had she gotten involved in something that was clearly not her concern?

David and his father talked about ten minutes, their voices low, words muffled, and then they came into the living room.

"David, thank Mrs. McCall for helping you."

David looked up at his father and smiled, his blue eyes sparkling with love and admiration. Walking over to Michael, he said, "Thanks for helping me and for lunch. My dad says we're gonna go to Los Angeles to see Grandma together. And you know what? Maybe you could come to my house for lunch. What do you think?"

Michael looked over the boy's head to his father, who offered no indication of what he thought of his son's invitation. Dr. Hampton just stood there watching her intently, his face a blank, although she believed she saw a faint smile beginning to form over his closed lips.

"We'll see. You take care of yourself, okay?" She dropped to her knee, pulling his shirt together at the collar, softly patting his chest. Running her fingers through his hair, Michael looked up at the father.

9

"David, let me give you my phone number, and if you want, you can call me sometime. Any time," she added.

She went to her antique desk, wrote her name and number on a piece of paper, and handed it to David, who had moved to her side. He put the paper in his jeans and threw his arms around her waist and hugged her tightly.

"Come on, David, it's time to go." Dr. Hampton held his hand out to the boy.

The rain had stopped. Michael waved good-bye to David as his father helped him into the car. She turned to go inside when the doctor called her name. He moved from the side of the car to the porch and stood beside her.

"Mrs. McCall, I haven't gotten the whole story yet, but from what David has told me, I owe you an apology. Actually, I owe you more than that. He has never done anything like this, ever. I'm just starting to realize what could have happened to him if he'd asked some nutcase for help instead of you."

He ran his hand through dark, wavy hair, that half-smile again playing at the corner of his mouth. However, his eyes were serious when he said, "I love my son, Mrs. McCall, and I am truly thankful he met someone like you."

Before Michael could reply, Richard got into his car and drove off.

CHAPTER TWO

MICHAEL RAN FROM THE SHOWER, hopping on one foot as she clutched her toe, and fell across the bed, her wet hair and body soaking the antique quilt as she reached for the ringing phone.

"Mrs. McCall, please."

"Yes, this is Mrs. McCall."

"One, moment."

Michael heard the click and realized she'd cut her toe on the shower door just to be put on hold. "Of all the rude, dim-witted..." She slammed the receiver back in place, muttering aloud as she was prone to do, and inspected her throbbing toe. *It's a good thing I'm going home,* she thought, rolling off the bed, *before I break every phone in the house.*

She stepped back under the water, and the phone rang again. Her toe still throbbing, Michael took her time, wrapping a dry towel around her long curly hair before picking up the phone.

"Do you hang up on everyone, or just me?"

"I beg your pardon. Who is this?"

"Richard Hampton, David's father. I asked if you always hang up when people call you."

Michael stared into the receiver, stunned.

"Mrs. McCall? Are you there?"

"Yes, Dr. Hampton, I'm here. What do you want? Is David all right?"

"Yes, David's fine. Actually, that's why I'm calling. I need to discuss something with you, and I wondered if you're available for lunch?"

"I don't think so. No, I mean, I'm very busy, and I don't think I—"

"Mrs. McCall, I want to apologize for the way I acted yesterday. There was no excuse for my behavior."

11

"Dr. Hampton, please, I don't—"

"You're not making this easy, Mrs. McCall. I'm trying to apologize."

"Dr. Hampton, I accept your apology, even though it's not necessary. It was a natural reaction; let's leave it at that. Thank you for calling. I appreciate the gesture, I certainly do, but as I said—"

"Mrs. McCall, please hear me out. I said David was okay, but something has come up. I really do need to talk to you and not over the telephone. Would you consider giving me thirty minutes of your time? Please."

The carpet felt like soggy grass, her toe hurt, and it didn't look like the good doctor was going to take no for an answer. "Thirty minutes, Dr. Hampton, I will meet you for thirty minutes. Where shall we meet?"

"Would you mind coming to the hospital? We could meet in the cafeteria, say in about an hour?"

One hour? It would take her that long to dry her hair. "I don't think so. Not in one hour. No, I don't believe—"

"You should have plenty of time to get here. Come to the doctors' parking lot; it will be quicker if you park there. I'll call right now and tell the guard to let you in. The cafeteria is on the second floor. See you at the door. Bye."

For the third time, Michael stepped into the shower. *Why didn't I just say no?* She had other things to do. She had to pack. She had to call Sarah. There was no way she could get dressed and be in San Rio on time. Besides, even if he had a problem with David, what did that have to do with her? Well, she would do her best, and what did it matter how she looked? This was not a date; it was about David.

San Rio was a small town nestled between the Muir Woods and Richardson Bay. With its half-timbered shops and restaurants, it looked more like a quaint European village than home to the San Rio Medical Center. In 1930, a group of doctors bought the property for pennies on the dollar from a millionaire who had lost his fortune during the 1929 crash. They built a small sanitarium and health spa. Over the years, it had grown into the renowned facility it was today.

The guard at the gate gave her a smile and directions to a parking spot. She followed the signs and scents to the cafeteria, surprised, and more than a bit annoyed, to realize he was not there to meet her. Nor was he in the dining room. Michael glanced up and down the corridor, wondering if she would even recognize him from all the other doctors in white coats. Of course she would. He was tall, with a straight back and an arrogant attitude, thick dark hair, and deep-set eyes. She had seen those eyes filled with silent rage, but when he'd looked at his son, his face had changed. She was sure she had seen another change, a slight glimmer of mischief, when David had invited her to lunch.

Michael moved out of the doorway, brushing a wayward curl off her shoulder, wishing she had tied back her hair. "When I get home, I'm cutting it short," she muttered, loud enough to get a strange look from an older man with a cane. She stared back and then turned away, feeling foolish.

One level below, Richard stripped off his surgical gloves and dropped them on the tray next to the operating table. His mask and gown came off as he rushed out of the OR and headed for his locker in the doctors' lounge. Reaching for his hairbrush, he checked his watch. Damn, he was late. He had asked her to meet him in an hour, thinking he'd have plenty of time to finish in the OR and be waiting for her. Richard quickly brushed his hair, pulled on his white jacket, and headed for the stairs to the second floor.

He saw her as soon as he stepped through the door, but rather than hurrying to her, he stopped, just out of her sight. When she'd opened the door yesterday afternoon, he had looked into deep green eyes of a woman dressed in jeans and a baggy sweater with a mass of curls held back with a ribbon. Today, in the brightly lit corridor, she was exquisite. Dark auburn hair, kissed red and gold by the sun, danced around her shoulders. As if sensing him watching her, she raised her hand to push unruly curls behind her ear. He watched as her hand moved slowly down her side. Past full breasts that pushed against a white blouse, over a small waist, to the short denim skirt, smoothing imaginary wrinkles. His gaze took in slender tanned legs and a foot that tapped out a warning signal. She reminded him of a teapot about to boil over. Still, he held back, gazing like a schoolboy at those incredible eyes that dominated a delicate oval face, a dainty nose, and just enough lipstick to define a pouting mouth.

His lips curved unconsciously into a smile. What a spitfire! But it wasn't only her spunk that had made him call her. It was the compassion he had seen yesterday when she'd said good-bye to David, the way she'd bundled him up as if sending him out into a cruel, stormy world, like a mother lion... guarding her cub. David had talked about her most of the night, begging Richard to let him see her again. *Will she agree to my idea?* No way to know until he asked her, but the tensing of her jaw, which clearly reflected her frustration at having to wait for him, made Richard reach into his pocket for his glasses. Maybe she wouldn't hit a guy wearing glasses.

Michael checked her watch for the third time in as many minutes. *You don't suppose he's going to stand me up?*

Richard reached out and tapped her shoulder, and she quickly spun around. "I was just leaving," she said.

"I gathered as much." He smiled. Knowing he shouldn't, but unable to stop himself, Richard said, "You don't have any more patience in person than you have on the phone, do you?" His hand was still on her shoulder, and he felt her body tense and start to pull away. "I'm sorry. I shouldn't have said that."

"Then why did you? Never mind, it actually doesn't matter because I have better things to do than wait—"

Richard let go of her shoulder and held his hands in front of him, easing back from the sarcasm that carried her words across the small space separating them. "Please, Mrs. McCall, how about a truce?"

He didn't give her a chance to respond, just took her hand and walked through the double doors and toward the serving line. Still holding her hand, he picked up a tray and pulled her behind him.

Michael didn't know whether to laugh or stay mad, let alone how to recover possession of her hand. He had insulted her and then thought he could just say he was sorry and buy her lunch. Well, she didn't want any lunch, and she would tell him so, but he had already loaded the tray full of food and was paying the bill.

Richard pointed to a table on the patio. Yellow daffodils and purple crocuses danced in hanging pots, and a light breeze spread their fragrance as it circled its way across the veranda. He deposited her in a chair and sat across from her.

Michael picked up her fork then put it down again. "Dr. Hampton, you said you needed to talk to me about David. You said it was important and—"

"Why don't you eat your lunch? We can talk after we've finished."

"Must you always interrupt me? Do you know how rude that is?"

Richard stopped eating and patted his lips with his napkin; his eyes locked on hers as he lowered it to his lap. "I'm sorry, Mrs. McCall, I didn't mean to be rude. Look, let's start over and maybe we can be a little less formal. Do your friends call you Mikie?"

"Do your friends call you Dickie?"

"Do you always answer a question with a question?"

"Do you?"

"Okay, I give up, but why Michael? Did your father want a son?"

It was time to go. This conversation was going nowhere, and it was none of his business what her father had wanted. She stood and reached for her purse. "I have to go. I've—"

He jumped up, interrupting her again. "Okay, I'll get right to the point. Just sit, please?"

She lifted her chin, meeting his steady gaze straight on. Her posture was stiff and proud, but her mind was a mess, submerged in a murky bog where suddenly all decisions and actions seemed impossible.

"Please, Mrs. McCall, sit down and give me five minutes, just five minutes."

She sat.

"I would like to employ you as a companion for David."

Michael stared across the table, thrown off by his words. What made him think she wanted a job? Besides, she was leaving for home at the end of the week and then back to work at the university in three months. What was he thinking? *I'm not a baby sitter; I'm a college professor.* She taught history to young adults, not the three R's to a third-grader. No, his request was impossible. She needed to think about her own life. She was going home, back to a world that had crumbled around her a month ago, a crash she had fought off for two years.

"I'm sorry, Dr. Hampton, but you have the wrong person. I mean a blind man could see that David needs someone to be his friend, but I'm not that someone. I have a job, and I'm leaving Sausalito at the end of the week."

"I'm prepared to pay you an excellent salary, a lot more than you earn teaching."

Michael leaned toward him. "You're not listening to me. I've made my plans. I have commitments. Besides, how could you even consider turning your child over to a stranger? Yesterday you believed I had kidnapped him or something worse. And how do you know I'm a teacher?"

"I know all I need to know about you. I had you checked out."

"You did what?" Her voice was low, fraught with disbelief and violation. "What do you mean you checked me out? What right did you have to do that?" Shock, then anger lit up her green eyes, but he continued. "I gathered information from people who know you, people we both know, like the ones who own the house where you're staying."

"You spoke to Sarah?"

"Mrs. McCall, listen to me."

"I don't believe you. Sarah Clark is my best friend. She wouldn't tell you anything without asking me first. You really win a prize for this one. Not only are you rude but now I know you're a first-class liar."

Michael grabbed her purse and jumped to her feet, but before she could walk away, he was in front of her, his hands on her shoulders, forcing her to look at him. Richard turned and guided her to the railing at the far side of the patio. She was trembling. She wanted to leave and never set eyes on this man again. Michael felt him behind her, his warmth, his strong hands. Why did she just stand there? Why didn't she leave? Michael reached for the railing and pulled away from him.

"Okay, I didn't actually speak to Sarah and Tom Clark. My attorney is Marc Bosworth, and he knew... Well, this gets a bit complicated. You see, Marc's wife Amy is Tom's sister, so most of the information came from them." *Damn, I'm blowing it.*

Richard felt her pull away, but her delicate scent, like soap and sunshine, quickened his pulse. "I believe the information I got from Mark and Amy was enough, and I'm sure Sarah would have called you if

16

I'd actually spoken to her about you. I don't doubt she is extremely loyal. Mrs. McCall, there is nothing dishonorable about what I've offered you. My son needs someone, a special someone, and I will do anything to make him happy. He likes you, and I think, especially after yesterday, that you're the one for the job."

Michael stood remarkably still, listening; his words close to her ear. His voice was soft and coaxing, filled with reason.

"I can't. No, there's—"

A voice came over the loud speaker, calling Richard's name. "Please don't say no," he pleaded. He stepped back. "I have to go. Please, consider what I've said. Think about David. That's all I ask."

She didn't turn around, but she knew, just like the last time, before she could think of a reply, he was gone.

CHAPTER THREE

MICHAEL FOUND HER WAY BACK to her car, but instead of turning toward Sausalito, she took Highway 1. When she reached the entrance to Mt. Tamalpais State Park, she headed toward the ocean. Two hours later, she turned around and drove back to the cottage. Michael didn't remember much of the drive, only the words that had passed between Dr. Hampton and her this afternoon, like a tape—playing it through, then rewinding it and playing it again.

Now, parked in her driveway, Michael drew a deep breath. She was past the point of anger, beyond the feelings of hostility that had surged through her when he told her he had checked her out; that he would do anything to get what he wanted. Well, he could do whatever he pleased, but Michael would not let him ruin in a few hours what she had worked so hard to achieve. The man was a fool if he thought he could change her mind. She was going home, and that was the end of it. After another deep breath, she felt better. No, she didn't.

Her mind raced, battered by emotions that refused to let her forget the way her pulse had bolted when he touched her, the sudden warm sensation that had surged through her body. She was being silly. Dr. Hampton was just the first man to touch her since her husband had died. It was only natural that his touch would make her feel uncomfortable. Why am I making such a big deal of all this? And why should I wait? She would start packing tonight and go home tomorrow, rather than the end of the week.

The snug little cottage welcomed her like an old friend, easing the despair that had accompanied her home. When Sarah married Tom, she moved across the bay, away from the home where she'd grown up, but the idea of selling the old place was out of the question. She leased out the main house, but kept the caretaker's cottage for times when she needed to get away from the city. Although small, the cottage was a refuge, a place of peace. The large bay window in the living room looked out toward the woods, and the gravel path that meandered through the pines, linking it to the main house.

Sarah had filled the cottage with antiques found in the attic, and the combination of oak furniture and vintage wallpaper, tile floors, and leaded glass windows made it a place Michael hated to leave.

It was dark by the time she finished packing. Michael stripped off her clothes and pulled on a red sweater and white slacks. She stood on her toes and checked the top shelf of the closet one last time, wishing for the umpteenth time that she were taller. Although small and slim, she was strong, tightly muscled from years of cycling and swimming. But she hated snivelers, and it was time she started counting her blessings. She had a terrific job, good health, and people who loved her. What more could she want?

As Michael walked into the kitchen, the clock on the mantle struck seven. She reached for a bottle of wine she'd been saving for a special occasion. *Well, no better time than now,* she told herself, pulling the cork from the bottle and filling a crystal glass to the top. On her way to the sofa, she turned on the stereo. The soft music and rich wine mingled together, transporting her into a long overdue state of peace.

She heard the knock at the door as she returned from refilling her glass. Bringing the bottle with her this time, she balanced it under her arm as she opened the door. "Why I am not surprised?" she said, staring at him. "Would it do me any good to tell you to go away?"

Richard Hampton stood before her with an apologetic look on his face and slowly shook his head.

"No? I didn't think so. Well, just don't stand there; come in." Michael walked back into the room and stood by the fireplace as the doctor's presence filled the small space. His powerful, well-muscled body moved with an easy stride, giving off a powerful air of self-confidence. He wore his dark wavy hair brushed back, and although not shaggy, he looked as if he had missed his last haircut by a week or so. His mouth was closed, but a hint of a smile revealed a small dimple on his right cheek. He wore a navy sport coat and gray slacks, and the top button of his white shirt was undone, his tie loosened. He took off his glasses and unconsciously twirled them in his hands as he waited for her to say something.

Feeling extremely relaxed and surprisingly hospitable, she held the bottle toward him and asked, "Would you like a glass of wine?"

"No thanks, I'm still on call. I'm sorry—" He stopped speaking, and a half smile covered his face. He replaced his glasses. "I actually have lost count. Was that the sixth or seventh time I've said I'm sorry? What I meant to say is, well, I should have called first, but I had some time to kill, and I thought we might talk."

Michael turned and placed the bottle on the mantel. The mirror over the fireplace reflected his image, making her acutely aware of how tired he looked. The shadow of his beard suggested many hours had passed since he'd started his day. His face looked drawn; a mixture of weariness and strain filled his eyes.

"Dr. Hampton, please sit down. Would you like a cup of coffee or maybe something to eat?"

He hesitated, but only a moment. "I would love a cup of coffee if it's not too much trouble."

"Nothing to eat, you're sure?"

"No, coffee will be fine."

As she moved toward the kitchen, Richard sank into the large chair by the window. Only minutes passed before Michael returned to the living room with the coffee and found Richard with his glasses in his hand, his eyes closed, and his long legs stretched out in front of him, fast asleep. She quietly set the tray on the oak table and then curled up on the sofa across from him as the sounds of soft music and the ticking of the old clock filled the room.

"How long have I been asleep?"

His voice made her jump. He hadn't moved a muscle nor opened his eyes.

"Only about ten minutes."

Richard pulled himself up into the chair. He opened his eyes and folded his glasses, slipping them into the pocket of his sport coat. "Do I dare say I'm sorry?"

"No, it doesn't take a college professor to see you're on the short side of empty. Why don't you go home and go to bed?"

Richard stood and stretched the kinks out of his body. "I can't, but does that offer of coffee still stand?"

"It's probably cold. I'll make some more." Before she could move, Richard picked up the tray and walked toward the kitchen with her following behind. He set the tray by the sink and reached for the same stool David had used the day before.

Michael dumped the cold coffee down the drain and drew water for the espresso machine. "I never thought to ask if you liked it strong."

The rich aroma of coffee quickly filled the air. "Sure, that's fine. Have you had a chance to think about what we discussed this afternoon? Maybe changed your mind?" His voice was calm, and his steady gaze never left her face. She adding a twist of lemon peel to her cup, busy work, anything to avoid his eyes, and placed the cups filled with espresso on the counter between them.

"You don't give up, do you? What makes you think I'm going to change my mind? I gave you my answer this afternoon." Her eyes finally locked with his, and she knew this would be their biggest battle yet. If she turned away and walked back into the living room right now, without any more words, she might win this scrimmage, but she couldn't. Michael couldn't force her eyes to leave his face. His smile brought an instant softening to his features, and that smile was as intimate as a gentle kiss.

Richard took a deep sip of his coffee, and his soothing voice probed further. "I know you said you were going back to your old job, but what if you consider my offer for, let's say, six months. I mean, if for some reason it doesn't work out, you could still go back to the university at midterm. I have never seen David like this. He cannot stop talking about you. He has called me at least six times since he got home from school today."

"I find it hard to believe that David has talked about me. He was only with me a short time and part of that time he was asleep."

"Well, I don't know what you talked about, but you really made an impression on him. You know, Mrs. McCall, this is the second time you've implied that I lie. No, the last time you didn't imply, you called me a liar. I do not lie. I want you to know that. Where David is concerned, I might be tempted, but only tempted."

"I stand corrected, Dr. Hampton. Seems like it's my turn to apologize, and I do if I've spoken out of turn."

From the living room came the sound of the clock, the constant ticking invading the silence that enveloped the kitchen. Although she had no thoughts of changing her mind, Michael was curious to know what he had found out about her. "Just for the record, how can you be so sure you can trust me? How could your attorney and his wife possibly know that much about me? I only met them once, at Sarah and Tom's wedding."

"I felt it was enough. I know you teach at a private university and that your late husband also taught there." Richard saw her wince when he mentioned her husband and knew he should stop, but she had opened the door. Knowing this was probably the last chance he would have, he continued. "I know your husband and young son were killed in a car accident. They said you'd pushed yourself at work for the last two years, teaching extra classes, but eventually it all caught up with you and you ended up in the hospital. Then you came here."

Michael was sorry she'd asked because now she felt like a spectator, watching her past race by. She wanted to run, simply disappear. But he had taken hold of her hands and held them tightly. She could not look at him, just stared down as his thumbs gently rubbed the back of her hands.

Richard leaned forward and lowered his voice. "I know you were orphaned when you were about fifteen and that you have no other relatives. Yesterday you made me realize what a lousy father I've been. I need help. Maybe it was wrong, coming here tonight, hoping to change your mind, but I'm not sorry I came. Anna has taken care of David since he was born, and she means well, but there's too much of an age difference. And it's not just age; it's more than that, like a significant gap that gets bigger every day. David has such high hopes of someday having a family like most of the kids at his school. Well, I can't give him that, at least not now. But if you changed your mind and accepted my offer, it would be a start."

Michael did not want to run anymore. She didn't even feel the violation she'd felt earlier today. She felt a little bleak; no one enjoys having their life spread out like yesterday's picnic. But he had spoken the truth; she had no one. She had a hundred friends, a few close ones, but no family. Michael had lived with that fact after the accident because she wanted it that way. She didn't want anyone close to her while she hid from her grief, anyone who might slip and remind her that she still had to come to terms with the rest of her life.

Slowly, Michael pulled her hands from his and walked out the back door. She left the porch and moved into the yard to a place where you could see the bay. The moon rode high, spreading its light on the water like an abstract painter moves colors on a canvas. The damp evening breeze swirled about her head with the scent of the pines, lifting her dark curls into soft disarray. He came up behind her, and although he didn't touch her, she felt his presence.

"Is that the famous tree?"

She turned at his words and found him looking up at the old oak. "That's the one."

"I can see why he was so impressed. It's a fine tree. Last night we went out into our yard looking for a suitable one for a tree house. We have many trees, yet nothing like this. But David wants more than a tree house; he wants you. He told me to be tough and to say please."

Michael knew he was smiling, even though she couldn't see his face.

"If I agree to what you've asked, we would have to have a very clear understanding about my duties, and I will only consider a commitment for six months as you suggested. Do you agree?"

Richard had been smiling, but now he beamed. "Anything, I'll agree to anything," he exclaimed. He felt like a thousand pounds had fallen off his shoulders, and he almost reached out and hugged her when she said she would come, but he didn't. He just followed her to the chairs on the patio, feeling decidedly lighthearted after winning her over.

"David talked about Mary and Allen, and now you've mentioned Anna. How many people work for you?"

Relieved to have the issue settled, Richard answered her question with rapid dialogue. Mary Barnes was an employee, his housekeeper for about two years now, but Allen Dean had lived with them for as long as Richard could remember. Back in the fifties, he'd come home with Richard's father from Korea and had never left. He was like a second father. Anna Kolle had taken care of David since he was two days old. She was a RN, who had worked at the hospital where David was born. When Richard offered her the job of caring for his baby son, she moved into the Hampton house the day they brought the baby home. But after all these years, Anna was getting married. She was fifty-five years old and head over heels in love for the first time in her life. The wedding date was in a few weeks.

"Anna started looking for her replacement months ago, but not one of the applicants seemed to be what she was looking for."

Michael asked Richard when he wanted her to start and almost fell off her chair when he said tomorrow would be fine. "That's out of the question. I can't possibly start tomorrow. I have a million things to take care of before I can take on a new position."

"What do you have to do that can't be done after you move in with us? David is still in school for another week and—"

This time Michael interrupted. "What do you mean, move in with you? I am not moving in with you. I'll come each day and—"

"McCall, that's ridiculous. You have to live at the house. You must know by now what crazy hours I work. I need you there. I mean, I cannot simply tell David to hold tight if something happens until someone can get back to him. What I'm trying to do here is to emulate a family, even if it is of my own design. Just pack what you need for now. David wants to come and get you, so we'll be here a little after three o'clock tomorrow."

Michael started to tell Richard his demand was unreasonable when his beeper went off and he asked if he could use the phone. She showed him to the phone in the kitchen. Using her own version of sign language, Michael informed him the last issue was far from settled. She waited for him to get off the phone so she could tell him what an absurd idea it was for her to move to his house, but she didn't get the chance.

"I have to go. I have an emergency. Thanks for the coffee."

"Dr. Hampton, we haven't talked about what this job involves. I need guidelines; what you expect of me." Michael followed Richard into the living room, talking to his back.

"Don't worry, we'll work it out. I really have to go." He was gone, well, almost. The door closed, then flew open again as Richard leaned in, holding on to the door handle to keep his balance. "Michael McCall, I hope you know you have made one little boy extremely happy. Thank you, thank you very much."

He was gone again, into his car and down the drive. She went through the house turning out the lights, and then sat in the dark, sipping her wine and thinking about what she'd just done. The only reason she'd accepted his offer was David. What would have happened if she'd died in the accident instead of her husband and son? Ryan would be where Richard was now, in desperate need of someone to love and care for his child, her baby. She pulled her long legs up to her chest and wrapped her arms around them, slowly rocking back and forth, fighting her tears. She was not going to cry. She was past that. It would be okay; everything would work out okay. And if it didn't, well, she could stick it out for six months and go back to the university at midterm. First thing tomorrow morning she would call Dan. She didn't want to leave him hanging. When she had talked to him last week, he had not hesitated when she asked if she still had a job. Dan McClaren was her boss but also a dear friend. If she called him right away, he would still have three months to find a replacement for her position. She knew it would be okay.

Michael rubbed the back of her neck. As her hand moved over her tight muscles, she realized how exhausted she was. It had been a hectic day, and she suddenly longed for her soft bed, but fifteen minutes later, she was still wide awake. Her mind wandered to Richard, who she had been trying to avoid thinking of since he left. He was David's father, she reasoned. She couldn't take one without the other. Michael had not thought it possible to talk to Richard without one of them getting mad, and although they had not actually fought, tension had filled the room. Not anger this time, but a new emotion, one she couldn't entirely explain. This new feeling bothered her deeply. Michael tried to force her muddled emotions into order, willed her heart to reject the thoughts that raced through her mind. It was only natural she would be attracted to Dr. Richard Hampton. He was an extremely handsome man. Was it merely a physical reaction? She'd felt so vulnerable tonight when he'd

25

held her hands. *He was just trying to be kind,* she told herself, and she honestly believed he had not meant to hurt her with his words.

"My God, I'm not dead yet," she said aloud. Michael fluffed the pillow and let her practical mind take over. She would just have to overcome her involuntary reactions to that maddening smile of his. Now she needed to relax and go to sleep. After all, he was gone most of the time. That's why he'd hired her. She was just being silly; she was worrying about nothing.

CHAPTER FOUR

RICHARD ROLLED DOWN THE WINDOW as he pulled out of the driveway and breathed deeply of the brisk night air. For the first time in years, he'd welcomed the sound of his beeper, although he swore the piercing noise resonated from his mind, warning him to get out of her house and away from the strong current drawing him to her against his will, each beep telling him to forget it, hire someone else—, maybe a nice older lady, someone's grandmother.

He switched on the radio and tried to concentrate on his driving, but his thoughts shot back to Michael McCall. As he drove to her cottage tonight, Richard had prepared himself for another verbal war, but when she opened the door, dressed in pink and white like a peppermint candy cane, she actually smiled. The prolonged anticipation of wondering if she approved of what she saw as her captivating eyes appraised him became almost unbearable. He half expected her to shut the door in his face; instead, she invited him in and offered him wine. Until that moment, he had not realized how nervous he was, but then he relaxed. In fact, he relaxed so damn much he fell asleep.

Richard turned onto the street leading to the hospital and thought about this afternoon's meeting. Confrontation was a better word. He had it all planned out, even worked on a speech guaranteed to win her over. He thought he would have plenty of time to finish in the OR and be waiting for her, but no such luck. And then he'd baited her with that stupid comment about her lack of patience. *Great move, Richard!* He doubted Mrs. McCall could hide her emotions if she wanted to. To say he'd made her mad was an understatement, but he'd stood his ground, although mesmerized, staring into eyes like polished jade, hot with fire. He'd wanted to reach out and touch the soft curls that played about her face. Only years of discipline stopped him. That had been the first time he heard warning bells, an alarm from the deep corners of his mind, and they still rang loud and clear.

Richard pulled into the parking lot and turned off the engine of his black sedan. Today Michael McCall had toppled his applecart, forcing him to confront feelings he'd locked away years ago. He took off his glasses and rubbed his eyes and tried to put today into perspective. She was gorgeous. But he was surrounded by beautiful women all day. No, it was more than the way she looked that sent his pulse racing. He'd almost hugged her when she agreed to his plan, and that was not like him. He'd spent the last eight years building up a wall against beautiful women. He never dated. Well, not formally. Years ago he'd become involved with a nurse at the San Francisco Medical Center. They usually met once a month, when he was in the city to teach or perform surgery. It wasn't a relationship, just sex—for both of them. They were always discreet. They weren't looking for any compliments, just safe, compatible sex.

He got out of his car and headed for the OR and his patient, knowing he needed to clear his head before he tackled the operation that would probably take most of the night.

The stiff brush dug into his skin as Richard scrubbed for the surgery alongside his team, but he hardly noticed. Needing to put an end to the turmoil rolling around inside him, Richard rationalized that first, David wanted Mrs. McCall, not someone's grandmother, and second, he was a mature man, equipped with self-discipline and strength that had brought him back from the grips of hell eight years ago.

She was a beautiful woman. True. She had awakened feelings Richard believed no longer existed, also true, but now that he thought about it logically, he could deal with it. He would stay out of her way. He was a busy man, hardly ever at home. After the newness wore off, she would be like any other attractive woman he knew.

Richard breathed easier as he approached the operating room. Now he could direct his mind and skills to the job he did best. Standing at the operating table, he smiled under his mask. He was alert and ready to start. Other than David, surgery was the most important part of his life, and he felt a deep satisfaction knowing he was damned good at it.

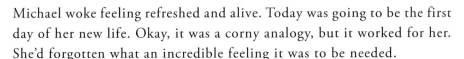

Michael woke feeling refreshed and alive. Today was going to be the first day of her new life. Okay, it was a corny analogy, but it worked for her. She'd forgotten what an incredible feeling it was to be needed.

Michael would never forget the devastating fear and panic that surrounded her when her parents died. She had no relatives, no one to take her in, and no prospects other than a succession of foster homes. Certainly no one in their right mind wanted to adopt a teenager. Michael did have a few things going for her, or so the social worker said. She was healthy, an excellent student, and had never been in trouble. It should have been enough, but it seemed her guardian angel had left town without leaving a forwarding address.

The county placed her in a foster home that already had one girl her age. The man of the house was a real bastard, a pervert on the prowl. She'd only lived there a month when the older girl, Patty, ran into her room late one night. She told Michael the son of a bitch had tried to rape her, that if he hadn't been so drunk, he would have gotten the job done. She wasn't going to hang around and give him another chance. Patty told Michael she better get out before he came after her. They left together but split up two blocks away. Michael spent her first night alone under a picnic table at the city park. After she'd cried herself dry, her fear became anger and she convinced herself she would be all right.

Early the next morning she went to the bus station and cleaned up in the restroom. She rented a locker, stuffing everything she owned into the small space, and then marched off to join the Navy. They told her to come back when she grew up. It was all she could do to keep from crying, except she never cried, but she knew one thing for sure; she wasn't going back to the foster home. Before the day was over, she had tried the Army, Air Force, Coast Guard, and Marines; she even went to the Salvation Army. They were her last hope, and they did not send her away.

The elderly woman was surprised when Michael marched in off the street and announced she was ready to join up, but her angel must have gotten back to work because no one told her to come back in a few years. Mrs. Woods got her something to eat, then took her to the man in charge. Michael remembered the softness of his voice and the reassuring way he put her at ease. It didn't take him long to pull the whole story from her. Then he made three phone calls that turned her life around.

First, he called the police, next the Department of Social Services. His last call was to Beth and Paul Williams. For the first time in her life, all fifteen years, Michael Jay Lydon began to believe there were people who actually cared.

Michael's new foster parents were in their sixties and had no children of their own. They had met in college and married during their post-graduate work. For five years, they traveled the world with backpacks, finally settling in California where Paul landed a job with the history department at Lowell University. Although the county paid them to give her a home, they also opened their hearts, and their love stripped away the armor she had pulled around herself.

Beth taught Michael everything her mother had not. Each night, from his comfortable old armchair, Paul's voice transported her all over the world to places she'd only dreamed about. After high school, Michael enrolled in college. While working on her master's degree, she met Ryan McCall, a widower who taught Political Science and was fifteen years her senior. They were married two months before she started her new job with the department of history at the university.

Andy was born five years later, and Michael's world was complete, perfect. She had everything, until one rainy night it all disappeared—stripped away in a mass of twisted metal and flames.

Michael realized she was crying. Tears came so easily now, held at bay for so many years. She pulled the blanket up around her chin and wiped her face with the back of her hand. Paul used to tell her that tears were God's way of cleansing the heart. Hell of a lot easier than sending it out to a laundromat. He always made her laugh. Paul died the year Andy was born, and it didn't surprise Michael when Beth followed him six months later. After all, they spent over forty years doing everything together.

Now it was time for her to move on; she'd had nine years of love and happiness. Michael was going to get out of bed, and all her self-pity and sad thoughts of the past were going into the washing machine with the dirty sheets.

Across town, at the same time Michael was getting out of bed, Richard longed to go home. The operation had taken most of the night and twice he'd almost lost his patient. His stiff and tired body screamed for a hot shower, but he needed to check his patient again. He'd just finished his notations in the medical chart when his partner, Hal Green, lumbered into the room with his usual bright-eyed greeting.

Hal Green had the voice of a bear, a solid-gold heart, and the body of a linebacker. One look at Richard told him what kind of night his partner had spent. "Hey, buddy. Time you got out of here and went home."

Richard handed over the chart. Hall flipped through it and then said, "Good Lord, Richard! No wonder you look like hell." In a quiet voice, so different from his natural bellow, he added. "Go home, buddy. Take the day off; it's going to be a great one. I'll mind the store."

Richard muttered a few words of thanks and headed to the lounge to change. When he stepped outside into the sunshine, he had to admit Hal was right. It looked like a beautiful day.

Twenty minutes later, he walked into his kitchen, savored the smell of baking bread, and accepted a cup of coffee from his housekeeper. "I know you want your shower, but you better take a few minutes and talk to David. He just informed me he wasn't going to school until he talked to you." Mary wiped her wet hands on a towel and continued. "I don't suppose you know anything about her yet? I told him it was too soon, but he's set and determined to have his way."

The edge in Mary's voice when she spoke of Mrs. McCall was not lost on Richard. He'd told Mary he didn't blame her for David's actions. As she said, once he made up his mind about something, David was determined to have his way. Richard knew Mary thought Mrs. McCall had overreacted two days ago, but at least she'd started the ball rolling. Now he was doing something he should have done months ago.

"Daddy, where are you?" David's voice reached the kitchen seconds before he burst into the room. "Have you talked to Mrs. McCall? Is she coming to live with us?"

31

"Hey there, calm down. I just walked into the house. You might say hello to your old dad."

"Hello. Now can we talk?"

Richard sat at the table and pulled David between his legs. "Aren't you supposed to be on your way to school by now?"

"I'm not going until this issue is settled."

Richard tried not to laugh as David stood in front of him with his small arms crossed over his chest, his chin set, waiting for his answer. "Well, it's settled. She's coming, but if you don't hustle and go to school, you'll be late. If your teacher makes you stay after school, you won't be able to go with me to get her."

David's arms flew around Richard's neck, covering him with hugs and kisses between squeals of delight. He ran out of the room, shouting for Allen to start the car, he had to get to school. But as Richard reached for his coffee, David was back, sliding through the door. "You'll wait for me? You promise?"

"I promise.

Now get out of here."

CHAPTER FIVE

RICHARD LEANED AGAINST THE WALL of the shower and let the hot water beat into his back, coaxing tight muscles to relax. His mind told him to get out of the shower and get some sleep, but his body didn't respond. He needed to go to the office in a few hours and catch up on paper work. He also needed to talk to Anna. And where was he going to put Michael?

Stepping out the shower, he reached for a towel and tried to collect his thoughts. Anna never wanted more than the two rooms downstairs. She was connected to David by an open intercom at night, but far enough away to enjoy her own space. Richard didn't want Michael in the rooms off the kitchen, and he couldn't put her in the guest rooms. That might be okay for a few days, but he wanted her to have more than just a place to sleep. Wrapping a towel around his waist, he reached for his razor and pictured the cottage where she'd been staying. She fit so well in that cozy place, and he wanted her to feel comfortable here.

His mother's room had the most space. It was big, with a sitting area, a fireplace, its own bath, and plenty of closet space. French doors opened onto a deck with stairs leading down to the patio and pool. She only used it a few times a year. "Let David have it," she'd told Richard. The guest room was just fine when she came to visit, but David didn't want to move. It was the perfect place for Michael.

Richard reached for the phone and pressed the intercom button. "Mary, I'm going to try to get some sleep, but call me when Anna comes in or if the hospital calls. And Mary, I want you to clean my mother's room. No, my mother is not coming. I've decided to give the room to Mrs. McCall."

33

Richard eased his naked body into bed, his warm skin absorbing the coolness of fresh sheets, but after ten minutes of turning from side to side, beating his pillow into a ball and counting the tiles on the ceiling, he decided sleep wasn't on his agenda. As he swung his long legs out of the bed, the phone rang.

"Dr. Hampton, Anna is here. She says she can't stay too long. I hate to disturb you, but you said to call, and I'm only obeying your orders."

"It's okay Mary. I'll be right down. You can start my breakfast."

Richard entered the kitchen and found Anna sitting at the table with a cup of coffee in one hand, shifting through a stack of papers with the other.

"How's the blushing bride this morning?"

"Just about ready to take off for Reno. Whatever made me think I wanted a traditional wedding?"

"Everything is going to be fine, and guess what? I've hired your replacement, not that anyone can ever replace you."

"Who is she? Where did you find her?"

"She's a friend of Sarah Clark. You know Sarah; she's Marc's sister-in-law. Well, anyway, I didn't find her. David did."

Anna raised an eyebrow, and Richard realized he'd better start at the beginning. He told her about the last two days, and by the time Mary placed his breakfast in front of him, he'd finished the story.

"I know you're running short on time, but she'll need to talk to you. There are things about David only you can tell her. I hate to ask, but I don't want her to be overwhelmed and decide to back out."

"Sounds like that's just what you expect her to do. Are you sure you're telling me the whole story?"

"Anna, don't look at me like that. It's just that I had to kind of twist her arm to take the job. But I think it's going to work out. Wait until you meet her. You'll see."

Richard ate his breakfast as Anna worked on her wedding plans. What started out as family and a few friends had escalated into a large affair. Martin was a widower with five grown children. Soon Anna would have a ready-made family. She would be a grandmother without ever having been a mother, although she would always think of David as her own. But the wedding could wait another few minutes. She wanted to know more about this lady, David's Mrs. McCall.

"So when can I meet her?"

"David and I are going to pick her up after he gets home from school. I thought we could have dinner together, and then you two could talk."

"Richard, that's impossible. I mean, dinner's okay, but I'll never be able to get all my things out of the room by this evening. I'm sorry. I just never thought about it. Of course, you need the rooms."

Richard walked around the table. "It's okay. You don't have to move a thing until you want to. I've decided she should have Mother's room. Don't worry about anything. If you can make it for dinner, we'll take care of the rest. Bring Martin with you; David and I will entertain him while you talk with Mrs. McCall."

"Hello, Sarah, it's me"

"Hello, me. Why are you up so early? Are we still on for lunch?"

"You bet, but can you do it earlier? Like eleven thirty?"

"Sure, I think so. What's up?"

"I have to be back here before three. Oh, Sarah, I have so much to tell you. You're going to think I've gone mad."

"Tell me now."

"No, not over the phone; you have to wait."

"Damn you, I hate it when you do this to me. Okay, I'll meet you at the ferry at eleven thirty, and you better not be late."

As she dressed for lunch, Michael tried to decide how much she should tell Sarah, and then realized there was only so much to tell. Besides, how could she put into words feelings she didn't understand herself? She was hired to be a companion or was it a nanny? The title didn't matter; she was going to work with the child, not the father, or so she told herself for the hundredth time.

Michael spotted Sarah before the ferry docked and she felt her chest tighten. She loved this woman like the sister she never had, ever since the day Sarah had waltzed into her room their first year in college and asked Michael to be her roommate. For the next four years, they were closer than peanut butter and jelly. A month ago, after Dan rushed Michael to the hospital, he called Sarah. She came that first night, and never left. When the doctor told Michael she could go home if she obeyed his orders, Sarah took charge. She booked a flight to San Francisco where Tom met them. Sarah gave her husband a quick kiss and a pat on his exquisite backside, a promise of better things to come, and drove to Sausalito and the tiny cottage with Michael in tow. For three days, they talked and cried, slept a little, and then talked and cried some more. When it seemed they had finally hashed over all the pain and sorrow Michael had refused to deal with, Sarah loaded the fridge, restocked the tissue supply, and returned to San Francisco, leaving Michael alone to find closure. To face, by herself, the private suffering no one, not even her closest friend, had a right to share.

Michael waved to Sarah and then ran off the boat and into Sarah's outstretched arms.

"I am so glad to see you. Girl, you look fabulous. Now tell me your news"

Michael smiled. "No. Let's get a table and a glass of wine first."

The waiter walked slowly in front of them, and along with the pair, thoroughly enjoyed the admiring glances they received. Sarah stood five foot seven, four inches taller than Michael. Her radiant red, shoulder-length hair danced above a dove-gray Georgette dress that draped beautifully on her slender figure. Michael's Armani, a cream delight that hugged every curve was crowned with a mass of dark curls and her favorite gold earrings.

Sarah told the waiter to bring them some white wine and to wait a bit for their order.

"Okay, toots, what's the big secret?"

"I have a job."

"Of course you have a job. That's not news. You're going back to the university in September."

"Not the university, in San Rio. I was hired yesterday."

"You're going to teach here? If you don't stop laughing and tell me what's going on, I'm going to make a scene."

It feels so good to laugh, Michael thought. "Okay, but you're never going to guess where I'm going to work, or what I'm going to be doing."

"Michael, I'm going to hurt you if you don't stop this and just tell me."

"Okay." Taking a sip of wine, Michael straightened in her chair and said, "Dr. Richard Hampton has hired me to be a companion to his eight-year-old son. I start this afternoon. I've only committed for six months. I talked to Dan McClaren this morning, and he's agreed to keep my job at the university until the spring semester."

Sarah just stared at her and then narrowed her eyes and asked, "Is this some kind of a joke? I mean, I didn't know you even knew Richard Hampton. You're kidding, right?"

"No. It's all true." Michael told her friend the whole story, starting with when she first met David. By the time she reached the part about moving into the Hampton house today, they had finished lunch.

Michael waited for her friend to say something, but Sarah just sat there, toying with a spoon. Finally, she said, "Well, I didn't think you could do anything that would surprise me, but I was wrong. I thought you'd gotten a new puppy or maybe a new car, but this—I don't know what to say. Are you ready for this? I mean... I've got to say what I think. You know how I am."

"I know, Sarah. It's okay."

"Michael, have you seriously thought this through? Because I don't think you have. It's only been a month since you collapsed because you could not or would not accept the fact that Ryan and Andy were gone. You said you agreed to do this job for only six months. What happens then? What's going to happen when you have to leave this boy? I know you. Unless he's a real pain, you'll be so attached to him it's going to hurt like hell to leave."

"You're not telling me anything I haven't already told myself, but don't you see if I go into this knowing I'm only staying for six months, I won't form any permanent attachments. Sarah, if I'd died in that crash, leaving Ryan to raise Andy by himself, he would need this kind of help. I have to do this... I want to do this."

"I understand what you're saying, but I know you. You will become attached. I think you're kidding yourself, thinking you can walk through a doorway and retrieve all you lost. Think about it: a ready-made family with a dad, a kid, and you as the mommy. I don't like it, not at all."

"Sarah, I'm through living in the past, and believe me, I've played the devil's advocate, and this still feels right."

Sarah finished her coffee and laughed softly. "Okay, I'll get off my soapbox. But wait until I tell Tom you're going to be living in the same house with Richard Hampton."

"Why? What's so funny?"

"I've told you before that Tom has been dying to introduce you to all the eligible men he knows. He has decided in all his immense wisdom that it's not right for you to be alone. He keeps muttering something about taking care of your biological clock. Wait until he hears you're going to be living under the same roof with one of the greatest looking guys in long pants. You'll have to have us over for dinner, and soon, so he can chart the progress."

"You didn't hear what I said I'll be doing. Sarah, stop laughing. Listen to me. I'm going to be the nanny, you know, like a servant? I'll probably have a room in the attic. Dr. Hampton hired me to take care of his son, not issue invitations to dinner. Besides, I'm not interested in socializing with him. I don't even like the man. He's rude and self-centered, and he expects you to jump when he says to."

"Oh, it's like that, is it? But you may be right. From what we've heard, your Dr. Hampton doesn't like women, not that there is anything wrong with him; it's just that since he lost his wife, he spends all his time with his son or his medical practice. Damn, what a waste. Sad too, when you think about all he's been through."

Michael gave her friend a questioning look. "What are you talking about?"

"Never mind. Besides, it's mostly hearsay. Just promise me you're going to be happy playing with this kid and that you'll call me every day."

"I promise," Michael said, looking at her watch. "Geez, I've got to go. I'll call you with my new phone number when I get it. Where should I leave the key to the cottage?"

"You keep it. No, now listen to me. You might want to get away for a while. The cottage is yours forever, so keep the key. If I need to run away, I have another one. Girl, give me a kiss." As the two embraced, Sarah told Michael to remember she was only a phone call, and thirty minutes away.

CHAPTER SIX

ICHAEL CHECKED THE BEDROOM AGAIN to make sure she hadn't forgotten anything before going into the bathroom. She looked into the mirror as Sarah's words echoed in her mind. Had she honestly thought this through? Or was she lying to herself, as Sarah suggested. Maybe, but only where Richard was concerned. Michael had told Sarah she didn't like the man, but the truth was she didn't want to like him. She didn't want to identify, let alone deal with the way she felt every time they were together, the way her heart bolted, sending her pulse racing out of control. Michael took a deep breath and repeated the same words she told Sarah. *I'm going to be a nanny, nothing more.*

"David, buckle your seat belt." It was half past three when they finally pulled out of the driveway, and Richard mentally kicked himself for going to the office today. He'd planned to catch up on his charting, but he'd no sooner walked in the door before Sylvia Grant appeared, demanding access to his private domain, to discuss a charity event sponsored each year by the medical staff and the auxiliary volunteers, or so she said. Working with Sylvia, the volunteer coordinator, was generally not too intense as long as everything went her way, but today she was in one of her moods and refused to be put off when his nurse told Sylvia he wasn't available.

There was another reason why Richard didn't want to see her. He did have work to do, but he was also having a hard time convincing Sylvia their relationship was non-personal. Months ago he'd asked her to attend a benefit with him, only to help Amy fill her table. A big mistake! And although he never asked her out again, she hounded him like a bitch in heat.

Today she barged into his private office and told Richard they needed to talk about the picnic. "Not today," he'd told her and set up a meeting later in the week, then had all but thrown Sylvia out of his office as a picture of Michael, her foot tapping out her frustration because he was late, again, raced through his mind.

"When we come home, I'm gonna ride with Mrs. McCall in her bathtub." David's hands worked the strap of the seat belt, pulling it out, letting it snap back against his chest.

Richard gave his son a quick glance. "What did you say? What bathtub?"

"I want to ride in her car when we go home. Her car's a bathtub. She told me so. We talked a lot, about bicycles and cars. She said her car was a bathtub."

"Son, you probably misunderstood her. I didn't even know she had a car. Why are we picking her up if she has a car?" Richard realized he was talking to himself, not David. Damn, he was tired. What he needed was a decent night's sleep.

Michael glanced at the clock; it read 3:45, but she wasn't going to get upset. She wandered around the room, straightening magazines on the coffee table. She had loaded the Porsche. That left the two boxes by the front door that held her CD player and discs, plus her favorite books Tom had brought when he'd driven her car up from her home down south.

Richard pulled into her driveway for the third time in as many days and stopped behind a bright-red 1964 Porsche Roadster. "I guess you were right, David," he said, pointing to the car. "There's the bathtub."

David gave his Dad a quizzical look. "The car," Richard said. "It's a classic Porsche, sometimes called a bathtub." He dropped his arm around the boy's shoulder as they walked to the door. Richard raised his hand to knock, but Michael opened the door, and David rushed into her arms.

"Why didn't you tell me you had a car and that you didn't need a ride?"

"You didn't ask. You just told me you would pick me up. I just assumed you didn't have anything better to do." Her mouth curved into a smile, showing him she was beyond intimidation.

His questioning frown eased into softness, followed by a chuckle. "Is there anything else I don't know? Something I've forgotten to ask you?" He tried to be serious but was losing the battle.

Michael mimicked his smile. "Doctor, you have no idea what you don't know about me."

As they moved into the house, Richard curbed his expressive smile, kind of disappointed that she chose not to elaborate.

The mood was gone, but as Michael pointed to the boxes by the door, she continued to smile because she felt relaxed for the first time in the presence of the good doctor, and she believed it would be okay; they could work together... for David. She locked the front door and turned toward her car.

"Can I ride with you, please?" David was at her side, his blue eyes bright and begging.

"Oh David, no... I mean, the passenger-side seat belt is broken. It wouldn't be safe." Michael saw the beginning of a serious pout cover his cherub face. She leaned over and hugged him. "I promise to get it fixed, and then we'll go for a long ride, but until I do, I just can't take a chance."

Richard knew David was going to ask, but he was unprepared for the look of sheer terror that covered Michael's face when his son asked to ride with her. It lasted only a moment, but long enough for him to see panic in her eyes, stripping away the laughter that just moments before had lit up her face. She was right, he reflected silently; there was a lot he didn't know about her. But it didn't matter, he told himself. All that mattered was keeping David as happy as he was today. "Come on, David, you can ride with Mrs. McCall another time."

Michael followed the black sedan. After they passed San Rio Medical Center, the road began to twist and climb. Scattered among giant redwoods, the laurel and gnarled oak trees stretched their thick branches over the narrow road, forming a lacy canopy. Michael basked in the opulent beauty surrounding them, following Richard when he turned into a driveway guarded by a weathered split-rail fence.

He drove up the driveway, past the front door of the stately Queen Anne design, decorated with gingerbread carvings and a wrap-around porch, toward the back of the house. Stopping at the edge of a walkway between the house and a large garage, Richard motioned for her to park next to him. Michael got out of her car and gazed in awe. Meandering paths of old brick led her eyes past the house and the pool to a knoll above a sloping lawn where a white gazebo, royally dressed in purple wisteria and pink roses, beckoned. Michael turned to the smiling doctor.

Richard walked to her side. "Close your mouth, McCall. You've been living in the city too long. If you like this, you're going to love the rest of the place."

David bounced after them, carrying one of her smaller bags as they entered the house through the back door, and Richard started the tour. He pointed out doors leading to Mary's room and Anna's suite. On the other side were doors to the wine cellar, a large pantry, and laundry and storage rooms. Richard entered the massive kitchen and then realized Michael had stopped short of the door. He reached back and took hold of her hand, pulling her to his side.

"Come on, McCall, I want to introduce you." His voice softened as his mouth curved into an unconscious grin.

"Michael, meet Anna, and that's Mary." Mary nodded from a distance. A tall man with gray hair and a smile from ear to ear reached for her hand as Richard introduced him. "And this is Allen, my friend and keeper." As Michael's hand disappeared between Allen's she returned his smile and somehow knew she had found a friend.

David edged next to Michael. "Come on," he said, taking her free hand, "I want to show you my room."

"Wait a minute, cowboy. Why don't you help Allen and me bring in the rest of Mrs. McCall's things? She can see your room later. Anna needs to spend some time with her before dinner." Richard dislodged her hands as he spoke to his son and turned her toward Anna.

Anna, like Allen, made her feel at ease. She was an attractive woman with short salt-and-pepper hair and sparkling gray eyes.

"Let me show you the rest of the house. Richard's grandfather built it a long time ago, but the old place just seems to hold on, although there have been some changes over the years, little things, like upgrading the electricity and the plumbing and jacking up the sagging floors." Anna laughed and led Michael out of the kitchen and into the hall. "Despite its age, it really is a very comfortable place to live."

From the two-story foyer, Michael looked into the formal dining room and on the other side, the library. Past the wide staircase, with its carved oak banister, Anna pointed to the living room at the end of the long hall. Richard's rooms were next to the library.

The upper level held David's room, a guest room, and the suite that would to be her home for the next six months.

"But your room is downstairs. I thought I would be staying there."

Anna opened the door and stood back, discreetly keeping her smile in check as Michael stared in amazement, finally recovering enough to shut her mouth, again.

The carpet was the color of sand, and the furnishings were exquisite antiques, mostly golden oak, but the rest of the room was blue and white. The room was almost as big as the cottage and practically divided in two, with a king-size bed adorned with a blue paisley quilt and pillows and the bathroom to the right. On the other side was a sitting room with a brick fireplace. Two loveseats, covered in blue-and-white striped linen, sat on each side of a coffee table. The far wall held several bookcases, a writing desk, and a chair with a navy-blue linen seat. The room was alive with color. A large fichus tree gathered the afternoon sun that radiated through the window and the French doors that led to the deck, with stairs to the pool below. Baskets of dried blue hydrangeas graced the tops of the antique chests and bookcases. A wreath of dried roses and herbs adorned the wall above the oak mantel, and a large bouquet of fresh roses on the coffee table filled the room with the scent and beauty of the garden.

Turning to Anna, who waited by the fireplace, she said, "Are you sure this is where I'm supposed to stay? I can't believe that all this…" She waved her arms expressively, "doesn't belong to someone."

"Why don't we sit for a minute and I'll explain a few things? I can see Richard has not." Michael sat across from Anna and immediately felt a bit apprehensive.

"When I moved here after David was born, this house belonged to Richard's mother. Richard couldn't stay in the house where he and

David's mother had lived. When David was about two, Richard and his mother did some remodeling. They redid the bottom floor, and she moved up here. You should have seen them, tearing out walls like children tearing paper from a tablet. It was such a mess; Allen finally threatened to leave if they didn't stop."

Anna stood and adjusted the wreath above the fireplace, then continued. "Two years ago, Richard's mother decided to move to Los Angeles. I could have come up here, but I chose to keep my rooms downstairs."

"Dr. Hampton must have loved his wife very much."

"Michael, I... May I call you Michael?"

"Yes, of course."

"I should not have mentioned Eve. I really must be tired. My dear, that's a topic we don't talk about, ever, and never, ever, around David. Please, forget that I mentioned her name."

Michael tried to register the significance of Anna's words. It was obvious Anna was momentarily upset with herself and Michael wondered what had caused the sudden change.

"Well, I can't take his mother's room. What is he thinking? I mean, where will she stay when she comes to visit? I don't want my coming here to create an upset. I can stay in Sausalito. I told Dr. Hampton I could come each day—"

"No, that wouldn't do. Richard wants you here, and his mother would want you to take this room. Actually, it's a brilliant idea. The suite is empty most of the time, and it's too lovely not to be used. For over a year now, Mrs. Hampton has tried to give her room to David, but for some reason David didn't like it. So Richard didn't force the issue. He doesn't like change," she said and added, almost as an afterthought, "He's very schedule-oriented."

Michael had so many questions to ask but didn't know where to start. Richard expected her to move into the shoes of a woman who had cared for the boy since birth. They could talk for hours, and there would still be so much she wouldn't know. Michael would require phone numbers; places David could and could not go. A cold knot formed in her stomach, and she felt a moment of panic as her mind jumped from one scenario to another. How could she ever pull this off? She just wanted to help David, but maybe Sarah was right. Michael tried to quell the warning voice in her mind that shouted at her to back out while she still had time.

"I'm not going to be far away," Anna reassured her. "You can always call me if something should come up that you think you can't handle. Although, I honestly doubt that will happen. David is just a normal little boy who needs lots of love and attention. Everything will be just fine; it really will."

Anna smiled, hoping her words had helped eliminate some of the skepticism she knew had briefly gripped the young woman. She sat still for a moment; giving Michael time to absorb all that had been thrown at her today. *I like her,* Anna thought. *She's honest with her feelings, and she's decisive. She'll do just fine.*

"Allen is a great help. He has David help him with all the guy things, especially on the weekends. Mary takes care of the house and meals, but she'll tell you right up front she wasn't hired to take care of David. Oh, she'll cover in a pinch, or at least she used to. After David's escapade this week, she's made it clear she cannot accept that responsibility again. I must tell you that Mary feels you overreacted the day David ran away, the day he met you. Richard has tried to make her understand he blames no one. She might be a little unfriendly to you at first because of that, but it will be okay. Now, I think it's time to go down to dinner. My almost-better-half should be here by now."

Three hours later, Michael snuggled deep into her new bed. She was tired, but she wasn't sleepy. Dinner had gone off without a hitch. Anna's future husband was a natural extrovert, and she found herself laughing at his stories. After dinner, David had shown her his room. He had a list of things he wanted to discuss with her. Things like joining the Cub Scouts, getting a pet, building the tree house. She finally cried uncle and told the little manipulator with his million-dollar smile to give her time to settle in before they tackled all his projects. Why wasn't he already a scout? It seemed there were a lot of things he had missed out on. Well, she would look at his list and manage each item, one at a time.

CHAPTER SEVEN

ICHAEL SURVIVED THE NEXT FEW days, barely. Her first morning, David knocked on her door before dawn, begging her to get dressed, and then off they went to explore the woodlands behind the house, raiding the pantry for provisions on their way out. David pulled her behind him as they climbed high above the lawn to a shaded glen—his super special place. Seated on a large rock, eating apples and graham crackers, they mapped out plans for the next twelve months... or so it seemed. David wanted so many things, but most of all he just wanted to be with her, and he told her so, hugging her tightly as if afraid she might not be real.

But a routine quickly evolved. Michael got up early, leaving the house before David woke up, to jog the peaceful trails and enjoy the calm of the morning illuminated by the rising sun. Then came breakfast, usually just the two of them, as Richard left for his office about the time she returned from her run. After David went to school, her day was free until he came home in the afternoon, racing through the door with his list in hand and a dozen more things he wanted to add to it. Michael realized she needed to take control, and soon. No wonder there was such chaos. The child was adorable but unintentionally spoiled.

Michael needed to talk to Richard. They'd never gotten around to discussing what he expected of her. She needed guidelines, but it was about as easy to pin him down as it was to say no to David. She called Anna. Realizing the wedding was not far off, Michael apologized for bothering her before explaining her predicament. Anna told her to make an appointment with him at the office, just call Ruthie.

She called his office that day and asked for Ruthie. Ruthie Coleman was Richard's right-hand, a RN who managed his office. According to

Anna, this woman wasn't the least intimidated by her boss. Michael explained her problem, adding that Anna told her to call. Ruthie understood perfectly and set up an appointment at five o'clock. After making sure Allen would watch David, Michael showered and changed her clothes.

Michael arrived at the offices of Hamilton Green, M.D. & Richard Hampton, M.D., Cardiovascular and Thoracic Surgery, at a quarter to five. She had dressed with care, donning a navy skirt with a matching a blouse and white blazer. She'd brushed her hair back severely and tied it with a thin red silk scarf. Last week Dr. Hampton had felt the need to comment on the fact that she rarely wore shoes, so today she wore three-inch navy heels and black stockings. She needed him to take her seriously.

"Hi, there. You're Mrs. McCall, right? I knew you were Michael. You look just as he described you."

Michael smiled and shook hands with the tall, good-looking blonde who had a slight southern drawl and a smile from eyes to chin. "And you must be Ruthie. I'm a bit early, but I didn't want him to slip away if he finished early."

"Oh, Tiger's still here. Whoops, I guess I shouldn't call him that, but then, he knows I call him names. Good nurses are hard to find, so he pretends not to notice. Well, I'm sure glad to meet you at last. And listen, anytime you need anything, you just let me know. He's dictating but thinks he still has a new patient to see, so I'm going to have you wait in his office."

The room reminded her of Richard. Two maroon leather chairs sat across from the large desk. A beautiful oxbow credenza, framed by tall bookcases with leaded-glass doors, occupied one wall and a sofa of beige leather the other. Indirect lighting gave a soft focus to the room, and there was not a file or a book out of place.

Richard finished his dictation and headed for his office. "Hello," he said. "I hope I haven't kept you waiting—"

Richard's words hung in his throat, and his legs froze. He had last seen her early this morning, waving to him as she continued up the drive, her jogging clothes damp, dark curls flying. Now she looked like

47

she'd just come from high tea at the St. Francis Hotel. "What are you doing here? Is something wrong? Where's David? Where's my patient?"

"I'm here to talk with you. Nothing's wrong, and David is with Allen. As for your patient, there isn't one; this is my time. So as the clock is running, please sit down. Look," she said, pointing to her feet, "I even wore shoes."

He admired her shoes and her slender legs as he straightened his tie that didn't need fixing and ran his hand through his dark hair. "Couldn't we have talked at home? I mean, it would have saved you a trip."

"Dr. Hampton, I've been trying to talk with you for over a week, and all I get is we will do it later. Now please sit down. You make me nervous."

Richard walked to the other side of his desk and dropped into his chair "I must say you look very nice today. Not that you don't always look charming."

"Thank you, Doctor." She acknowledged his compliment with a lop-sided smile and a racing pulse, wishing he would stop staring at her. "Now, if we can get down to business. I told you when I agreed to take the position I would require explicit directions about what I'm to do or not do. I understand you are an exceptionally busy man, and I wouldn't bother you with something as trivial as bedtime or what he eats for breakfast, but this is about the welfare of your son. Now, I've made a list." Michael handed him his copy. "If you would like to take a moment to review what I've written, I'd like to discuss each item in detail."

Richard took the piece of paper and glanced down the page. "What is all this? David is untidy, not responsible." He lifted his eyes from the list. "What's this about? What do you mean he's not responsible?"

"Dr. Hampton, David is a captivating, sweet child, but he's a slob."

"I resent that."

"That's really beside the point. When was the last time you looked in his room, really looked? His clothes fall where he takes them off. His things are scattered all over the room. David has enough toys to start his own store, and while I'm on the subject of toys, how much allowance do you give him?"

"What?"

"How much money do you give him on a regular basis?"

"He gets twenty-five dollars a week. Why?"

"You give David twenty-five dollars a week? Good Lord! And how does he spend it? Have you set any guidelines? Have you ever discussed with him how he spends his money?"

"What do you mean guidelines? What has his allowance got to do with anything?"

"Apparently nothing; that's my point. Does he have a savings account? Does he give to charity? Do you have any idea what an eight-year-old does with thirteen hundred dollars a year?" She waited for a reply. "Don't stand there looking at me that way. Say something, and please sit down."

Richard didn't realize he was standing, but he didn't sit, just leaned over the desk, glaring at her. "What way am I looking at you? And why are you calling me Dr. Hampton? What happened to Richard, Mrs. McCall?"

Michael rose to her feet, and leaned over the desk, meeting him halfway. "You don't know, do you? Well, let me enlighten you, Doctor. He couldn't tell me what he does with it. He told me he just spends it on stuff. David buys toys, but most of them end up broken. He doesn't know anything about saving money or about giving to a charity. And the worst part of all is that he doesn't seem to understand why I was so concerned."

Michael pulled back and walked toward the door, then spun around. "This is not going to work. I thought we could work together, but it's obvious we can't. I thought you wanted more from me than just seeing to it David doesn't skip town again, but I guess I was wrong."

"No, you're not wrong. I didn't hire you to be just a baby sitter."

"Then why are you so upset with me? I'm trying to do what I thought you wanted." She stopped talking and started silently counting to ten. When she reached six, she adjusted her voice to a calmer tone and tried to choose her words carefully. "David will not be equipped to deal with life without some sense of discipline. Taking care of his room and his belongings, and learning to be responsible in the way he spends his money, it's all part of that."

"But he's so young. There's plenty of time to teach these things."

"Good Lord, Richard, I don't claim to have all the answers. No one gave me a license that said I was qualified to raise a child. Actually, I think it's rather ridiculous that you need a license to catch a fish or shoot a deer, but not to raise children. All I know is that somewhere between potty training and puberty, a child has to learn about values. He has to have rules, rights and wrongs, like a road map, something he can follow. And that includes learning the meaning of the word no."

Richard sat, calmer now. Actually, he agreed with her completely, well almost. "A steady dose of no can have an adverse effect on a child, McCall."

"I'm not suggesting a steady diet, but he has to know that rules are there, governing and guiding. Sure, there can be compromise, but consistency is the key word here."

"Your remarks sound as if your parents were very strict."

"Sure, I had rules, but we led a simple life, so they were few but firm. And it was different with Beth and Paul."

"I'm sure it was. I'm sure it's an entirely different kind of responsibility raising a child that's not your own. Were they exceedingly strict, like your parents?"

"Not really," she said as a small smile softened her lips, wondering if he realized what he'd just said. "They taught me values, to help me grow and mature. Actually, Paul only told me no once, and once was enough"

"Well?"

"Well, what?"

"Come on McCall, tell me about the lessons you learned."

"We've gotten off track here. My life growing up has nothing to do with David. I think you need to find someone else for this job. I'll stay until you find someone, but—"

"No deal. I'm not interested in someone else. Besides, you promised to stay six months, so don't try to weasel out on me."

"But..."

"No buts. I would think keeping one's word would be somewhere on that list of yours?" Richard gave her a smug grin and continued. "When we first crossed horns, you thought I was a terrible father. Don't try to deny it. I know what you thought. Don't ever try to play poker, McCall; you're so easy to read." Then his expression changed. It projected authority and a bit of arrogance in the set of his jaw, determination in the thrust of his chin.

"I totally agree with everything you've said. So I want you to come to me, any time, and tell me what you want me to do, and I'll do it. We can work through this together, and I promise I'll do anything you ask. Agreed?"

"Anything?"

"Yes, anything." Her green eyes sparkled, and he knew he'd won her over. "Now, what else is on this list?"

"He would like a pet. He told me you're not crazy about a dog, so he thought something smaller. Anyway, I thought you could talk to him about it. He would also like to join the Cub Scouts, and take swimming lessons. There's something else. I need to go home for a few days. I have a chance to lease my house, but I have to put some things in storage. It will only take a couple of days."

Richard felt a momentary feeling of apprehension. If she left, would she come back? He was overreacting. Of course, she'd come back; she'd given him her word. "That will be fine. I'm sure we can make out for a few days, and that will give me time to talk to David about the things on this list."

Michael walked to the desk and picked up her purse. She hadn't expected him to be so agreeable. "There is one more thing. I know you're an extremely busy man, but you need to spend more time with David. After all, I'm just the hired help, and I'll only be here for six months. He needs to spend more time with you."

Richard stood and walked around the desk to her. He was about to address her last statement when the door flew open, and Peter Farrell walked in.

"Oh, sorry Rich, I didn't know you were busy. I thought I'd walk with you to the meeting."

Michael found it impossible not to smile at the man who'd just burst into the room, his movements swift and full of grace and virility. His grin and his deep-blue eyes were captivating, and she couldn't help but notice his air of confidence or the size of his shoulders. His light-blond hair was a stark contrast to his deep tan, and his strong features displayed a captivating sensuality.

"I was just leaving," she said with a trace of amusement in her voice.

"Peter, I'd like you to meet someone." Richard stood by her side as he introduced them, his hand resting lightly at the small of her back.

"I'm glad to meet you, Dr. Farrell. Are you a surgeon also?" Michael took a step away from the hand at her back, immediately sensing the void.

Richard frowned at the way Michael smiled at his friend, and he navigated her toward the door, "Peter's an ob-gyn. Ladies and babies, right, Peter?" He meant his words to be light, but his forced smile was without humor.

Her face remained just inches from his. "Do you need a ride?" Richard asked, realizing only after the words were out that she didn't.

Slowly shaking her head, she replied, "No, I have my car."

"That's right, the bathtub."

It took her a moment to understand what he was talking about. Then she shot him a smile. "Yes, the bathtub. Will you be home for dinner?"

"Yes, I'll be home for dinner if it can wait until seven."

After saying good-bye to Peter, she replied, "We'll hold dinner until 7:10."

Richard closed the door and found Peter staring at him. "What?"

"You cagey old bastard."

"What are you talking about? You think…? Come on, Peter, she's David's companion."

"Yeah, right, what a perfect setup. Where can I sign up for a kid?" Peter sat on the edge of the desk, grinning.

"I told you… She's David's companion."

"So? Don't tell me you haven't noticed, friend, but that woman gives a new meaning to the word gorgeous. I think I'm in love."

Richard's aristocratic jaw lifted slightly as he gave Peter a disapproving look. "You're still on the rebound. Anything in a skirt would look good to you right now. Besides, you always were horny, divorce or no divorce. Come on, we're going to be late for the staff meeting."

"Wait just a minute. Are you saying you don't think she's beautiful?"

"No, of course not; Mrs. McCall is an exceptionally attractive woman."

"You didn't say she was married."

"She's a widow. Can we get going? I promised I'd be home for dinner tonight."

In the elevator, Peter picked up where he'd left off in Richard's office. "Well, if you're sure I won't be treading on your turf, I think I'll see if Mrs. McCall would like to have dinner with me."

The thought of Peter asking Michael out to dinner infuriated him, but only for a moment. Richard loosened his tie and the top button of his shirt and slowly regained a perspective that helped level out his breathing. He unclenched his hands and rotated his neck, coaxing his taut muscles to relax. Son of a bitch! He'd almost lost it with one of his best friends.

Maybe she was right. Maybe she should leave; he could find someone else just as qualified to take care of David. Anna hadn't done such a terrible job. Richard laughed aloud, and the sound echoed through the small elevator as Peter gave him a questioning look. Damn, he was doing it again, backing away from the truth. Richard wondered how long it would have taken him to become aware of all the problems Michael brought up today. Would he have replaced Anna, even if she hadn't decided to get married? He doubted it.

The elevator came to a stop, and Richard relished the cooling air from the lobby. Maybe he just needed a night with Sue in San Francisco. It had been some time since their last romp. One thing he knew for sure; he wasn't going to let himself go crazy every time he came within ten feet of Mrs. McCall, and that was another promise he meant to keep.

CHAPTER EIGHT

WHEN MICHAEL ARRIVED IN REDLANDS, Dan McClaren met her at the airport and insisted she stay with them. Maggie, Dan's wife, volunteered to help her pack the things she needed to put in storage, and soon it was done. She felt good about her new tenant, a young man doing graduate work for his Ph.D.

Michael knew the party that took place her second night in town happened by design, not chance. About seven-thirty, people started to drop by; old friends and co-workers marveled at how fabulous she looked... so different from a month ago. Laughter soon filled the house as they stuffed themselves with pizza and beer and stayed up most of the night reminiscing about the good old days.

Ah, the good old days... gone, but not forgotten. *What a fool I've been.* Michael hated to think about those days because to remember hurt; it hurt like hell, but nothing like what she'd gone through the last two years. She had buried her son and husband but refused to deal with the anger and despair, emotions that had become her constant companions. She taught more classes, drove herself night and day and brilliantly sidestepped her friends when they offered love, support, and especially advice. Then one day she fell apart. Her body had had enough. Dan had found her, alone—ice-cold and trembling—in the dimly lit classroom, and tears were the only answers she had to his frantic questions. Michael vaguely remembered the wild ride to the hospital, the staff milling about, fine-tuning the miles of tubing attached to hanging bottles that seemed hooked to every part of her body. Then Sarah arrived and took control. She browbeat the doctor and hospital personnel, had a bed brought into Michael's room, and informed everyone she was not leaving until she could take Michael home. Those issues settled, she turned on Michael, giving her holy hell for being such a fool, telling her that, by damn, things were going to be different. When the doctor released her, Sarah bundled Michael up and deposited her at the cottage in Sausalito. Then she left, forcing Michael to reach deep and touch the pain… and finally put it all to rest. It had taken a month, but as her despair lessened, replaced by a sense of strength, she basked in the knowledge that she would be okay. Now she was on her way home. Well, maybe not home, but the address she would use for the next six months.

"Ladies and gentleman, this is your captain speaking." Michael half listened as he told them it was a beautiful evening in the city, about sixty-eight degrees, and that they would be starting their descent momentarily.

The flight attendant picked up where the captain left off, her sweet voice repeating her canned speech as she prepared the cabin for landing.

When the door opened, Michael reached for her carry-on, eager to be back on solid ground. Sarah was picking her up, but since she didn't believe in parking lots, she would be waiting at the curb and had given Michael strict orders to hustle because Tom was being a bit testy about all her parking tickets.

When she stepped into the waiting area, a squeal of delight greeted her. "We called Sarah and asked if we could come get you. She said it was okay. I sure missed you." She knelt to receive David's giant hug and smiled up at Richard, wondering how it was possible to have missed them so much.

Somehow they managed to collect her bags in record time and then headed for the car. Richard drove the black Mercedes out of the parking structure, easing safely into the Sunday night traffic.

David took off his seat belt and leaned over the front seat, patting her shoulder. "David, you have to sit back and fasten your seat belt."

"But I want to talk to you. I gotta lot of things to tell you."

"Okay Sport, fire away, but stay buckled up."

"Well, Friday we went to the bank, and now I have my own savings account. I gotta put fifteen dollars a week in the bank and in six months I take… Dad, how much do I give away?"

"Fifteen percent of the total," Richard replied, grinning at his son through the rear-view mirror.

"Yeah, fifteen percent of what I got in the bank I give to people who need it more than I do. Then I give two dollars and fifty cents a week at church. That's ten percent, right, Dad?"

Richard confirmed David's question, feeling rather pleased that his son remembered their contract so well.

"And I get to keep the rest, but I don't have to spend it just 'cause I got it. Allen gave me an old cigar box, and I can keep my money in there so I'll have it if I need it. And guess what? I can have a pet—something small to start, a little creature in a cage. And best of all, Dad's gonna pay for the animal, but I gotta pay for the upkeep, buy food and all. We didn't go to the pet store yet. I wanted to wait until you came home. Can we go tomorrow?

"And guess what? I get to join the Cub Scouts. Tommy Walker says being a scout builds you a character. I don't know what that means, but it's gotta be true 'cause scouts are good, so that's what I'm going to do. We signed a contract, didn't we, Dad? We each have a copy. I'm keeping mine in my cigar box. My part is to keep my room clean, and Dad's going to come home earlier. But if he has to be at the hospital, to help people who are sick, that's okay. He told me he'll do his best. That's all we can do, you know, is do our best. And wait until you see my room. It's maculate… No that's not the word. What's that word, Dad?"

"I think you mean immaculate"

"Yeah, immaculate, but wait till you see it. Allen says you can eat off the floor, but we're not going to do that, huh, Dad?"

"No, David, we'll still eat downstairs."

The car suddenly purred with silence. Michael continued to watch David for a moment, so relaxed his chest barely moved at all as his heart beat evenly. How she envied the nature of a child. Life was so simple; he'd told her all his marvelous news and then, pleased and content, had fallen asleep.

The traffic thinned out as they approached the bridge, and Richard turned on the radio, keeping the volume low. "I hope you don't mind that we changed the plans tonight. He wasn't kidding; he truly missed you. David suggested we call Sarah last night. I've had a devil of a time trying to get him to pace himself. He could hardly wait to tell you about our contract and his room. Really, McCall, I think you're going to be surprised. He worked all weekend cleaning and sorting. He packed three boxes of toys to give to the church, toys he doesn't play with anymore. I wish I could bottle some of his energy." Richard turned to look at her and realized he was rambling on, just like David. "I don't want this to go to your head McCall, but you were right, again."

Even in the dimly lit car he saw her brows arch, draw together, questioning his words. "When David and I had our talk and I brought up the subject of his messy room, he told me he didn't know he was supposed to keep it clean. David actually believed cleaning his room was Mary's job. He thought someone would always pick up after him. I have to agree with you, what you said about needing a license to raise a child. I used to think I was rather smart. You know, you feed them, keep a roof over their heads, read them a story when you can, and tell them you love them. I always thought I was a super dad. Wrong! I guess I should have read more Dr. Spock... or something."

"You're over-reacting. If he'd thrown a fit because he had to clean his room, then you might have something to worry about. Sounds as if you two had a busy weekend, and I think you did a terrific job."

Michael looked at Richard, her head still resting on the back of the seat. She studied him as he came to a stop at the tollbooth and dropped the token into the slot. His profile, outlined by the light from the booth, was strong and confident, a contradiction to the words he'd just spoken. She knew he knew she was watching him, and although he kept his eyes straight ahead, his handsome face shifted into a broad grin.

His smile did crazy things to her. Michael felt her heart beating wildly against her breast, in the tips of her fingers, and she had the strongest urge to reach out and trace the corner of his mouth, his smiling lips. She closed her eyes and exhaled, trying to block out her awareness of him. It was impossible. Michael settled in her seat and gave in to her desire. She luxuriated in delectable warmth that surged from her heart to her toes, filling her with a gentle quivering she never wanted to stop. She smiled and tried to burrow deeper into the soft leather seat, so relaxed, finally admitting the truth she had refused to accept since the first time she'd seen him. She was falling in love with this outrageously self-confident, truly arrogant, wonderful man. She opened her eyes to make sure he was still there. Her pulse slowed. The insistent pounding of her senses mellowed. Then, like David, she closed her eyes and fell asleep.

Richard eased the car to a gentle stop at the back of the house. The light above the garage cast an amber halo around her sleeping face. She'd pulled off the ribbon holding back her hair and it fell in a soft shimmering mass, curling protectively about her face and shoulders. So many times during the past few weeks he'd wanted to touch the dark strands playing about her face. Slowly he reached out and gently caressed her hair. How easy it would be to move just a few inches and touch her lips with his, but as he stroked her hair with the tips of his fingers, he knew one kiss wouldn't relieve the tension coiled inside him. He was wrapped up so tightly he could hardly breathe.

"Oh, Mikie, Mikie," he said softly, knowing she was still asleep. "What am I going to do about you? Should I send you away? I should, but I don't think I can. What pleasure it would be to love you. I could love you so easily... if I dared. But I can't. I can't let myself love you."

He drew away from her and frowned. Partly because he was sitting in the dark talking to himself and because remembering the past was hard. The remembering overrode her beauty and his desire for her, and it made him pull away. He started to shake; deep down in that private place he had locked away from everyone, even David. Richard gripped the steering wheel with both hands and waited for the tremors to subside. *How could I be such a fool?*

"McCall, wake up." He gently shook her shoulder as he opened the car door, flooding the interior with light. "Come on, you sleepyheads, we're home."

Michael came awake with a start and realized where they were. Her small laugh was half embarrassment, half disbelief she had gone to sleep. "Is David awake?"

"No, he's out for the night. We'll get him tucked away, and then I'll get your bags. Here," he said, turning to give her his keys, "get the door for me."

Michael unlocked the back door and held it open for Richard and his son. She led the way as he climbed the stairs, turning on lights as they went. When they reached David's room, she opened the door and flipped the light switch.

"Close your mouth, McCall." Richard gently nudged her out of the way, moved past her and lowered his son on the bed. "I told you he worked all weekend on this room. Some job, huh?"

The room was spotless. The books in the wooden case under the window stood like tin soldiers, straight as a pin. Richard went to the closet and opened the door. All the clothes were in order: robe first, then coats, shirts, pants. Shoes on the floor—military perfect. Even the stuffed bears in the toy box sat proudly upright and alert.

After Richard left to get her bags, Michael sat on the edge of David's bed and called his name. He woke up slowly, rubbing his eyes with the heel of his hand. It took him a moment to realize they were in his room, but when it clicked in, he smiled with excitement and pride and jumped to his feet.

"What do you think? Does it pass muster?" He pulled her into the closet, pointing out the shelves where he'd sorted his toys by categories. "And you know the best part? I know where everything is. When Mary cleaned up, I couldn't find some of my stuff for weeks. Allen says being shipshape makes you feel good. He was in the Navy, you know. Anyway, I'm gonna be shipshape from now on."

"David, I'm so proud of you. It's the cleanest room I've ever seen, and I think it deserves a special hug." Michael wrapped her arms around him and squeezed tightly, ruffling his blond hair with her hand. "Better get undressed now and ready for bed, and David, thanks for coming to the airport and bringing me home."

She left him to get ready for bed, just in time to open her door as Richard topped the stairs with two of her bags. "Damn, McCall, what have you got in here?" He pushed his way into her room and dropped the bags to the floor.

"Are you always this cantankerous when you have to do a little manual labor?"

"I'm not cantankerous, and I'll have you know I've been doing manual labor all weekend. David piled everything he owned out on the landing, and I mean everything that was in his room, except the furniture. Mary had a fit. First, because she's supposed to have Saturday afternoons off, and David wanted her to vacuum his room and clean the bath, and then when she couldn't lift the vacuum over the four-foot pile to get to his room. She's not been a happy housekeeper anyway, so to keep peace, I did the vacuuming. After I finished with his room, I decided to clean the second floor. By then I was on a roll; I even cleaned the attic. Now I hurt in places I didn't know I had."

"Poor baby," she said with an unsympathetic grin. Richard slumped against the wall, dramatically dropping his hand across his heart. He looked wounded, or tried to. An actor he was not. His grin got the best of him and his rich, warm laughter mingled with hers around the room. "You're a heartless woman, McCall. No sympathy for a worn-out man."

"Well, maybe it's time you took your worn-out body downstairs and put it to bed." She pulled him off the wall and turned him toward the door. "You could have waited until I got home, you know. I would have helped him and saved you all your aches and pains. Besides, the cleaning company is supposed to do the heavy cleaning every two weeks. You could have waited for them."

Richard turned slowly, letting her do most of the work as she guided him across the landing to the top of the stairs. "I guess I'll live," he said with a final chuckle. Halfway down the stairs, he looked up at her. "McCall, I'm glad you're back. I'm glad you're home." He took two more steps then turned again. "Oh, McCall, do me a favor? Find us a new cleaning company. I fired the old one this weekend. Thanks, and sleep well."

Richard locked up and turned out the lights. He needed to do some reading, but his mind wouldn't cooperate. Finally, he gave up the idea and took a shower, letting the hot water beat against his tired muscles. He hadn't lied to her about hurting. Well, maybe a bit, but tonight it was so easy to talk with her, just joking around. Maybe it is going to be okay. There was no reason why they couldn't be friends. She made him laugh. Just keep it simple, he told himself as he dried off and crawled into bed. Just don't think about things that can get you into trouble, like how great she looks in jeans and a T-shirt. Richard stretched his long arms over his head, gripping the top of the headboard. He flexed his toes under the sheet, letting go just before his calf muscles screamed. His body relaxed, and his mind drifted into the night, but his last conscious thought was of his fingers slipping beneath the softness of her teasing curls.

CHAPTER NINE

S HE OPENED HER EYES AS splinters of sunlight pushed the last remnants of the night behind Mount Tamalpais. Michael snuggled deep in the warm bed, knowing it was time to get up and start her morning jog. She needed to get out of bed, but not yet. She eased her naked body deep into the warmth and succumbed to the liberation of her mind, warm body, and soul. Contentment and a wondrous sense of peace flowed through her and the joy she felt was pure and explosive. She was in love. Silly in love, she thought, muffling her sudden laughter with the edge of the blanket. When Richard left her last night, pleading his aches and pains, she'd wanted to reach out and pull him close. Michael wanted to know the feel of him—to hold him in her arms, to kiss that part of his neck, there, just below his ear, and feel his heartbeat with her lips, but she hadn't. She'd stood perfectly still and suffered a dull ache of need and desire.

Michael pulled the covers up to her chin and imagined his hand touching her face, the side of her neck where her pulse raced double-time now, as she imagined her skin under the tips of his skilled fingers. She closed her eyes and plunged deeper into her erotic aberration, as his hand slid from her neck to the top of her breast and his lips explored her mouth. Their tongues met, mated, and then danced to a silent melody. His fingers caressed the swollen globe, bringing the tip to a crested peak, holding her close until they were hot and wet, melting in harmony, totally consumed with the need of each other.

Michael drew up her legs into a fetal position, about to be reborn. She wet her dry lips with the tip of her tongue, as her breasts ached and her legs grew tense. Her most sensitive flesh grew damp and pulsed with a desire that begged for release. She sucked in her breath as nerves and muscles tightened, as an explosion of rapturous delight washed over her, suspending all thoughts—all movement—drenching her in the glory of lush, moist heat. Michael lay trembling but still, trying to prolong the rush of exquisite pleasure as tight, lingering spasms charged through her.

The moment of fire passed, leaving her cleansed and shaken but needing more. She didn't want to be alone now but curled in the arms of that man who slept below, the man who didn't even know how much she loved him.

Michael refused to open her eyes, but her mind tried to focus. "I have to have a plan," she muttered to her secret self. "I can't simply tell him I love him. That would scare him away. He doesn't even know he needs me, but he will..." Burrowing deep into the bed, Michael's words trailed off, lost to the pull of sleep, pulling her back to her dreams, to his touch, back to the pleasure.

Richard finished dressing and decided he would have breakfast with David and Michael. Everyone should start the day with a good breakfast. Besides, it would reassure David he meant to fulfill his part of their contract. As he walked into the kitchen, Richard wondered why it had taken him so long to realize what a lucky guy he was. He had wallowed in self-pity for eight years, never seeking help for the problem that was his and his alone. Richard had never sensed David's sadness or realized how lonely the boy was, and he'd almost missed out. What he needed years ago was a swift kick in the ass, but he was on track now.

David sat alone at the table, fidgeting with his spoon.

"Where's Mrs. McCall?" Richard asked, pouring a cup of coffee. "I thought she's usually back from her jog by now."

"She's not jogging. She's still in bed. Do you think she's sick? I peeked in her room, just a little. I was real quiet, but she didn't move. I know she's there, 'cause I saw her hair. She's always up by now. Do you think she's sick?"

"Let's not jump to conclusions. You were so tired last night you fell asleep in the car. She did too. I'm sure Mrs. McCall just worked too hard this weekend."

"Don't you think we better go check, just to be sure? I think we better go check."

Out of the corner of his eye, Richard watched Mary and realized she was not only listening to their conversation, but also mimicking their words with a look of disgust on her face.

"Mary? Do you have a problem this morning?"

He'd seen her and knew what she was doing. Mary also knew the smart thing to do was just come right out and tell him she wasn't happy about that woman moving in, or about all the changes. Rather than doing the smart thing, Mary said, "Nothing's wrong. I don't have a problem, except..."

"Except what, Mary?"

"Well, are we changing the schedule again? You never used to come in here in the mornings, not even for coffee. I suppose you're going to want breakfast now?"

"I suppose I am. I may even decide to change a few other things, and if you find that too much of an adjustment, maybe we'd better discuss it."

Richard finished his coffee and placed the cup on the counter next to the sink. He turned to face her, staring her down as he'd tried doing to his mother when he was a boy. Unlike his mother, who usually gave Richard a swat to the back of his head, Mary lowered her eyes and acquiesced, silently admitting she realized who signed her paycheck.

Turning back to his son, Richard said, "I'll go up and make sure Mrs. McCall is okay. You finish your breakfast. I'll be right back."

He knocked softly on her door a couple times and then opened it and walked in. As David had said, you could only see the dark sheen of the top of her head. He moved to the side of the bed and bent over, lifting a mass of curls off her face with the back of his hand. She felt warm, but not feverish. Michael didn't look sick. In fact, she looked rather amused. She had a silly grin on her face, and he half-expected her to laugh out loud at any minute.

"McCall, wake up." He sat on the side of the bed, his hand still against her cheek. Michael turned slowly onto her back, and the side of her face caressed his hand as she stretched like a contented kitten. Her slender arms unrolled from the blanket like petals of a flower awakened by the morning sun. Richard watched the blanket inch lower, revealing a glimpse of smooth skin as the rounded tops of her breasts lifted slowly, moving with the beat of her heart.

Michael opened her sleep-filled eyes and smiled, thinking what a pleasant surprise it was to see him sitting beside her. She looked into his black eyes as his magnificent smile sent her over the edge. Michael started to reach out and touch the small dimple on the right side of his cheek when alarms went off, and an explosion of reality reeled through her head. Good Lord! She wasn't asleep, and Richard wasn't part of a dream. He was real. And he was sitting on the edge of her bed. Her arms were flung over her head like Betty Boop, and if the blanket moved any lower, he'd see her as naked as the day she was born.

"Well, good morning, sunshine."

Michael jerked the blanket up so hard she all but knocked him to the floor. "What are you doing here? What time is it?" Her eyes searched the foot of the bed for her robe. How was she going to put it on with him standing there watching her? And what was he doing in her room? She rolled over to look at her clock by the bed. Damn! She'd gone back to sleep. "Where's David?"

"Downstairs. It's about 6:45, and I'm here because David thought you might be sick and in need of a doctor."

"What?"

"You asked me—"

"Why would I need a doctor?"

"I didn't say you needed a doctor. I said David thought you might—"

"Well, I don't. I'm fine. I just overslept. You can go now."

"You interrupted me, twice. Do you know how rude that is?"

He's laughing at me, Michael thought, pushing curls behind her ear as she tried to figure out a way to hold the blanket up to her chin and reach for her robe at the same time. "Well, remind me to apologize next week. I would appreciate it if you would leave so I can get dressed."

Richard held back his smile and tried to be serious, although he thoroughly enjoyed watching as she struggled to recapture her composure. "You don't have to get up. In fact, I'm sorry I woke you. Stay in bed. Allen and David have some things they can do this morning." He crossed the room, but when he reached the door, he turned back to face her. "David will be very happy to know I didn't have to administer CPR." Richard heard the shoe crash against the quickly closed door. At least it sounded like a shoe, but as he reached the top of the stairs, he hoped she hadn't gotten her hands on one of his mother's antique lamps.

Michael looked into the mirror and shuddered. Both cheeks were bright red. Great! Good morning Raggedy Ann! The flush would subside, but her humiliation and the anger that whirled inside her for being so stupid would last forever. Michael couldn't remember the last time she'd gone back to sleep in the morning. She rinsed her face with warm water and ran a brush through her unruly hair. She felt like Lady Godiva, without the horse. Michael knew Richard had wanted to laugh at her. Well, so much for her brilliant plan to seduce the man. As she pulled on her clothes, Michael told herself she'd just have to start over at square one… and stay awake.

Feeling better in mind and spirit, but hungry as Godiva's horse, Michael headed for the kitchen. Mary sat at the table reading the morning paper. Michael walked into the room and said hello, but Mary ignored the greeting.

"Is there any coffee?" Michael's question was redundant because she could see the pot was empty. The lady at the table, complete with a sour face, uttered a few undistinguishable grunts. This was no good. She needed to break the ice between Mary and herself, and since they were now alone, Michael figured this was the time to do it.

"I'll make another pot. Maybe you would like a fresh cup." The room was silent, no answer from stone-face. Michael went to the pantry and got a banana, then waited at the counter for the coffee to brew. She filled two cups and took them to the table, placing one in front of Mary.

"I suppose you want breakfast?"

"No, this will be fine." Michael waved the half-eaten banana in the air. "But I think we need to talk."

"I don't see as how we have anything to say; seems like you already did your talking to the doctor. It's not fair, you know. I never was hired to take care of that child, and I shouldn't be blamed when he goes off and does whatever comes into his head."

"Mary, I don't think Dr. Hampton blames you for what David did. But would the situation be better now if I'd just let you come and get

David that day? Can you be sure he wouldn't have tried to do it again the next time he got a chance?"

"That's not my problem. I was hired to cook and straighten up, not babysit that kid. If you ask me, that boy needs the strap taken to him once in a while."

Laced with bitterness and resentment, Mary's words shot across the table. Unconsciously, Michael pulled back as if struck.

"Have you told Dr. Hampton how you feel?" *No, of course you haven't.* Michael silently answered her own question and realized Mary was looking for a fight.

"No need for me to say anything to the doctor. I just do my job. I know my place, but I don't run a boarding house, so if you're going to keep special hours, don't expect no favors." Signaling she considered the conversation over, Mary dramatically snapped the folds from the paper and started to read again.

I'm an adult. I can handle this. I'll just stay calm. Like hell I will! Michael reached across the table and ripped the newspaper out of Mary's hands, then sent the paper sailing across the floor. "I thought we could have an adult discussion and work out any misunderstandings, but apparently you don't know how to act like an adult. That's fine with me, but you'd better listen to what I have to say. I don't want, or need, any special favors from you. I suggest you do your job, and I'll do mine, and if I need anything from this kitchen, I'll get it myself, and if that doesn't meet with your approval, take it up with the doctor. Another thing, you mind your own business when it comes to David, and you might try wiping that nasty look off your face. Try a smile for a change; you'd be surprised what it can do for you."

Michael didn't wait for a reply. She stormed out the back door. Damn, she was mad. Why was Mary being so unreasonable? Michael walked past the pool and toward the gazebo, trying to think. Had she been rude or condescending? She didn't think so; she thought she'd gone out of her way to be tactful so they could get past any misunderstandings. Well, so much for diplomacy. Michael wondered how you dealt with a person steeped in so much resentment. Well, let the old sour puss soak in her misery. She'd just better stay away from David. The more Michael walked around the gazebo, the calmer she became. She needed to speak to someone about Mary, but who? Anna was getting married soon, and Michael didn't feel right about discussing this conversation with Richard. Well, she was sure of one thing. She had to stay on her toes about David. When Mary said he needed a good spanking, Michael knew she wanted to be the one to do it, but there was no way in hell she would allow Mary touch a hair on his head, let alone paddle his butt.

Allen and David drove up to the garage as Michael rounded the pool. David jumped out of the old pickup and ran to meet her. "I'm glad you're not sick. Dad said you were just tired. Have you had your breakfast? We went to the church and gave them all the toys I don't play with anymore. And guess what? Allen says we can plant a garden. We can grow things to eat. He says we haven't had a garden since Grandma moved away. You'll get to meet her at the wedding. Maybe she'll want to help with the garden."

"David, slow down. You wear me out just listening to you." Allen stood behind his young charge and shook his head. "We've got a lot of time to get the garden in. And besides, your grandma is coming for a wedding, not to muck in the ground. How you doing today, Mrs. McCall?"

"I'm fine, Allen. But please, call me Michael"

"Seems kind of strange, calling a lovely lady by a man's name. I guess your daddy wanted a boy."

"That's what most people think. I mean that my dad named me Michael. But actually, it was my mother who wanted a boy."

Allen watched the two of them laughing and jumping around like a couple of June bugs. Bringing her here was the best thing Richard's done in years. Didn't think he'd ever get Anna some help. Allen had no doubt Richard was a terrific father, but raising a boy was hard. Allen also knew, probably better than most, what Richard had gone through with his wife. He should have sent that one packing right off. Richard's mother saw through her from the start, but she was smart enough to keep still because she knew he wouldn't listen to her anyway. But now we've got Michael.

CHAPTER TEN

RICHARD PHONED AT TEN O'CLOCK, just a friendly call to see how the patient was getting along, or so he said. She could tell he enjoyed catching her off guard this morning and was having a good laugh at her expense. Michael wanted to hang up, but she didn't. Instead, she took a deep breath, and in a very controlled voice, dripping with sweetness, informed him she was perfectly fine.

She lied. She wasn't fine, just glad he couldn't see that her cheeks had turned bright red again when he mentioned this morning's escapade. She held the receiver to her ear, just wishing she could think of something to say, something brilliant to make him squirm, a bit of his own medicine. Suddenly Richard said he had to go, quickly telling her he was pleased to hear she was well and he would be home for dinner around six.

Michael planned to spend the morning writing letters, but David had another idea; the three of them were going fishing. She packed a lunch, and they piled into Allen's old truck, heading for the hills. Turning onto a dirt road lined with giant redwood trees, Allen drove slowly toward a small lake hidden at the bottom of the canyon.

David told Michael they were going to the same spot Allen used to take Richard when he was a boy. "Allen says my grandpa would go along sometimes, but most of the time they went alone. My dad caught his first fish, right down there." David pointed over the dashboard. "Today's my lucky day; I just know it. I'm gonna catch a real big fish. Huh, Allen? Today's the day."

As the two anglers set about their business, Michael spread a blanket on the ground and poured a glass of lemonade. She tried to picture Richard as a small boy, dropping his fishing line into the clear pool. She could see him biting his lower lip as he listened intently to Allen's instruction, just as David did now. Michael felt David's anticipation as he sat quietly, anxious for his first strike. Had it been the same for the young Richard? Suddenly she wanted to know all there was to know about him. Until today, she'd never thought of Richard as a child, but now she wondered if he'd been a whirlwind like David or just a smaller version of the straight-laced, quiet professional he was today. Had his overwhelming smile made the third-grade girls fall at his feet... or had all that come later?

Michael snapped back to the present as water tickled her face, compliments of the tiny fish dangling on the end of David's fishing pole. "Look! Michael, I caught one, but I gotta throw him back 'cause he's too small. But I caught a fish and on my first try. Wait until I tell my dad." He ran back to the edge of the water where Allen helped him remove the hook and lower the small fish back into the water, and then the mighty fisherman honored Michael with a smile and a thumbs-up, grinning ear to ear.

"What we got to eat? I'm starving. Next time I'm gonna catch a whole bunch of big ones so we can have fish for lunch. We should have brought the camera. We'll bring it next time 'cause I'm gonna catch bigger ones next time."

After lunch they headed home, with David planning their next trip as soon as Allen started the car. But after ten minutes, he settled against her shoulder and dozed off until they pulled into the driveway.

Michael left David with Allen and climbed the outside stairs leading to her room from the patio. She wanted to stay away from the kitchen as long as possible. Before leaving on the fishing trip, she'd left Mary a note telling her Dr. Hampton would be home for dinner at six o'clock.

The afternoon passed quickly. She wrote her letters, listened to music, catnapped, and roused herself in time to take a leisurely shower before dinner. As Michael ran a brush through her damp hair, she heard a knock on the bedroom door. She walked into the room and found a note on the floor under the door. It was from David. They needed to talk about their list. Michael got dressed and went to his room. She found David on the floor with his list and a large calendar from the local grocery store.

"We got lots of work to do," he told her, turning back to his list. "Allen says I gotta set priorities 'cause he says I can't do everything. I showed him our list this afternoon, and he says I gotta choose which ones I want to do the most. He says I gotta talk it over with you, so we better get to work." David patted the floor beside him.

A little before six, Richard pulled to a stop at the rear of the house and reached across the seat for the tray of fresh strawberries he'd bought from the local fruit stand on his way home. He'd never stopped there before. Hell, he'd not been in a grocery store in years; he'd just hired someone else to see that there was food in the house. Sometimes he'd buy wine from a small shop he'd found in the city, and once a year he went to Collin & Burke's for his clothes, but he'd never bought a sheet or towel for the house, or a plant for the yard. As he'd paid for the strawberries, Richard realized he'd been living his life in a vacuum, and he had pulled David in with him. He went to the office and to the hospital. He taught, he operated, and he did research. Occasionally, he would go to the club or out to dinner, and the only social functions he attended were those that raised money for the medical center. He bought season tickets to the ballet and symphony, but never went, just gave the tickets to the girls at the office. Richard hadn't played golf or tennis or gone fishing in years. No wonder David wanted to run away.

Richard greeted Mary as he put the tray of berries on the counter top. She gave him a garbled reply, then turned away to stir something on the stove. He obviously needed to talk with her, but not now. Now, he needed to see his son. How could he ever make it up to David for the past years? Take one step at a time, he reminded himself.

Dropping his briefcase on the bottom step, he headed for David's room. The door was open, and he stared in amazed silence at the two on the floor. They were head to head, stretched out on their stomachs, legs bent, with bare feet suspended in air. David had on shorts and a T-shirt, and his cheeks were bright and rosy, as if he'd been scrubbed and polished. Michael wore a sleeveless blouse tucked into blue denim shorts, her long slim legs crossed at the ankles as her painted toes kept time to the music coming from David's radio. She had tied her hair on top of her head with a ribbon, and ringlets of blazing mahogany swayed back and forth, keeping time with her toes.

Michael turned around, causing her blouse to draw tightly across her breasts. She felt the heat rise to her cheeks and almost moaned aloud, realizing how she must look stretched out on the floor. Without being coy or flirtatious, she gave him her best smile. Michael knew she should get up, but she couldn't turn away; she just stared like an idiot as the corners of his mouth turned into a smile and a mischievous look filled his black eyes.

"Looks like some high-level stuff going on here." Richard had no idea what he'd just said. Caught off guard and stunned by the sight of her, he could only smile as a bolt of excitement spiraled through him.

"Dad, guess what? I caught a fish, on my first try, but I put him back 'cause he needed to grow some more. We went to the lake where you used to go. And guess what? We're gonna go back 'cause now I know how to fish so I'm gonna catch enough for dinner. And guess what? We're planning the whole summer. Want to see our schedule?"

David pulled Richard to the floor and snuggled between them, tighter than a hot dog in a bun. Their eyes followed his small finger as it flipped through the next three months and all the things he wanted to do before he had to go back to school in September.

"We had a lot more things we wanted to do, but we can't do everything, huh, Michael? And you can come with us anytime you want."

Richard combed his fingers through his son's blond hair. "Thank you, David. I'll have Ruthie make a copy of this so I'll know what you're doing, and if I can get away, I'd love to go with you."

Look at me, Richard, she said with her eyes and heart. Michael willed him to glance her way, but it wasn't working. She wished she were a witch so she could cast a spell over him, to make him want her as much as she wanted him. That thought made her laugh as a vision of Richard, with glazed eyes and outstretched hands, moved toward her, ready to obey her slightest wish. But it was David who asked if she was all right as Richard continued to study the calendar.

"I'm fine, David. I'd better go see about dinner. It's almost six, and we don't want to keep Mary waiting." Her words sounded ridiculous. What did she care if Mary had to hold dinner? Before she could utter any more profound statements, Michael snapped her mouth shut, biting her bottom lip in the process. *Good Lord,* she thought, *I've got to get out of this room before I make a complete mess of my brilliant plan to seduce the master of the house.*

Now he looked at her with that questioning arched eyebrow of his as she tried gracefully to maneuver her long legs under her and stand up. *Now he looks.* Michael decided Richard just wasn't going to help her at all with his seduction.

After dinner, Richard told Mary that from now on he wanted their meals served in the kitchen where it was more relaxed and family-like. Mary didn't say a word, but her eyes narrowed with icy contempt as she stared at Michael, then nodded her head and left the dining room.

"Richard, we need to talk to you." Someone had to pick up David's tuxedo for the wedding, get his Cub Scout uniform, and go shopping for the new pet. Michael started to suggest that she take David and spend a day in the city when the "Master of Schedules and Timetables" told her he had it all worked out.

Tomorrow they would go to the city. It was his regular day to teach at the hospital in San Francisco. Michael and David could drop him off and take the car, giving them all day to get everything done, and they could even stop for dinner on the way home if they wanted to.

Early the next morning, they were on their way, across the bridge and straight into the commuter traffic. After ten minutes of weaving in and out of the morning rush, Michael decided she wasn't crazy enough to take over the wheel of the black car. Just finding a place to park would be a challenge.

"I don't want the car. We can get around by BART or by cable car. There's too much traffic. I might wreck your car."

"Don't be silly, McCall," he said, moving from street to street, managing to stay a few seconds ahead of stalled traffic. "Nothing can happen that our insurance won't cover."

He pulled into the circle driveway of the medical center and set the brake. Michael finally gave up, not wanting to buy into his monumental production of dragging her out of the passenger seat and pulling her around the car. After he had her buckled in place, her hands gripping the steering wheel, he said, "Have a great day, and try to be back by five." Then he was gone.

Actually, she had worried for nothing, and at one minute to five they were back where they started that morning, waiting for Richard. Michael had stashed the pint-sized tuxedo and Cub Scout uniform in the trunk, and the new pet rode in the back seat with David, who beamed like a proud new parent.

"Here he comes, Michael. Here comes Dad. I can't wait to show him what I got. Do you think he'll like Runaround? I just love him. I can't wait to show Allen."

"It's going to be okay David. Just give your dad a chance to get in the car."

Michael rolled down her window and waved to Richard as he walked toward the car. For the past hour, she'd been somewhat ambivalent about the new pet. Maybe she should have discussed the matter more thoroughly with Richard, but he had said something small and in a cage. Well, that's what they'd bought. Runaround was small... and he had a cage.

"You're right on time. Good girl. I told you it would be okay." Richard opened the back door on the driver's side to put his briefcase on the floor. A big smile covered David's face as he held up his new pet, minus the cage, for an introduction.

"Good God, David, what have you got in your hands?" Richard jumped back, bumping his head against the headliner of the car. David immediately pulled the small bit of fur to his chest, holding him tightly, trying not to cry. Richard extracted himself from the back seat and headed for her door, bending down to her open window as Michael tried to calm the tearful David.

"What in the hell is that? That's not a guinea pig. I thought you were going to get a guinea pig or a hamster. McCall, what are you doing?"

"I'm trying to get out of this car, so back up. Richard, back up and stop swearing, and lower your voice." He stepped back and Michael shot out of the car, slamming the door. She grabbed his arm and pulled Richard away from the car, then whirled around and said, "Damn you, Richard. You scared David; you made him cry."

"I'm sorry; I didn't mean to yell like that. It must be the lighting because it looked like he was holding a rat. What is it?"

"A rat."

"You bought him a rat? You were supposed to buy a guinea pig, or a hamster."

"You never said we were supposed to buy a guinea pig or a hamster. You said something small, in a cage. Well, Runaround is small and—"

"Runaround?"

"That's his name, Runaround, and he has a cage. We could have bought a bigger one. They grow quite large, you know, but we got the smallest one they had. Of course, he'll grow some, a little."

"Tell me something I don't know, McCall. I've seen rats bigger than house cats. That thing in the car, that rat, is not small, and he will, I assure you, get bigger. He has to go back. I said David could have a small, domesticated pet, but I meant something like a hamster, not a rat. It has to go back, and that's that."

"Major news flash, Doctor! Runaround is domesticated. He even has papers. Really, Richard, do you think we got him out of some gutter? We spent hours today learning about rats, how they make exceptionally devoted pets, especially for someone like David. Okay, fine, if you won't let David keep him, you better come up with a legitimate reason why the little guy has to go back. Your son and I acted in good faith when we bought Runaround. You said small and in a cage, and that's what we bought."

"So now I'm the bad guy. Is that what you're trying to tell me?"

"HELLO! Have you heard anything I've said? Okay, let's try this again. You don't have to be the bad guy. I just said you better have a valid reason why the rat has to go back. On the other hand, you could give David and the little guy a chance to prove it will or won't work. I mean, he's had all his shots, the rat, not David, and what harm can that little bit of fur do anyway? Huh?"

Richard ran his hands through his hair as he paced back and forth. Well, actually, he just walked in a small circle, muttering something indistinguishable under his breath. He stopped in front of her and held out his hands. She waited for him to say something, but he didn't. He just walked to the car and got in the back seat with David, who still held his new friend on his chest. The item in dispute seemed calm enough. His pink eyes gave Richard the once over, and his long tail whipped back and forth as he waited for his fate to be decided.

"David, I'm sorry I frightened you. It's just that I hadn't expected this, a, kind of... I guess I thought you would buy a hamster or something."

David and Runaround looked at Richard and waited for him to give the final verdict. "Michael explained to me that it's now acceptable to have a... a rat as a pet. I didn't know that. That's why I reacted the way I did. Do you understand what I'm saying, David? I'm not mad at you. I was just surprise."

"Do I have to take him back? I heard you tell Michael I have to take him back."

"No, David, you don't have to take him back. We will give it a try, but there will be some rules you'll have to follow."

"Thank you, Daddy. I'll take very good care of him, you'll see." David threw his arm around Richard's neck and Runaround offered his thanks too as he snuggled against Richard's chest and thumped him with his powerful tail.

With the little guy back in his cage and David buckled in, Richard finally pulled out of the driveway. "Where do you want to eat?" he asked as he threaded his way into the traffic.

"Well, we could hang a left at Mickey D's, or we could just go home. I vote for home. What about you David?"

"Home, I vote for home too."

"Home it is." Richard picked up the car phone and called Maria's in Sausalito. He placed an order for three grinders. Then he turned to Michael, trying hard to keep a straight face. Trying not to laugh, he said, "Should I order one for the little guy?"

CHAPTER ELEVEN

MICHAEL HAD DECIDED NOT TO go to the wedding, but Richard and David overruled her decision. Okay, she'd go, but only if she could take her own car so she could leave after the ceremony. Richard ignored her words, just as he ignored the scowl on her face when he took her arm and escorted her to the front seat of his car, fastening her seat belt. Why did he do that? *Does he think I'm not smart enough to attach my own seat belt?*

Ten minutes after arriving at the church, panic set in. Martin couldn't find the rings, David declared he didn't want the cute little flower girl to kiss him, and no one could find Richard's boutonniere. How could he give the bride away half dressed? Michael took control.

Much to Martin's chagrin, she searched his pockets and found the rings, which she gave to David. She helped him tie them to the tiny satin pillow and told him not to move and then positioned the flower girl next to Martin, giving her the same command before telling Richard to chill-out. Then she went in search of Anna.

Michael found the nervous bride, her future stepdaughter Sally, and Ruthie, the tearful maid of honor, in the dressing room. After a quick introduction to Martin's daughter, Michael suggested Sally might want to check on her own daughter, the precocious little flower girl who had unwittingly terrorized David, then found a tissue for Ruthie.

The missing boutonniere was just gone. "No problem," she told Anna with a reassuring smile, pulling a sprig of greenery and a rosebud from the bridal bouquet. "No one will ever know." Retracing her steps Michael pinned the makeshift boutonniere on Richard's lapel. After a final pat to his chest, she stepped into the sanctuary and found an aisle seat at the back of the church.

Touching him hadn't been so bad; it was looking into Richard's dark eyes that made her shake. Well, he wasn't going to turn her into Silly Putty today. She glanced around the church and counted at least ten men who were as handsome as Richard. Maybe she needed to rethink her feelings. Why did she assume she was in love with Richard? Maybe it was just lust turning her to mush every time she looked at him. Michael had not made love in over two years. *Maybe a good romp in the sack would calm me down, get my hormones working again.* This feeling of limbo stunk. What she needed was a different perspective. She needed to call Sarah.

A hush fell over the church as the organ music filled the air. Her chest tightened at the sight of David, looking very smart in his tuxedo as he walked toward the altar. When the wedding march announced the arrival of the bride, she stood with the rest of the congregation, but when Michael turned to face the bride, all her reasoning about love and lust flew out the door.

Anna looked lovely, but Michael's eyes locked on Richard, at the tender look on his face as he stood proudly beside the bride. The word handsome simply didn't describe how he looked, tall and strong— his magnetism so powerful. Richard started back, his gaze bold and provocative, a soft smile tipping the corners of his mouth. He stood close enough for Michael to smell his cologne and feel the warmth of his body. Her reaction to him was so intense her heart jumped to an erratic rhythm and Michael prayed her legs would hold her until Richard moved down the aisle.

Then his expression changed; his eyes narrowed, an eyebrow shot up, and his smile dissolved into a frown. Michael took a step back, right into the arms of Peter Farrell.

"Hi, Rich. Beautiful day for a wedding." Peter spoke softly, as if he were whispering in her ear rather than talking to Richard, who gave a curt nod to Peter before starting toward the altar, muffing his first step.

When the pastor told Martin he could kiss his wife, Michael knew what she had to do. If she left before the bride and groom waltzed up the aisle, she would be long gone before Richard could make her stay, but then a thought froze in her brain. What if he didn't care if she stayed or not? Sure, he'd smiled at her. *But wise up dummy*, she told herself. *You're just his son's nanny. Chill-out, like you told him to do. Enjoy yourself—eat some cake and have a glass of champagne.*

Michael's desire to run out of the church and call a cab dissolved, and she stood quietly with the rest of the guests and honored Mr. and Mrs. Martin Shaw.

David ran up the aisle. "Did I do good, Michael? Didn't Anna look pretty? We gotta take some pictures and then we're going to the party."

David looked over his shoulder at his father, but Richard was looking at her. Or was he looking at Peter, who stood behind her like a second skin?

"The pictures should take about fifteen minutes, and then we'll go to the reception. You can wait down front." Richard maneuvered her into the aisle, and although he spoke softly, Peter heard every word.

"These things always take longer than expected. Why don't I drive Mrs. McCall to the club? You can join us there."

Smiling ear-to-ear, Peter reached for her arm as Richard shook his head, refusing the offer. Michael looked from one to the other as the two men stood firm. Well, this wasn't Richard's decision.

"That's a good idea," she heard herself saying as she turned away from Richard's frown and smiled at Peter. "If you're sure you don't mind?"

The trip didn't take long, barely enough time for their conversation to cover the weather before Peter pulled his expensive sports car to a smooth stop at the front door of the club. Richard must have bribed the photographer because he and David walked through the door just as Peter handed her a glass of champagne.

Michael took David to get him a soft drink, and when they returned to the table, Richard handed her another glass of champagne. "I haven't finished this one," she objected

He took the half-filled glass from her and put the fresh one in her hand. "Champagne goes flat very quickly."

Men! He was just mad because Peter had given her the first one, and the champagne was just the beginning. She wasn't allowed to finish one dance all night. If she danced with Peter, Richard cut in. If Richard held her tightly, Peter arrived, tapping his friend on the shoulder. They acted like a couple of fools... like little boys, only wanting something because the other one had it. Michael was not sorry when it was time to go home.

Two nights later, Michael dove into the pool, set her pace, and let instinct take over. After everyone had gone to bed, she came to the pool and swam. Swimming usually relaxed her, but not tonight. Tonight the feeling of tranquility she usually felt evaded her. She was tired but couldn't sleep, and she knew why. No matter how hard Michael tried not to think of Richard, there he was, his image so clear, shuffling around in her brain, creating chaos and confusion. It had to end, but she didn't know how to make it stop. Every time she thought she'd figured him out, he sent new signals. Why couldn't he tell her how he felt or leave her alone? She felt like a yo-yo on a piece of silly string.

Michael swam to the side of the pool and got out. She wrapped a towel around her head and pulled on her robe. If he just kept his hands off her and stayed ten feet away, maybe she could keep things in perspective and avoid falling all over herself. She sneezed. She was stiff and cold. If she didn't get out of her wet suit, she was going to be sick, and right now she had enough to think about without catching a cold.

Michael crept up the stairs and pulled off her suit. After a warm shower, she crawled into bed and made a mental note to call Sarah in the morning. Damn! Tomorrow was Monday. David had a boat trip with the Scouts to Angel Island for a cookout, and she'd signed on as a chaperone. Maybe she could meet Sarah in the city tomorrow night.

An hour later, sleep seemed impossible, and she couldn't let go of Friday night's fiasco. She'd avoided Richard all weekend, refusing to go fishing on Saturday. After church today, they planted the garden, but she made sure Allen and David never left them alone. *What a mess I've made of everything.* She not only had Richard to figure out, now she had Peter Farrell knocking at her door, figuratively, but he was calling on the telephone.

Early the next morning, Michael threw the alarm clock under the bed. After killing the clock, she pulled the covers over her head. She wanted to go back to sleep, but she had to get up, right now.

Half an hour later, Michael struggled to finish the last quarter mile of her morning jog. She longed for a cup of coffee, but she thought of bitchy Mary and her evil eye. If she couldn't face Richard and didn't have the stamina for David, she sure didn't need a confrontation with Mary.

Michael had spent a miserable night, and it was all Richard's fault. She had no business going to the wedding. The first time he'd pulled her into his arms and onto the dance floor, drawing their bodies together, she had willingly surrendered to the sweet agony surging through her like an electric current. When his hand moved gently up and down her back and his warm breath brushed her neck, she'd whirled toward a higher arousal that grew to dangerous proportions. Who was she trying to deceive? She wasn't in lust; she was in love. She knew it because every time she thought of Richard, her heart beat at warp speed. Peter had held her just as tightly, as intimately as Richard had, but she'd not felt the same rush. Peter was a grab-your-heart scrumptious looking man, an honest-to-goodness hunk. He had the right moves and danced like a dream, and Michael believed his sexy voice could charm a saintly nun out of her habit. But when he'd held her in his arms, there was no magic, no chemistry, and no passion. God help her, she didn't want a roll in the sack or a casual affair. She wanted Richard. Michael wanted him to love her, but she didn't think he did because after Peter left the reception, Richard had not asked her dance again.

Richard wasn't having a good day. "Damn it, Ruthie, have you called the maintenance department again? How can I work if the power keeps going on and off?"

"Yes, Doctor. I called them again, and their response was the same as when I talked to them ten minutes ago. They didn't expect this storm. The emergency generator is working on the hospital wing, but they can't tell me when they'll have it up here. Hopefully the regular power will be back on by the time they get the generator fixed."

"Son of a bitch, we have a multimillion-dollar facility and they can't keep the damn lights on. How many patients do we have left to see?"

Ruthie handed Richard a glass of iced tea and told him to drink. They were behind, had been all day. It was well after six, and the unexpected thunderstorm had caused the power to switch off and on for the last hour. The patients Ruthie could handle, but not Richard. Today, Dr. Cool was not cool. She didn't know what was biting at him, and she knew better than to ask.

"Mrs. Briton is one week post-op; she has to be seen. Then we can call it a day."

"Okay, let's get to it, but call the house again."

"I just did. There's still no answer, just the machine."

"Well, try again. I can't believe she's still out in this weather. Don't look at me like that. You can be replaced, you know."

"So you keep telling me, but you know what, Doctor? Today that threat sounds really good to me."

"Okay, calm down. Give me Mrs. Briton's chart and go call the house again."

Ruthie handed over the medical chart and reached for the phone. She let it ring until the answering machine came on. She didn't know why Richard was so worried. Although Ruthie didn't know her well, she didn't think Michael was a stupid woman and surely she would not take any chances, especially where David was concerned. Why was Richard so upset? Well, she'd had a lousy day too, and she wasn't going to make it worse by asking him any questions. Ruthie went to room three and looked in. When he turned to her, she just shook her head and quickly closed the door.

One hour later, Richard punched the accelerator and the speedometer registered the response. *Where are they?* The windshield wipers labored to keep up with the torrent of rain, but the storm was passing.

No one was home. Mary had the day off, and Allen was at his weekly poker game, but where in the hell were Michael and David?

He roared up to the house and shot out of the car. Richard fumbled with his door key, swearing aloud as his skilled fingers dropped the key ring. When he finally got the door unlocked, Richard was almost hyperventilating.

Then he heard the music. The foyer was dark, but a faint light beckoned from the living room at the end of the hall.

The room glowed softly with a tranquil light coming from the fireplace. A tiny flame skipped and danced between bright-red coals. A propane lantern, turned low, sat on the coffee table, and an empty picnic basket was propped up in front of the fireplace. Michael was on the floor, her back against the couch with David asleep in her arms. Soft refrains of The Mamas and The Papas, singing about Monday morning filled the room.

Richard swallowed hard. He couldn't speak until he got his heart out of his throat and his pulse below ninety. Richard felt his blood pressure ease back to normal, so relieved to find them home and safe he couldn't speak… Or was he tongue-tied because of the way Michael looked? The frown she'd worn for the last two days was gone, replaced by a dreamy smile. She was radiant with the light from the fire sparkling in her hair. He shoved his hands in his pocket and fought to stay focused.

"You're home," he said.

"Of course we're home. Where else would we be in a storm like this? What happened? You look like you were chasing a ghost."

"I've been calling for the last two hours. Why didn't you answer the phone? Good God, McCall, I've been out of my mind with worry. I've imagined you capsized, stranded on Angel Island, and God knows what else, and all the time you've been here. Why didn't you answer the phone?"

"Really, Richard, you don't give me much credit, do you? And lower your voice. You'll wake David, although I think he needs to go to bed."

Richard moved into the room and sat beside her on the floor. "Why didn't you answer the phone?" This time he asked his question in a soft, low voice.

"Because David was tired and fell asleep. I couldn't get to the phone without waking him."

"It looks like you've been having a party, but why the fire?" Richard loosened his tie and unbuttoned his shirt. "McCall, do you realize it's hotter than hell in here?"

"I know. I had David open the French doors, but it didn't help much. We had to have a decent size fire to get enough coals to cook the hot dogs."

Richard stood up and removed his jacket and rolled up his shirt sleeves, then sat beside her again, only this time his shoulder rested against hers. "The last time I checked we had a kitchen for that purpose. I know Mary's gone, but surely you could have managed to fix a couple of hot dogs."

"For your information, Doctor, I'm an excellent cook, but David wanted to roast hot dogs and marshmallows. That's what we were going to do at Angel Island, but we never got there. We waited at the dock for over an hour, but eventually the scoutmaster decided the storm was going to get worse, so they called off the trip. We came home, tramped all over the hillside in the rain until David got hungry, and then built a fire and roasted the hot dogs. Do you know he has never roasted a marshmallow before?"

"Here, let me take him. You must be stiff." Richard stood and lifted David to his feet. "Come on, pal, time for bed." He held the boy with one arm and offered his free hand to Michael. When she touched his hand, his pulse took off, pounding with a fierce inner fire that matched the heat of the room. As he pulled Michael to her feet, her thigh brushed against him, and his desire for her was as violent as the storm that had just passed. "I'll take David upstairs."

"I better clean up this mess," she said, pulling her hand from his grip. Michael gave the sleepy David a kiss. "I'll be up in a minute to tuck you in."

"No, I'll do it. But you better be careful, McCall. If you back up any farther, you'll be in the fire."

She hadn't realized she'd backed away. He was right; it was too hot in here. "Maybe I'll go for a swim after I get things put away."

David muttered goodnight as he and his dad turned to leave the room, but at the door, Richard stopped and drew his son closer to his side. "Sounds like a great idea. It looks like the storm has passed us by."

Michael grabbed the poker, spread the hot, glowing coals, and placed the fire screen tightly against the opening. She threw the rest of the picnic into the basket, turned off the lantern, and took the basket into the kitchen. She would deal with Mary tomorrow if the surly housekeeper had anything to say about the mess.

In the pool, Michael cut through the water, swimming as fast as her arms and legs could propel her, sending her into the wall where she pivoted and swam the other way. She saw Richard standing by the edge of the pool, holding two glasses and a bottle of wine. She would keep swimming and pretend she didn't see him, just turn and swim the other way, but she didn't do either. Michael just stopped and reached for the lip of the pool.

"David is all bedded down for the night. He said to thank you for a great day and the funny stories. I thought you might enjoy a glass of chilled wine," he said as he filled the glass and held it out to her.

Say no. Swim away, fast. Of course, Michael didn't listen to the warning. She swam to the corner and walked up the steps as tiny droplets of water slid off her body, leaving a shimmering radiance to her skin.

He placed the glass in her outstretched hand. "This is supposed to be a fresh new Chardonnay. See what you think. Marc says I should buy a few cases before the price goes out of sight." Richard frowned and shut his mouth. He was rambling, but he couldn't help it. He felt so heady, terrified and excited at the same time. Her swimsuit was a simple tank, black spandex that molded itself over her full breasts and slim waist. The material stopped just above her slender hips and long, lithe legs that a moment ago had propelled her through the water like a rocket. Richard set his glass on the patio table and took a step toward her, but the sound of his pager shattered the air and halted his steps.

He swore under his breath as he reached into his pants pocket for the device that had stopped him from taking her into his arms. Richard looked at the display. "I'm sorry. I have to take this call."

Michael watched him go into the house. She sipped her wine, so unnerved by the sudden change in his mood before his pager penetrated the air that her head reeled with confusion and doubt. Never mind the rest of her emotions that he'd managed to gift wrap with ribbons of hope and hysteria. Michael drank deeply from the glass he'd placed in her hand. She reached for the bottle and refilled her glass, then paced beside the pool. He was going to kiss her. She hadn't imagined it…

Or had she? Michael knew she couldn't go on like this, hoping, always wondering how he felt.

He's not coming back, she thought as she continued to pace. A cool breeze whirled about her. She willed it to wash away the feeling of rejection that knotted inside her. A feeling she'd never known before lodged in her throat as she fought off a panic that would bring tears if she allowed it. Michael put her glass on the table and went to her room. The small lamp by the side of her bed created shadows around the room but offered enough light to find her way. She wouldn't cry. She would not behave like a young girl with her first love. Michael took off her wet suit and put on the white terry robe, then turned off the light in the bathroom and walked past the bed.

Richard stood just inside the room by the French door, the door she hadn't bothered to close.

"You didn't finish your wine."

Michael doubted she could hold back her tears, so she just turned away. "Please go away, Dr. Hampton. I've had more than enough for one night. Please, just go."

He set his glass on the coffee table and walked to her. Her hair rode high on her head, held by tortoise shell pins, and the soft light caressed the damp curls like slivers of amber. Richard touched her shoulder, felt her quiver as his hands reached deep into the mass of ringlets and removed the pins. Her dark hair spilled down, engulfing her like a shroud, embracing his hands as he lowered his face to her hair and drew in the scent of her.

Slowly, he turned her around and her face drew the light. He raised his hands to her face, and his thumb lightly traced the outline of her cheek, then her lower lip. Richard looked into her deep-green eyes as his hands gently cupped her troubled face. She closed her eyes, and thick, dark lashes rested gently on her delicate skin.

Richard heard her breath catch as his lips brushed hers. He kissed one eye and then the other, his touch light, whisper light, but leaving a burning trail as he moved over her. He felt hot and exhilarated, but he forced himself to go slow as he kissed her ear, moved lower as his lips then the tip of his tongue tasted the side of her slender neck.

Richard held her away from him, and when she opened her eyes, he softly told her to look at him, and when she did, a fragile thread began to develop between them. He drew her into his arms as ragged whimpers of sheer need escaped her lips. She moaned his name, and her words caressed his ear as he instantly responded to her intense cry, driving them to the edge, toward the fire as he crushed her to him and buried his face in her hair. The air stopped, and their world became silent and still as his senses screamed with the feel, the scent, the need of her. Then his mouth claimed hers.

Michael shook violently, fed by her passion and the power of his kiss as his firm mouth demanded a response. Her lips parted, and she rose to meet his kiss as his tongue sought hers, gloriously meeting, then mating... just as she'd dreamed. His lips seared a path down her neck, returning quickly to recapture her lips, demanding more this time. The sweet trembling of his lips made her move closer as he explored her mouth and their tongues danced together to a silent melody.

Richard's hands moved beneath the robe and explored the smooth lines of her back, her waist, her hips as his hard, searching mouth continued to savor hers. His hand outlined the circle of her breast. He placed his palm on the smooth globe, pushed in a slow circle, and felt the soft nipple instantly harden under his touch, felt the rapid beat of her heart. Richard molded his hand to her, caressing her long and slow, as he drew her body to his.

Michael withered with erotic pleasure as his hands created a symphony throughout her body. Her arousal reached a staggering height, and Michael thought she couldn't absorb anymore, but she was wrong. He kissed the pulsing hollow at the base of her throat. Then his lips moved to her temple with such overwhelming tenderness as his hands moved downward, once again skimming the sides of her naked body, coming to rest on her hips before his powerful hands molded her into the contours of his hard frame. Michael's arms tightened around his neck as she pressed her open mouth to his. Instinctively, she arched toward him as he gathered her close to his warm, pulsing body, binding her tightly to the hardness of his desire.

She could feel his body tremble and push into hers as she captured his tongue and sucked it gently, inhaling the sweetness of his mouth. A fierce tempest raged through them, erasing all logic... almost.

Then Richard moaned and pulled his lips away. He buried his face in her hair and his arms held her tightly as their heated bodies trembled. He held fast to her as the tremors of their arousal slowly began to subside. Then he took her face into his hands as he had done a lifetime ago.

"My God, Michael, what have I done?" Richard let go of her and backed away, turning from her as he ran his hand through his hair. He spun around to face her again. "You are so beautiful, and I want you so badly I ache just looking at you, but I can't do this. I can't get involved. After Eve, I just. . ."

She opened her mouth to speak, but whatever words she might have said wedged in her throat. Words were impossible; at least until her mind stopped spinning. What was he saying? She put her hands over her mouth as her head moved from side to side in denial. She wouldn't listen. He couldn't mean the words that ripped at her heart. He couldn't.

Richard wanted to turn away. He didn't want to watch the tortured look of disbelief that covered her face as she tried to understand what he'd just said, but he couldn't turn away. He would not play the coward. "I'm so sorry. I didn't set out to hurt you. But I can't do this. I can't get involved... I just can't."

"Why? I thought that you..."

The pain in Michael's eyes cut to the deepest part of him, to the exact place where he had locked away all of the memories of Eve. When would he ever be free of her? When would it all end? What could he possibly say to Michael? She stood so still, waiting for him to answer her simple question, but all he could say was, "I'm sorry." Then he turned and left the room.

Michael stood where he'd left her, slowly dying, shaking all over. Her pulse pounded in her temples, and a chill invaded her body, which had burned so savagely just a moment ago. Her legs gave way, and she crumbled to the floor. She bit her swollen lip until it throbbed like her raging pulse. A raw, primitive grief overwhelmed her as she fought to find a meaning to his devastating words and some way stop the tremulous waves of yearning that still burned in her. She swallowed hard as hot tears slipped down her cheeks. Then she wept aloud, huddled on the floor, slowly rocking back and forth.

CHAPTER TWELVE

ICHAEL WATCHED RICHARD DRIVE AWAY and wondered if he'd had a lousy night. Maybe he'd just decided to change his morning routine again and leave before the happy family gathered around the breakfast table. Either way, she hoped he was miserable.

She was so cold. A thick fog had rolled in from the ocean and hugged the hillside, blotting out the early morning light. Michael turned away from the window and wrapped a wool shawl around her shoulders. It was covered with sand from last night, but she didn't care; she would shake it out later. She sat on the floor by the loveseat and knew it would be better if she did it now. Anything would be better than thinking about last night, but she couldn't help it.

How long had she cried last night after he'd left her room? She couldn't remember. All she remembered were wrenching sobs coursing through her until there were no tears left. Why? She'd asked that question a hundred times, and no matter how hard she tried, she still didn't understand.

Michael pulled her legs to her chest and rested her throbbing head on her knees, holding the shawl tightly around her. Tiny granules of sand, lodged in the garment, bit into her face, but she didn't brush them away.

Long after he left, after her tears had stopped, she'd thrown on some clothes and driven away. Her sweater and jeans and the shawl she'd grabbed as she ran out the door weren't enough to ward off the deep chill that still raced through her. She had driven aimlessly, finally stopping at a small bay facing the ocean where she sat in the sand near the water and cried again. The thunderous roll of the surf, as the waves crashed against the rocks down the beach, echoed the pain in her heart. She walked the beach, lost in a cold gray mist like the sea birds whose mournful cries rose from a ghostly depth of a darkened place to lead her way.

Michael heard a knock on her door. It was David, but she couldn't let him see her like this. "Just a minute," she called toward the closed door. Michael rolled the shawl into a ball and brushed her clothes with her hands. She was freezing, still damp from the ocean spray and wet sand.

She opened the door, but only enough to put her head into the opening. "Hi, Sport. Ready for breakfast?"

"Yeah. Dad had to go in early so he won't be eating with us, but he said to tell you he would call you later. Are you ready to eat?"

He wore cutoff jeans and a T-shirt with a pocket, and from this front-row seat, Runaround peered about. "I'll be down in a minute. Why don't you ask Mary to fix us some fruit and cold cereal? We'll have our breakfast in the gazebo."

As soon as David and the rat took off to do as she'd said, Michael stripped and jumped into the shower. She brushed her hair and put on clean clothes. Her room was covered in wet clothes and sand, but she'd take care of it later. As she rounded the hallway leading to the kitchen, she could hear David's strained voice, clearly on the verge of tears as he repeatedly said he was sorry. Mary stood over him with a wooden spoon in her hand, shouting at David. "Get that filthy rat out of my kitchen."

"David, take Runaround and go find Allen. I'll meet you outside." Michael took David by the shoulders and eased him out the back door and then swung around to face Mary.

"I won't have that nasty thing running around my kitchen. I just won't have it." Mary shook the spoon at her, waving it through the air, swishing it close to the side of Michael's head.

Michael grabbed the spoon as it sailed by her face, forcing Mary's arm to stop midair. "Stop yelling like a fool and give me that damn spoon before you hurt someone."

"I don't want that rat in here. I won't have it, I tell you." Mary lowered her voice as she rubbed her wrist.

"Well, I actually don't care what you want. In fact, the last time I checked, this kitchen belongs to David and Dr. Hampton, and unless you're blind, you could see that Runaround was in David's pocket and not running around this room. I think you better calm down."

"You can't order me around. I get my orders from Dr. Hampton."

"Fine, I'll just call the doctor and tell him you were yelling at David and about to hit him on the head with a wooden spoon. We'll just see what he tells you to do."

"Wait, there's no need to bother the doctor. Maybe I will go to my room. That boy is driving me crazy."

"Just go. And I think it would be a smart idea if you keep your remarks to yourself." Michael realized she was shaking the spoon at Mary as the housekeeper backed away from her.

When Mary slammed her door, Michael threw the spoon toward the sink. Her aim was true, hitting two glasses that tumbled to the counter with a crash, sending glass flying into the sink. She suddenly felt better. She fixed a tray for their breakfast and went in search of David and the little guy. Michael found them with Allen at the gazebo.

"Am I in trouble? I just told her we wanted to eat outside, but she started yelling at me, and she wouldn't let me tell her anything."

Michael gently pushed the hair out of his eyes. She looked over his head at Allen and rolled her eyes. "You are not in any trouble, my sweet. I shouldn't have asked you to tell Mary we wanted to eat outside. I should have talked to her or just done it myself, but you didn't do anything wrong. Look, I brought some fresh peaches." She smiled at the child, who still wore a worried look on his face. Trying to get his mind off what had just happened in the kitchen, she said, "Look, David, look at Runaround getting ready for breakfast."

The little guy was washing his face and combing his hair with his busy front feet. He seemed totally unaffected by all the shouting and was ready to enjoy whatever David wanted to do.

It did the trick. She gave David a damp towel to wash his hands and filled his bowl with sliced peaches and corn flakes, placing a small pile of flakes in front of the little guy. Michael walked with Allen away from the table and told him what had happened.

"That woman better not touch the boy or else she'll have me to deal with. Never did like the old witch. It's a good thing you walked in when you did. Good Lord knows what would have happened if you hadn't stepped in, and she'd have denied it. That woman tells lies. I know she does."

Michael looked at her watch. "David has a swimming lesson in about an hour. Then I'm going to take him to the library in Mill Valley. He's never been to a library, except at school. I think we'll have lunch at the park, and that should take most of the day. I'm sure Mary wouldn't do anything stupid, but I'd feel better if we left the little guy with you if you don't mind?"

"That's okay with me. I thought we could get some materials and David can help me build a bigger cage for Runaround. I'll let David do most of the work. I know the little mouse stays pretty close to him when they're inside, but David can't watch him all the time, so just somewhere we could stick the little mouse when he's outside."

"Allen, he's a rat. It takes a little getting used to, I know, but he is a rat, not a mouse." Michael watched Allen laugh, and the way his face softened when he talked of David and their plans for the summer. Life actually had its checks and balances, she thought. For all the crazies like Mary, there were people like Allen, and she realized how fortunate she was to have him here as a friend.

The rest of the day was a joy. David was a natural swimmer and quickly made friends with the other children in his class. She was glad she had insisted he learn to swim at the club instead of teaching him at home. He spent too much time in the company of adults and needed to be around kids his own age. They stopped at the deli and went to the park. After lunch, they headed to the library where David checked out five books, signed up for the summer reading program, and got his own library card, now tucked safely away in the new wallet his father had bought for him.

Later that afternoon Michael left David in his room, reading to the little guy. She cleaned her room and then stretched out on her bed, hoping to relax before dinner. Although she was exhausted, sleep played a game of tag. Michael hugged a pillow to her chest and took a deep breath, rolling her shoulders as she tried to work out the stiffness that had plagued her all day. *What am I going to do?* She had to leave; she couldn't stay in the same house with Richard, seeing him each day—reliving last night every time she saw him. She had promised to stay six months, but there was no way she could honor that commitment, not now. Sarah had been right. *I'm not ready for this. How could I have been so stupid?* She should have taken care of David during the day and kept to herself the rest of the time, instead of trying to fit in like family.

The whole scenario turned out just as Sarah predicted. *I wanted to be the mommy and wife. What a mess that caused.* Michael rolled onto her side, and it started again. No hysterical sobbing this time, just hot tears rolling down her cheeks fueled by a deep despair she could not shut out.

Michael woke up to the phone ringing in her ears and a dark room. She turned on the lamp by the bed and realized she'd been asleep for three hours. As her feet touched the floor, her head started to spin. She ached in every part of her body, and her head throbbed so badly she wanted to scream, except she was awake enough to know that if she screamed, her head would hurt even worse. The phone by the bed continued to ring. She didn't want to talk to anyone, but the ringing hurt her head.

"Hello?"

"Michael, is that you? What's the matter? You sound terrible. Michael, answer me."

"Sarah, if you'll hush up for a minute and give me a chance, I'll answer you."

"Okay, I'll shut up, but what's wrong. Are you sick?"

"No, I'm not sick. I just have a headache. I must have slept wrong last night or something, I don't know. Really, I'm okay. What are you up to?"

"Nothing that would make the six o'clock new. I just haven't heard from you in a few days. How was the wedding? I understand you were the belle of the ball. Filled your dance card right up, or so I heard."

"Well, you heard wrong. I only danced a little. The wedding was fine, as weddings go. No, that's not fair. It was a beautiful wedding. The bride was beautiful; everything was beautiful."

"Girlfriend, you don't sound well. Are you sure you don't need the good doctor to take a look at you? There's a lot of flu going around."

"Sarah, believe me, the last thing I need or want right now is to have Dr. Hampton anywhere near me."

"I'll wait one minute for you to explain that last remark. What's going on out there? What happened?"

"It's nothing. Nothing happened, really. We had a disagreement, and with this headache, I'm just not up to continuing the argument."

"You haven't convinced me. Care to try again?"

"Sarah, let it go. Really, I have to lie back down. I think my sinuses are plugged or something. If I don't feel better, I'll see a doctor, I promise. I'll call you tomorrow."

"I'm letting you off the hook, but only until tomorrow, and you better call me, or I'll be on your doorstep before the sun goes down. Take a pill and go back to bed. Love you, babe. Bye."

Michael went to the bathroom and pressed a cold cloth to her throbbing head. She sat on the edge of the tub and tried to pull off her shoes without bending down. Damn, she hurt, and she couldn't take a pill. She didn't have any.

Michael finally managed to remove her clothes and slip the oversized football shirt she slept in gently over her head and crawled into bed. She placed the damp washcloth over her eyes. *If I don't move and just relax, the pain will go away,* she told herself, trying to apply her own generic brand of biofeedback, hoping it might work.

The knock on her door was soft, but she knew it wasn't David. Even with all her pain, she knew it definitely wasn't Mary, and she doubted if Allen was paying his respects at this time of the night. It was Richard, and she didn't want to see him. *Did I lock the door?* No. She never locked the door.

"McCall, open the door. Are you all right? Please, open the door. David is worried. He sent me to check on you. McCall, if you don't answer me and open this door, I'm coming in anyway. Can you hear me?"

"Go away. I'm fine. Just go away."

"I can barely hear you. Are you okay? McCall, are you sick?"

"Go away."

Richard opened the door and walked into the dark room. It took him a moment to adjust his eyes to the darkness. The lamp from the landing didn't offer much light, and he stubbed his toe. He swore softly under his breath as he moved to the side of the bed. "Don't you believe in night-lights? I just hit my toe."

"Good. I hope you broke it. You're not welcome here. Go away and leave me alone. I have a headache, and I don't want to talk to you. Go away."

"Are you sure you don't have a fever? Maybe you're coming down with something. Let me feel your pulse."

Michael screeched and pushed the washcloth tighter over her eyes when he turned on the lamp by her bed. "Don't you dare touch me. I just have a headache. Turn off that light and get out of my room," she moaned at him as he reached for her wrist.

Richard quickly turned off the lamp. He went into the bathroom and turned on the light over the sink. "I'm sorry," he said, returning to the bed. "But I really need to take your pulse. What if you have something that's contagious and David gets it?"

"That's right, use David to get me to do what you want. You never play fair, do you, doctor?" She turned on her back and lifted the cloth, her eyes squinting against the dim light. "You don't understand, do you, Richard. I don't want you to touch me."

"I understand perfectly, but it won't be Richard examining you. It will be Dr. Hampton. Now give me your damn wrist."

Too tired and hurting too much to argue anymore, Michael flung out her arm. *Why is he always right?* Maybe she did have something more than a headache, and it was true; she didn't want David to get sick.

"I'll be right back. Stay put."

"Of course, I'll stay put. Where do you think I'd go?" Michael threw the words at his back as he left the room. She didn't want to argue with him anymore; she just wanted to go to sleep. Michael had just replaced the cloth over her eyes, trying not to move, when he dropped his black bag on the bed and pulled the cloth off her face. She opened one eye in time to see his hands coming toward her with a tongue depressor in one hand and an instrument with a small light on the end in the other.

"Your pulse is crazy. Let me look in your mouth" Richard watched Michael shake her head and squeeze her lips together. He couldn't believe she refused to let him look at her throat. "I can wait all night if that's what you want." She had yet to open her mouth, although he held the tongue depressor on her lips, tapping lightly. Still squinting and muttering something under her breath he couldn't make out, she finally gave in and opened wide, much wider than was called for.

"Good girl," he said and started a thorough examination, including her throat, ears, and the glands of her neck. Then he gave her his diagnosis. "I can't find anything. Your throat's not red, your ears are clear, and the glands in your neck are well within normal limits. But I have to tell you McCall, you do look like hell."

She wanted to kill him. How dare he tell her how she looked? Did he have any idea what she'd been through the last twenty-four hours? Instead, she said, "I told you so. Not as smart as you thought, huh, Doctor? Now go away."

Richard went into the bathroom and brought her a glass of water, then dug in his bag. "Here, take this. It will ease the pain in your head." He tried to help her sit up, but she brushed his hand away. Michael balanced herself on her elbow and swallowed the pill, then fell back on her pillow. "Maybe I better check your heart." He reached for his stethoscope.

Michael wanted to scream at him, but she couldn't, not without blowing off the top of her head. "There's no way you're going to get anywhere near my heart, and if you won't leave, then I will." She started to climb out of the bed, her football shirt riding high on her tanned thighs.

Richard jumped off the bed, trying to keep his balance as she threw the covers off and kicked him with her foot. "Get back into bed. McCall, stop kicking me. I'll leave, just get back in bed." He shoved the stethoscope back in his bag. "I'm going." But before he got to the door he circled back and stood at the end of the bed.

"I'm going, but well… Allen told me what happened this morning between Mary and David. I'm sorry it's gone this far. I should have talked to Mary a long time ago, but I had a very frank discussion with her this evening and I think she now understands just how things are going to be. Thank you for being there for David. I hope you feel better in the morning. Just stay in bed and rest. I want you to feel better for a small dinner party we're having tomorrow night. I want you to meet some friends of mine."

"You said you were leaving. Why are you still here? And I don't care who's coming to dinner because I am not going to any party tomorrow night, next week, or next year, or next—"

Michael heard the door close. She rolled into a ball and spoke into her pillow. Had he heard her? She hoped so because she wasn't going anywhere he might be.

Her tears tasted salty as they saturated her cheeks and slid past her mouth onto her neck. "I didn't cry in front of him," she said proudly. "I didn't." Although when his fingers touched her neck, checking her glands, she'd almost lost it. *What am I going to do?* "I have to leave," she said to the pillow as the pill cut through the threads of reason. "I have to run away, far away."

Richard looked at his watch. It was eleven o'clock. He had installed a night-light on the landing. It wasn't much, but it was enough. He opened the door slowly and listened, then walked to the bed. Michael was asleep; he knew she would be. Richard watched her sleep, her mouth open slightly, and was relieved to see that her face wasn't as drawn, not like earlier this evening, so etched with pain. The pill had done its job.

"I never wanted to hurt you, Mikie," he said to her, knowing she didn't hear him. "I don't know how, but I'll make it better, I promise. I will make it right. Somehow I'll make everything all right." He leaned over and kissed her forehead, brushing damp curls off her face. His hand cupped the side of her cheek, and she pushed into it like a kitten about to purr, but she didn't wake up.

He shouldn't be here. He'd only come to make sure she was all right. He should leave, but he didn't want to pull his hand away. He had no right to be here. He took a deep breath and removed his hand. No, he didn't have the right, but he bent over anyway and gently kissed her parted lips, then walked out of the room and closed the door.

CHAPTER THIRTEEN

WHEN MICHAEL OPENED HER EYES the next morning, the sun was up. She rolled onto her back and stretched. It felt so good, after the last few days, just to stretch her arms and legs, point her toes at the ceiling, but then her mind took over.

Four weeks ago, Richard offered her a job and a new direction toward getting on with her life. Taking the job was step one. Step two required getting her lazy bones out of bed and finishing what she'd started, with a few exceptions. Michael knew she'd promised, but there was no way she could stay the six months. She would wait until David started school in September, and that would give Richard more than two months to find someone else.

Thankfully, her headache was gone. She'd slept like a baby, although she dreamed Richard had kissed her. How long would it take to get him out of her mind? Probably not as long as it would take to get him out of her heart. But Michael wasn't going to think about Richard today. She'd take a shower and go find David.

The smell of coffee pulled her to the kitchen. Richard said he'd talked to Mary, clearing the air, so Michael decided to start the day off with a clean slate. She plastered on her best smile and walked into the kitchen.

"Good morning, Mary. Your coffee always smells so fantastic. May I have a cup?"

"Suit yourself. You know where the pot is. I hope you plan to take the boy somewhere today. I'm almost finished cleaning the house. I only have the bathrooms to clean, but then I have dinner to cook for seven people, and I don't have time to be cleaning up after that boy."

Okay, so much for clearing the air. Michael filled a cup with coffee but kept her smile in place, feeling like she had super glue on both cheeks. "We hadn't planned to go anywhere, but I'm sure he won't cause you any problems. Where is David?"

"He had his breakfast and went outside with that rat of his. He's somewhere with Allen, I guess."

Michael went in search of her charge and found him with Allen, weeding the new garden, making up silly stories as they worked in the dirt.

Sunshine and laughter prompted Allen to suggest they pack a lunch and go fishing. Michael and David would go to the pool for his daily practice while Allen finished with the garden, and then they all would to go fishing.

"Mrs. McCall, you're wanted on the phone," Mary yelled from the side door, not too happy, as usual.

"David, get out of the pool and wait for me. I'll only be a minute." David climbed out and reached for his towel. "Remember, David, do not go into the pool until I come back."

Michael ran to the phone in the hallway. It was Sarah. "I was going to call you a little later. I'm okay, really. I feel a lot better. I even let the good doctor check me over, so you can rest at ease."

"You do sound a lot better, but I was worried. Last night you didn't sound like you were still among the living and—"

David's scream pierced the air, cutting through Michael's heart with fear and panic. Had he gone back into the pool? No, his cries came from inside, from the kitchen. "Sarah, I've got to go. Something's wrong."

Michael threw down the phone and ran into the kitchen. David's hands were over his head, trying to repel her blows, as Mary slapped at the boy with both hands.

"Get away from him," Michael yelled. "Stop it; stop hitting him." She lunged for David, pulling him behind her as she grabbed the front of Mary's dress and hurled her toward the sink. Michael wrapped her arms around David and held him tight, kissing his hair and telling him not to cry when Allen ran in the back door.

"Oh my God, Allen, she hit David." Charged with rage, Michael turned back to Mary. "You're fired. Allen, get the truck. Get her out of her. I want her gone, now."

"You can't fire me. Only the doctor can, but I quit. I'm not going to stay in this house any longer."

"Allen, take David to his room, and then I want you to get her out of here. Just take her to the ferry. David, go upstairs; I'll be right there. It's going to be okay, love, I promise. Please go upstairs. I have some things to say to Mary." As Allen took David and left the room, Michael spun around and marched toward Mary, eyes narrowed and ready for battle, not once questioning who would be victorious.

Allen pulled his truck to the back door and Michael threw Mary and her two suitcases into the truck and slammed the door, then walked to the driver's side. "Just dump her at the ferry, Allen. No, take her to the bus station in town It's closer, but hurry back."

David sat on his bed, shaking and sobbing, trying hard to hold back his tears. She gathered the scared little boy into her arms. "It's okay now. She's gone. Mary's gone, for good."

"I had to go to the bathroom. I was... I wasn't dripping water. She said I was dripping water all over her clean floor. Michael, she wouldn't listen to me. She just started hitting me, and it hurt. Why did she hit me? I wasn't dripping. I wasn't."

Michael held him until his sobs and tremors lessened, rocking him back and forth, holding him against her breast—next to her heart that raged with anger and disbelief. *How can I explain to this child why Mary would do something so hateful?*

She was still holding him when Allen came up the stairs, and then the phone rang. Michael looked over David's head at Allen and asked him to answer it. A few minutes later, he came back into David's room, running his hand through his hair.

"It was Richard. He asked me to tell Mary there would be another guest for dinner tonight. He said there's now going be eight people. I didn't tell him anything. I just said okay. He said everyone would get here about six, and she should plan to serve dinner between six-thirty and seven. I should have told him; I better call him back, tell him to call it off. He'll just have to call everybody and tell them the dinner's off. What a hell of a mess."

"We're not going to tell him. Furthermore, we're not going to call off the dinner. David? David, do you think you could help me? Would you help me get the house ready and fix dinner for your father's friends?" Michael saw the questioning look on Allen's face. She shook her head, silently pleading with him to go along with her.

"I don't know. Maybe I… I think I could help. If you tell me what to do, I… I could. But I don't know how to cook, except I can make a peanut-butter and jelly sandwich,"

"We can do it. If you'll help me, we'll make the best dinner in the whole world, and you won't have to cook. I can cook. Did you know that I'm a great cook? Well, maybe not a great cook, but I am good."

Allen's face lit up when he realized what she was doing. "I can help too."

"Okay! Now, we need a plan, so let's go to the kitchen and get started."

David washed his face and combed his hair, leaving most of his sobs but all of his tears in the bathroom. The first order of business sent them looking for a menu or some idea of what Mary had planned to cook for dinner. After a few minutes, the three gathered around the old oak table to reconnoiter.

"I have no idea what she planned to serve, so we'll just have to start from scratch. Mary told me she'd cleaned the house except the bathrooms. Okay, here's the plan. First, we do the bathrooms, but only the guest bathroom downstairs, then on to the kitchen."

So began their adventure and the diversion she hoped would help David forget what had happened with Mary. Michael needed help. *I'll call Sarah.* Good Lord! She'd forgotten about Sarah.

"Sarah, I'm so sorry I haven't called you back sooner. Let me tell you what happened, and then I'm going to need your help, big time."

The greatest thing about having a best friend, one so outrageously rich, with connections to serve up an elephant if it struck her fancy, was you could ask anything, and she'd pull you out of the muck first and ask questions later. After a few minutes of explanation, Sarah took control of the wheel. "Stay off the phone. I'll call you right back."

While they waited for Sarah to call, Michael directed the project into the dining room and the table setting. Allen had reclaimed the household keys from Mary, something Michael would never have thought to do. He unlocked the butler's pantry, where they found the china and silver. Michael let David pick out the color of the linens for the table and then sent him outside with Allen to check on fresh flowers for the table.

Michael answered the phone on the first ring. "Okay," Sarah said. "Here's the plan. Veal chops, glazed carrots Marsala, and haricot verts, and for a starter, the shrimp recipe you make, with the mustard sauce, then a salad of asparagus and baby lettuce with the hazelnut and tarragon vinaigrette. Are you still with me?"

"I'm with you, Sarah, but where am I going to find veal chops and asparagus in time to serve by seven?"

"Not to worry, my dear. I'm turbo-charged and on a roll. I've already checked; everything's available. If the menu is okay with you, I'll have everything delivered before noon, but if you want something different, I'll have to go back to the drawing board."

"No, it's fantastic. I mean, I can do everything you mentioned."

"I know. That's why I chose what I did. Now then, I don't know what the wicked witch has in the cupboards, so I'm sending everything, spices, garlic, fresh bread, and the whole nine yards. Right, let's see, cross that off, and that. Oh, and don't worry about hors d'oeuvres. All they'll need is a few minutes in the microwave, and they'll be ready to serve. You're only going to have so much time. After the way you sounded last night, I don't want you killing yourself. I can send someone to do all this, you know. Just say the word and I'll have one of the best chefs in town on his way in an hour."

"I'm okay, and I really need to do this."

"All right, I'll go along with you, but I am sending a couple of ladies over there to help you. You're going to be tied up in the kitchen, and you'll need the help. Let's see, I can scratch that off the list, and that. Now, about dessert, I can send something yummy, or if you think you'll have the time, your pear tart would make a perfect finish."

"You've been reading my mind."

"Okay. Now, how about wine? Does the doctor have a wine cellar?"

"Beats the hell out of me. We've not gotten around to discussing the finer things in life yet."

"That's okay. I'll make sure you have whatever goes best with the food. I think that just about takes care of everything. Do you want me to come and help you? You know I can't cook, but I can peel something, or supply moral support."

"Thanks for offering, but I think we're going to be okay, and Sarah? Thanks. I owe you, more than big time."

"Forget it, you don't owe me anything. I'll have the stuff there before noon, and I think Cassie and her friend should be there about four-thirty or five. She's a gem. Just tell her what you want her to do. Oh, one more thing, what about flowers, I forgot all about flowers for the table."

"Covered. Allen and David are standing here right now telling me we have plenty in the garden. Wish me luck pal. I'll call you later."

"Oh, one more thing. I'm going to send some smelling salts. I think the good doctor might need it when he sees the bill for all this. Bye now."

Michael replaced the receiver and turned to her compatriots. "Well, guys, looks like we're in business."

Dr. Hampton's kitchen was a dream. The small breakfast table sat in an alcove surrounded by windows that filled the room with morning sunlight. The rest of the kitchen offered enough space to kill and cook a cow if that's what you had an itch to do. Michael surveyed her new domain: two double ovens, a six-foot range, stone counter tops, one with a vegetable sink, another long enough to stretch out and take a nap. Over this counter hung a pot-rack with every kind of pot and pan ever made. An old oak plank table, big enough to seat at least twenty people, divided the room.

She loaded the utility cart with china and silver and wheeled it into the dining room. David followed her lead, and in no time, they had the table set. As Michael placed the last of the crystal around the table, she wondered if Richard realized what beautiful tableware he owned. The whole house held a wealth of superb furnishings and decorative pieces.

Someone had taken exceptional care to fill the house with the best of everything. Had it all belonged to Richard's mother, or had he brought it all with him to remind him of Eve? Had the woman Richard loved so much and still couldn't forget, even after eight years, owned all these things? No wonder he still loved her when each day all this reminded him of the beautiful home she had created for them.

Cassie and a young woman named Rose arrived a little after four, dressed in jeans but carrying a garment bag. Cassie looked about fifty, with brown hair pulled back in a bun. Her eyes were a bright aquamarine blue and her smile put Michael totally at ease.

"I thought we might be able to give you a hand, set up the bar or whatever you need, and then we can change into our work clothes."

Michael showed Cassie and Rose the dining room and then the living room where she assumed Richard would like to serve the drinks and hors d'oeuvres. The large room dropped two steps lower than the main hallway. A French door divided one wall, with tall grilled windows on each side, offering a magnificent view of the pool and patio. The far wall opposite the fireplace held a long narrow bar crowned with a large beveled mirror, reflecting the furniture in shades of hunter green and deep burgundy, grouped in front of the fireplace and around a large coffee table. A second grouping, across from the bar, held wingback chairs around a circular antique English gaming table. They covered this table with a pad and linen cloth and arranged cocktail plates and cutlery for the hors d'oeuvres.

While Rose peeled and deveined the shrimp, Michael and Cassie worked out the serving schedule. She made one last check of the dining room and her cooking schedule, and then arranged the flowers David and Allen had gathered from the garden. Everything was finished. If there were no major disasters, like an earthquake or another power failure, they would pull it off. Before she took her shower and changed, Michael drew Allen to one side.

"We have one last problem, and I need your help. Richard thinks I'm one of the guests, that eighth guest he told you to add. Allen, there's no way I can prepare and eat at the same time, so here's what I want you to do. It's not the truth really, but it's not a lie; I would never ask you to lie. When Richard comes home, this is what I want you to tell him."

Richard pulled into the driveway at fifteen minutes after five and Allen met him at the back door. "We better go in by the side door. Things are pretty hectic in the kitchen right now." As they walked around the house, Richard noticed Allen was dressed in slacks and a sports jacket.

"Hey, you look spiffy. Big date?"

"Nope, just thought I'd help out tonight. Never know; something might come up where we'd need another pair of hands."

"Are Michael and David ready?"

"David is all spit and polished, but Michael won't be joining you for dinner. She wanted me to tell you she'd already made other arrangements for tonight."

Richard stopped on the path and looked at Allen as if he'd not heard him correctly. "What plans? Where is she? I better talk to her because this is totally unacceptable."

Allen rubbed a hand over his freshly shaven chin. Now what was he going to do? There was no way in hell he could let Richard know Michael was in the kitchen at this very moment, cooking dinner. She told him not to lie, and the story they cooked up an hour ago had sounded reasonable then, but Richard wasn't buying it.

"Richard, she's not in her room; she's already gone. You can talk to her later. Right now you better get your butt in gear, pal. You only have a little time to shower and change."

They went through the double doors with Richard muttering under his breath. Allen walked down the hall with him, making sure Richard went into his bedroom and not into the kitchen. He was about to go find David when Richard spun around.

"Any trouble with Mary today?"

Allen almost choked. He tried to swallow the lump that kept him from talking. "What do you mean?"

"Her attitude. I talked to her last night about her attitude. Did she say anything to you today? I sure don't need any of her lip tonight."

"Oh... ah... sure, everything's okay. I can guarantee you'll not get any negative vibrations from Mary tonight."

Allen waited until he heard the shower running in Richard's room, and then flew up the stairs to find David. The boy was on the floor with the little guy. "David, put Runaround in his cage and go wash your hands, but first let's go over one more time what we're telling your Dad about Michael."

"I remember everything. We're gonna tell him she had other plans. That's 'cause she wants his party to be special. So we're gonna tell him she went out, but she'll be cooking dinner in the kitchen, and I should kinda stay out of the way so Dad won't grill me. But we won't be telling a story 'cause she said she was gonna go somewhere else. She never was gonna go to the party, and after she gets dinner on the table, she's gonna leave. Did I get it all right, huh, Allen?"

"Yes, David, you have it right. You probably won't even be asked. I've already told your Dad that Michael will not be joining him tonight, so he may not even ask you about it. Now go wash your hands and don't play with Runaround anymore tonight. I'll see you downstairs, and David, don't go into the kitchen. Okay?"

Richard walked into the hall, the back of his hair still damp from his shower, just as Allen came out of the kitchen with an ice bucket. Behind him stood a very attractive woman Richard had never seen before. Allen introduced Cassie, explaining she came to serve dinner and help in the kitchen. "I'm pleased to meet you. Allen, I think I'll just check in the kitchen before our guests arrive."

Before Allen could pass the ice bucket off to Cassie and tackle Richard, the doorbell rang. *We must be living right,* Allen thought, thankful that he literally had been saved by the bell. When this night was over, he was going to get drunk, not just wasted, totally shit-faced, drunk as a skunk—if he could wait that long. He was getting too old for this kind of fun.

The doorbell hadn't stopped ringing before Marc and Amy Bosworth walked in. They were the perfect picture of Mr. and Mrs. America. Marc and Richard were the same age, but the resemblance ended there. A few inches shorter than Richard, with sandy hair and brown eyes, Marc could still pass for an Ivy League college student. Same for Amy, whose blond hair and hazel eyes glorified her brilliant smile.

Marc looked at his watch. "Right on time. See that, Richard?" Marc held his arm with the watch under Richard's nose. "I told you I'd be on time. Gill and Holly are right behind us. Give Richard the wine, Amy, because as soon as he greets his other guest, Richard is going to make us a drink. He bet me the bartender's job that I wouldn't be on time."

Richard kissed Amy and removed the two bottles of wine from her arms. "How do you stand this guy? Is he always this smug when he wins a bet?" Turning back to Marc, he said, "It's the first time in six months you've been on time so stop gloating and take this wine into the kitchen."

Cassie appeared out of nowhere and reached for the wine. "I'll see to this," she said, taking the bottles from Marc. "The hors d'oeuvres are ready in the living room, Dr. Hampton."

"Thank you, Cassie. Gill, it's great to see you." Richard shook hands with his white-haired mentor as Holly Merrick followed Gill through the door and walked into Richard's outstretched arms. Holly was not the typical wife of a renowned college professor. Her gray hair, cut in a carefree bob that mirrored her lifestyle, perfectly framed her round face with a mischievous smile and large blue eyes. After a lingering kiss, Richard said, "You look younger every time I see you."

"You, my love, must be losing your eyesight, but that's okay, I love it. Richard, let me look at you. Now you, you do get more handsome each time I see you, and my eyes are fine. Where's that son of yours?"

"Hello, Richard."

Richard took two steps back as Sylvia Grant closed the space between them. She stood about five-foot-seven, had blonde shoulder-length hair and plain brown eyes. Sylvia was an attractive woman, but Richard knew that every time he came within three feet of her, he wanted to run the other way. Hal told Richard months ago that the grapevine at the hospital said Sylvia wanted his body. Well, it was never going to happen. "Hello, Sylvia, glad you could join us tonight. Although, I must have misunderstood you. I thought you told me you were related to Holly?"

"She's not related to me," Holly said. "She's just pushy."

"Oh, Holly, that's a dreadful thing to say, even if you are only joking."

"Who's joking?"

"Be nice, dear." Dr. Gilford Merrick gave his wife a half smile and took Richard by the arm. "I think I need a drink. Lead the way, bucko. Don't worry about the ladies; they've been trained to heel."

"Where did you say you were going to sleep tonight, dear?" Holly spoke the words lightly to her husband's back as she took Amy's arm. "How are the girls, Amy? We've been gone for so long it will take me months to catch up on all the latest backdoor gossip."

"I guess I'm stuck with you, Marc." Sylvia didn't want to be on the arm of Richard's best friend, or four steps behind Richard. She wanted to stand next to him, and although she wore a fake smile, Sylvia fumed as they stepped into the living room. She had told a bit of a white lie regarding her relationship to Holly Merrick, but so what? Her mother and Holly were old friends. She'd only learned about the dinner by accident when Ruthie had called to reschedule an appointment. Well, she didn't want to reschedule; Richard had already rescheduled three times, but Ruthie said it couldn't be helped. The Merricks had just returned from a lecture series in Europe, and Richard had invited them to dinner. Sylvia had hung up the phone and decided to take matters into her own hands, cornering Richard that afternoon, suggesting she was somewhat related to Holly Merrick and would just love to join them at dinner. She knew she'd caught him off guard. Richard had been in such a hurry; he was always in a hurry, but he finally told her he guessed it would be okay and that they would be dining at seven.

Allen assured Michael that Richard wasn't going to come into the kitchen. "But I'm going to hurry them up. With all this food, they don't need to fill up on hors d'oeuvres. How long before you're ready?"

"Oh, Allen, you have such style. I love it. Okay, tell them dinner will be served in twenty minutes." This was no time to start giggling—they were trying to deal with a crisis here, but Allen and Cassie were snickering, and Michael couldn't help laughing. "Stop it, you two. I'm trying to be serious, so stop making me laugh." Michael coughed, to clear her head not her throat, and then raised her wine glass in a toast. "Well, here goes nothing. Battle stations, everyone."

Allen delivered the announcement, and fifteen minutes later Rose, quietly eased into the living room and removed the remaining hors d'oeuvres.

"Richard? Shall I be your hostess tonight and sit opposite you?" Sylvia stood at the end of the table offering her biggest smile.

"Actually, Sylvia, I've already told David he may sit there."

Alert and on his toes, David didn't miss a beat. "That's right. When Michael's not here, I get to sit there."

Rolling her eyes, Amy took over. "Marc and I will sit on this side, and the three of you can sit there." *So simple,* she almost said aloud.

"Yes, for God's sake, Sylvia, sit down. No, not there, I'm sitting next to Richard. Sit in the middle so Gill can talk to David." Holly decided that tomorrow she would send a note to Karen Grant, Sylvia's mother, explaining why it had been necessary to kill her daughter.

The dinner began. Cassie and Rose moved about the table, refilling glasses with water and wine, removing empty plates, replacing them with the next course.

As they took away the salad plates, Amy asked, "Richard, where is Michael? I was really looking forward to talking with her. We had to leave shortly after Anna's wedding, and I only had a little time to talk to her. The girls thought Michael was so funny and ever so beautiful. Their exact words, I might add. They're just dying to come over and go swimming. She told them they could come any time."

"Michael is the best swimmer. She's teaching me how to butterfly."

Richard smiled at his son. "David, you mean she's teaching you to swim the butterfly stroke."

"Yeah, that's what she's doing. I'm taking swimming lessons at the club, but Michael still teaches me a lot."

"When you do come over you better bring your ear plugs. They love their music loud, and I'm talking loud. It's not so distressing when they're outside, but I came home the other day and thought we were having an earthquake. The whole house shook; I thought we were going to lose Mother's chandelier."

"Oh Dad, it wasn't that bad. Michael is teaching me to dance. You gotta get down and feel the beat. You gotta go with the program."

"Richard, you didn't answer me. I thought you said Michael was going to be here tonight?"

Richard had heard her the first time, and he'd tried to change the subject with that stuff about the music. He tasted a spoonful of sorbet that Cassie had placed before him and then looked at Amy. Did Michael honestly have prior plans, or did she just want to be someplace else, some place he wasn't? "She had a previous engagement," he finally said, hoping he sounded convincing.

Cassie checked the table one last time and returned to the kitchen. "Well, they either liked what you fixed or they fed it to the dog. The plates are all but licked clean."

"We don't have a dog."

"So there you are. I don't think they're going to have any room for dessert. Maybe Allen and I should take care of the tart. What do you say, Allen? Want to share with me?"

For the first time today, Allen felt relaxed. "We better tone it down or we'll have the master of the house in here wanting to know what's so funny." The tide had turned, and Allen was having a ball. Of course, the wine had gone down easily, helping them all to unwind. He gave Cassie a sad look as Michael playfully pulled the pastry away from the two.

"Okay, guys, I'm out of here. Allen, would you make sure David doesn't stay up too late?" Michael turned to Cassie and gave her a gigantic hug. "Thanks, lady. You and Rose truly saved the day, or should I say the night. Anyway," she said with her best upper-crust voice, "let's do lunch."

"You got it, toots."

For the first time tonight, the dining room was void of small talk and laughter.

"Richard? When did you get a new cook?"

"Amy, I don't have a new cook. Mary's my cook."

"Are you sure? I've eaten Mary's cooking before. She's okay, but I'll bet the bank she didn't prepare this. When was the last time you checked the kitchen? This is great."

"I agree with Amy. This is the best dinner I've had in years." Gill kissed his fingertips. "Holly, you have to get the recipes."

"I admit I don't spend a lot of time in the kitchen, but believe me, Mary is still my cook."

"It sounds to me as if you've been a widower too long." Sylvia offered Richard her best smile as she continued. "What you need, Richard dear, is a woman to take care of things."

David glared at Sylvia and made a face; he also made a decision. He lifted his chin and said, "Mary didn't cook dinner. Michael did. Mary's gone."

"David, what are you talking about?" Richard asked. "What do you mean Mary's gone?"

"Oooooh yeah, she's gone! But we're not supposed to talk about it tonight."

Everyone at the table looked from son to father. "Well, I want to talk about it tonight. David, please explain."

David tried to choose his words carefully, praying Michael wouldn't be mad at him. "Well, see, a terrible thing happened this morning. Then Michael told Mary she was fired, but Mary said Michael couldn't fire her. She said only you could fire her, Dad, but then Mary said she quit anyway because I was spoiled rotten and you always took Michael's side. So then Michael told Allen to get me out of the room, but I heard Michael tell Mary that she'd messed with the wrong kid and that before the next ten minutes were over, she was going to be Mary's worst nightmare because that was the amount of time Michael gave Mary to get her sorry ass off the property."

No one said a word. Marc bit his lip to keep from laughing. Amy dug her nails into her hands and tried to look serious. Gill and Holly waited for David to go on, and Sylvia couldn't wait to give Richard her support. Only Richard seemed in control.

"Go on, David. I want to know what terrible thing happened. It's okay, son. Just tell me what Mary did that caused Michael to fire her."

"She hit me, and she kept on hitting me until Michael heard me screaming and she ran into the kitchen and pulled me away from Mary. Then Michael threw Mary in the sink. Mary said I dripped water on the kitchen floor, but I didn't. I wasn't wet, and I didn't get any water on the floor. Anyway, Allen took me out of the room, and I couldn't hear anymore, but Allen said Michael would take care of things. He said Michael was like a she-cat protecting her cub. Then later, Allen said we would have to call the party off, but Michael said the party was important to you, and we could still have the party if I helped. She said if I helped her, she would cook dinner. So that's what we did, we all helped. Allen and I cleaned the bathroom, and I got to chop the carrots, but I washed my hands first. Michael called her friend and a man delivered all the groceries and everything, except the flowers. Allen and I got all the flowers from our own garden. But Michael fixed them all pretty for the table, and she did everything else."

The mood in the room turned serious. All but Sylvia knew and understood the implications of what David had actually said.

Now was not the time to intervene, but Sylvia didn't seem to understand that. "Richard, I don't think I know this person, this Michael, but it seems she has overstepped her position regarding the running of your household?"

Richard wasn't in the mood to answer any of Sylvia's stupid questions. He needed to talk to Allen, but first he turned to her and unleashed some of the anger boiling inside him. "For your information, Sylvia, although it is none of your business, Michael McCall brilliantly runs my household, with my blessings. Now, if you will all excuse me for a moment."

Allen looked up from the table where he and Cassie were playing cards and could tell right away that Richard knew what was going on. He stood and said, "How did you guess?"

"I didn't. David told me. It just came out. You want to tell me what happened?"

"What did David tell you?"

"That Mary hit him. Is that true? Did she really hit him?"

"It's true. The old bitch really exploded, and David was the victim."

"Where is she now? I want to face her and—"

"Just calm down. Mary is long gone, and Michael saw to it she had a proper send off."

"Where's Michael? David said she did all this." Richard waved his hand through the air, hardly aware that Cassie and Rose sat quietly, trying to look invisible.

"Richard, Michael isn't here, not now anyway, and yes, she took care of everything, cooked the dinner, everything, but you have to understand one thing right up front. She didn't do it to interfere or so you could have your damn party. She did it to take David's mind off what Mary had done to him. It was awful, Richard, and the boy was hysterical. Hell, no one has ever touched him like that. No one has the right to punish a child that way. It worked though. In no time she had him peeling carrots and believing she couldn't do any of it without his help. So don't get mad at her. She did the right thing, at least that's what I think."

"Allen, I'm not mad at her. I want to thank her. Do you honestly think I'd be mad at her for defending David? It's a damn good thing I wasn't here. I would have done something to that bitch that would have landed me in jail. Did Michael actually throw Mary in the sink?"

"Well, not in the sink, just up against it, hard. Oh yeah, sure hope the old biddy doesn't get a lawyer when she checks out her bruises. Although, Michael said it was justified."

"The she-cat and cub thing?"

"David told you about that?"

"You bet. He was extremely proud of the fact he was her cub. Where is she?"

"Who?"

"Allen, don't play games with me. Where is Michael?"

"She's not here."

"Goddamn it, I know she's not here. Where is she?"

"I think she went for a drive. She's done in. Been on the go since early this morning, and David said she was sick last night. I expect her back soon. Michael said she wanted to go to bed at a decent hour. How did your guests enjoy their dinner?"

"Great, in fact, it was one of the best they've ever had. I didn't know she could cook like that."

"Richard, I'm sure there's a lot we don't know about our Michael, but I do know she'll have my head if we don't finish this party up right. So go back and play it out. Just tell me when you want us to serve the dessert."

Richard returned to his guests and suggested they all retire to the living room. Coffee and dessert were on the way. "Would anyone like an after-dinner drink?" he asked.

Excitement buzzed through him, but Richard tried to relax. Michael had not run away from him. How could she be a guest at his table when she'd been his mainstay? Michael had held everything together, including using the party as a ploy to help blot out the trauma David had experienced with Mary. If he ever got his hands on that woman, he'd... But then, Allen said that was another thing Michael had taken care of.

"Dad, can I..., I mean, may I be excused?"

"Sure David, but don't you want any dessert? Allen says Michael baked a wonderful pear tart."

"I can have some tomorrow." David kissed Amy and Holly good night and shook hands with the others. Except Sylvia. He didn't like her, and he decided he wasn't even going to say good night to her, except that might be rude and reflect on his Dad, so he just muttered a quick good-bye and hurried out of the room.

Ten minutes later, he tore into the kitchen and asked Allen when Michael was coming home. "I gotta know, Allen. Did she say what time she was coming home?"

"No Sport, but it shouldn't be long. What's up?"

Allen had told David not to play with Runaround so he couldn't tell Allen what had happened. He needed Michael. She would help him— she would understand and help him. "Nothing's up, but I need to talk to Michael the minute she comes home. It's very important. Will you tell her I need her right away?"

David paced the floor, running to his window every time he thought he heard a noise. What was he going to do? His dad would never understand. Then he heard her car. He flew down the stairs and ran into Richard, who had also heard the car.

Michael knew the moment she saw the look on Allen's face the fox had been in the hen house. "How did he find out?"

"David. But it's okay; everything is okay. I explained what happened, and Richard is fine. We were just getting ready to serve dessert and coffee. Go on and go to bed. We've got it all under control. Oh, David said he needed to talk to you, right away. Maybe you could look in on him when you go up."

Michael walked out of the kitchen and into the hall and ran straight into father and son.

"Michael, I gotta talk to you right away. It's very important. Please, right now."

"David, give her a chance to at least say hello."

"But, Dad, you don't understand. It's a... I mean, I need to see her in my room, right now."

"David, you're acting like the house is on fire. It's not, is it?" That would be all he needed tonight.

"No, Dad, it's nothing like that. Well, I mean, please Michael, come to my room." Not waiting for an answer, he pulled her up the stairs.

As they climb the stairs, Richard realized he'd been outmaneuvered by his eight-year-old son. He called after her. "Do I have to take a number?" He was trying to be funny, trying to keep it simple. He didn't want to blow it, not now. "When you have the time, I'd like to talk to you, also."

David dragged her into his room and shut the door. "David, what is so important that it couldn't wait?"

"Runaround is out."

"What do you mean out? He's out in your room?"

"Yes, no! He's out! He's not in my room. I've looked. He's not in my room, anywhere. We were playing on the bed, and I just turned away for a minute. Then he was gone."

"Have you looked on the landing? David, you should have kept your door closed."

"Don't be mad at me, Michael. I'm sorry. Allen told me not to play with him anymore tonight, but I just took him out for a while. Please, don't be mad."

"I'm not mad at you, David, just tired." She was about to suggest they check the landing, when they heard the screaming.

"Well, it sounds like someone just found the little guy."

David looked at Michael, guilt all over his face. "Guess you're right."

When they reached the bottom of the stairs, the hallway looked like a subway platform at rush hour. Michael thought it was a good sign to see more people laughing than screaming, all except the hysterical woman hanging on to Richard, screeching at the top of her lungs.

Richard pointed to the living room, and the rescue team went into action. Runaround sat on the floor, thoroughly enjoying the show. Michael gathered him up and asked David, "Who's the screamer?"

"That's old Sylvia Grant. She works at the hospital. I don't like her. She tries to get Dad to pay attention to her, but I don't think he likes her either."

"Well, I can't stand that noise. Guess I can't get in any more trouble than I'm already in. Stay here and keep our friend with you." Michael handed the rat to David and headed toward Sylvia. She was tired and still upset by what happened this morning. Well, she was leaving anyway, so what did it matter? She'd already thrown Mary out on her ass, might as well try for a record.

Michael gently took Sylvia by the arm, and without missing a step, walked her to the front door. "You poor thing, scared by that tiny little rodent. You better go home. Richard, why don't you take this poor woman home? She seems about ready to faint, and we wouldn't want that, would we?" Michael opened the door and pushed Sylvia out onto the porch. "He'll be right with you," she said, then close the door.

Holly almost wet her pants. She hadn't had this much fun in years. Hot damn, this Michael had balls, solid gold. She didn't know who this lady was, but Holly sure liked her style. She was still laughing as Richard opened the door Michael had just shut in Sylvia's face and decided she had to add her two cents. "He doesn't have to drive Sylvia home my dear, she has her own car. Here's your purse, Sylvia. Drive carefully."

Sylvia stopped screaming and just managed to catch the purse Holly threw at her. She gave Holly a dirty look. "I don't want to go home," she said and walked back into the foyer. Sylvia didn't want to go home. She wanted Richard to hold her as he'd done when that horrible furry creature had climbed up her leg. Besides this Michael person needed to be put in her place.

"You can't send me out of the house. How dare you tell me what to do? You're probably the reason why that boy is so incorrigible."

"Lady, tonight I'd venture to do just about anything I damn well please. Would you like to see me do it again?"

Somehow Richard found himself between the two women as Michael moved toward Sylvia, ready to launch her out the door again. Sylvia held on to Richard's arm, using him as her shield.

"Richard, please, I don't want to go home. Anyone with eyes can see the problems you have, how crazy things are. Poor dear, let me help."

The hair on the back of Richard's neck bristled as he spun around to face her. He'd actually felt terrible when Runaround had run up Sylvia's leg, really thought she might pass out, but now he didn't care because she'd said the wrong thing. "Thank you, Sylvia, but you see, I rather like this craziness, and I don't know what problems you're talking about. I'm sorry you have to leave. Let me see you to your car."

When Richard returned to the house, he followed the sounds of laughter to the living room, not the robust kind that had followed Runaround's escapade, but soft laughter, bonding his friends and family. Allen and Cassie moved behind Michael, offering coffee as she served the tart. Richard watched from the archway and felt the warmth pull him into the relaxed atmosphere that hadn't been with them earlier. She was a natural. In the time it had taken him to take Sylvia to her car, Michael had turned a difficult situation into a cohesive gathering of friends.

Best of all, Michael wasn't mad at him. She hadn't stayed away because she was upset. She'd been working her fabulous magic in the kitchen, saving his party and his son's peace of mind.

"Richard, come in and have some dessert." Amy patted the cushion beside her on the sofa.

An hour later, the party was over. After the last kisses and good-byes, Allen took David up to bed, making sure Runaround was secure in his cage, and then left to find his own bed.

Richard locked the front door and turned out the lights, then went in search of Michael. He found her in the kitchen.

"You know... I'm sorry. I didn't mean to startle you." Damn! He should have banged on the door, anything except sneaking up on her. "I wanted to thank you. I mean, I should have fired Mary the day David found you." Richard walked across the room, but she moved away, putting the long oak table between them.

"You don't owe me anything, Dr. Hampton. Don't you know by now how much I care for your son? That makes what I have to say all the more difficult. No, please stay over there, but I need to talk to you. I've done a lot of thinking, about the other night, and I realize I've been extremely foolish. Anyway, what I want to say is I think it's better for all concerned that I leave. Please, let me finish. I'll wait until September, until David starts back to school. That will give you over two months to find a suitable person to take my place. I know I promised to stay six months, but that's just not possible. What happened two nights ago was my fault, and I'm sorry, but it's best that I go. We both know I have to go. I don't know what you're going to tell David, but I'm sure you'll think of something. Now, I'm going to bed. It's been a difficult day, and I'm tired. Good night, Dr. Hampton." This time it was Michael who left the room before Richard could reply.

CHAPTER FOURTEEN

ICHAEL TURNED THE VOLUME ON the radio up a notch and
finished slicing the melon. It was too early to wake David,
and it didn't say anything in her job description about getting
the boss out of bed. Hell, she didn't have a written job description, and
even if she did, she wasn't about to go into Richard's bedroom. After
all, thanks to yesterday's fiasco, she was only the part-time temporary
housekeeper, chief cook and bottle washer, and soon-to-be-unemployed
nanny.

After leaving Richard last night, walking out of the kitchen with her
chin high and her step light, trying to look so smug, she'd teetered on
the verge of tears. She had stood up to him, told him how it was going
to be. Sure, she had, and all the time she kept hoping he would ask her
to stay. Well, one should beware of playing games, especially with the
heart. She'd done such a fabulous job convincing him she meant to leave
he hadn't bothered asking her to stay. Michael took a sip of coffee and
burned her mouth. Served her right. She was acting like a sixteen-year-
old. What ever happened to the educated, levelheaded woman she used
to be? Gone..., long gone. Since his first smile, she'd been duck soup.

When she'd reached the top of the stairs last night, she was shaking
so badly it was all she could do to open her door. How could she have
been so stupid to think Richard might want her to stay after she'd
thrown his date out his front door? What had she been thinking? She
hadn't thought, just reacted. Why had she assumed that just because
David didn't like Sylvia, Richard felt the same? But it was done, and
there was no way she could undo it, any more than she could change the
fact she'd told Richard she was leaving. She had made her bed, only now
she didn't want to lie in it.

Last night, after pacing the floor for over an hour, she'd told herself to take a shower and relax and go to bed, but the shower hadn't helped. Why had she told Richard she would stay until September? Allen and David managed just fine during the day. Let him hire a cook and housekeeper. While beating her pillow to death, Michael seriously considered packing up and sneaking out like a coward at first light, but she couldn't do that, not to David. *Who am I trying to fool?* Michael didn't want to go at all. As she lay in the dark, staring up at the ceiling with tears just a sob away, she would have made a deal with the devil to have Richard beside her. Sarah had warned her about lying to herself. Could she keep up the charade until September? Could she pull it off and get out of town with at least her dignity intact? She didn't have an answer.

"Good morning, McCall. I'll just get some coffee, and then I have to go. By the way, I've decided to take David to Los Angeles. I have to make rounds this morning, but I should be back around ten. Would you pack a bag for David? Enough for three or four days, and you'll have to tell David that we're going. I didn't have a chance last night."

Richard filled his cup, but Michael didn't say a word. Was she uptight because she'd spent a rotten night as he had? Maybe she couldn't stand the sight of him. Not trusting himself to look at her face, Richard looked just a bit to the left of her shoulder as he spoke to her about the trip. *Take it easy, Richard,* he told himself. *You're both adults. Just tell her what you want her to do and then get the hell out of here.*

"I spoke to my mother yesterday afternoon. She's not feeling well. That's why she didn't come to Anna's wedding. It has something to do with her blood pressure. She says she's all right, but I want to make sure. I think David will enjoy the trip; maybe we'll have time to go to Disneyland. Anyway, I told her we were coming to town because I'd promised David a trip to Los Angeles. Now seems like a good time."

"I'll see that he's ready to go before ten. Should I pack a lunch?"

"Don't bother; we'll stop along the way. McCall, I guess we should discuss a few things before I go, about the house, I mean. It seems we've run out of help. We still don't have a cleaning person, and now we don't have a cook."

"Dr. Hampton, I'm sorry about yesterday. I should not have taken it upon myself to fire Mary. I should have let you address the problem."

"That's nonsense, McCall. What you did was keep me out of jail. If I'd been here, well, let's just say it would not have been pleasant. No, you did the right thing, but I need you to find a replacement. Maybe while we're gone, you can work on that project." He looked at his watch. Richard didn't give a damn what time it was; he just needed an excuse to look away from her. "I have to go. You can page me if you have any problems."

Richard swore under his breath as he fumbled with the key, finally starting the car. He had come so close to asking her to change her mind, to stay, but he hadn't. She had almost jumped out of her skin when he'd said they needed to talk, as if she wanted to tear out the door, but when she realized he'd only meant to talk about the sudden lack of domestic help she turned all soft, even apologized to him for having fired Mary. The engine roared. Richard took his foot off the accelerator and put the car into drive, but as he spun out of the driveway, he called himself every kind of a fool, a wimp. He'd lacked the courage to ask her to stay.

"So?"

"Sarah, you could start a conversation by saying hello."

"That's redundant. Just tell me. How did it go?"

"The dinner was superb. In fact, as I'll be out of a job by mid-September, maybe you could use your connections to get me a job as an associate chef or something. I can probably come up with a few references."

"Holy night in hell, what did you just say?"

"I said the dinner was great."

"Forget the dinner. What was that little tidbit you slipped in there about your job? Geez, Michael, with a friend like you, who needs the soaps? Did I just miss something? Maybe you better start over from the beginning, and I don't mean the dinner."

"You didn't miss anything, but you were right a few weeks ago. You're always right, you know. I wasn't ready for this, and now I've really screwed it up. I quit last night. It's as simple as that. I said I'd stay until Dr. Hampton could find a replacement, or until David goes back to school in September."

"You should have let me bring in a chef or just called the party off. I knew it would be too much on such a short notice. Baby, I'm sorry."

"Sarah, my quitting has nothing to do with last night. I mean the party had nothing to do with it. Oh, hell, I don't know what I mean. Yes, I do. What I mean is if I'd had the sense God gave a piss ant, I'd never have taken this job in the first place. And come September, or sooner, I'm out of here."

"Oh, baby, don't cry. Please don't cry. Pack a bag. I'm coming to get you."

"No, you can't do that. I have to get David ready to go to Los Angeles. They're going to visit David's grandmother over the weekend. She's sick or something. Anyway, I'll have time to be by myself and come Monday, I'm going to have it together. I'll be a new woman, or as least maybe I can find some of the good parts of the old one. Sarah, I have to do this myself. I love you. I'll call you tonight, promise."

Michael waited to tell David about the trip until after breakfast, and he just assumed she was going with them. When he asked where her suitcase was, and she told him she wasn't going with them, he came unglued.

They couldn't go off and leave her alone. As soon as Richard pulled in the driveway, David took his case to his dad. Now the three were at a standoff.

"Michael, we might go to Disneyland. You gotta come with us. We're gonna have a lot of fun, and you just gotta come with us. Dad, tell her. Tell her how much fun we're gonna have. Please?"

"You're welcome to come with us, McCall. In fact, I think it's a terrific idea. We can wait while you pack a bag. We're not in that big a hurry. Why don't you come?"

It was wrong; she knew it was wrong to think about going with them, but maybe. Michael would never know what she would have decided because before she could say anything, the doorbell rang.

"Hello Tom, it's good to see you. It's been a long time. What brings you out here?"

"Hi, Rich, I've come to get Michael."

Tom stepped into the house and shook hands with a confused Richard, who glared at Michael, standing at the bottom of the curved staircase. "Sarah sent me to get you."

"That was thoughtful of her. I'll be ready in a minute."

Richard dislodged his hand from Tom's and gave her a questioning stare. "You said you'd stay until—"

"David, why don't you take Mr. Clark and show him Runaround. I'm sure he'd love to see your new pet." She felt like a character in a B-movie as she flicked her head to one side, trying to tell Tom, without words, that she wanted him to go with David. She was just about to resort to sign language when the lights came on, and Tom realized she wanted him and the kid gone.

"I'd like that. Come on David; show me your new pet."

David didn't need any encouragement. He took Tom's hand, and they went to find the little guy.

Richard waited, almost, for them to leave the room. "What the hell is going on here, McCall? You said you'd stay until September. What were you going to do? Leave me a note?"

"Richard, what are you talking about?"

"You're leaving. Tom is here to pick you up. He said so."

"You think? You think I am leaving for good?"

"Well, I..."

"First of all, I didn't know Tom was coming, but it's only for the weekend. Maybe I should check the verbiage in the contract we don't have. Maybe it states I have to stay on the property for a specified number of hours a week. Well, you can just dock my pay.

"Dr. Hampton, what is the matter with you? Do you honestly think I would sneak out and leave David like that, without a word? If you think that badly of me, maybe you better make sure your silver and valuables are locked up tight before you leave town."

Michael knew as soon as she'd said the words that her last comment was totally uncalled for, but she was mad. "You better get your son and go on your trip. I'll be here when you get back. That's what I told you I'd do, and I'll do it, but I suggest you get your act together and get a replacement for me because the sooner you do, the sooner I'll be out of your life."

Richard took a step toward her. "Michael, I'm sorry. I just assumed…, I thought—"

"Don't touch me." Michael jumped back, tripped, and fell on her butt, but she didn't want him to help her up. She needed him gone. "Please, don't help me. Just get David and go."

"The son of a bitch, if I could get my hands on him right now, I'd pull him apart. But I'd make damn sure he knows exactly what he's going to miss when you're gone. The bastard! I hope you know I'm pissed. He has seriously pissed me off."

Michael watched Sarah pace the floor, her arms flailing about, spilling some of the drink she clutched in her hand. "Sarah, please don't be so upset and sit down. You're supposed to drink that scotch, not pour it on your expensive carpet. I should never have told you what happened between Richard and me."

"Now you're going to piss me off if you think like that. You're my best friend, damn it, the sister I never had. Did you think I wouldn't know? Did you think you might just pack up and leave in September with your broken heart buried beneath your underwear, and I wouldn't have known?"

"Sarah, come here. Please, sit down."

Sarah paced a few more steps just to show Michael she wasn't in any mood to be told what to do, and then she sat beside the person she loved more than anyone on earth, except Tom, who picked that moment to walk into the living room of their fashionable San Francisco high-rise.

"Are we through with our ranting and raving?"

"Don't you use that condescending tone with me, and who's ranting? I never rant. Well, maybe I was just a little, but the nerve of the guy. You're damn right I'm ranting and maybe I'm not through yet."

Tom bent and kissed Sarah on the top of her head. "It's okay sweetie. I know how you feel, but look at me. Sarah? I said look at me."

Sarah obeyed and looked at Tom as he hovered above her, with a look that plainly stated she wasn't about to give it up so easily. But she was wrong. "Tom, what are you up to? I know that look. Do you know something we don't?"

Thomas Sinclair Cook, Chairman of the Board of TSC Global, six feet tall, steel-gray hair and deep-blue eyes that beckoned with a promise of mystery and mischief, dropped to the floor in front of them and sat like an Indian chief willing to trade off his only daughter if offered enough ponies.

"Tom, don't do this to me." Sarah watched her husband, suspicious of his sweet Boy Scout look. As his go-to-hell smile slowly chipped away her defenses, Sarah told herself to stay on guard, knowing that smile was not always to be trusted, a smile that could send mortal fear into the heart of any man foolish enough to try to outmaneuver Tom Clark on the corporate battlefield.

"It's so simple ladies. Do we get mad, or do we get even? Do we stay down or get on top? I'd rather be on top myself." Tom let his words simmer for a minute and then asked the only question that needed an answered. "Sister dear, do you honestly love this guy, or do you just need Richard to warm your bed? There is a vast difference and only you know the difference, or maybe you don't. Can you separate the two and make that kind of judgment call? You couldn't do it six months ago."

Sarah reached for Michael's hand and squeezed tightly. "Tom, that's mean."

"No, it's not, and Michael knows I'd never hurt her. I'm just sorting the wheat from the chaff so we can develop a game plan here, or worst scenario, a way to smuggle the girl out of town. Michael, can you answer me?"

She closed her eyes and reached deep. She knew what Tom wanted. A few months ago, Sarah had been her rock. She'd built the fortress and stood guard, but Tom had been her champion—had fought off the dragons. He'd held her for hours as a father might have done if she'd had one, or an older brother. But she'd had no one, except Tom, and he had been there—, soothing, steadily coaxing all the emotions she'd locked away for so long back to the surface. He had demanded with his gentle voice that she face the demons head on, fortified by his strength and determination.

Could she be honest with herself now? Would she even know the truth? Michael leaned forward and opened her eyes and then her heart. "I love him, Tom. God help me because I do love him, but it doesn't matter what I feel because he doesn't feel the same about me. He may want me. I mean, he may want to make love to me, but he'll never love me. His wife has been dead for eight years, but he still loves her. My God, to be loved like that. But to answer your question, am I capable of making a rational decision? Yes, I think so. I'm confused, I'll admit that, but I do know one thing for sure. I can't fight a memory. I don't know how. That's why I have to leave."

Inside, Tom churned with anger, and even though he continued to smile, the mischief was gone, replaced with frustration. He wanted to tell Michael she was wrong, to tell her he would bet the store it wasn't love Richard felt for his late wife. He wanted to take her by the shoulders and make her understand what was pulling Richard Hampton apart, but Tom was a man of honor. No matter how much he wanted to ease her heartache, to make her realize that Richard did not love David's mother, he couldn't reveal what his sister had shared with him in confidence. Amy had told him years ago that Richard had been driven to the very edge of reason, that his state of mind was so fragile, so adversely twisted by Eve, that she feared for his sanity.

But Tom couldn't disclose any of this. Well, there was more than one way to shuck a guy out of his shorts, so he said, "I thought you were a fighter? Why don't you quit whining, get all your feminine tools shined up, and go get your man?"

"Tom, what's gotten into you? Michael's not whining. She's not up for a fight; she just wants to go home."

"Well, she can't go home and hide. I won't let her, and my money says she is up for it. I say go after the bastard with all the tricks you women have been taught since the beginning of time. It's war, baby. No holds barred."

"Tom?"

"Yeah, Michael?"

"I need a drink."

"Shall I make it champagne?"

CHAPTER FIFTEEN

MICHAEL AND SARAH HAD ARRIVED at Temple Door Spa on the outskirts of San Francisco at nine o'clock this morning with the worst kind of a killer hangover. Now, as she moaned into the pillow and the six-foot, two hundred pound woman with hands of a Swedish angel rubbed sweet oil into her back and shoulders, Michael calculated it had been less than six hours since the limo driver had dumped them on the doorstep of the spa. During that time, she'd survived a workout with a trainer from hell named Dante. When that hour was up, the two hauled their aching, hung-over, misused bodies to the next torture chamber. Sometime during the day, they experienced the wonders of yoga, with several unsuccessful attempts to fold themselves into impossibly difficult pretzel-like contortions, but with a little help from another sadistic staff member, they actually got in touch with their aura.

Finally, they hobbled into paradise, a womb-like room draped with pastel chiffon, where they floated in a state of pleasant, aroma-therapeutic semi- consciousness from which they'd refused to leave, thus missing out on astrology, dream analysis, and the much needed mental edge training.

Looking like flamboyant gypsies in their colorful, flowing robes, Michael and Sarah drank the three glasses of water required each hour, thus becoming drunk again. They then moved on to the next level of pleasure. Miracles do happen though, because somewhere along the way, they managed to lose most of their hangovers.

The day at the spa was a direct result of the infamous plan the three had cooked up after they established the fact that Michael loved

Richard, and they were willing to do just about anything to help him realize it would be in his best interest to love her back.

As they toasted their project with champagne, Tom decided he needed to make notes, and then they were on their way with Operation Seduction, the campaign to transform Michael into a woman Richard simply could not live without. The first item on his list was her hair.

"What's wrong with my hair?" Michael asked, refilling her glass.

"Nothing, if wild is your thing. It's just too thick and too long. If you braided it, you could stick a few feathers on top and convince Richard you'd make a proper squaw. You have beautiful hair, babe. It just needs to be styled; maybe cut off a foot or so. Now then; about your clothes."

"I am so glad I'm perfect," Sarah said, a small chuckle escaping her lips as she poured more champagne into her glass.

Michael cocked her head. "Okay, smart ass, so tell me what's wrong with my clothes."

"Don't get testy, my love. Remember, I'm on your side, but for a gal who used to be such a classy dresser, I have to tell you, I've seen better coordinated bag ladies. Those black high-top tennis shoes you wear, when you wear shoes at all, are straight out of the late 1950's. Your shirt is usually large enough for three people. The colors you wear would give a blind man a headache, but I have to say, I do like the tight leggings you wear most of the time, and those cropped tops. You've got fantastic legs, lady, and a beautiful top side."

"Hey chum, just stick to the facts and forget her body."

Tom only smirked, and then continued. "What we're trying to accomplish here is a look out of *Vogue,* not the *Beach Volleyball Gazette.*" Item by item he continued his critique, but after a couple of hours, he decided he couldn't continue his duties as a critic and recording secretary because he was starving. He ordered in.

When the sun invaded Michael's bedroom the next morning, almost blinding her as she forced one eye open a quarter inch, all the events that transpired in the mighty war room the night before were pushed to the dark recesses of her mind. Michael carefully walked to the kitchen and made a pot of coffee, which she consumed in a semi-prone position. When silently joined by her fellow conspirators, they made and drained another pot, but they were still drunk, only now they were wide-awake drunks. They showered, one at a time, but after their allotted twenty minutes, each having to sit on a chair covered with a plastic bag, the census of their tiny kingdom totaled three exceptionally clean, waterlogged, wide-awake drunks. They needed the Spa.

At seven o'clock that night, while Sarah fixed them something to eat, Michael counted several empty champagne bottles, four bottles of beer—empty of course—, and a bottle of Bailey's Irish Cream nestled among the brut bottles. She'd never actually been a drinker, and as she tried not to make any sudden moves, she vowed to abstain from the lure of the vine in the future.

Sarah announced that dinner was ready, and after viewing the table, Tom couldn't resist adding. "Really, dear, you shouldn't have gone to so much trouble."

"Don't mess with me tonight, love, not tonight. Now eat up and then I suggest we retire at an early hour. Shall we say in about fifteen minutes?"

The vote was unanimous. It took thirteen minutes to finish their clear broth, burned toast and hot tea.

The next morning found the three tremendously improved. Michael was up and had breakfast on the table before her fellow companions washed the sleep out of their eyes. The day was a bit overcast, but the guy on the radio promised sunshine before noon.

Tom walked into the kitchen and took Michael into his arms. "Did I do anything I need to apologize for?"

Michael returned the hug. "No, except I'm still miffed about losing the best dressed award to a bag lady." Michael took a playful bite out of Tom's earlobe just as Sarah entered the room.

"Stop nibbling on my husband, and Tom, keep your hands to yourself. If we're going to have an orgy, we need another male member."

"Oh, Sarah, you're good, and so early in the day."

Sarah looked at her husband. "What? Oh yeah, right."

With no more talk, they devoured French toast and ham, fresh fruit, and hot coffee before moving to the terrace where Tom inhaled the damp air into his lungs. "Do we dare continue with our plans?"

"No, I vote we cancel the whole project." Michael stood at the railing, toying with her coffee cup. "Tom, it's no good—, the plan I mean. We need to burn the damn thing. If you hadn't had an endless supply of the bubbly, we would have realized it was all wrong two nights ago instead of almost drinking ourselves to death. You said it yourself. There's just too much of me to make over. It's hopeless."

"I never said it was hopeless."

"Yes, you did. I remember distinctly. You said I was hopeless, a throwback to the flower-children of the sixties."

"I did not."

Michael marched into the living room and returned to the terrace with Tom's notes.

"It says right here. It says she's a throwback to a flower child, a reject from Woodstock."

"I wrote that? Maybe that was when you started to undress and dance on the sofa. I can believe I might have said it, but I can't believe I was sober enough to write it down."

"It's all there, Tom, and I did not undress. I remember what I did; I just opened a few buttons. Anyway, drunk or sober, you're one hell of a secretary. Look, you even drew pictures."

"Honey, I'm sorry. Maybe this was a lousy idea, but it did accomplished one thing. You were laughing."

"Yeah right, until it hurt to breathe. I never want to see another bottle of champagne. I'm going to stick to my original plan, stay focused until he gets someone to take my place. I'll chalk it up to a learning experience, like the last two days, and I will get over it."

"No, now wait a minute. This can still work. We just took the wrong approach. There's nothing wrong with the way you look. Hell, Amy said you looked like a million dollars at Anna's wedding, and I know how great you look when you're all dressed up. Maybe all we need are a few adjustments, and a new pair of shoes. You have to understand that all men look at the same woman with a different kind of yardstick. Richard has always been quite up tight. Even in college, Marc said he was a

Serious Sam. But the women in his life have all been extremely social. His mother was the leading pillar of society in San Rio until she moved south, and his wives were right behind her."

"Wives? As in more than one? Tom, what do you mean wives?"

"Oh, geez." Sarah waited for her husband to get his foot out of his mouth, because she didn't know what to say.

"Sarah, you knew about this? Are you two telling me Richard has had more than one wife?"

"Oh, baby, it never crossed my mind to bring up Carol. It was so long ago." Sarah took a sip of cold coffee, searching for her next words in the bottom of the empty cup.

"Sarah, do me a favor and stop calling me baby. I'm almost thirty-four years old, and even though I've been acting like a child, I'm not ready to throw in the towel and crawl back into the womb. Now will one of you please explain about this other wife?"

"Okay," Tom said, "but don't be mad at Sarah. She's always called you baby, and I doubt she'll ever stop."

Michael reached for Sarah's hand and squeezed, the contact conveying her apology before Sarah went inside, leaving Tom to tell the tale.

"Richard and Carol were only married a few years, but they'd been together since their days in the sandbox. Carol Remington grew up next door to Richard. They were the same age; started kindergarten together, even went off to college together. When Richard finished his general surgery residency and Carol received her master's in nursing, they got married, just a few months before his father died."

Tom waited until Sarah refilled his cup with the fresh coffee she brought from the kitchen. "They'd only been married a short time when Carol was diagnosed with breast cancer. She died a year later."

Tom slumped in his chair and continued. "They couldn't cut it out, burn it out or wash it away with chemo, and no matter how hard he tried, Richard couldn't find any way to save her. Six months after her death, Richard decided to go back to school, to specialize in cardiovascular surgery."

Michael looked up and realized Tom had stopped talking. She wanted to say something, but what could she say? Was there a parallel between Richard and her? She had lost her parents, her foster parents, a husband, and her son. Richard had lost his father and two wives. Was there any common ground left for them to bury their pain from the past and move on together?

"Good Lord, I almost said I needed a drink." Michael tried a forced smile, but it came off badly.

"What we need, I think," Sarah said, "is to move on. All this sad stuff happened to Richard a long time ago, and I can't believe someone as intelligent as he is hasn't put it all behind him by now. I'll bet my next month's allowance that all he needs is a push in the right direction for this saga to have a happy ending."

"That much? Wow, you are confident," Tom said.

Over a pitcher of lemonade, they formed a new plan. Sarah and Michael would take the rest of the day and spend Tom's money on new clothes and a few hours at Chez Chic with José, known to perform miracles with wild hair. Tom would go to the club and play some golf, and they would meet at McGregor's at six o'clock for a bowl of onion soup. Beyond that, well, they agreed to let fate keep the dice.

Leaving the apartment an hour later, Tom yelled. "Michael?"

"Yes, Tom?"

"Lose the shoes."

Michael and Sarah really worked it as they swished their way to the table on the patio. They looked fabulous, and they knew it. The dining room at McGregor's, with its mustard-yellow walls and shiny copper-topped counter in front of the open kitchen, was already full as they navigated their way outside.

Sarah planted a light kiss on the cheek of Alain, owner and chef, who stood next to Tom. To her husband she said with a grin, "Close your mouth dear."

The weatherman's choice of crystal balls had been spot-on, predicting it would be a beautiful day, or else Fog City just happened to remember it was summer. A light breeze circled the patio, delivering the sweet scent of roses and gardenias among the patrons as the two settled into place at the table.

"Why is the table set for four? Are you expecting someone?"

Tom took a sip of wine and shook his head yes, then no.

"My God, I think you've suffered brain damage, and what are you drinking?" Sarah put her hand on Tom's forehead, as if expecting an answer to her question to emanate from his head.

"Sarah, what are you doing? Please remove your hand." Tom studied his watch. "In about five minutes, if he's on time, the male member you ordered this morning should arrive."

"What?"

"You said we needed another male member. Well, I found one."

"You found one what?"

"A male member."

Sarah looked at Michael as the same image appeared in their dirty little minds. Michael tried to keep a straight face, trying not to laugh, but it didn't work. "Does this mean we're going to have an orgy, right here?"

"Who's going to have an orgy? Damn, Tom, I would have gotten here sooner if you'd said anything about an orgy."

Michael shot up in her chair as an automatic process called mortification shut off her laughter, almost. If only she hadn't turned to look at Sarah as Peter Farrell loomed above her in all his golden glory, Michael might have swallowed the last remnants of laughter bubbling in her throat, but it was no use. Sarah's laughter gave her the hiccups, and every other second she bounced on her chair.

Tom stood and shook hands with Peter, rolling his eyes. "Glad you could make it, Peter. Have a seat, if you're not embarrassed to sit with these crazies. I swear to God, I can't take them anywhere."

Peter sat between the two women, who coughed and swallowed and fidgeted, and tried to be serious. He couldn't keep his eyes off Michael. She looked stunning in a simple sleeveless dress with a low V-neck, the color of ripe strawberries. The soft light on the patio sparkled in her dark hair that danced about her exquisite face. The light, and the color of her dress, accentuated her deeply tanned skin and Peter wanted, more than anything he'd wanted in a long time, to bend over and kiss the spot where the silk crepe rested gently against her ample breasts.

Instead, he leaned toward her and said, "You've cut your hair. It looks beautiful. You look beautiful."

"Different yardsticks," Tom muttered, "just like I said."

"Tom, shut up, dear." Sarah then turned to Peter. "How delightful to see you. It's wonderful you could join us tonight." Sarah had managed to get her act together but obviously needed a few minutes alone with her husband. What was he thinking inviting Peter Farrell to have dinner with them? Didn't they have enough irons in the fire already? Michael didn't need this distraction now. Anyone with eyes could see Peter Farrell was planning a picnic with Michael as the main course. *My God,* she thought, *I believe he's about to start drooling all over her.*

"How's your golf game, Peter?" Sarah didn't give a rip about his golf score, but at least he was looking at her and not sizing up Michael like she was little red riding britches.

Peter recovered his manners and offered a toast to dear friends, and the tone of the evening rose to a new level. After Alain's onion soup, the merry foursome planned what to eat next. Tom got on the phone, securing a table at Vivande. They left Peter's sports car behind and took off.

Dinner consisted of herbed lamb chops at Vivande, then over to Fillmore Street for caramel-coated cream puffs, before ending at the Top of the Mark, where they danced, sipped B&B— sip being the operative word— and gazed at the lights of the city.

It was after midnight when Tom pulled to a stop beside Peter's car. "Come to Stern Grove with me tomorrow," Peter asked.

Michael looked at Peter and felt the warmth of his shoulder as it rested against hers. They'd had fun tonight. Even Sarah relaxed as they had danced and laughed their way around town. Michael felt remarkably comfortable with Peter Farrell, but she had to get back to San Rio.

"How about it you guys? Michael, say yes. You'll love it. We can have a picnic and enjoy the symphony, and I'll have you home early."

It was impossible to resist his pleading smile. "Peter, it does sound like fun, but I have to be home very early."

"No problem. We'll all be back at Tom and Sarah's anytime you say."

"No, I mean I have to be in San Rio early."

Michael really didn't get a chance to say anything; it was settled. They would all go to Stern Grove, and then Peter would take her to San Rio, saving Tom a trip across the bay.

Okay, she told herself as she got ready for bed, *a picnic in the park, listening to the symphony; that will be fun.* But when had she said yes to dinner and dancing? "Maybe I have brain damage too, like Tom," she said to the sheets, because she couldn't remember saying she would go with Peter next Saturday night. She did remember the twinkle in Tom's eyes and Sarah acting like Peter was a long-lost friend, but before he'd gotten out of Tom's car, Peter had signed her up for the musical picnic tomorrow, a night on the town next weekend, and a promise that she'd think about going with him to the annual charity gala at the club.

CHAPTER SIXTEEN

ICHAEL FELT WARM AND EXCITED, like a kid waiting for a promised ice cream cone. She gripped the armrest as the top of the Widow's Walk came into view. They were almost home. Home, what a comforting thought, but only in pretend-land could she call this place her home. *Don't start,* she told herself. Nevertheless, wistful threads of melancholy tightened around her heart. Michael had had a good time this weekend—she'd had fun, but she missed David and wished now she had gone to Los Angeles instead of running around town shopping and eating and dancing and almost drinking herself to death.

Michael thought about her past life, her son, Andy. So many times during the last few weeks she had relived the special times they'd spent together. But then it was all special because their time had been so short. It still hurt—like ripping her heart out while she fought for air—, every time she remembered his trusting little face. Why did he have to die, stolen away before she'd had a chance to experience the joy and wonder of her sweet little boy? When he'd needed her, trapped in that burning, twisted car, calling her name, she hadn't been there to help him. In the beginning, Michael truly believed that she could care for David, help him to laugh and feel secure, but that she would not love him, not like she loved Andy. But it was a lie, just another lie, because she did love David, and what was she going to do when she had to leave him?

The door opened before Peter pulled to a complete stop in front of the house, and Richard walked out onto the porch. Her heart lit up when she saw him, but then Richard made a big production of looking at his watch and Michael felt like a teenager who'd just shot down her curfew. "A hello might have been nice," she muttered to herself as she dug in the back seat of Peter's car for her bags and boxes.

Michael had always wanted to walk out of a store after shopping with the chauffeur marching behind her, carrying stacks of fancy wrapped boxes, just like in the movies, and that's what she and Sarah had done. Now, instead of having a few large bags with handles, she had twelve boxes tied with elegant ribbon and six garment bags mocking her from the tiny back seat of the car.

"Hi Rich, want to give us a hand?" Peter couldn't believe the look on Richard's face. *Well, what do you know? The sneaky green monster has Richard by the ass with both hands. Come on Richard; try to convince me again how you only think of Michael as David's companion,* Peter silently told himself, deciding to stick the knife deeper, twist it a bit.

"Hey, it looks like we bought out the whole town. Here," Peter said, pushing several boxes against Richard's chest. "There's nothing like watching a beautiful woman shop."

Michael wanted to throttle Peter. *You put them in long pants and out pops a strutting ego.* "Never mind, Richard, I can do it myself." She balanced two boxes and a garment bag with one arm and reached toward him with her other hand, only to drop one of the boxes on the porch. They both reached to pick it up. His shoulder knocked her off balance and boxes went flying in all directions as his hands shot out to save her from falling off the steps.

"For God's sakes, McCall, just go in the house. Please, before you break your neck." His mouth was near the side of her face, and the warm, clean scent of her slammed against him like a brick wall. He drew Michael to her feet and turned her toward the open doorway. "Besides, can't you see Peter is dying to tell me all about your shopping spree? You wouldn't want to ruin his chance to tell me all about your fun-filled weekend, now would you?"

Her back shot up straight, and her nails cut into her clenched hands. She wanted to tell him to go to hell; it was none of his business what she had done this weekend, or with whom, for that matter. He needed to know she just didn't care what he thought. *Liar, liar, pants on fire.* She shut her eyes and tried to turn off the stupid nursery rhyme rolling through her head.

"I didn't go shopping with Peter Farrell. He simply offered to drive me home," she said as she lifted her chin and stared into his eyes. Then she turned around and walked through the door.

Both men realized the game was over. With a few mumbles and a bit of small talk, the last of her packages were brought in, and the round table in the foyer disappeared under the fancy boxes and bags. Peter stepped around the table and thought briefly about kissing Michael, then decided not to push his luck. He patted her arm and told her he would call her tomorrow.

Richard closed the door, picked up the remaining boxes, and followed her up the stairs. She flipped on the light with her elbow and dropped the boxes and garment bags on the sofa. "Thank you. I could have made two trips. What?"

"Your hair, what did you do to your hair?"

Michael's hand automatically reached for her hair. "I cut it. I've been meaning to do it for a long time. I'm sorry you don't like it."

"What makes you think I don't like it?"

"Well, I just…"

"Don't put words in my mouth, McCall. I like it. But what happened to the curls?"

José had cut off six inches of hair and used some super-duper stuff that relaxed her natural curl. He cut her hair one length, and then curled the ends under slightly, so it fell just below her chin.

"The curls are still there. They're just resting or something like that. I should go see David. Do you think he's still awake?"

"Of course he's awake. He was terribly disappointed when we got home and you weren't here. He said he'd wait up for you. I'm really surprised he hasn't come out to find you." Richard followed her out of her room and across the landing. He opened David's door and they found David on his bed, still dressed but curled into a ball, sound asleep.

"I'll do it," she said as Richard moved to the bed. "I should have been here. I honestly meant to be home… I mean, I had planned to be here before you got home. I'm sorry."

"Don't be silly McCall. As you said before, you're not on any time clock. He's just become accustomed to having you whenever he wants you. You look tired. I'll put him to bed."

"I'm fine. Please, I—"

David opened his eyes and sat up. "Michael, you're home! I wasn't asleep. I was just resting my eyes, but I'm awake. What did you do while we were gone? Allen said you were gone the whole time. Did you have fun?"

"Not as much fun as I have with you. I missed you. Do you think I can have a hug?"

Richard left them and started to go downstairs. He turned back and poked his head through the door. "Good night, David."

"Good night, Dad."

"McCall, when you get this rascal in bed, I'd like to talk to you. I'll make us a cup of tea."

It didn't take long. David tried to tell her he wasn't tired, but couldn't hold his yawns back. Ten minutes later, he let her tuck him in bed with a kiss and a promise to tell her everything they'd done on their trip in the morning.

When Michael reached the bottom of the stairs, Richard called from the living room. Deep within her, another voice cried out. *Go to bed Michael,* it told her. *You're only asking for trouble,* but she walked on toward Richard's voice. She knew about the fire now. She wouldn't let it pull her in, let it burn away her thin wall of defense, and she'd only been burned a little. As she walked toward him, toward his beckoning voice, she hardly remembered how badly it had hurt, and this time, she'd be more careful.

Allen and David took the little guy out for a romp in the backyard. Michael stood at the window and watched David run in circles around his little buddy and then drop to the ground so Runaround could climb all over him. Last night, Richard had told her that on the trip to Los Angeles, David had apologized for letting Runaround get out the night of the party. He told her they had discussed the situation, and David thought he should take the little guy back to the pet store. Richard told David he didn't have to give up his pet, but David decided it wasn't fair to Runaround. David had Scout meetings and swimming and fishing, things the little guy couldn't do. No, it wasn't right to keep him in his cage a lot and not play with him all the time.

Michael pictured David taking the blame for the night of the party. It was not all his fault, Richard had told him. Then he asked David if he thought a puppy would be a better pet. David had almost jumped through the roof of the car. Of course, he would like a puppy. That's what he wanted all along, but only if Richard thought it was a fair and responsible decision.

Well, at least they could return Runaround to the pet shop. Michael called, and they were more than willing to take the little guy back. Mr. Benton also informed her they had an exceptional selection of puppies, that is, if they were interested.

Michael turned on the CD player and started thinking about dinner. She opened the window and the fresh breeze rolling in off the mountain filled the kitchen with the scents of honeysuckle and jasmine and the pines on the hillside. She didn't mind cooking, but they would soon have a new cook. Michael had contacted three employment agencies, assured by all three she was not to worry. They would call her to set up the interviews, no problem.

Richard wasn't crazy about the Medical Center's food, but he only had a little time for lunch today. Better than not eating at all.

"Richard, it's been a long time. May I sit here?"

Richard stood and held the chair for Sue Kingsley. As he patted his lips with his napkin, he realized he'd not talked to her in a long time. Not since Mikie had walked into his life. He smiled and welcomed Sue, openly admiring the way she looked. Not many women could wear their hair as short as she did and still looks so feminine. It hugged her head like a cap, making her brown eyes look larger than they were, not as penetrating as Mikie's, but nice. Sue smiled at him as she put her lunch tray on the dining table. She had beautiful teeth and a terrific smile, but it didn't slam his heart into his chest like Mikie's smile.

"Sue, it's good to see you."

"I've missed you." Sue raised her head and her eyes locked on to his face. "I didn't realize how much until just this minute. Have you found yourself a new gal among the ranks, Richard?"

"I've never been interested in anyone else here. You should know that."

"I guess I do. It's just that I've missed you."

"I haven't stayed in town much. I'm trying to spend more time with David. He tried to run away. He knew I was busy and didn't want to bother me, so he just tried to skip town. I was so damn wrapped up in my work I didn't even realize what I was doing to him, shutting him out like some street kid with a bank account."

"Oh my God, Richard, I'm sorry. Has it helped, being with him more?"

Richard shook his head and took a sip of water then inched forward, "Tremendously. I never realized how much I've missed these past few years."

Sue played with her fork and didn't look up. "Richard, when can I see you? Is there going to be any time for us?"

He waited for her to look at him before he said, "No, Sue. You see, I've met someone. Actually, in the last month, my whole world has turned upside down. It's a lot to sort out."

"I see. Should I buy a wedding present? Have you set a date?"

"No, I mean, this is a new relationship, far too new to be thinking about a wedding, at least right now."

"You know I wish you well, I do, but I won't lie and tell you I don't wish it were me because I do. But that was never in the cards, was it? Maybe I'll just put an ad on the bulletin board, advertise for a new lover: Wanted, quick lay. No strings attached! What do you think?"

"Stop it, Sue. Don't do this. Don't make it sound cheap. Maybe what we had was unusual, but never degrading. Don't make it that way now."

"I'm sorry Richard, but you're right about us. It was wonderful and beautiful, and I'm going to miss you like crazy. Well, chief, I guess I actually wasn't as hungry as I thought I was. I better go. Be well, my friend." She picked up her tray and then turned back to him. "If it doesn't work out with your new lady, call me. I'll be here."

Richard shoved his plate away. He tried to blot out his last image of Sue. He'd never thought of her as vulnerable, not Sue, who could face down the worst S.O.B. in his profession with just a look. She was the one who had set the rules for their relationship, and he'd gone along with her because it had suited him perfectly.

Why had he just ripped apart a relationship that had worked so well for so long? Why had he told Sue he'd found someone else? Someone he might even marry. Why? Although he'd not meant to, he had hurt her. They'd known from the beginning their relationship would have to end someday, but not like this. Richard heard his name over the loud speaker. Damn, he was due in the OR. He had to put his thoughts of Sue aside for now, but he'd find her when he was finished. They would talk.

Four hours later, Richard walked out the front door of the medical center and looked for his car. The fog had cleared a little before noon, leaving the city bathed in crisp sunlight. Now the sun headed west toward the horizon, and the air was bracing. He breathed deeply. Richard hadn't thought of Sue since lunch because Michael's face crowded his mind. He wanted to see her right this minute. He looked again around the drive and out onto the street for the car. Then he heard the horn.

Michael stood by the passenger door of the big Mercedes, waving at him. Richard waved back and headed toward the car. "Have you been waiting long? I didn't see you at first."

"No, just a few minutes. We were talking and I didn't see you come out."

Richard walked to the back door on the driver's side and opened the door to put his briefcase on the floor.

"Hi, Dad. Say hello to Bo. Bo, this is my dad. Shake hands with my dad."

Richard looked past his son to the other side of the back seat. He heard, about the same time he saw, Bo. It was a low growl—not aggressive, just low and steady—, accompanied by an enormous paw held out in greeting. The paw was attached to the biggest, hairiest dog Richard had ever seen.

He retreated from the car, taking care this time not to rip the top of his head off, and said, "McCall, can we talk?"

He took her by the arm and walked a short distance from the car. "Is that a dog?"

"What do you mean is that a dog? Of course, that's a dog. That's Bo."

"McCall, you don't understand. What I mean is, McCall, is that a puppy?"

"Really, Richard, of course he's not a puppy. He's five years old."

"Thank God. Don't look at me that way. You said you were going to get a puppy. That guy has got to be over sixty pounds if he's an ounce."

"No, but you're close. Actually, Bo weighs ninety-seven pounds, and he's almost three feet tall at the withers. Shall I go on?"

"Please do."

"Bo is a Giant Schnauzer. Now, you're not supposed to get upset because we only have him with us tonight on loan so you can take a look at him. Bo belongs to the son of Mr. & Mrs. Benton, the people who own the pet store, and he works for the State Department—, the son works for the State Department."

"I've got that part. Please continue."

"Right, okay. The son was transferred to England, and he couldn't take the dog. The Bentons have been trying to find a home for Bo."

"But I thought we were going to get a puppy?"

"We looked at a lot of puppies. David played with every puppy they had, for hours, but he and Bo just seemed to gravitate to each other. David knows that if you don't approve, the dog goes back tonight. We'll just start the whole process over another day. He has a lot in his favor actually. He's already housebroken, obedience trained, and they told us he's in serious demand as a stud dog and fetches a very tidy sum. He does that too, fetches things. Anyway, the money would come in handy because we will have to build a dog run for him in the back yard."

Michael waited for Richard to say something. She'd already told David not to get his hopes up, although she thought Bo was the perfect pick for the boy.

"Richard? What do you think? He's unique, you know. He comes from the working breed of dogs. His ancestors used to herd cattle in Germany years ago. He's remarkably calm and mellow, for a dog."

"McCall, the last time I checked, we didn't have any cattle, or have I missed something else?"

Michael slowly shook her head and watched as Richard ran his hand through his thick hair, a sure sign he'd made his decision.

"What does Bo stand for? Beauregard, I suppose."

"No, actually it stands for Bodacious. He does kind of make his presence known. Can we keep him?" Michael mimicked David. "Huh, Dad, can we?"

Richard's smile turned into a full laugh. She looked like a little girl, staring up at him with a silly, pleading look on her face. All she needed was a balloon on a string and a straw hat. She was wearing green-and-blue plaid walking shorts with a white sleeveless blouse and a navy-blue cardigan draped over her shoulders. Her new hairdo bounced as she playfully turned her head from side to side.

"I suppose David wants him to be an in-the-house-dog? I thought so. Does he chew on shoes?"

"No, he's been obedience trained."

"That's good to know. He's had all his shots?"

Michael nodded.

"Right, he has papers, I suppose?"

"Yep, he has papers and great blood lines, going back forever."

"Does he come with a thirty-day trial period?"

"Yes, sir, in writing."

"Well, I guess we can give him a try."

Michael didn't think; she just reacted, throwing her arms around Richard's neck and kissing his cheek. "Oh, thank you. He'll be good. You'll see." And then she was off, running to the car. "He can stay, David. We get to keep him."

Richard watched her lean in the back window to give David the news, but then she turned and looked at him, and her happy face was gone. Michael walked back to Richard. "There is one more thing you have to consider."

"McCall, did someone just die?" He was trying to be funny, but something was genuinely bothering her. "McCall, what is it?"

"It's just that not everyone might appreciate a dog like Bo. I mean, Richard, you're going to have to make sure that if we keep Bo, well... Richard, whoever you hire to replace me has to know that the dog stays, that he is a member of the family. The person you hire will have to be able to get along with Bo. Do you understand?"

"Yes ma'am."

CHAPTER SEVENTEEN

ICHAEL ROLLED HER NECK AND hung up the phone. The employment agency was still working on finding a new cook and housekeeper, but she had better things to do than listen to their excuses. She had to get back to work.

They were deep into producing the Hampton family's contribution to tomorrow's Fourth of July Picnic. The doctors on staff had agreed to donate the food for the fundraiser, and Richard had drawn desserts. He told her to buy something from the baker. But not her, no sir; she decided to make cookies, lots of cookies.

David and Allen, with Bo as third in the pecking order, were helping, and when Michael walked back to the kitchen and saw David and his dog, her tension vanished.

The radio blared as David danced around the room, leading an imaginary band with his wooden spoon, his tall chef's hat held out of his eyes by a wooden clothespin on the back. Allen sat at the long oak table with his own set of spoons while Bo followed in David's path, all keeping time to the music. Bo didn't have a hat, but David had tied a white dishtowel around his neck. Despite her hassle with the agency and a crick in her back, Michael felt carefree and happy. She checked the batch of cookies in the oven and then fell in line behind Bo, marching to the rhythm of the song.

This sight greeted Richard and Marc when they walked in the back door minutes later.

A week ago, Michael might have felt a little stupid, but not today, and it was just as well she hadn't taken her designer makeover too seriously. She wore a baseball cap, turned sideways, a bright-red T-shirt with a giant number one on the front, and white shorts hidden under her shirt, plus her favorite black high-top tennis shoes.

"Hi! I'm afraid the cook's gone round the bend," she said, "or is it over the edge? Anyway, she's lost it, so dinner will be a little late. But the dessert's ready." Michael's eyes danced with laughter as she waved her arm in the direction of the table full of plates, piled high with their culinary accomplishments. Her hair was a mess, and she had flour all over her shirt, as did the rest of her crew. She decided it was better to laugh than worry about how she looked.

Only a cantankerous old grouch, or a dead man, could help but notice the infectious mood that filled the room, and Richard was neither. Michael had brought fresh flowers along with sunshine and laughter into his home. He couldn't remember when he'd experienced so many different emotions, and it was all her doing. She'd made him angry, happy, passionate, and frustrated. She'd even brought to the table a few feelings he decided not to explore right now.

A week ago, she acted as young as David, begging Richard to take a chance with Bo. She had looked like a china doll, but today, with flour on the tip of her nose and down the front of her shirt, she sparkled like a shiny red wagon. He looked at David, amazed at the change in his son. For the last two years, until he met Michael, David had hardly said a word, was considered shy and withdrawn. Now he was so alive, so eager to experience new things. He no longer held back, afraid to think for himself or to ask a thousand questions. David was no longer afraid to be a child.

"Well, seeing as how I'm such a terrific guy, I thought I would take everyone out for dinner."

Marc Bosworth usually marched well with everyday life, but every now and then, it would sneak up and knock him on his ass. Who would have thought the key to his prayer for the past eight years would be a hot little number wrapped in a red T-shirt with flour on her nose. How many years had it been since he'd seen Richard this relaxed, this happy? Marc and Richard were like brothers. And from their first trip to the principal's office in the first grade, they'd stayed together... through it all, good and bad. Tonight, one look told the whole story. Richard was infatuated with this sexy little enchantress in a baseball cap. He might not realize it yet, but Richard was hooked and set, just waiting to be hauled into the boat.

"Marc and Amy and the girls are going with us. In fact, has Amy called yet? Loren had a dentist appointment this afternoon, and Amy was going to call to find out where to meet us."

"Nope, only the people who were supposed to find us a new cook," David said as he unconsciously snuggled his back against Michael's chest.

"Who?"

"Never mind. Richard, I can't go out anywhere. I mean, just look at me." Michael did a quick sweep of her hands, head to toe. "Sorry, guys, but I'll need a rain check."

"McCall, don't tell me you have nothing to wear. I know better, and we don't have to go anyplace fancy. With a little water and a clean shirt, you'll be fine."

"With a little water, Richard, I'll have glue. Okay, but I'll need a few minutes."

Allen popped a piece of sugar cookie into his mouth. "I'd better take Bo outside." He started toward the back door when the phone rang.

"Marc, that's probably Amy. You get it. Hurry up troops, where do we want to eat so Marc can tell Amy."

"Pizza, let's go to Gino's and have pizza." David swung around to Allen "That sounds good to you?"

"Well, I was just going to heat up some soup. Bo can stay with me"

"You don't like pizza, Allen?" Richard asked.

"Sure I like it, but—"

Richard yelled to Marc. "Tell Amy to meet us at Gino's. The vote is for pizza."

David had Allen by the arm. "Then you gotta hurry, Allen. It's gonna be fun, but you only got a few minutes to get cleaned up 'cause that's when we're leaving, huh, Dad?"

"That's right, Sport, so you better go get washed up."

The two men watched David tear out of the kitchen with Bo on his heels. "Look Richard, I don't want to intrude. I can fix something in my apartment."

"Allen, what do you mean intrude? We're all family here, just a bunch of hungry people. Now, do you want to go for pizza or not?"

"I guess I better go wash up."

Even while talking to Amy, Marc caught most of their conservation, and Richard was right. Allen was family. When Roger Hampton returned from Korea, Allen came with him, broken in mind and spirit. He'd lived in the small apartment over the garage ever since Marc could remember, doing odd jobs for Richard's father, helping Mrs. Hampton when her husband was out of town, and keeping a fledgling Richard out of trouble—, not an easy task.

When they were fifteen, Marc and Richard learned that Allen had been a prisoner of war, and although Allen never talked about it, Marc knew now, as an adult, that experience must have been beyond hell. Back then, all Allen wanted was to be left alone. That wasn't a problem for Roger and Caroline Hampton, but a little why-bug named Richard didn't follow the rules. Bit by bit, as the boy grew to be a man, all Richard's whys helped draw Allen back to the human race.

Marc accepted the drink Richard handed him. "They're going to meet us at Gino's as soon as they can get across the bridge." Marc held his glass in a salute to his friend. "Way to go, pal. We all know Allen couldn't love you more if you were his own son, and he's the grandfather David never had, but it's always gratifying to be told you're family, loved and needed... and most of all, appreciated"

"I know. I shouldn't let a week to go by without telling him how much he means to us, but I can be a real bastard, Marc, pure and simple. Where have the years gone? I thought I was doing everything right. I thought I was the ideal parent. I never raised my voice, never struck the child. But I've been so busy with myself I've let the last few years of David's life just slide by."

"That's a bit of overkill, I think. You didn't have to pay a lot of attention to David because you could hire someone else to do it for you, but Richard, no one can say you don't love David."

"Is it just me, Marc, or do you see the change in David?"

"Sure, I see the change, and not only in David. Let me tell you something, my friend. You don't know how good it is to see you like this. I was beginning to think you would never get over the wall."

147

"What do you mean? See me like what? You think I've changed? I haven't changed, except I'm more tuned in to David, and that makes me happy. I want to make up for all the years I kept him on the shelf. I guess you just put more of yourself into… What?"

"Who do you think you're kidding? Yo, buddy, it's me, remember? I'm the guy who knows all about you, the guy who's been along for the whole ride. Richard, don't tell me you haven't changed. And I can tell you the exact time it happened—, the day David found Michael."

"Well, sure, okay. I admit Michael has had an impact on the way I see certain things."

"No shit, Sherlock! Now tell me she hasn't had an impact on you. Forget David. Forget Allen. Forget the house and the damn dog, everything except Richard Hampton. The guy who never smiled much, who never, and I mean never, trusted anything a woman had to say or do, except your mom, and maybe Ruthie, but then she's been with you forever."

Marc paced the kitchen, surprised that he'd said so much, but every word had been bottled up for so long and now he was on a roll. "Good Lord, Richard. I almost fell on the floor last week when you defended Michael to Sylvia, and then when Michael threw Sylvia out the door, I mean, you should have seen the look on your face. Pride, Richard, pure pride and admiration. It was worth a million dollars."

Marc took a sip from his glass. "Don't give me that dumb look. I wasn't the only one who noticed. Gill called me the next day. We were ready to pony up an offering to the guy upstairs for finally deciding you were worth saving.

"Richard, I swear to God, if you think you haven't been touched by this funny little elf with flour all over her face, then there's no hope for you." Marc stopped and drained his glass, then pointed it at Richard's chest. "And another thing, I'll tell you right now I'm not going to stick around and watch you wallow in self-pity anymore. If you blow this, then you're a damn fool. And I don't believe you are a fool."

"Dad, Michael said I needed to ask you about Bo. Dad, can he come with us?" David had a habit of sending his words ahead of his feet. They heard him coming and silently agreed to continue their conversation later, much later as far as Richard was concerned. He'd never seen Marc like this. It wasn't only what he'd said that had Richard troubled; it was the intensity of his demeanor as if Marc were trying to get through an invisible wall to make his point.

Richard knew he was acting differently these days. Ruthie asked him last week for the name of his new happy pills, but then she was always needling him about something. Why shouldn't the fact that he had a stronger relationship with his son be reason enough for him to be in a happier mood? Marc and Amy had tried for years to get him to date, to find someone, if for no other reason than to give David a mother, but they didn't understand. Richard wasn't ready for a wife, or even a steady significant other. Maybe he never would be. Sure, he liked to be around Michael. He thought about her all the time; he thought she was funny, exciting, and so beautiful. Sure, he liked being near her. He had thought about her after his conversation with Sue. He tried to imagine what it would be like married to Michael, or any woman. Well, he wasn't ready for that kind of commitment. Richard appreciated what she had done for David, and he liked being with her, but he wasn't ready to commit. Not yet.

Besides, he had a feeling Michael felt the same as he did. Hadn't she told him she was leaving? If Michael had felt any romantic inclination after the night of the storm, she would have said something. She wasn't shy; hell, she spoke her mind all the time. She was leaving, and soon. Sure, she was leaving, because he'd let his brains sink below his belt. He knew Michael hadn't appreciated the fact that he had taken advantage of a fierce summer storm and sexual magnetism that set off a chain reaction, destroying all his reasoning powers. Their chemistry had met, run wild, and instantly exploded.

Marc said he was a fool if he let her get away. Hell, he'd be a fool if he got out of line again. David meant a lot to Michael. He could see it every time the two were in the same room. Richard knew he could talk her out of leaving, but not if he didn't get himself under control and keep his hands to himself.

"Hold up there, cowboy. The two of you have to stop running in the house. You'll tear the walls down."

David and Bo had just completed a not-so-perfect one-eighty into the kitchen. Bo was definitely having a difficult time with traction on the tile floor, but when the pitch of Richard's voice changed, Bo came to a sudden stop.

"What did you do to Bo?" Michael walked up behind David and the dog that stood looking up at Richard.

"I didn't do anything to the dog. McCall, why is he in my face?"

"Don't ask me. I just came in. Bo, sit, over there."

The dog went and sat, two feet away, but kept his eyes glued on Richard.

Richard ran his hand through his hair. He wanted to eliminate the last twenty-eight minutes. First Marc, and then the dog. The next thing he knew, his mother would be calling to tell him to go wash behind his ears. He was the dad here. He was the one who said what would be done and when. Richard stood up straight and tucked in his shirt, although it didn't need tucking in. He was just about to tell David how it was going to be when Michael changed his mind.

"I told David to ask you about Bo, but we have to take him, Richard. They couldn't deliver the dog run until tomorrow. It's warm, so we can sit outside at Gino's. He can stay in the car, but we can watch him."

Richard smiled and shook his head in agreement. What else was he supposed to do? He definitely needed to talk with her about who had the last word on issues like this, but not tonight. Tonight they were going to celebrate.

Peter said he would pick her up before seven thirty. Michael had tried to back out, but Peter wasn't listening to her. She told him at the picnic she didn't think she was ready to start dating again. They'd been dancing at the time, but he wouldn't listen. He just held her tightly and hummed in her ear. No pressure, no strings, just relax and enjoy, that was his prescription. Take one each day and call him anytime. By the way, the prognosis was excellent. He promised.

This was wrong. She'd given up trying to convince Sarah she didn't want to make Richard jealous. She wanted him to want her because he felt the same desire she felt for him, and she was not going to use Peter Farrell to force the issue. Tonight she would tell Peter she couldn't see him again. September would be here before she knew it, and it was time to cut all loose ends.

Michael finished with her hair. It was easy to style, just as José had promised. She pulled it back and up, twisting it once. A set of silver combs held the dark tresses in place, and only a few unruly curls danced about the back of her neck and the sides of her face. Michael heard the car on the drive. She picked up her evening bag and started toward the stairs.

"Come in, Peter. I'm sure McCall is almost ready."

Peter stepped through the door and looked up just as Michael started down the stairs. Richard's eyes followed. Bo stood beside her with his head at an angle, his gaze directed at the two men who waited at the bottom of the stairs. Michael's evening gown was emerald velvet, a one-shoulder classic, hugging every curve from her tanned shoulders to the top of her black silk sandals. The dress was slit on one side, just below her knee, revealing an alluring glimpse of her shapely leg. Her long, slender neck was bare of adornment, but diamond and emerald earrings danced at her ears.

With one hand on the banister and the other on the top of Bo's head, she moved slowly down the stairs. Richard's smile widened. Is this the same woman who'd danced like an elf with flour on her nose a few days ago?

"Michael, you look divine." Peter stepped forward and held out his hand, trying to ignore the low growl from the gigantic hairy dog at her side. "Are your slippers made of glass? Do I have to have you home before midnight?"

Michael glanced over Peter's head at Richard. He was shaking his head in the affirmative to Peter's question. Was he trying to tell her something? *Just ignore him,* she told herself. But then, what if…? Michael tried to subdue the pesky mischief-maker living deep inside her, knowing this could be dangerous territory. Really, she did, but—

"I can stay out past midnight, can't I, Richard?" She dared him to say no. She narrowed her green eyes and challenged him to speak up for himself. *Tell Peter I'm not going anywhere with him. Tell him, Richard. Tell him that I belong to you.* She screamed out the words, but of course, he couldn't hear her. Neither could Peter because it was her heart speaking, urged on by an ache that rocked her soul. *Do it, Richard, and I swear I'll make you forget about Eve and Carol and any other woman you've ever known.* But he didn't say a word. He didn't tell Peter that she was his and his alone.

"We better be on our way. Our reservations are for eight."

The door flew open, and David and Allen walked in with an arm full of videos. "Look what we got, Dad. We got a couple of old cowboy ones."

Allen pulled David aside as Michael and Peter crossed the foyer with Bo right behind them. His smile reflected he liked what he saw as he reached for Bo's collar. The dog was going to soil her gown, but he didn't need to worry. Michael was Michael, no matter how she was dressed. She bent down to kiss David and then told Bo to stay.

"I bet it will be great. Don't eat too much junk food tonight."

Richard watched as his son returned Michael's kiss, but before Peter took her arm and escorted her out the door, Richard swore he heard Michael tell David she wished she were staying at home and watching movies with them.

The night was warm, and the lights of the city sparkled like tiny ballerinas on a stage of glass. Michael relaxed against the back of the seat, her eyes closed, as soft jazz resonated from the radio. Peter had given her a wondrous night. The dinner was five-star, and conversation came easily as they laughed and danced and enjoyed the night. All evening Michael tried to ignore the mocking voice inside her that kept asking why this wasn't enough. When was the last time she'd thoroughly enjoyed herself like she had tonight? And she had enjoyed herself, with Peter.

Being with him was so easy. Peter was as handsome as Richard, smiled a lot more than Richard did, and he'd made it clear he wanted her. Michael opened her eyes and came back to reality. A reality dredged up from a place beyond logic and reason. She was in love with Richard, not Peter, and right now, she wished it were the other way around.

Parked at the top of a high ridge overlooking Sausalito and a pristine view of the city, Peter watched her as she listened to the music and wished he were inside her head, privy to her thoughts. She enjoyed herself tonight, he knew she had, but he also knew something was bothering her, and not just the need for air, he thought, as she tried to put down her window. Peter reached over and helped her, admitting a breeze from the bay. Slowly he raised his hand to her face and his fingers caressed its softness. His gaze was bold and seductive as his thumb outlined the contour of her lips. Then he kissed her.

Peter's kiss was slow and gentle as his fingers teased at the tip of her ear. His tongue traced the soft fullness of her lips, tasted the sweetness, drugging him with desire. Then his mouth recaptured hers and demanded a response.

This kiss was intense and coaxing—his lips like warm honey as he moved his mouth over hers, devouring its softness. He sought the dormant sexuality he knew was there, hidden away. Then Michael opened her mouth to him, and he was lost.

Michael knew he would kiss her. The cool breeze did nothing to restrain the need she saw in his eyes. Peter's lips were warm and eager, but he didn't rush her. He gave her time to become accustomed to his touch, time for her to turn away, but she didn't turn away. Michael waited for her body to respond to his gentle demands as he softly called her name before his mouth covered hers and all words stopped, lost in the passion of his kiss.

Help him, she told herself. *Give him something back.* Wishing it could be her heart, she opened her lips and heard a low, painful moan of pleasure as he took what she offered him with a fierce intensity, and in one forward motion, she was in his arms, pulled tightly against his trembling body.

He held her close, his face against hers, his lips, just inches away from her mouth. They were both trembling. "I'm sorry if I hurt you." Peter lifted his head and gently touched her lower lip with his finger tip. He knew. He guessed he'd known from the first, but then the male ego had a way of disguising the truth.

Michael waited until she could trust her voice. She needed to do this right. She couldn't hurt Peter. She'd kissed him with all she had to give, but it just wasn't the same.

Michael pulled back. She needed to put some space between them. "Peter, I can't do this. I mean, I—I told you"

"I know. It's okay. Please don't cry. Michael, please don't. I'll really feel terrible if you cry." Peter took his handkerchief from his pocket and handed it to her.

"It's not your fault. It's me. You're a wonderful man, and you don't deserve this. I told you I couldn't do this. I told you... I did." Michael opened the car door and got out. She walked to the edge of the cliff and tried to clear her mind. She felt Peter behind her, and when he wrapped his arms around her, it felt right to give way, to let him hold her.

"It's Richard. No, don't pull away. Michael, I've known from the beginning. Deep down, I knew that you had this feeling for him." He squeezed her tightly. "I've got eyes. Anyone who sees the two of you together can see how you feel about each other, but I had to try. I could have been wrong, you know."

"You are wrong. Richard has no feeling for me, none at all. I should never have accepted the job with him, but I felt so sorry for David. I made a very big mistake, but I'm leaving soon. I've already told Richard I'm leaving. He'll just have to find someone else. I've agreed to stay until school starts, then I'm going back to the university, back to teaching."

Her tears stopped. She felt warm and safe in Peter's arms, and she knew he wouldn't take her being there the wrong way. He didn't deserve this. He deserved so much more, but she didn't have anything more to give. It was time to go home. There was that word again. She would never again refer to the Hampton residence as home.

Michael turned, and Peter kissed her again, but it was a peace offering and she accepted it that way.

Peter pulled into the driveway and turned off the key. "I can't say I liked the ending so much, but I did have a marvelous time tonight. Thank you, and one more thing. I still want to take you to the gala. That is unless you plan to go with Richard."

"Peter, I told you, Richard has no designs on me, none at all. It would never enter his mind to ask me to go to a dance. I'm just the hired help. I look after his son, and I won't be going to the gala. If I were, I'd be happy to go with you, but I'm not going."

Peter opened the door and helped her out of the car as if she were a porcelain doll. He stood beside her as she searched for her key in her bag. "Please give it some more thought." When she started to answer him, he put his finger on her lips. "Wait, don't say anything now. Just think about it." Then Peter bent and placed a light kiss where his finger had been.

CHAPTER EIGHTEEN

THE MOISTURIZING LOTION DISAPPEARED INTO her skin faster than Michael could squeeze it out of the bottle. If she wasn't careful, she was going to end up with permanent dishpan hands. Sure, she had a dishwasher. This was uptown; they had two, but each day she found new places that needed a good scrubbing.

Michael gave the sink a final wipe. She definitely needed to buy some gloves. With these hands, she couldn't pass for one of the idle rich at Richard's club. She laughed. That sure wasn't something she had to worry about. It wasn't that she couldn't associate with his crowd. Michael knew better than that, and it wasn't the money. She had money, more than she would ever need. Drawing interest in several accounts were large sums of money—insurance money, assets belonging to her because people she loved had died. And it could stay there. Michael still couldn't think about the accounts without wishing she could trade it all and have her family back.

She rolled her shoulders and wondered how her financial situation had taken over her thoughts. Dealing with money wasn't her favorite pastime, neither was cleaning house, but by damn, she knew when she was being cheated, and Mary had cheated. The house was a mess! Michael couldn't understand how someone with Mary's demeanor and apparent IQ could have fooled an intelligent man like Richard Hampton for over two years. But then, how long would it have taken him to realize that his son had an identity crisis and needed a lifeline?

Thank God David had decided to take matters into his own hands. He finally had his dad's attention. Michael might have helped, but now it was up to Richard, and the sooner she went back to the life waiting for her, the better it would be for everyone.

Then there was Peter. He just wouldn't take no for an answer. He'd called twice before she'd gotten home from David's swimming lesson. When he finally reached her, he said he needed to know what color dress she would be wearing to the gala. He just wouldn't give it up, but she wasn't going to the gala or anywhere else. She held her ground as Peter tried to convince her to change her mind, but then his beeper went off. Although she had said all she'd wanted to say, he told her the issue wasn't settled, not by a long shot, and that he'd call her back. But he hadn't called back, and Michael felt relieved. After thinking it over, he probably decided to let it go.

Michael finished sweeping the kitchen floor and turned off the light. She just stepped into the hallway when she heard the doorbell ring. Bo raced past her toward the door, followed by David and Richard coming from the library. David called the dog to his side as Richard went to the door, giving her a questioning look.

"I have to talk to Michael." Peter looked tired and drawn and in no mood to take no for an answer. He saw her and didn't wait for Richard to ask him in, just walked to Michael, took her by the hand, and headed for the kitchen.

"This will only take a minute, Richard, but I need to talk to Michael." To her, he said, "Come on, let's go outside."

"What's the matter with Dr. Farrell, Dad?"

Richard put his hand on David's shoulder and wondered the same thing. "I think he wants to talk to Michael."

Of course, Dr. Farrell wanted to talk to Michael. David was only eight years old, but he could see that. Sometimes grownups sure acted strange.

"I gotta go upstairs and work on my budget. Michael says I have to fact in…, No, that's not it. What's that word, Dad? Means I have to look over my money 'cause Bo is eating more than Runaround did."

"I think you mean factor. It means you might have to make some changes with your money." Richard wondered what Peter wanted. It was obvious he was in a real twist about something, and by taking her outside, Peter had made it extremely clear his words were for her and her alone.

"Dad, did you hear me?"

"I'm sorry, David, what did you say?"

"I said you should put your dirty clothes basket in the laundry room. That way Michael doesn't have to carry it in there tomorrow when she does the laundry."

"David, what are you talking about?"

"The laundry, Dad, I said—"

"I heard what you said, son. What about the laundry? Does Michael do the laundry?"

"Sure she does. Who did you think was doing it now that Mary's gone? Dad, Michael does everything around here except mow the lawn. Allen does that. She even helps us weed the garden. Allen says we gotta get her some help. She's talked to a bazillion people, but they all have some hang-up, so she doesn't hire them. I just thought it would help if you did your part, like I do."

As soon as Richard promised David he'd get his act together, help out from now on, David was off to work on his budget, with Bo following on his heels. Richard walked into his room to get his dirty clothes but stopped at the French doors leading to the patio. He knew they couldn't see him because the lights were off in his room. He also knew what he was doing was wrong, and he felt like an intruder. What were they saying? *Let it go,* he told himself. *It's none of your damn business.* But he couldn't move away; he just watched and wished he could hear.

"Peter, will you stand still and say what you came to say? You're going to fall into the pool."

Peter Farrell didn't want to stand still, and he wasn't going to leave here tonight until she understood a few important facts. "I want you to listen to me."

Michael held out her hand. Peter looked haggard. He was without his suit jacket and tie, shirt open at the collar, and he needed a shave. "Peter, I'm listening. I'm not going anywhere until you tell me what you came to say. Just sit down, please."

Peter pulled a chair in front of her. He took a deep breath and rubbed his hand over his five o'clock shadow, then took her hands in his. "Guess I should have gone home and cleaned up. I must look like hell. I started to come here hours ago, but one of my babies decided it was time to enter the world. Michael, I don't want to be your lover. Or marry you."

"What?"

"Wait, that came out all wrong. Let me start again. Okay, what I want to say is I want us to be friends. It's only been a year since my divorce became final, and let me tell you, I made a lousy husband. Pat and I were married for three and a half years and, in all reality, it was over after the first three and a half weeks."

Peter rolled her fingers between his as she waited for him to go on. Was he choosing his next words or reflecting on his recently deceased marriage? Michael almost suggested they put this conversation off until he could get some rest, but he tugged her fingers and continued.

"Pat's a great gal. We get along great now that we're not married. She's a CPA in San Francisco. I'm rambling, aren't I? Yes, I am... I'm rambling. Michael, I was well on my way to falling in love with you. When I first realized how you felt about Richard, I was pissed. I mean, it kind of smashed the Farrell ego to discover I wasn't number one. And the more I thought about it, the madder I got, and the madder I got the harder I worked to make you want to be with me, and that's when I realized why I was so upset. Love is not a game, and if you're going to love someone, you have to work at it, and right now, I don't want to work that hard. Well, if I thought I had a chance, I would. The truth is you love Richard, and I know that.

"But I don't want to be alone either. I know I'm crazy, but please hear me out. I worked on this speech between contractions this evening. I want to laugh and dance and go out to dinner, or just munch-out with a bowl of popcorn and a movie, but I don't want to do these things alone. I don't like single bars; the women look you over like you're a side of beef. And I sure don't want to end up another notch on some divorcee's garter belt. What I want is a friend, someone I can truly relax with. I want you to be that friend. You make me laugh. I can tease you, and you tease back. I know you wouldn't get upset if I said let's go grab a beer and a hot dog and to wear your jeans.

"I'm trying to be as honest as I can because it hit me, like a sledgehammer that this is something I want very much, as much as I thought I wanted to make love to you. Well, let's just say it balanced out about even. Lady, there is nothing I'd like better than to strip down and spend about a month between the sheets with you.

"I may be mixed-up, Michael, but I'm not stupid. I realize I can't have it both ways. You never played games with me; you were honest from the very first. You could have used me to get to Richard. Believe me, kitten, most women in your situation would have used me good, but you didn't. I want to see you. I want to do all those things I said, go dancing, go to a movie or just hang out. Do I make any sense at all?"

"Oh, Peter, of course you make sense."

"You said you're leaving soon, but that doesn't bother me. Planes fly in and out of here on a regular basis. Go with me to the dance. We'll have a blast, and you have my scout's honor I'll behave. Say something, Michael. Say you'll be my buddy and say you'll be my special friend."

Peter stood up before his final plea and paced with determination. Now Michael stood and held out her arms, and in less time than it took a smile to cover his face, Peter had her in a bear hug, swinging her round and round.

Like a Peeping Tom, Richard watched the scene by the pool. *Well, that settles that,* he told himself. *She's made her choice.* No, that wasn't fair. There had never been a choice to make and he knew it.

Peter had declared his intentions from the beginning, the first time he saw Michael, while Richard held back, telling himself he couldn't get involved. Peter had actively pursued her, and now his perseverance had paid off.

Richard tore the lid off his dirty clothes basket and sent it sailing across the room like a missile. It hit the lamp on his desk, knocking it to the floor, sending glass flying in all directions. "Screw it," he muttered as he went out the door with the basket in his arms. "And screw the lamp. I never liked the damn thing anyway."

CHAPTER NINETEEN

"**D**AVID, TAKE YOUR WINDBREAKER. IT looks like rain."

"Good, Allen says the garden could use some."

Michael watched David race up the stairs, his long legs skipping every other one. He was growing faster than the weeds in their garden. David had a Cub Scout meeting and Mrs. Compton was picking him up. Michael had to quit fooling around and get the seatbelts fixed in the Porsche.

She'd completely forgotten Allen had to go to San Francisco today, and when she called to see if Richard could bring her his car, Ruthie told Michael that Richard had an unscheduled trip into the city. In fact, he'd already left. At least Allen could go to the grocery store for her, but she knew he wouldn't be back in time to take David to Scouts.

Mrs. Compton hadn't minded picking David up at all. David and her son Jerry had joined the Scouts on the same day and became fast friends.

The afternoon passed much too soon, but Michael enjoyed every minute. Although she loved David dearly, she savored her afternoons alone, if you could call having a three-foot shadow with a black beard and bushy eyebrows and wearing a bright-red neckerchief being alone. Michael indulged herself with a bubble bath, a manicure, and a hot-oil treatment for her hair, with Bo resting contentedly close by. Her prediction of rain came true. In fact, what started out as a light drizzle progressed into a heavy downpour.

Michael made a salad and had the rest of dinner ready to hit the stove the moment her men came home. She'd just fixed a cup of tea when the phone rang.

"Hi. This is Alice, the assistant den mother. Yes, well, we've had an accident, and I need you to come get David."

"Is David hurt?"

"No, it's not David. One of the other boys cut himself and Clara, the den mother, well; she's taken him to the hospital. Poor kid was screaming and bleeding all over the place. Anyway, she left me in charge to send the other boys home."

"Has Mrs. Compton picked up Jerry yet? David should go with them."

"Oh, she's come and gone. I didn't know David was supposed to go with Jerry, but they're gone now, so I need you to come and pick up your son."

Michael started to explain to Alice that she wasn't David's mother, but decided not to confuse the poor woman any more than she already was. "Tell David I'll be there soon."

Michael called Richard's office again, hoping he might have returned from San Francisco, but his receptionist said they didn't expect him to return to the office today. Damn! Michael looked at the clock. Allen wouldn't be back for at least another hour, and Anxious Alice might not last that long. She would have to take the Porsche, broken seat belt and all.

She put Bo in his kennel before backing her car out of the garage. A whipping wind sent ribbons of water in all directions and played havoc with the trees lining the streets. Michael had to detour several times to avoid broken branches blocking the road. Although it was only four-thirty, storm clouds darkened the skies.

David saw her pull up and get out of the car and tore out the door before she reached the porch. Michael held David's jacket over his head as she said good-bye to the frazzled assistant den mother, and they ran to the car. Michael made a U-turn and headed for home. The rain hadn't let up; water ran onto the road from the already swollen ditches running parallel to the road.

David bounced in his seat, giving her a play-by-play account of the accident. "Well, see, we were making these model cars, and you had to cut away these little thingy-bobs that hold the good pieces to a sheet of plastic, so the best parts don't get broken. Anyway, Mrs. Bowen—, that's our den mother—, well, she told us we had to be real careful. She even showed us how to use the knife so we wouldn't cut ourselves, but dumb old Bobby started horsing around, acting like he had a sword and was going to stab someone."

Michael listened to David but kept her eyes on the road and not on his hands as they swished through the air, imitating the swordplay. Sheets of water coursed across the road as the windshield wipers whipped back and forth, unable to keep up with the heavy rain pelting the glass, making it almost impossible to see out. Michael slowed down, silently wishing they were in Richard's big car. Stupid mistakes like this always got her in trouble. If she were by herself, it would be bad enough, but with David in the car, she was more than uptight; she was terrified.

"David, I want you to—"

Michael never got the chance to tell David to sit up straight and lean back into the seat. Halfway through the intersection, a pickup truck roared out of the darkness and slammed into the rear of the driver's side of her car. She didn't have time to do anything except throw herself in front of David in a desperate attempt to keep him away from the dashboard. The impact sent the Porsche into a 360-degree spin, propelling it toward the side of the road. With so much water on the road, traction was impossible. Later, much later, she would remember feeling caught in a whirlpool, spinning totally out of control.

It had taken less than a minute, but Michael died a thousand lifetimes. Another crash blazed before her eyes as an image, painfully etched in her mind, played over and over again. She felt the heat of the flames; saw the slashing of flesh by twisted, jagged metal that claimed the lives of her son and husband. She couldn't breathe; hysteria threatened her sanity as it siphoned the very breath from her lungs.

They were in a residential neighborhood, and the sound of the impact brought people out into the street. Hands appeared out of nowhere, pulling aside the crumpled door panels to get them out of the car. Michael heard the sounds of heart-wrenching screams, and then realized the sounds came from her. Where was David? She had to stay calm—she had to get David out of the car.

"Please, God, don't take him," she yelled to the air. "He doesn't belong to me. You have Andy. You took everything I had. You can't have

David." Then Michael was out of the car. Where was David? She had to find David.

"DAVID, OH MY GOD!" She saw the soles of his shoes and pushed away from the arms trying to hold her. She tore at the man who stood in front of David, shoving him aside as she dropped to her knees, taking his face into her hands. Then she cried.

"You're alive. Oh, thank God, David, you're alive. Where do you hurt? Thank you, Lord, thank you."

In the distance, she heard the sirens. An older man asked her name. Whom should he call? Where was she hurt?

"Oh MY GOD!" She had to call Richard. How was she going to tell him she'd let David get into her car? He had trusted her to take care of his son and she'd almost gotten him killed, but he was alive. In fact, David was smiling at her. Why was he smiling? It must be shock; he was going into shock.

Two ambulances edged their way through the crowd and stopped a short distance from her car, or what was left of her car. Flares placed around the accident scene gave off a distorted reddish glow as a police officer directed traffic away from the damaged vehicles. The pickup truck had slid past the intersection and rolled off the shoulder into a ravine.

Almost simultaneously, men poured out of the ambulances. Two paramedics hurried toward David and Michael while the other crew ran in the direction of the upside-down pickup truck. When the paramedic dropped beside Michael and asked her name she told him not to bother with her; David needed his help.

His partner was already talking to David as he wrapped him in a blanket. He checked his pulse, the pupils of his eyes, following a set routine but talking to David at the same time. After his preliminary examination, the paramedic pushed his cap to the back of his head and declared David one lucky kid. It looked like he had only sustained a broken arm, other than a few superficial cuts and bruises. Of course, when they got him to the hospital, David would have to undergo X-rays, lab tests, and a more thorough examination, but his breathing and pulse were within normal limits, considering the circumstances. His blood pressure, skin temperature, and the response of his pupils convinced the paramedic that David suffered only a slight case of shock.

While the EMT named Josh worked with David, splinting his right arm and getting him ready to transport, his partner, a man named Harry, addressed Michael. She was still on her knees in front of David, and he wouldn't let her move until he conducted his preliminary examination. He worked the same as his partner, checking her pulse, pupils, and respiration, all the while keeping up a running dialog with her. Deciding she had no broken bones, Harry wrapped her in a blanket and let her sit on the curb by David. As Josh checked in with the hospital emergency room, Harry continued to monitor Michael, who displayed signs of respiratory shock. Her blood pressure dropped; her pulse, rapid and bounding, combined with her gasping and irregular respiration, hastened his attempt to keep her calm, but he wasn't getting through to her. It was normal for an accident victim to be frightened and upset, especially a mother, but this gal was wired. No, it was more than that; she was terrified.

Harry figured that fright brought on the hypertension and her irregular breathing. Plus, she had taken a pretty strong blow to her chest and side. He tried to check her vitals again, but she pushed him away, whiter than Casper's sheet and colder than ice.

Harry tried to start her on oxygen—, she told him no. He wanted to place her on a backboard—, no again. When he tried to insist, she told him to bug off, poking her finger into the center of his chest.

"Look, if I'm going to cause additional damage because I refuse to be immobilized, the odds are I already did that when I climbed out of the car under my own steam." Since she had never lost consciousness, was able to ambulate without assistance, and could certainly verbalize her thoughts, Harry backed off. She was just a little bit of fluff, no bigger than a mouse, weighing, he guessed, a little over a hundred pounds soaking wet, but as she poked her finger into his chest and narrowed her eyes, he felt a chill skate up his spine when she told him what he could do with his backboard. Hey, he was bigger than she was, so he stood his ground and finally she agreed to the oxygen, but only if he allowed her to explain.

"This boy's father is a doctor at San Rio and I want to be taken there right now." Michael stood up, with help and a smirk from Harry. The smirk quickly disappeared when she took the oxygen from her nose and grabbed the front of his shirt, pulling him a few feet away from David.

"You don't understand. I am not David's mother; I'm only the nanny. How am I going to explain this to his father? You have to help me here, get us to the hospital. I can't let anything else happen to David. Please, I'll be good, I promise. I'll get on your stretcher, use the oxygen, anything. Just help me…, please."

On the way to San Rio Medical Center, Harry rode in the back, checking Michael's and David's vitals every few minutes. He stayed in constant contact with the hospital and advised them more than once that they needed to contact Dr. Richard Hampton right away. And Michael kept her promise.

Harry regulated the flow of oxygen and checked her pulse. She was quiet, and he knew she fought her tears. When she'd pulled him away by his shirt so she could talk to him without the boy hearing her, he had never seen anyone look more desperate. It had only taken a moment until he'd understood.

"Take it easy. Just breathe normally; we'll be there real soon. The boy is doing fine. He's going to have quite of a story to tell his pals, but we want this story to have a happy ending, so please, try to relax."

Harry hovered above her, checking her eyes again, and Michael was glad he spoke softly. She didn't want David to think she was hurt. She had told him she was fine, and he seemed to be okay with that.

Michael jumped when the ambulance came to a stop. Harry led the way, with Josh in hot pursuit as they wheeled the stretchers through the automatic doors leading to the emergency department of the San Rio Medical Center, bypassing the receptionist at the front desk. They stopped long enough for Harry to punch the metal plate that opened the door leading to the treatment room, then rolled down a pea-soup-green corridor and into a waiting cubicle.

Harry and Josh drove into the cubicle and parallel-parked the rolling stretchers beside the metal exam tables. "I told you to trust me. I ordered a twin suite and here we are."

"On my count..., one, two, three." The tall, redheaded nurse took control and moved David and Michael to the exam tables, transferring data onto the hospital chart as Harry rattled off his initial findings and admitting diagnosis.

"Have you talked to Dr. Hampton?" Michael tried to sit up, but Big Red's associate had other ideas.

She removed the oxygen apparatus from Michael's nose, threw the tubing into the trashcan by the table, and then replaced the entire application with clean tubing hooked to the wall and adjusted the flow of oxygen.

The two women in green moved about the room without saying a word, hooking David to a series of machines. "Harry, come here," Michael said. When he stood by her side, she told him, "Do something, Harry. They're frightening David. He doesn't understand what they're doing, and he's... Just look at his face. Harry, tell them I'm all right so I can get off this damn table and let him know it's okay."

"I can't do that. We have to wait for the doctor to examine you. What I say doesn't carry weight here."

"Mrs. Hampton, if you don't cooperate, I'll have to use restraints. It's for your own safety. We can't have you sustaining more injuries."

The room echoed with the words, "I'm not—"

"She's not Mrs. Hampton."

Michael, Harry, and Peter Farrell all corrected the nurse who had her hands full of table straps.

"Peter, oh, Peter. Tell Attila here to let me up. I need to find Richard."

"Easy, kitten, easy. I've already talked to Richard. I'd just finished with a patient in the ER when the call came over the radio about the accident. We beeped him right away, and he called from San Francisco. Richard's on his way. He told me to call him just as soon as you got here so he could talk to you."

Peter held her hand as he dialed Richard's number. His eyes scanned her face and mirrored his concern. "Are you okay? I've been out of my mind. Wait a minute. Richard? Yes, they're here. No, not yet. They just got here. Talk to Michael while I go check." Peter handed the phone to Michael. "I'm going to find Dr. Singer. Talk to Richard; tell him I said I'm staying right here."

"Richard, I'm sorry. I'm so sorry."

"Mikie, it's all right. Don't cry; please don't cry. I'm on the bridge right now, and I'll be there before you know it. Just stay calm. Everything will be all right. Mikie, this was not your fault, just remember that; this wasn't your fault. Is David close by? Let me talk to him."

Michael gave the phone to Harry to give to David. "David, it's your dad."

Harry gave the phone to David and had a few private words with Attila the nurse, who, against her better judgment, relinquished her hold on the tie-down straps.

Just as David ended his conversation with his dad, Peter and a short, baldheaded man came into the cubicle. "Michael, this is Miles Singer. He's an orthopod, and he's going to take care of the two of you."

Dr. Singer smiled and rubbed the top of his shiny head, but when he took a step toward David, Michael jumped off the table before anyone could stop her.

"Do you know what you're doing? I'm not going to let just anybody touch David. Peter?"

Dr. Singer stopped dead and looked at Michael and then at Peter. "Peter?"

"Michael, it's okay. Dr. Singer is Chief of Orthopedic Surgery. He's the best and Richard told me to call him. He'll take good care of David. Now, you have got to be still." He moved to her side and gently eased her back onto the table. The movement caused her to clench her teeth and her hand came to rest on her abdomen. Peter retrieved a stool and sat by Michael's side.

After a few moments, Dr. Singer had the place jumping. A tech wheeled a portable X-ray machine into the room and set up to take pictures of David's arm. Then he turned to Michael, and after he examined her, Dr. Singer explained it would be less painful for Michael to go upstairs for a series of X-rays. When she shook her head, telling him she was fine, he smiled and told her it was his call, not hers. He did give her the option of a gurney or a wheelchair, but that was the only choice she had. He explained about David's arm, which he would set while she was gone. It was a simple break. David would have to wear a cast for about six weeks, but he would be good as new. His vital signs were fine and Dr. Singer couldn't see any reason why David couldn't go home with Richard tonight.

Michael didn't like the sound of his last sentence. Was he implying she had to stay in the hospital? "Dr. Singer, I'm fine. I mean, I know I've been a bit outspoken, but I'm sure."

He had her number. "Miss McCall."

"Mrs."

"Right, Mrs. McCall. The sooner you follow my instruction, the sooner I'll know what I'm going to do with you. Okay? Good. First we'll get some X-rays, and then we'll go from there."

Michael opted for a wheelchair and a light blanket to take over where the skimpy hospital gown, hastily applied to replace her wet clothes, left off. Peter wanted to go with her, but she convinced him to stay with David, at least until Richard got to the hospital. She wished Harry hadn't left. He had become her champion, but he was still on the clock and had to go back to work.

A cute kid from dispatch wheeled her into the elevator at top speed. The radiology department was quiet this time of the day, and it didn't take them long to have her on her back again and in a few other positions that hurt like hell. When the tech finished with her, Kenny, the wheelchair jockey, bounced into the room with a set of scrubs sent by Dr. Farrell, who thought they would be more comfortable than the airy gown.

Dr. Singer walked into the room. "I want to look at the films before we go back downstairs," he told her. "Try to relax. Are you warm enough?"

"I'm fine," she told him, "Is Dr. Hampton here yet. Who's with David?"

"You're not to worry about the boy. His father is with him, and I think Richard sent someone to the cafeteria. Seems Mr. David is starving. Now, let's see what we have here.

"Mrs. McCall, it looks like you're just battered and bruised. All the pictures are negative. That's good news, but I'm afraid you're going to be extremely stiff and sore for a while. I'd like to keep you overnight. I know you don't want to do that, but let me finish. If you promise me you'll stay quiet, and if Richard will monitor you tonight, I'll agree to release you, but only if you give me your word you'll behave." Dr. Singer laughed gently at the questioning look she gave him.

"Yes, my dear, your demeanor precedes you. In the short time you were in the ER, your chart already wears the label uncooperative and hostile. Having an attitude, I think the nurses called it, but we're not going to worry about that right now. Just give me your word and you're out the door. I'm going to give you a shot now to help you relax, then we'll go downstairs and Richard can take the two of you home."

Dr. Singer personally delivered her back to the ER, still wrapped in the blanket and gown, with the set of scrubs on her lap. She tried to keep herself covered with the blanket but failed miserably. One hand held the blanket together at her chest while the other clutched the material at her knees but from there down, just bare legs and feet.

Richard waited with David in the corridor. Instead of showing signs he'd just been pulled from a car wreck, David proudly displayed his cast.

Michael tried to suppress her tears; she didn't want to frighten David. Richard ran his hand through his hair, then over his face. There were lines of weariness at the corners of his firm mouth, and he drew his thick brows together, making it impossible for her to read his thoughts. Her stomach churned violently, then clenched into an agonizing knot. Michael turned away so David couldn't see her as hot tears boiled up and then slid down her face.

Too humiliated to look at Richard, Michael tried to brush away the flood of tears streaming down her face. If she didn't get out of his sight quickly, she knew she would fall apart.

"Dr. Singer, please push me into the cubicle so I can get dressed." She got the words out, barely, and then lowered her head. Feeling guilt as bitter as bile, she wished she could just disappear. As Dr. Singer turned the wheelchair around and pushed her through the curtains, she shifted in the chair, sending a bolt of pain radiating through her arm.

"Do you need some help?" he asked as he bent over her, patting her hair as a father might comfort a child. Dr. Singer mistook her tears for pain and fatigue. *The shot should be kicking in,* he thought as he turned to leave, *but Richard needs to get her home and into bed.* "We'll be right outside if you need any help."

"Is she all right? What did the X-rays show? She looks like she's in a lot of pain. Miles, I don't want her hurting if there's something you can do."

"Richard, for God's sakes, calm down. The last thing we need right now is for you to fall apart. She's going to be fine. The films were negative. I did a spinal and neck series, as well as several shots of the chest and arms. No breaks, everything looks good, but her ribs are bruised, and her arms are going to be sore. In fact, she's going to hurt like hell all over for a few days. I've given her a shot to calm her down and help with the pain. She's pumped enough residual adrenaline to power a freight train. Before you got here, she was ready to take on the whole nursing staff because they wouldn't let her go to David when he bumped his arm and started to cry."

"I'm not surprised. When it comes to David, she would walk through fire to fight off the devil if need be."

"Richard, she blames herself for what happened. But she's wrong. There was no way she could have prevented it. I talked to the police myself. They wanted to interview her, but I told them, as her physician, I didn't think she was up to speaking to them tonight, so they'll probably call her at home tomorrow. The police officer told me a couple of kids were in the pickup that hit her car. They'd been drinking. Seems they rolled out of the truck without a scratch but couldn't stand up when the sheriff started to question them. My guess is they'll be spending the night in the county jail.

"You'll have to watch her tonight, wake her up a few times. I'm sure she doesn't have a concussion, but we better be on the safe side. She's probably ready to go, and Richard, I'll want to check David's cast tomorrow. Just call the office."

Richard thanked Miles Singer for taking care of his family and pulled the curtain apart slightly to see if Michael was dressed and ready to go. Michael leaned against the exam table with her head down. She had managed to put on the scrub pants, but her shoes were on the floor and the hospital gown hung from one arm, leaving most of her chest and her back bare. Her shoulders shook as tears streamed down her face. She looked toward him when he walked through the opening in the curtain but quickly turned away.

"I cou-couldn't get the top on. I can't raise my arms over m-m-my head."

Richard carefully pulled the gown across her breasts, and then drew her against him. He held her close, gently folding his arms around her as he buried his cheek in her hair and ached for her. What could he say that would give her comfort? He needed to say something, and quick. And his words needed to penetrate deeply and calm her anxiety.

"Mikie, I'm going to wrap the blanket around you, and then I'm going to take you home and take care of you. Now I want you to put away your tears. There's no reason for you to be crying, not now. David is fine. He loves all the attention he's getting, and you're going to be fine too."

Richard turned her around and held her at arm's length. He brushed the curls off her forehead and then lifted the tears off her pale cheek with the back of his thumb.

"I'm so sorry, Richard. I should not have let David get in that damn old car. How can you ever forgive me or trust me again?"

Richard took her face in his hands. "Sh-sh. Mikie, don't. Baby, I'm not upset with you. It was not your fault. Everything is going to be fine. We're going home, and everything is going to be okay." He reached behind him and pulled the blanket around her quaking body. "Do you want to sit back down in the chair?"

She wiped watery eyes with the back of her hand. "Richard, I'm so cold."

"I know, baby." He pulled another blanket off the exam table and wrapped it around her for good measure and then helped her into the wheelchair. Richard balanced on one knee as he slipped her favorite shoes onto her feet and tied the strings.

He pushed her out into the corridor where David still held court, dressed in a set of scrubs rolled up at the legs about ten times. "Come on, Sport. Tell your new friends good-bye. We're going home."

"Look, Michael, I already have five signatures on my cast. I'm going to get lots more and have everybody sign my cast. Did you get a cast? You gotta be real careful until the plaster dries, but then you can even draw pictures and everything."

"David, let's wait until we get home. I don't think Michael feels very well right now."

With David in tow and a nurse following behind with a bag full of their wet clothes, Richard led the way to his car, which he had left outside the front door of the ER when he arrived at the hospital.

Peter had told Richard he would call Allen before leaving the ER. He also called Hal Green to cover for Richard tonight. Richard made a mental note to call Peter in the morning and thank him for all his help. Peter had stayed because of Michael. Richard knew that, but he'd also helped with David—sitting with him while Miles got him ready to reduce the fracture and cast his arm. Richard had arrived at the hospital as the procedure was taking place and comforted his son while Dr. Singer set the arm before David even knew what was happening.

When Richard pulled up to the garage, Allen stood waiting. He opened the car door and helped Michael out of the car while Richard unbuckled David in the back seat. "Oh, Michael. Lord, I'm so sorry I wasn't here to help you. I should have remembered about David's Scout meeting."

Richard caught Allen's attention as they went through the back door. He motioned to Allen with his eyes as if to say, not now. "Allen, will you take David up and get him undressed and into bed? I'll help Michael."

"Sure, Richard. Come on, pal."

"Allen, look at all my autographs. Dr. Singer said I should wait until it completely dries, but I had everyone be real careful. Michael didn't get a cast, but she doesn't feel very good. She held on to me so I didn't hit the windshield, and she got hurt real bad."

Richard reached gently under Michael's knees and lifted her into his arms. There was no way he could hold her without hurting her, but she shook so badly he didn't think she could manage the stairs on her own.

"Richard, I can walk," she said, resting her head on his chest. She had stopped crying, and she wasn't going to cry anymore. He wasn't mad at her. Richard had told her that the accident wasn't her fault. Michael relaxed against him as he carried her up the stairs and hoped he was telling her the truth. She hoped he wasn't just waiting until she felt better to tell her what he really thought. She didn't think she could stand it if he blamed her.

Richard eased her to the edge of the bed. "Where do you keep your nightgown? Mikie, I know you're sleepy, but you have to stay awake long enough to help me get you ready for bed."

Michael tried to focus her eyes and look at Richard. Why did he want her nightgown? She didn't own a nightgown. She was so tired. She just wanted to go to sleep.

He lowered her head to the pillow and went to the closet and then her dresser. He couldn't find anything that resembled a gown. Richard made sure she wouldn't fall off the bed before going downstairs to his room where he pulled the top of a new set of pajamas from his drawer and headed back to her room.

"Here, Mikie, put this on." He tried to sit her up, but she fell over like a rag doll. The shot Miles had given her had gone to work. Richard gathered all the pillows on the bed and wedged them behind her in an attempt to prop her up. He unlaced her shoes and pulled them off.

Richard stripped off all her clothes and replaced them with the silk top. Her feet were freezing. He threw all the decorative pillows on the floor and eased her back onto the bed before searching through the dresser again for a pair of dry socks. When he returned to the bed, she had rolled onto her stomach, but she was shaking, her muscles tight and jumpy.

Richard gently turned her over and lifted her up. He pulled the covers to the end of the bed and lowered her onto her stomach again. "Work with me, Mikie. You've got to relax or you're going to feel worse in the morning." He knew he was talking to the air as he put the socks on her feet. Slowly, he massaged her neck and shoulders. His hands moved over her bruised body with a gentle strength, coaxing her to relax.

Michael floated in limbo. Richard's hands gently kneaded her tight muscles as she drifted into a troubled sleep, guided by his soft voice that promised he would stay with her. She wouldn't be alone as she moved deep into the darkness. She would not have to face the shadows by herself, but still she was afraid.

Richard felt her relax as her body responded to the shot and the coaxing of his hands. He moved beside her, and his hands moved lightly up and down her back, kneading the taut cords in her neck and shoulders. The pajama top was too large, but as his hands moved over her, he could feel her small waist and slender hips. In the semidarkness, he could see the shape of her bottom under the silk and her long, firm legs stretched out beside him on the bed.

Richard lowered himself beside her and gazed into her sleeping face. He lifted her hair from the side of her face, and his fingers lingered on her temple. The need to touch her was so great. An undeniable magnetism drew him to her, and he felt a strong stirring in his loins. He waited for his quickened pulse to subside, but it didn't. Richard wanted to take her in his arms and hold her forever, but he knew he shouldn't. He wanted to lie beside her for the rest of his life, but he knew he couldn't. He wanted to kiss her delicate mouth, her eyes. And he did.

Richard lay beside her, his eyes closed, and thanked God, again, that she was going to be all right. When Pete called him from the hospital, he'd assured Richard that the initial report said David was fine, but he didn't know about Michael. All Peter could tell him about Michael was that she was conscious but in a lot of pain. Until Dr. Singer had her X-rayed, there was no way of knowing how badly she was hurt. Her car was totaled, Peter knew that much, but there wasn't much more he could tell Richard about Michael.

As he'd raced through traffic, Richard couldn't deny any more how he felt about Mikie. He loved her. God help him, it had taken an accident and the knowledge she had been hurt for him to admit to himself how desperately he needed her, how much he loved her. He didn't care what she felt for Peter; he would make her want him.

She moved beside him, still fitful. Richard knew he needed to leave her alone. She needed to sleep. Michael started to mutter as she had done before, her rambling words lost in the pillow, their meaning locked in her dreams. He turned on the small lamp on the desk and quietly left the room.

Richard stripped off his clothes and took a shower. After checking his two patients again, he went downstairs and into the kitchen.

Allen had fixed him a sandwich and filled a glass with two fingers of scotch. He raised the glass and looked at Richard. "This is strictly medicinal, bucko, but I think you need it. Do you want me to sit with the troops while you get some sleep?"

"No, I'll be all right. Go to bed. I'm going to need you tomorrow. I have to take David to have his cast checked, and I don't want to leave Michael alone." Richard stared into the glass of amber liquid. "Peter told me her car's totaled. She loved that car, Allen. Goddamn kids, drinking and raising hell. The police told Miles it was a lucky thing they weren't going very fast and that they hit in the rear end and not up front where the gas tank is located. The way the doors were smashed, if the car had caught fire, they would have been trapped inside."

Allen poured them another drink. "Stop it, Richard. We don't need any what ifs. We've got them back, now we just have to make sure we take care of them. You try to get some rest. Call me if you need me. I sleep light."

Every hour he checked them both. David slept soundly, with Bo on guard beside his bed. Each time he checked Michael, he hoped to find her resting easier, but she slept fitfully, still fighting her demons.

A little after midnight, just as he left David's room, he heard her screaming. Richard ran across the landing and into her room. Michael was on the floor, her face looking at the ceiling, screaming just one word.

"ANDY, ANDY, ANDY."

Richard dropped beside and cradled her in his arms. "Baby, sh-sh-sh. Mikie, it's all right."

"Andy's not buckled in. He's bleeding. Ryan, why didn't you strap him in? He hit the dash. The flames, oh my God, Andy's burning… He can't get out. Oh God, Ryan, help him. He's so little, and he can't get out. David can't get out. Ryan, help David, please help David."

His tears mingled with hers. Richard held her to him and rocked back and forth. Why hadn't he guessed what had been tearing her apart all night? He'd thought she was worried about David. He had never once stopped to think she might be reliving the accident that had killed her son. Amy had told him it had rained that night, that the car had caught fire, trapping Michael's son and husband inside to die in the flames and twisted metal. After the fire was out, it had taken the Jaws of Life to tear

176

open the car in order to remove the charred remains of the two people she had loved so much.

"Wake up, Mikie, wake up. David's fine. He's in bed. Oh my God, Mikie, wake up."

Michael heard his words, but she didn't understand. He said David was sleeping. She fought through layers of fog to clear her thoughts. She needed to understand. Richard said David was all right, and Michael needed to believe that. Calling on every bit of reasoning power she possessed, she tried to remember. Michael remembered the car spinning out of control. She recalled Harry and the trip to the hospital. Michael took a deep breath and settled into the safety of Richard's embrace. David was fine; she could see him now. He had a cast, with names written on it, but he was smiling and he was all right.

"Richard?"

"Yes, Mikie?"

"Is David really all right?"

"Yes, baby, he's fine. He's sound asleep, and Bo is right by his side, standing guard for the night."

"Richard?"

"Yes, Mikie?"

"Did you tell me you weren't mad at me?"

"Yes, I did, a thousand times, and I want you to believe it."

"I didn't see the truck coming, Richard. It was raining so hard. I just didn't see it."

"It wouldn't have made any difference if you had. The kids were drinking, not paying any attention at all to the road. I don't want you to think about it anymore. David's okay and you're going to be fine, and right now I'm going to get you back in bed."

She felt as light as a swan's feather as Richard picked her up and placed her on the bed. He got her a glass of water and watched as she took a few sips, her hands shaking, but the tears were gone.

"Richard? Have I been saying strange things?"

"No... Yes. Michael, you had a bad dream, that's all."

"Did I talk about Andy? Richard, tell me the truth."

"Yes."

"I thought it was over, but it all came back—; all of it, so real."

"Do you want to talk about it?"

"No. I... Yes."

"I'll stay if you want to talk"

"Would you?"

Richard took the glass from her hand and put it on the table. Without hesitating, he crawled into bed with her and drew her into his arms. Well into the night, he held her while she unlocked and then opened the door of the secret place where she had hidden the horror of the accident. He held her; he listened, cried, and loved her with all his heart, and finally, she slept. She'd told him all of it, then sighed, snuggled against his chest, closed her eyes, and drifted off to sleep.

CHAPTER TWENTY

BEFORE RICHARD OPENED HIS EYES, he knew he was still in her bed. He breathed deeply, drawing in the scent of her. Sometime after midnight, he'd gotten up to check David, but instead of going to his own bed, he came back to Michael. She lay on her back with her head turned toward him, her arms crossed over her chest, her breathing, even.

She had talked for hours—and he let her. As he held her, Michael had told him about her childhood. A few funny stories had made him laugh, but most of her tales echoed sadness. He would never know if she shared all her secrets with him willingly or if the shot had opened the door to her private place without her full consent. Either way, he knew if he hadn't already realized he loved her, he did now.

Long after she had fallen asleep in his arms, he held her tightly as sleep eluded him, and her words echoed in his mind. He had teased her about so many things, issues that had been a constant source of pain for her. Almost from day one, he taunted Michael about her name. A name he assumed given to her by a jock of a dad who had wanted a boy. But her mother had wanted the boy and apparently never missed an opportunity to tell Michael how utterly worthless girls were, especially her daughter.

When she was five, Michael turned to her father, hoping he might find her worth protecting, worthy of his love, but he just turned to his books, shutting himself away from the child. She had not understood, although his lack of interest hurt badly. Not with the cutting edge that always accompanied her mother's harsh words—it was different, but it hurt more; it still did. Michael defended his actions. She told Richard she had always felt her father might have loved her if he had been strong enough to stand up to her mother.

For many years, Michael lived in her own private world, never asking anyone in. She had cried when she was five and fifteen years old, but never again, until two months ago when she finally lost the will to go it alone. Michael had taken the name, given to her as punishment, and worn it proudly. Only Sarah, who had comforted abused kids and stray dogs since kindergarten, had totally broken through Michael's defenses, until Andy.

Still asleep, Michael pushed into his hand caressing her cheek and a spontaneous smile moved over her soft lips. Just as Richard leaned over to kiss her, the phone rang. Feeling like he'd just been caught stealing, Richard pulled back and fell out of the bed, taking the phone with him.

"Hello," he whispered into the receiver.

"Who is this? Richard? Is that you? Richard, where's Michael?"

"Who is this?"

"It's Sarah. Amy just called and told us that Michael and David were in an auto accident last night. Is she okay? Are they all right?"

"Yes, Sarah, they're fine. David has a broken arm and Michael is pretty battered and bruised. The doctor gave her a strong shot before he let me bring her home, so she slept most of the night. In fact, she's still asleep."

"No, I'm not."

Richard looked over his shoulder and saw Michael leaning near the edge of the bed, staring down at him.

"Good morning, princess. I'm sorry the phone woke you."

Her eyes squinted in confusion. "Richard, why are you sitting on the floor in my bedroom with no clothes on?"

"Richard, who are you talking to? Richard, are you still there?"

He heard Sarah yelling at him from the receiver. "Yes, Sarah, I'm here. Michael just woke up. Do you want to talk to her?"

"Of course I want to talk to her."

"Talk to Sarah, Michael. I'll answer your questions later," he said as he handed her the receiver.

Michael kept her eyes on him as she took the phone.

"Hello, Sarah."

"Babe, are you okay?"

"Sarah, may I call you right back? There's something I need to do right now. I promise I'll call you back in a few minutes."

Michael rose to her knees as she hung up the phone. The top button of the pajama top had come undone during the night and the dark-green silk top hung off one shoulder. Richard stood by the bed, waiting, his tanned legs set firmly apart and his arms folded over his chest, dressed only in his shorts. *What is he doing here,* she thought? *And where were his clothes?* Michael rocked precariously on her knees, lifted her chin, and stared back at him.

Looking confident and secretly amused, he just stood there. Michael fell back on her legs. She waited for him to say something, but he just stared at her. Every inch of his tall, lean body radiated raw power and disciplined sensuality. Beneath his straight dark brows and thick lashes, his eyes glinted with humor as a faint smile touched his mouth, but his heavy-lidded gaze was bold and seductive, issuing a challenge... Or was it an invitation?

"Richard, I asked what you are doing here. And where are your clothes?"

The tension around them was almost palpable. He should do the right thing and just leave, but Richard felt a surge of excitement and desire race through him, and this feeling, this wanting, drove every rational thought from his brain.

"Don't you remember, McCall? You asked me to stay with you last night, and I did."

Her beautiful green eyes widened in disbelief, and he savored the delights of her sweet, pouting mouth and the delicate flush on her skin. After a moment's hesitation, she gave him a direct, assertive look.

"I don't remember any such thing. Really, Richard, you choose the most inopportune moments to be funny."

A smile of admiration broke across his face. "Okay, here's the truth. I spent the night going between you and David, professionally that is, checking your physical condition, as I'd promised Miles I'd do. I admit I should have gotten dressed before I came up this morning, but you've slept so soundly. It would have been okay except the damn phone started to ring and woke you up. Now that I see you're okay, I'll go take my shower. You stay in bed, doctors' orders."

"Where's David? Richard, is David all right?"

"He's fine. His arm was hurting him, so I gave him some medicine about four this morning, and he went back to sleep. He's still asleep. Why don't you do the same? Go back to sleep, McCall."

Richard knew he had to leave. God, he loved the way she blushed when he told her they'd spent the night together. He actually had her believing it for a while. Richard walked slowly to the door, knowing she hadn't taken her eyes off him. He turned as he reached the door. "Better not jump around too much, McCall. You don't have anything on under that pajama top." Richard quickly shut the door, and then remembered her throwing arm was out of commission. After so little sleep, Richard should have felt like hell, but he didn't. When he reached the bottom step, Marc opened the front door just as Allen came out of the kitchen with a cup of coffee for Richard. Marc said hello and started to ask about the accident when Michael marched out of her room and into the landing. Having learned a trick from David, her words shot over the railing before she reached it.

"Richard, you wait just a minute. How do you know what I don't have on under this—?"

Oh sweet angels, she wanted to die. She never dreamed Marc and Allen would be standing at the bottom of the stairs with an almost naked Richard.

"What did you say, McCall?" Richard would choke to death before he would utter the laughter rolling in his throat.

Michael gritted her teeth, whirled around, and trudged back into her room.

Allen watched Michael retreat, then looked at Richard and threw his hands over his head. "I don't even want to know what that was all about," then went back to the kitchen, shaking his head.

"Well?"

"Well, what, Marc?"

"I came here expecting to find Michael on death's door, according to Peter Farrell. Instead, I find the two of you half-clothed and barking at each other."

"Just goes to show you how strong she is. Comes from healthy stock, I hear."

"Richard, I swear to God I don't know what you're talking about."

"Forget it. Want some coffee? Get a cup while I take a shower. I won't be long."

Safely back in her room, Michael leaned against the closed door and waited for her pulse to fall below a hundred. Why had she run after him? What a stupid thing to do. Of course he had known she was naked except for the silk tent she was wearing—he had undressed her. He had dressed her at the hospital, and then undressed her when he got her home. Had they really slept together? She remembered Dr. Singer had given her a shot before she left the hospital. She vaguely remembered the undressing part, something about a nightgown, but then the shot had taken hold, and she must have fallen asleep. She did remember waking up on the floor, him holding her. He put her back in bed and then they had talked and..., and what? He had gotten in bed with her and held her while she rambled on, but then he left, or at least she thought he had. Michael rubbed between her eyes. *You're no Aladdin*, she told herself. *You can rub all day, and all you'll to get is a bigger headache.*

Sarah. She had promised to call Sarah. Michael pulled away from the door and was instantly sorry. *Damn, I hurt.* She went into the bathroom, unbuttoned the silk top, and stared into the mirror. Her chest and the tops of her arms were thirty different shades of blue, green, and bits of orange and yellow, and when she pressed a fingertip into the center of her chest, tears came to her eyes. Very carefully, she ran her hands over her ribs, and the tears increased. She couldn't look or feel any worse, even if a herd of elephants had used her for a doormat. How could she look like this and still have managed to walk away from the car on her own? Her special angel must unquestionably be back in town.

Michael rolled up the sleeves and buttoned her tent. She dialed Sarah's number and sat on the edge of the bed. "Sorry I took so long. I had to go to the bathroom," she lied.

"No problem, I figure I'll be there in about fifteen minutes."

"What do you mean you'll be here in fifteen minutes?"

"I'm just crossing the bridge. I decided not to wait for a medical report, so I forwarded my calls to the car phone. I'm actually having a rip playing with all these techno-toys Tom keeps giving me. I just push a few buttons and watch out, world. Are you still there?"

"I'm here, and I'm okay. I could pass for a dirty rainbow right now, but I'm fine."

"Save your words, toots. You never tell me the truth anyway, so I'm going to see firsthand. Do you have anything to eat at the ranch? Or should I stop and pick up something sweet and gooey?"

"Sweet and gooey sounds good."

Michael carefully pulled on her panties and jeans. She reached for her bra—big mistake. She muttered a few chosen words as she tried, unsuccessfully, to muscle her way into her bra, then gave up and slipped her arms into a big button-down oxford shirt. After wiggling her feet into a pair of sandals, brushing her hair seemed like a good idea, until she found it hurt too much to lift her arms enough to accomplish the deed. Everything hurt too much.

Michael opened her door and saw David sitting on the top stair, with Bo taking up the next step down.

"You're up. Dad said I could wait here if I didn't make any noise. He said you needed your sleep. So we decided to wait here until you got up. I gotta go have my cast checked this morning, but I wanted to see you first. So I'm glad you got up. I can't go swimming until I get the cast off. I'm not supposed to get it wet."

Michael cautiously sat down beside David and tenderly pulled him into her arms before his first tear fell. "It's okay to cry, you know," she whispered in his ear. She held him close, her lips dispersing tiny kisses in his blond hair. "I was really scared. Weren't you?"

"Yeah, but I didn't want to be a baby and cry. Harry said I was really brave. He said I acted like a grown-up. And you know what? I hardly cried at all when the doctor pulled my arm and fixed it like it used to be. Dad was there, and he was proud of me."

"Oh David, you are brave, and I am so proud of you too. I guess I really messed up when I came to get you in the dumb old bathtub."

"No, Michael, Dad says it wasn't your fault. He said the same thing would have happened if we'd been in his car, and it's big." He hugged her with all his might, careful not to bump her with his hard cast.

"Michael?"

"Yes, David."

"Michael, I'm sorry about your car. Allen says it's done for. Are you real sad?"

"No, David, it's only a car, and I can always get another. I could never get another you, and that's the important thing."

Richard came out of the library and saw the two at the top of the stairs. "What are you two doing up there?"

"Hi Dad, we're swappin' spit."

"What did you say?"

"Tommy Walker says when people who love each other kiss; it's like swappin' sweet spit."

Michael tried to stop laughing. It hurt.

Richard was still laughing when he opened the door to Sarah.

"Richard, don't you know it's obscene to be so cheery this early in the morning? Want a sweet gooey?"

Not waiting for an answer, Sarah pushed a large pink box into Richard's arms and walked past him, her other arm loaded with fresh flowers. "I know, you have a garden full of flowers, but it's something Mother taught us when we were young. Always bring flowers to the sick and ailing, but I do believe I've come to the wrong house. No one looks sick to me."

For the next hour, they partied. Amy and the girls came by. Marc was still there. Allen had called Cassie, and she arrived, a suitcase in hand, ten minutes after Sarah. Peter called; Ruthie called. After talking to Gill and Holly, Richard let the answering machine take over so they could enjoy Sarah's sweets, washed down with milk and Allen's coffee.

Marc and his family left before Richard and David headed to Dr. Singer's office. Sarah stayed long enough to help Michael wash and dry her hair and to extract a promise from her to call if she needed anything at all.

Michael went upstairs to lie down. Not because she'd promised Richard, but because she still had a headache. Everything ached, especially when she forgot and moved the wrong way, which was almost any way she moved. Her front end had taken a real pounding. Richard had left a bottle of medicine for her to take if the pain got too bad, but so far, she'd not taken any.

Allen saved the day by asking Cassie to help with the house. Michael would never have thought to call her, but then, she hadn't been dating Cassie since the crazy dinner party. Michael wondered if Richard knew Allen was dating Cassie. It didn't matter. Cassie told them she was here to stay as long as they needed her. She could cook, clean, and still spend time with her new friend. Allen thought it was a terrific idea. He could save a bundle on gas, with her living just across the walk.

Her thoughts wandered back to Peter. He had called again, wanting to come over, just to visit and check her out for himself, but she'd begged off, telling her new friend she just needed sleep. He understood. Michael had a feeling Peter always would understand. He told her to rest well and he would call her tomorrow.

It was dark when Michael woke. She could hear voices coming from downstairs, but she didn't have any idea what time it was. Michael was stiff, but her headache was gone. She had gone to sleep before noon, and now it was dark. As she debated whether to get up and go downstairs or just stay in bed, there was a light tap on the door.

Richard opened the door and walked to the bed. He bent close to her.

"If you've brought a mirror to hold under my nose to see if I'm still breathing, you better turn on the light so you can see."

"Ho-ho, we're alive. I never thought of a mirror. I'll have to get one." A shaft of light filtered into the room from the landing and bathed her face with a faint glow. "It's after nine. I came up to get you undressed and into bed."

"Richard, is there a dark side to you I need to know about? I mean, you seem obsessed with taking my clothes off."

"Really McCall, you insult me. I'm a doctor, remember? When I take off your clothes, it's just academic. I see nothing I wouldn't see if I opened a copy of *Gray's Anatomy.* One of the first things they teach us in medical school is to be detached. The female anatomy is simply that, anatomy."

"Yeah, right, I suppose you've brought another piece of silk to drape me in tonight?"

"No, I figured if I found you awake, you could tell me where you keep your nightgowns. I felt like a sex-crazed second-story man last night sorting through all the lace in your dresser, trying to find a nightgown."

Michael tried to sit up, but her arms refused to help her. Richard reached out instinctively, gathering her against his chest. Her arms were between them, and her fingers touched his face and the side of his neck. She felt his strength, inhaled the fresh, intoxicating scent of his cologne, the warmth of his body pressed so tightly against hers. When she looked up at him, she was lost to the tenderness of his gaze.

Michael didn't stop to rationalize if what she was about to do was right or wrong, it didn't matter. "Richard, I don't think it's a smart idea for you to undress me tonight. I think you better ask Cassie to come up and help me." She was almost whispering. "There is something I'd like you to do for me if you wouldn't mind?"

"What do you want me to do?"

"I want you to call me Mikie, like you do when you think I don't hear you. And then I want you to kiss me."

"Oh my God, Mikie. Oh, Mikie." Blood pounded in his brain, leapt from his heart and sent years of discipline into oblivion.

He gently pressed his lips to hers, and his mouth played her a sweet melody, transporting her above reality—beyond the loneliness to a warm and wispy place that had no knowledge of tomorrow.

CHAPTER TWENTY-ONE

T HE NIGHT OF THE GALA arrived. Michael had spent the last two weeks doing nothing but resting by the pool, orders from Alan and Cassie, who together had taken over the house and the job of running David around town. Cassie even offered to help her get ready for her big night.

"You've missed your calling. It looks beautiful."

Cassie had gathered Michael's dark hair on top of her head, dividing it into simple curls. Wispy tendrils refusing to obey played at the back of her neck and the sides of her tanned face, next to her teardrop earrings. She gave Michael's hair a final pat and a squirt of hair spray.

"Hey, I just put some pins here and there, but girl, your hair is so thick, I just hope it stays put until you get home."

"It should. I'm not going to be bouncing around tonight. I shouldn't be going at all. Dr. Farrell doesn't seem to understand the word no, but he has promised I'll be in capable hands."

Cassie helped her into her gown. When she first agreed to go with Peter to the dance, she'd planned to wear her new white gown, but it was sleeveless, almost topless, just two thin straps holding the elegantly beaded satin in place. But it didn't work. Most of the bruising and the soreness were gone, but she still had discoloration on her shoulders and arms. She had bought two evening gowns on her wild shopping spree with Sarah. The emerald gown wouldn't work either; it only covered one shoulder. She hated the cliché but even though her closet was full, she didn't have a thing to wear.

When Sarah casually asked her what she was going to wear, Michael explained her predicament. And just like the dinner party, Sarah took over, promising to take care of everything. Last week, Michael received a special delivery package with a new gown from New York.

It was a beautiful creation of pastel-peach silk crepe by Versace. The simple cut of the gown accentuated her small waist before the soft crepe fell to the floor. The long sleeves were form fitting, with a small buttons at each wrist. Both the front and back were high but softly draped, and the unique design hid all traces of the accident.

"I'll make sure David is ready to go," Cassie said, giving a rebellious curl one last shot of hairspray. He was spending the night with Anna and Martin, but he refused to leave before he saw Michael dressed for the ball.

Richard was going to the gala, and he was going alone. Cassie told her that Allen said Sylvia Grant, alias: "the screamer," had the nerve to call Richard and tell him she was free and would be happy to go with him. After a polite no, Richard hung up and told Allen, who told Cassie, who told Michael, that the woman needed a keeper and that he, Richard, had other plans for the night, whatever that meant. Michael was glad Richard would be at the dance. When he'd kissed her the night after the accident, she'd wanted to pull him into her bed and never let him go, but he just kissed her gently into oblivion, making her body quiver and quake, then left. Since that night they had talked but didn't touch. Each day he wore a captivating smile that played at the corners of his mouth and nearly drove her senseless as they bantered over this and that.

Michael felt it was up to Richard to make the next move, but he hadn't mentioned the kiss, or that night, at all. Of course, he was exceptionally busy and not home a lot, but when they were in the same room together, she would catch him watching her with that silly, sexy smile of his, as if he knew a secret and was trying to make up his mind if he wanted to share it with her or not.

Sarah claimed he was jealous of Peter, but Michael didn't think so. He didn't seem to mind at all, even offered to deliver her to Peter at the club, but Dr. Farrell had declined the gesture.

Michael picked up her evening bag and crossed the landing to the stairs.

David and Bo waited for her in their favorite spot at the top of the stairs. "Wow! Michael, you look so pretty. Turn around and let me see."

Michael slowly turned in a circle. Anna and her husband waited with Richard at the foot of the stairs, watching the display. David offered Michael his arm and ordered Bo to the back as he escorted her down the stairs.

"Isn't she beautiful Dad? You can't even tell she's all banged up."

Richard's pulse jumped as it did every time he saw her. Even when she wore jeans and her terrible tennis shoes, it raced out of control. Now, looking like a princess on the arm of his gleaming son, it was all he could do to keep from throwing her over his shoulder and carrying her back upstairs to her bed. *Be patient, Richard,* he silently told himself. *Just stick to your plan.* So he just smiled and said, "Yes, David, she's as pretty as a princess."

Michael tried to look over Richard's head as she held on to David's arm. She greeted Anna and Martin, thanking them for taking David to the show and letting him spend the night, although she also assured everyone she would be home way before his bed time.

"We're not changing our plans now, McCall. Who knows? You might decide to party all night," Richard replied with a smile.

Michael watched as Richard handed David's overnight bag to Martin and opened the front door without taking his eyes off her. Why was he looking at her that way? Richard had the most devilish look on his face. He was up to something; she knew it. He was too accommodating, too cheerful. A few minutes later, Richard even joked with Peter, who arrived just as Anna and her two men were leaving, shaking his hand and lightly slapping him on the back.

"Here she is, Peter, all dressed up and ready to go. Careful now, we don't need any tumbles," he said as he handed her to Peter, resting his hand on her back just a fraction longer than was necessary. "See you two at the ball."

Peter's thoughts mirrored Michaels. *What the hell is Richard up to?* Although they had been friends for years, Richard's attitude had turned almost cold when Peter said he wanted to date Michael, but now, he was his old self. This new demeanor started the day after the accident. Richard had stopped by Peter's office to thank him for helping David and Michael before he'd gotten to the hospital. The look on Richard's face, when he spoke of Michael and how distressed he was when no one could tell him how badly she was hurt, convinced Peter to set the record straight.

He explained to Richard that he and Michael were just friends, platonic friends, in every sense of the word. He should have realized, from the immediate change in Richard, that his declaration had lifted a troubling weight. Tonight Peter was more mystified than ever by his friend's behavior. *If Richard cares for her, why in the hell doesn't he tell her so?* Well, he wasn't going to worry about Richard tonight. Platonic or not, he loved to be with her and relished the feeling of holding her close on the dance floor.

The club was lit up like the Golden Gate Bridge, and the strings of light that laced the tree-lined drive sparkled like crystal in the twilight. As the valet helped Michael out of the car, Peter draped his arm lightly across her shoulder as they moved toward the ballroom.

"Hey, wait for me."

Michael stiffened, startled by Richard's words. He had parked right behind them, and as they continued into the ballroom, he became their shadow.

Potted trees dressed with the same tiny lights decorated the ballroom. Tables crisscrossed the room, allowing easy access to the dance floor on the patio and the lush gardens overflowing with fragrant flowers. In the center of the dance floor stood a fountain. Water bubbled up from a pair of stone sea nymphs and shot a light mist high into the night, catching the overhead lights and sparkling like liberated fireflies.

Sarah and Tom, along with Amy and Marc, sat at a table by one of the doors leading to the dance floor. Gill and Holly were just taking their places when Michael and her escorts reached the table.

"Look, Tom, did I ace this or what? The dress, Tom, look at Michael's dress. Isn't it divine?"

She kissed Sarah's cheek, and feeling like cheese between two slices of bread, Michael said hello to their friends at the table as the handsome duo held her chair, then claimed their seats on either side of her. Once seated, Michael tried to listen as Sarah walked Holly and Amy through the steps she'd used to find Michael's new gown on the internet, but no such luck because Richard had slipped off his dress loafer and was caressing her ankle with his toes, inching up and down her leg with a feathery touch.

The combination of his sensual touch and the exquisite fragrance from the garden made her feel light headed but exhilarated. She wanted to reach out and touch him back. No, she needed more—, to escape from their friends who had no idea what he was doing to her under the table. She wanted Richard all to herself, but she was here with Peter. *Wise up Michael,* she cautioned herself. *Richard is just playing with you.* And he had trouble written all over his face.

She turned her back on Richard and pulled her leg away from his wandering toes. "Peter, the band sounds marvelous. Dance with me."

Peter jumped at her invitation and whisked her toward the dance floor. Halfway through the dance, it hurt to keep her arm around his neck, so she rested her left hand below his shoulder as Peter sang along with the band. They danced well together and stayed on the dance floor for two more tunes.

"What's up, kitten?"

"What do you mean?"

"You're tight. If you don't relax, I'll think you're not enjoying yourself. Come on now. Smile. We're supposed to be having a good time."

He was right. She had to stop worrying about Richard and relax. After all, Peter was her date, and he made her laugh as he sang in her ear. By the time the band finished the set, Michael was certainly relaxed and enjoying herself, even though she hadn't been able to put Richard out of her mind.

Michael stopped laughing as they neared the table. An irritating voice rang through the air. Sylvia Grant had waltzed by their table and taken a seat.

"Richard, I thought you had other plans tonight. You should have called me. I mean, I'm so glad you're here, but we could have come together." Before he could respond, the headwaiter appeared and told her she was needed in the lobby. "This will only take a moment. I'll be right back." With a scowl on her face and a flip of her head, she was gone.

Holly ordered something special to celebrate Sylvia's departure, and when the waiter brought champagne, the laughter started again. Tom pulled it together first.

"Ah... Holly, we don't drink champagne anymore," he spurted out between cackles. "We found it to be a... somewhat hazardous to our health."

"What's so funny?" Amy asked.

Sarah and Tom just shook their heads and continued to laugh. But Michael had stopped laughing and shot arrows of caution at Sarah and Tom. She didn't mind telling about their night from hell, but how could they explain and leave out the reason why the whole fiasco had started in the first place? Sarah's internal instincts got the message.

"You had to be there, Amy," Sarah replied. "The whole thing sort of loses something in the translation. Let's just say we drank too much champagne."

By the time the waiters cleared the table, the hilarious mood had turned melodious. They'd laughed and hooted and chattered away—devoured their dinner, drank the wine, and then mellowed out to enjoy the music and dim lights, each in their own way, thankful for true friends.

Without taking his eyes off Michael, Richards asked, "Peter, may I dance with your date?"

Peter wanted to knock the silly grin off Richard's face. "Don't ask me. Michael is over twenty-one, and we all know she's liberated. Ask her."

Just then, Peter's beeper went off. "Dance with Richard if you'd like, kitten. I'll be right back."

Richard stood and offered his hand. "Dance, McCall?"

"Oh my goodness, Mr. Rhett, you're just so eloquent."

"Do you want to dance or not?"

"Only if you promise to stay off my feet."

"I'm not promising anything. You buys your ticket and takes your chance."

"I thought you wanted to dance? Or do you plan to talk me to death?"

Richard carefully lifted her out of her chair and swung her around, facing the dance floor. "March."

Michael had only taken a few steps when Peter called her name. She turned around and walked to him.

"I have to leave," he told her. "Mrs. Ricco is about to deliver her third child."

"I'll go with you. I can wait for you at the hospital."

"Lord, no. I mean, no telling how long this is going to take. By the books, it should only be a few hours, but she has a history of dragging her feet. This could take all night. Stay here and dance some more. You can keep my car. I'll get someone from the hospital to come and get me."

"I won't need your car. Tom and Sarah will take me home." Michael reached up and brushed a lock of blond hair off his forehead. "Peter, I'm so sorry you have to leave. I hope you're not up all night."

"Kitten, kiss me good-by. Then I'm on my way."

Richard stood by the table and watched as she talked to Peter. Even as his hand reached for his drink and he emptied the glass, he never took his eyes off her. Richard wished he believed in mental telepathy. Was his desire strong enough to reach across the room? Could he draw her to him just by the strength of his need? *Look at me, Mikie. Feel my need; touch me with your eyes.* And she did.

Richard put the glass on the table and moved toward her. Son of a bitch, it worked! When he reached her side, it seemed so natural to rest his arm around her waist.

"Peter has to go deliver a baby. Be nice, Richard, and tell him good-bye."

"Sorry you have to leave Peter, but I'll take good care of our girl."

"See that you do. I'll call you tomorrow, kitten. Don't overdo."

Refrains of soft music filtered from the garden and into the dining room as the band started another set. Richard took her by the hand. "Dance with me, Mikie." This time he didn't wait for an answer, and she willingly followed him out into the garden.

Other couples danced close to the band, but Richard found a spot under a large tree where moonlight flickered through the leaves. He gently pulled her into his arms and began to sway, barely moving his feet at all.

Michael snuggled into him, both arms wrapped around his waist. She could feel the erratic beating of his heart against her own as he held her close, drawing her into him, his hands molding themselves over her body that vibrated with liquid fire as she felt the strong, hard pulsing of his desire.

All games were over. This was for real. "Mikie, I want to hold you this close all night." Richard's words were muffled as he kissed her hair, her temples, and her lips. "We need to go home. Right now, Mikie, let's go home."

Again, he didn't wait for a response, just turned her around and headed for the table. "McCall tells me I've had too much to drink. She's appointed herself my designated driver and thinks we better call it a night."

Richard could have saved his breath with his explanation because he fooled no one, and he knew it. But as they waited for his car, he didn't care.

The car arrived. He walked her to the driver's side and waited until she was seated, then reached across her and buckled her in. "Are you all right to drive?"

Michael's eyes were closed. How did he expect her to answer much less drive the car or think clearly as his mouth kissed her face like the flutter of a newborn moth? She took hold of the steering wheel and opened her eyes.

"Richard, if you'll just get in the car, I'm pretty sure I can drive us home. Get in the car, Richard, please."

He couldn't take his eyes off her as she maneuvered the car out of the circle drive and onto the road. His fingers reached out and touched her shoulder, moved to her neck, then up the tanned skin to the base of her ear. She bent toward him, bonding his open hand with the side of her face.

Michael continued to lean into his hand, almost purring as his index finger drew small circles around her ear. She felt the blood race through her veins, felt the heat between her legs as his skilled fingers moved over the side of her face with light butterfly strokes leaving her skin on fire.

"Richard, if you don't stop doing what you're doing and talk to me, I can't guarantee I'll be able to get us home."

Her words were playful, but not their meaning. His need to touch her was so great, but he realized she was wound as tightly as he was. The very air around them felt electrified, charged by the turbulent passion and emotions of the past few weeks. They teetered near the edge, like primed powder kegs, where even a look or the slightest touch could set them off. He moved to the far side of the car and pulled his hands into his lap.

"I've run out of words, Mikie. I'll be good. Just take us home."

CHAPTER TWENTY-TWO

T HE HOUSE WAS DARK. ALLEN and Cassie had gone into the city. Bo acknowledged their arrival with a low growl, then went back to sleep. Richard unlocked the door and held it open for her, but he didn't touch her as they walked through the kitchen and into the foyer.

Michael waited at the bottom of the stairs while he set the alarm, her whole body silently screaming for him to hurry.

"I have to check my service and then I'll be up." He didn't want to rush her. Richard wanted to give her time to decide if she wanted this as much as he did, or if at all.

Michael switched on the small lamp on the desk in her room and dropped her bag next to the lamp. She turned to the French doors and opened them wide. A cool breeze made its way into the room, but the coolness had no effect on her heated body. She kicked off her shoes and stood directly in front of the door with her arms crossed over her chest, then heard him come into the room.

Richard carried two wine glasses by the stems and a bottle of wine. He had taken off his jacket and shoes. His tie was gone, and his white dress shirt was open enough for her to see the dark hair curled tight on his chest. Every time he looked at her, just as he was doing now, the pounding of her heart shook her whole body. Every day her love for him had deepened—intensified, and now she prayed the smoldering flame she saw in his eyes was a silent admission that he felt the same.

Richard put the glasses and wine on the desk. His hands cupped her face and held it gently. He reached up and pulled the pins from her hair. As the mass of darkness tumbled down around her face, his hands moved to the fastening at the back of her neck. Again, his hands started to shake, skilled hands, trained to be disciplined and exact, to cut away death and to heal. But they couldn't undo the tiny clasp.

He wrapped his arms around her and Michael felt his breath, so warm, against her face. She stood still, waiting, hoping he would tell her he loved her. She waited… but he just held her with his head buried in her hair. It didn't matter. For the past three days, she had told herself it didn't matter if he loved her as long as he wanted her—to make love to her. She stepped away from him and the radiating hunger she saw in his eyes sent her spirits soaring. Slowly she raised her hands to the back of her gown and unhooked the clasp. As she lowered her hands, the gown came with them, revealing her firm breasts, nipples already hard from his touch. Michael continued to move her hands down her body, taking all the clothing she wore. Stepping out of the garments, she stood straight—naked and proud.

Tremors of anticipation shot through her, leaving her wet and wanting. Ever since Eve stood before Adam, dressed only in a mantle of desire, this primal need had never changed. It was simply passed down over the millennia, a wanting that said touch me… love me.

Richard's breath caught in his throat. She stood like a bronze statue, her skin glistening in the shadowy light, her hair framing her face like the dark night frames the moon. Afraid to take his eyes off her, he removed the rest of his clothes and closed the small space separating them.

He drew her into his arms and their bodies burned as bare skin touched. Richard kissed her soft lips, and his tongue spread moisture over their dryness. He sought the hidden depths of her mouth as his hands roamed over her body with a will of their own, easing her close against him. His kiss gained momentum—he felt drugged and demanded more as her moans and whimpers of pleasure guided him on.

Richard lifted his lips from her trembling mouth and started a slow burning trail down her neck to the top of one full breast. His tongue again became the bearer of sensual magic as it circled the heavy globe, coming to rest on the taut nipple as his free hand cupped her other breast, squeezing its fullness. Richard began to draw from the swollen sphere, unable to get his fill of her. He moved to the already hardened twin and repeated his caresses.

Michael felt the carnal desire rush through her with the force of a storm, the exquisite seduction bringing her to a new awareness. Gone was the wretched loneliness, the pain of the past two years. She was alive... and loved. She knew she was. Gone were her secret inhibitions, as Richard stripped away the last fragile remnants of the shell she'd built around herself. And he would never be sorry; she would show him, love him with every fiber in her body, return the exhilaration racing through her as he moved down to her flat stomach, down to the soft mound of darkness that ached for his touch.

Richard picked her up and carried her to the bed. He lowered himself on top of her, his desire and need evident and pulsating between them. He was hypnotized by her beauty, her lean, responsive body that arched to meet his.

"Did I hurt you?"

Michael shook her head. She pulled him to her, kissing his eyes and then his mouth as her tongue moved like a fiery comet. She hurried on, eager to explore all of him. Michael rolled Richard onto his back. She kissed tight nipples, gently nipping at the tips with her teeth while her hands sought the curves and contours of his lower body, moving over his hips and thighs.

A devilish smile lit her face when he shuddered as her hand came to rest on his throbbing hardness. He moaned and twisted as her fingertips slowly roamed up and down the swollen shaft. Michael held him with a delicate touch and felt his need, the wild pulsing in her hand matching that of his heart.

Richard pressed his head into the pillow and held his breath. He needed to be inside her, and this need sent a new wave of intensity sweeping through him. Richard pulled her beneath him as his hand sought the moist softness between her legs. He caressed her inner thigh, her smooth skin, so warm and wet to his touch. His fingers worked quickly now, circling again and again, stroking the hot, liquid core of her that throbbed at his touch. Richard heard her quick intake of breath, felt her muscles contract as her body arched abruptly and his hands lifted her hips toward him. Then he buried himself deep within her warm tightness.

Michael wanted to scream, overcome by this new awareness as her needs rose to the surface, coming now after so many months of denial. She opened her thighs and welcomed the full length of him.

Richard paused, then pushed deeper into the warm, enticing bliss. He wrapped his arms around her body, bonding them together as he began a slow, deliberate movement within her. His strong body obeyed his heart's commands as he set a pace she quickly followed. He buried his face in her hair and then sought her lips again. He tried to possess all of her as his hunger overrode all reason. Wave after wave gathered him up, binding him to her as he felt her body respond. The intensity of their passion covered their bodies with a satin sheen, a dampness that did nothing to cool the fever that raged between them.

Richard quickened the pace, trying to penetrate to the very center of her soul. He held her face in his hands as his eyes searched and found the answer he sought. *My God, I love her so much.*

Michael rose to meet his kiss. The strength of their need refused to be quenched. She felt the warmth of his breath on her face as she moistened his parched lips with her tongue. Carefully she rolled over, forcing him back so that he lay beneath her as she continued to hold him tightly within her, and slowed the movement of their bodies, rhythmically rotating her hips as she covered his face and chest with her kisses.

Richard's head sank deep into the pillow as his body rose to a new height of excitability and he luxuriated in the pleasure it brought him. He opened his eyes as his hands reached up to cover her smooth breasts and then raised his head to capture a swollen nipple in his mouth, seeking sublimity.

She moaned and purred, trying to absorb the agonizing pleasure that spread through her as his hands and mouth caressed her body. Michael arched her back, shifting her weight to the tops of his legs. Richard shuddered with spasms and moaned her name as her movement pulled tightly on his already engorged shaft still sheathed deep within her warm, protective flesh.

Michael heard his cry as she drifted away from reality, detached, tethered only by nerve endings that lay close to the surface as her body soared independently—cut off from her mind—toward a state of frenzy that threatened to consume her.

Richard maneuvered her long legs out straight and drew her to his chest. All movement ceased. They lay still, panting. The rhythm of their still unsatisfied mating beat strongly between them, keeping time with the pounding of their hearts.

He raised his head and brushed her damp hair with his hands, soft curls that held tightly to her face. Richard tugged gently on her lower lip, a slow, sensual pull that grabbed deep inside her. Their need to find a final release peaked as Richard rolled her onto her back and began to move within her with an uncontrollable urgency.

Totally oblivious of her bruised body, Michael wrapped her arms, her legs, and her very life around him as she followed Richard's undulating motion, overwhelmed by the turbulence and velocity swirling around them.

Richard felt the tightness of her as he continued to plunge deeper as they rode the final wave of fulfillment. Her nails bit deep into his back as her cry of pleasure came at the same time his own body shook with the release of the long overdue orgasm. His hands grasped her dark, wet hair and he buried his face in the tangled mass as the spasms continued, filling her with his seed as he trembled violently within her. Her name rushed from his parched lips, and Richard was carried over and up... up to the crest of the highest wave until it crashed over both of them. He held on tight, lost to the moment.

Michael savored the warmth, so different from the flames that just moments before had driven her to a perfect madness. She caressed his quaking body as he continued to fill her with the richness of their union. Smiling contentedly, her hands penetrated his soaked hair, pulling him close and holding him tight as his body quivered, still racked with the aftermath of his climax, and then Michael slowly, deliberately, tightened her inner muscles.

"Damn you," he moaned into her wet hair. "You're a witch. I always knew you were a witch."

A small shriek escaped Michael's lips as he pinched her butt. "Of course I'm a witch."

"Just remember you're my witch, my queen of the magic." Richard started to move off her.

"Don't move." She held him tight, enjoying the opulent abundance of their lovemaking. "Don't move," she whispered again. "I don't want you to move, not ever. I'll be good. Just lie still." She rubbed his back, easing her hands up and down his spine, over his strong legs, pulling him into her.

Richard relaxed but raised on his elbows, lifting his weight off her chest, and buried his head in the hollow of her neck. He lay quietly as the last spasm of pleasure passed through him and then rolled onto his side, taking her with him. Richard kissed her nose, her eyes, and then smiled as his hand traced a path over her face, roamed down her neck and intimately over her breast.

They were bound together, their naked bodies damp from their lovemaking—flesh against flesh, man against woman. Michael lay panting, her chest heaving from the joy and happiness she felt, and love flowed through her like warm honey.

She traced the shape of his lips with the tip of her finger. "I love you," she whispered.

He picked up a lock of her hair with shaking fingers and caressed it gently as his heart swelled with a feeling he'd thought long dead. She loves me. He had known it before her words, but those words filled Richard with a sensation that defied description. She was his, and he would love her and protect her for the rest of his life.

Richard gently eased into her, and she felt his need growing as a hot tide of renewed hunger raged through them again. He rode her with a desperate fury, insatiably draining away what little strength she'd held in reserve. Michael felt her mind give way as the awareness of her body took over. Knots of desire swarmed like bees inside her as they soared to a staggering height, binding her with a withering feeling close to pain in its intensity. With each thrust she soared higher, nerves stretched, quivering, tingling, bathed in a sea of fire. Wave after wave spread over her trembling body, inside and out, until she was totally engulfed. She moved her hands flat against his back and gently pulled his heart next to hers.

Within seconds of her pulsating tremors, he found his own release as he thrust into her with one last shuddering lunge. His chest moved up and down, his breathing became ragged as undulating currents of splendor surged through him.

Richard threaded his hands into her wet and tangled hair. He gently rubbed his face against hers as his fingers massaged her temples. "Have I hurt you?" he whispered.

Michael shook her head. She wanted to open her eyes—she would have to eventually. But she was afraid as she waited, prayed for the words. Words that, left unsaid, would hurt much more than anything he could have done to her body during their lovemaking. She knew that all her bravado and audacious declarations meant nothing. It did matter if he loved her. Michael fought back tears and willed him, with all her might, to say he loved her. Even if he didn't mean it, damn it, didn't a guy still say he loved a girl after making love, so she won't feel cheap?

Well, she wasn't cheap. She loved him as much as was humanly possible and she'd told him so. What more could she do? *Be patient*, she told herself. She had to remember this was new for him. He had come so far since the night of the storm. *At least he hasn't jumped up and run out of the room.* Michael told herself that it would be her love—not pushing or demanding, just steady and constant—that would help him forget David's mother and turn to her, Michael McCall, his Mikie, who was alive and loved him more than life.

She opened her eyes and put away her coward's cloak. She smiled and met his gaze. Was it love she saw in his eyes, blazing like black diamonds in the dim light? Could he have made love to her with such passion if he didn't love her? *Let it go, Michael,* she silently said. *Just hold on tight and take what he gives you.*

The phone crashed to the floor as she swung her arm across the table. The ringing brought Michael straight up in the bed, dragging her out of a dream and back to her darkened room. She reached for Richard, but he wasn't there. They had shared some wine, made love again, and then fallen asleep. He had gone to sleep. She knew he had because she'd watched him and then dozed off herself.

"Hello?"

"Michael, this is Marc."

"Marc? What..., what time is it? Do you want Richard? Wait a moment; I'll get him for you. He must be downstairs."

"Michael, wait, Richard's not there."

"What? Of course, he is. Marc, he's downstairs sound asleep. It will only take—"

"Michael, there's been an accident. Richard has been in an accident, and he's in the hospital. I'm with him now. The police called me. Michael? Did you hear what I said?"

She heard what he said, but she thought it must have been some kind of a joke. How could Richard be at the hospital? He'd been with her, in her bed, for hours. They had fallen asleep together. No, there had to be some kind of mistake.

"Michael, I'm coming to get you. I need you here. Michael? Answer me."

"Marc, I don't understand what you're saying. What kind of accident? OH MY GOD. Marc, is he all right?"

"Michael, I'm on my way. I'll explain when I get there, okay?"

"Yes, of course, just hurry. Please, oh God, please hurry."

She hung up the phone and started to shake. She still didn't understand how Richard could have been in an accident. *No, this is wrong.* This family had suffered more than their share of accidents. She had to think. Marc didn't say that Richard was hurt. Maybe he was called out on an emergency. That was it. He'd gone to the hospital for one of his patients, but how did he get into an accident? She had to get dressed. Marc was coming to get her.

Michael ran into her closet and pulled on her jeans and a shirt. "Screaming won't help find your damn shoe." Her shouted words echoed off the closet walls. "Calm down. Marc said he needed you. Just find your shoe."

When Marc stopped in front of the house, she stood waiting. Michael opened the car door and jumped in.

"I hated to wake you, but Richard is calling for you. He was unconscious when they brought him into the ER, but he's been in and out for the last hour."

"Marc, what happened?"

"Michael, I don't know. I mean, hell, I don't know. He was on the ridge road, not far from Mill Valley. They think a deer might have run in front of him. He must have swerved and then rolled over an embankment. Thank God another car was coming from the other direction. The police got there right away, but they couldn't get him out of the car until the paramedics and the fire department arrived."

Michael's nails cut into the leather seat. She had to keep her eyes open, no matter what. She had to stay focused, to hold the panic boiling within her at bay. This was now; this had nothing to do with the other accident. Richard needed her. Marc said Richard had called for her and she would not let anything detract from that.

"Are you okay?"

"I'm okay, Marc. How badly is he hurt?"

"We don't know yet. Dr. Singer is with him now. Richard has some broken bones, we know that, but which one or how many, that's what they have to find out. He was on his way to X-ray when I left. I haven't called anyone but you. I thought you would want to be the one to tell David."

"Oh Marc, I forgot about David. I can call and talk to Anna, but I can't tell David over the phone. And what do I tell him, Marc? What do I tell him about his father?" She wiped rebel tears away with the back of her hand.

"Hang in there, Michael. I know you want to see Richard. We'll be there in a minute. I guess I should have waited until I knew more before I called you, but—" His voice broke. Michael took his hand, squeezing hard.

She gave him a moment and then said, "No, Marc, you did the right thing. I'm glad you called." Michael waited until he turned to her. "I love him too. He has told me how close you two are, but I want you to know I love him too."

Marc held her hand as he drove into the empty parking lot. The receptionist at the desk told them Richard was in radiology and would probably be taken directly to the OR. Marc took her arm and headed for the elevator. The tech on duty in radiology said he would tell Dr. Singer they were waiting.

Michael paced up and down the small waiting room while Marc called Amy. Unconsciously, she rubbed her chest. She relished the tenderness of her breasts as she closed her eyes, recalling his touch, how just hours ago Richard had been with her, loving her body until she'd begged him for release. Even now, she felt the heat of their coupling. He had taken her to a place she'd never been and then she watched as he dozed off, like a child, totally sated and spent. What had caused him to drive off into the night? "Amy said to tell you to stay strong and call her if you need her. Here, I brought you some coffee. Be careful, it's not terribly good, but it's hot. I told Amy not to call anyone yet. There's nothing to report anyway. Come here and sit with me."

Ten minutes later, they wheeled Richard out of X-ray. Dr. Singer stood beside the gurney, holding his hand. He signaled for the orderly to stop. "You can have one minute, Mrs. McCall. He's overdue for surgery." Miles Singer took Marc by the arm and backed a few steps away.

Michael held Richard's hand and again fought her tears. She wasn't going to let him see her cry. He was so pale. A blood-soaked bandage rested above his left eye and cuts and abrasions covered his shoulders and chest.

"I'm sorry, Mikie. I've gone about this all wrong. I shouldn't have—"

His words were choppy, his breathing shallow. She placed her finger on his dry lips. "Hush, don't try to talk. Everything will be all right. Dr. Singer will fix you up, good as new. He promised. Please relax. All you have to think about is getting better. I'll be right here. Just rest." She bent close to his face, and the anguish in his eyes tore at her heart as she kissed him softly.

"We have to go. I'll talk to you again just as soon as he's in recovery." Dr. Singer took her hands as the orderly started down the corridor. "I've given Marc a preliminary overview of Richard's condition. You're not to worry now. I'm going to take excellent care of him, just like you said."

While Marc had listened to Miles, he also heard her conversation with Richard. He was afraid this would happen. Richard had been a damn fool to think they could live in the same house and not get involved. For weeks, ever since he'd seen them together the night of Richard's dinner party, Marc had wanted to talk to Richard about Michael, but he had taken the easy way out. It was none of his business, he told himself.

Well, it was his business. Richard was like his brother, even closer, and Michael didn't deserve this. She had a right to know.

"Come on, Michael, Miles said it's going to take some time. I can't stand this coffee, but I know where we can get a decent cup, and a better place to wait. I'll call the OR and tell them where we'll be."

Marc took her hand and led her to the professional wing of the hospital building. He unlocked the door to Richard's practice office and flipped on a light. He definitely knew where he was going as he led them through the waiting room. He unlocked Richard's private office and told Michael to relax while he put on a pot of coffee.

"The bathroom is through that door. It's going to be a long wait. Try to unwind and relax. There's nothing we can do now except wait."

Michael went into the bathroom. She wet a towel and held it to her face. She looked like hell. A mass of curls gathered about her face and her skin carried a reddish glow from his beard. Her breasts throbbed, her ribs were tender, and she hurt all over. Of course she was sore. What did she expect? She hadn't made love since Ryan died—and she had never, in her life, made love like she had last night. Michael leaned over the sink and felt a knot pulling deep inside her as she thought about last night, the way his hands and mouth had made her quiver and sweat and moan with delight. She took a deep breath; she couldn't think about that now. She needed to stay focused.

Michael dried her face and ran her fingers through her hair. Marc sat on the sofa, steam rising from the cups on the table in front of him. "You told the OR where we were?"

"Yeah, but it's going to be some time before Miles calls. Michael, I want to ask you some questions. You'll probably want to tell me to go to hell, but I have to ask anyway."

"Go ahead. What do you want to know?"

"Are you and Richard lovers?"

Michael couldn't believe she'd heard him right, but when she stared into his face, she knew she had. "You're right. I should tell you to go to hell. What right do you have…, I mean?" She took a sip of coffee and burned her mouth. Marc looked miserable, tired and drawn, fighting to find his next words.

"Yes, Marc, if you can call it that. We made love for the first time last night, all night, until early this morning, several times."

He pulled her into his arms and held her tight as the tears rolled down her face. He started this and now it had to be finished. After a while, the convulsive sobs lessened. He patted the back of her head, assuring her it would be all right. He only wished he could convince himself. She pulled away and asked him for a tissue. Marc pulled out his handkerchief and dabbed at her eyes.

Michael took the handkerchief and wiped her eyes and nose. "I'm sorry. I didn't mean to cry, and I didn't mean to be sarcastic. I know you must have a legitimate reason to ask me such a question. I'm not going to cry anymore, but I'd like you to explain yourself."

"I intend to, but first I have to ask more questions. Michael, believe me, I'm not trying to hurt you. Believe me, I'm trying to help."

"Go ahead. Ask your questions, as long as I still have the option of telling you to go to hell."

"You love him, don't you?"

"I've already told you I do. Yes, I love him, but he doesn't love me."

"Why do you say that?"

"It's true. Trust me on this one, I just know, that's all."

"You said last night was the first time?"

Michael didn't understand his question. What did he want from her? Okay. Sure, she could tell him where to go, or she could talk to him, but could she tell him all of it, all the things she had not told Tom and Sarah, anyone? She stared into the empty coffee cup, knowing she wasn't going to find the answer there. It was time to trust someone. Michael started at the beginning, from the first day they met and by the time she finished, she had cried again, and he had held her each time until she could go on.

"If only he could forget her. If only I could make him love me, like he still loves Eve."

"Son of a bitch! Michael, Richard doesn't love Eve. He's not pining away for his long-departed wife. He hated her. He still does. After all these years, he hasn't been able to forget or forgive. Richard is a gentle person by nature, and he's been trained to heal. He's taken an oath always to do the right thing. But if Eve was here right now, I believe he might kill her."

She listened to his words. She watched and listened and shook as the blood pounded in her head. What was he saying? This was all beyond her ability to understand.

He could see her confusion, mixed with panic and fear. "I have to go back, back at least twelve, thirteen years. Do you know about Carol? Okay, when she died, when Richard lost Carol, it almost put an end to his career as a surgeon, or any kind of doctor. When he finally got back on track, he went back to school. Richard did nothing but study and work hard for the next four years. He finished his residency in cardiovascular surgery, all the time trying to cram every bit of medical knowledge available into his brain. You see, he blamed himself; he found himself inadequate—found fault where others couldn't, and I don't think he has, even to this day, forgiven himself for not being able to save her. They're different, you know. Doctors are a different breed, Michael; if they're not careful, they start to believe they share the same zip code as God."

Marc went to Richard's desk and dug through one of the cabinets. "I need a drink. I know Richard keeps a bottle of brandy available for medicinal reasons. Ah, here it is."

He poured them a small drink and continued. "He accepted Hal Green's offer to join his practice. Then he met Eve. I never liked her, not from the very first. She was a beautiful woman. Even I can't deny that. You only have to look at David to realize how lovely she was. But she was evil. That sounds very sinister and melodramatic, but like you said, trust me on this one. She was rotten to the core.

"About... Let me see, David is eight. About ten years ago, they got married. I prepared a prenuptial agreement. Richard and Carol had taken out insurance policies on each other for a million dollars, and when she died, the money came to him. He wouldn't touch it, not one dime of the million bucks, but it was still considered an asset. Richard fought me on the agreement, but I fought just as hard. I had this feeling he might need it sooner or later, and he finally agreed. I didn't want that bitch to have anything if she decided to walk. Shit, if I'd only known—the poor bastard never stood a chance.

"Then she got pregnant. Everyone was in seventh heaven, except the mother-to-be. She wasn't about to have a baby. They fought for weeks, with Richard ending up a wreck. Damn it to hell, he didn't know what to do. Eve threatened to have an abortion. She would disappear for weeks at a time, then call him and say she'd found a place where she could get rid of the kid. One time, she was gone for a month. Then one day, she just walked into his office as if she'd been out shopping. Michael, he couldn't take much more. He wasn't eating or sleeping. It was all he could do to work."

Marc drank the brandy and poured a bigger shot into his cup. Michael knew with each word Marc spoke he also was reliving the whole nightmare. She tried to think of something to say, anything to help him through this, but he cut her off.

"Wait," he said, taking a sip. "It gets better. She must have worked out her plan while she was gone that month. 'Let's make a deal,' she says to Richard. 'I'll have the baby and give it to you. You give me a divorce and half a million dollars.' When he told me what she'd proposed, I could have cheerfully strangled her, except for one thing. Richard wanted his child more than he wanted his own life. Eve told him if he gave her the money, all of it and a divorce, she would give him the baby and he would never see her again. He agreed."

Marc paced in front of her, rolling the empty cup in his hands. "Of course, we had another problem. Richard didn't have that kind of cash. We'd put the million dollars from Carol's insurance into a trust. We couldn't touch it; it was all tied up and unavailable. Just before they married, Eve wanted a large house, so Richard bought it for her. Six months later, dear Evie decides she wants to build a bigger house, so he goes in debt for that. Now he has a house for sale—, real estate prices are at rock bottom—, and a half-built house that isn't worth a tinker's dam unless he can get it finished and sell it. And the bitch wants half a mill. But he agrees, and I start praying we hit the lottery."

Marc's face softened. He stood by the window and gazed at the horizon, but she knew he wasn't watching the sunrise. Michael's head reeled with all he told her, but it wasn't hard for her to imagine the anguish Richard must have endured. Now she understood what he meant the night of the storm, when he'd run away, telling her he couldn't get involved. Did he think she was like Eve? Of course he had.

"Michael, you're the first person I've ever told any of this to. Amy doesn't even know the whole story; no one does. Not even Richard's mother and Caroline had a great deal to do with making it all work. Richard simply asked her to love and trust him, and she did. No one knows the whole truth, except Richard and me."

"And Eve."

"Eve's dead."

"What? I don't understand."

"I know you don't. I was there, through it all, and I can't say as how I totally understand it all myself. One thing I've never been able to comprehend is how Richard managed to keep his sanity through the whole thing, but let me finish.

"I had the papers drawn and ready to sign the day David was born. As you probably know, Richard hired Anna to take care of the baby. He had moved in with his mother and that's where he brought David and Anna. Eve signed the legal papers. She was to receive the half million and nothing else. Believe me, I made sure everything was airtight and legal. She had no rights to David, then or in the future. We just wanted her gone. Caroline mortgaged her house; we all came up with some money. Richard cashed in some bonds at half their value. Anyway, we did it. Then three years ago, Richard gets a call at his office. It's Eve, and she wants more money. She tells him if he doesn't pay her a quarter of a million dollars in ten days, she will appear on his door step and tell David she's his mother."

"Oh God, no. How could she threaten to do such a vicious thing?"

"She was vicious, a real bitch—and she wasn't just threatening; she would have done it. I told you she was rotten. We didn't know what we were going to do. The well was dry. He had finally sold both houses, but by the time he repaid everyone, he was nearly broke. Oh, he still had the trust, but he'd been forced to use the interest from that to pay the money he'd borrowed. Plus he was making two, sometimes three payments a month on the mortgage for his mother's house. All we could do was meet her and try to get her to deal with reality. There was no money. I figured I could scare her into thinking Richard would have her thrown in jail if she went against the court order and tried to see David. We drove down the coast to a small airfield. She told him she would fly in, get the money, and fly off again. We waited in his car and watched when they tried to land, but something went wrong, or else her pilot friend was drunk. Who the hell knows? No one ever knew. Anyway, he came in too low; the plane hit some electrical wires, flipped over, and exploded as we sat in the car and watched the whole thing.

"Would it be callous and cruel to say we were happy she was dead? Because, honest to God, we were at first, but I like to think we were also civilized. Anyone who believes in God knows better than to flout death, or the working of the Man upstairs. Had we wished her dead? I did, I'll admit it, but I honestly believe Richard never wished her harm. What I said before, about him wanting to kill her, that's not so. Richard has always believed anything can be worked out with words. He just knew, someway, somehow, he could make things work out."

The first rays of the sun filled the room with arrows of dim light. Michael shuddered. She wasn't cold, just more troubled and confused than she'd ever been. How had Richard survived? She only had to deal with tangibles. Ryan and Andy had been in an accident, and they were killed, period. And as hard as it had been for her to finally deal with it all, she only had herself to keep from going over the edge. Richard had David to protect. Sarah and Tom, many others had stood ready to help her, but it was all after the fact. My God, to have a friend like Marc. He'd stood by Richard, never leaving his friend alone to deal with the demons by himself. Michael walked to Marc and took him in her arms, rocking back and forth. She didn't have to say anything. Michael knew he trusted her. He had shared Richard's darkest secrets with her because he trusted her to deal fairly with the knowledge. She wiped his tears with the tip of her thumb and kissed him on the cheek, then led him back to the sofa.

Marc let her hug him. He needed to be held because remembering was hard and it still hurt. He leaned against the back of the cushion and looked at the ceiling and uttered a small laugh. "You know what's so ironic? Doctors do some dumb things. I mean, most of them couldn't balance a bottom line if their lives depended on it. Richard had taken out an insurance policy on Eve when they got married. And for some reason, he could never tell me why, and I never figured it out, he kept paying the damn premiums, even after she left town. It was for one million big ones. The authorities identified Eve by her dental work and that insurance money got Richard out of debt, with some left over. Two years ago, he bought the house from his mother and Caroline moved to Los Angeles."

Marc looked at her intently as if trying to convey his thoughts to her. "I guess now is the time I'm supposed say, to make a long story short—but I think the reason Richard left you early this morning and went out in his car was because he couldn't deal with his feelings, and he needed to sort them out. Michael, he's been all but celibate for the past eight years. I firmly believe Richard loves you very much. He just doesn't know how to deal with it. He trusts his mother and... Well, that's it. Oh, Richard respects Amy and some other women he knows, but he made a vow the night we paid Eve off and she left town. He held David in his arms and vowed never, ever, would he trust another woman again as long as he lived. And he's stuck to his words, until you. You got under his skin the first time you hung up on him, the day David found you."

"Richard told you I hung up on him?"

"Oh yeah, he was scorching mad at first. He called me right after he got off the phone with you and wanted to know if I thought he should call the police or just go get David. I told him I thought it sounded like something David would do and I'd just go get him. Then bright and early the next day he calls and tells me to run a check on you. Oh, he told you about that too?"

"Oh yes, I considered it one of his better tools of persuasion. I guess he thought if he told me he'd found me acceptable, I would jump at the job."

"He loves you, Michael. I know he does. And you love him and the story should be that you live happily ever after, but it's not going to be that simple."

"What am I going to do? I've argued with myself, made plans, and then changed them. I told Richard the morning after that damn party I would have to leave. I told him I would stay until David started school or until he found someone else to replace me, but I don't think he's even placed an advertisement for my replacement."

"I know he hasn't. He told me he knew you would change your mind. He said you loved David too much to leave."

"That sounds like him. Richard uses David against me all the time, just to have his way, but then, I guess he's used to having his way."

"Don't get me wrong, but Richard's way is usually the right way, and whether you want to admit it or not, he's right. You don't want to leave, do you?"

Michael took a sip of brandy and welcomed the burning sensation as the liquid eased down her throat. "No, but if I stay, he will never have to make up his mind. I mean, I'm there, around the clock. All he has to do is walk up the stairs and into my bed. And even if I wanted to, I don't think I could turn him away. He has to decide, Marc. I won't force the issue, especially now. But the ball is in his court, and just as soon as he's able to pick up his racket, he's going to have to finish the game."

Michael put the empty cup on the side table. "What a stupid analogy. Life is not cut and dried; it's not a game, but just the same, how can he go on with his life if he can't forget the past? You say he loves me, and I hope to God you're right, but there's more to all this than love. From what you've just told me, how can Richard think about whether he loves me or not when he doesn't even know if he can trust me? I don't know what to do. I can only be me. I wouldn't know how to change even if I could."

She would never know what Marc planned to say, because the phone rang and they both jumped to answer it. Dr. Singer said he would meet them outside the recovery room. Marc replaced the bottle of brandy, and they left Richard's office and headed for the second floor.

Miles was waiting for them in the hall. "The Hampton family must have a good luck fairy locked away somewhere. Anyway, here's the scoop. The patella is badly bruised, but not fractured or displaced. That's the good news. He has a compound fracture of the proximal tibia shaft with a fracture of the neck of the fibula. There's some deep tissue injury at the protrusion site, but all in all, it could have been a lot worse. We debrided the area and reduced the fractures, which were relatively clean.

I had Hal check the lateral popliteal nerve because of the damage to the head of the fibula."

Marc looked surprised. "Hal Green was in the OR with you?"

"Hell, Marc, we could have held a board meeting in there, except our chairman was out cold on the table."

"May we see him?" Michael didn't understand anything Miles had just said, only the part about Richard being lucky.

Miles held her hand. "Soon. He should be coming out of the anesthesia in an hour or so, but he's going to be drowsy. We need to talk about his convalescence. He'll be in the hospital for at least a week, maybe longer. We'll start therapy right away, and we've already started pumping antibiotics into him. When he does go home, he'll be in a long leg cast for about ten to thirteen weeks. Hal is going to watch the site to make sure there is no vascular insufficiency, but I know Richard. He will hassle me for a walking cast so he can get back into the OR. Well, that's where his luck runs out. He will be able to use crutches if he can tolerate the pain, but no OR for a long time."

"I can't see Richard on crutches."

"I know, but he's not the doctor in charge here. I am. I'm just telling you all this because I doubt he will agree with me. In fact, I can almost guarantee you he's going to be a rotten patient. But I'll back you up to the hilt if you decide to put him in an extended care facility."

Marc laughed. "Yeah, right, but I guess we'd better keep that thought in mind."

Two hours later, as they entered the recovery room, Marc squeezed her hand. "Remember the pact, Michael. No tears."

Michael squeezed back. She wasn't going to let Richard see her cry. He had enough to worry him. She had called Anna. After the initial shock, Anna's training as a professional kicked in. She told Michael not to worry about David. Martin would help her keep David busy until Michael came for him, and they wouldn't say anything about the accident. Michael also called Allen. He wanted to come to the hospital, but she told him there wasn't anything he could do except maybe start looking for a rental car for her.

"Mikie?"

"Sh-sh, don't try to talk. I'm here. Marc and I are right here."

"God, I feel like hell. What hit me?"

"They think it was a deer. You're kind of broken up. You've been in surgery, but you're going to be fine."

"I don't feel fine. Are you sure it wasn't a Mack truck?"

"No, just a deer, Bambi's big brother, I think."

Richard closed his eyes and slipped away. Miles had warned them he would do this. It was expected.

CHAPTER TWENTY-THREE

"THERE'S NO NEED COMING NOW, Gill. They just moved him out of recovery about an hour ago. I doubt Miles will allow anyone see him, at least today. Yeah, do that... Or I'll call you if there is any change." Marc rubbed a throbbing spot between his eyes. He'd left Michael with Richard in recovery and gone home to shower and change.

Marc called Richard's mother. When she moved to Los Angeles, Marc promised Caroline he would take care of Richard and David. She only laughed. Now he wished he had waited to call her until he felt like being yelled at. After he explained all he knew about the accident, and reassured her that Richard was going to be all right, Marc let it slip about David. How was he supposed to know that Richard hadn't told her about David's broken arm? He listened to her angry words, not daring to interrupt her. Caroline Hampton was not one to argue with, especially when she was steaming mad. Finally, Caroline ended the conversation, telling Marc she would be on a plane the next day and to tell her son to try and not do anything else stupid, at least until she got to San Rio.

Hal Green said he would take care of the office schedule and Richard's obligations in San Francisco. Marc finally called Richard's closest friends, which created another problem. What happened? How do you explain something you don't understand yourself? What a mess. But right now, he had to get back to the hospital to relieve Michael.

Marc knew she would hold on, but there was a limit, and she still had to tell David. *Why? What had possessed Richard to drive off in the wee hours of the morning? Life had been so happy for him lately.* He hoped Richard had a legitimate reason for what happened. If not, when he got back on his feet, Marc was going to kick the shit out of his friend. Maybe he'd do it anyway, just on general principle.

Michael looked around for a clock as she rolled her neck and shoulders. She pulled herself out of the chair by the side of his bed and stretched, then bent over and touched the floor with her hands. She was tired; her chest hurt, along with every part of her body. What she wouldn't give for a hot shower.

Richard still slept. He'd been somewhat alert when they wheeled him out of recovery and into the private room. The people from physical therapy had come and gone after setting his leg in traction. With all the tubes and dripping bags, plus the beeping monitors and the metal frames and pulleys holding his leg in place, Richard resembled a high school science project. Marc told Michael he would make the necessary phone calls and come back. She hoped he wouldn't rush. He looked worse than Richard when he'd left, pale and drawn. He needed to rest, but he insisted he would be back to relieve her if she would stay. He wanted someone to be with Richard when he finally woke up.

When Richard opened his eyes, he hurt. The bandage over his eye burned; his leg felt like it weighed a hundred pounds despite resting in a sling hooked to a maze of trapeze bars at the foot of the bed.

"Mikie?" The word came out choppy. He ran his coated tongue over parched lips, but it was a futile gesture and he gained no relief.

Michael pushed her hair out of her eyes and reached for the glass of ice chips. "Sh, don't talk." She placed the ice in his mouth and heard his weak sigh of thanks. *Oh, Richard,* she moaned silently, placing more ice in his opened mouth. *What have we done?* She wanted to touch him, but she wouldn't, not anymore. Every moment they had spent together had played through her mind again and again as she waited for him to regain consciousness. None of this was his fault. He'd hired her to be a nanny, a surrogate mother for David, not to warm his bed. If he had left her alone, she would have spent her days with David and her nights in her room, as hired help was supposed to do. If he hadn't invited her into his world—if he hadn't looked at her with his mischievous and sensuous smile, maybe she would have done her job and not fallen hopelessly in love with him. But he hadn't left her alone. He had teased her, flirted with her, drawing her into his web. But she was the one who'd made mistakes. She had been so foolish, read the wrong signals, and like a couple of fools, they'd crashed head on.

The ice melted. Michael took a damp washcloth and carefully sponged Richard's face. His eyes were closed, but his expression said it all. She saw pain and perplexity, then release and calm. Or did she? Maybe she still saw only what she wanted to see.

"Richard, I'm going to get more ice. Try to sleep." Her eyes fell on the nurse call button. She could push the button and someone would bring more ice, but she needed to get out of the room. As she waited for a fresh cup of shaved ice, Michael took a deep breath and reaffirmed her earlier decision. As soon as Richard came home and was able to get around, she would move back to the cottage. Space—they both needed space—time to think. If his feelings for her were more than merely satisfying a moment of physical desire, he would have to tell her so. If she arrived at the house before David got up and didn't leave until he went to bed, Richard couldn't complain about her not doing her job. The nurse gave her the ice and Michael walked back into his room with, she convinced herself, a more determined stride.

"Mikie, go home."

His words and his hand on her face startled her. She must have dozed off. His fingers roamed over her scalp, tugged at her hair, touched her neck. Michael lifted her head from the side of the bed and gazed at Richard. He shouldn't be doing that. *I can't let him touch me,* she told herself as she carefully removed his hand, trying not to twist a long intravenous tube.

"I'm okay. I promised Marc I'd stay until he got back. Then I'll go home."

"What time is it?"

Michael looked at the clock on the wall. "It's almost eleven o'clock. You were brought to the hospital early this morning. You've been to surgery, through recovery, and now you're in your room. I should tell the nurse you're awake. Dr. Singer wanted to be called when you woke up."

"What does Miles want?"

"Well, since he just spent several hours putting your leg back together, my guess would be he wants to explain what he did. I do know you're going to be out of commission for at least three months, maybe longer. I've already informed him not to count on the Hampton household for any more broken bones, at least not this year. And Allen told me he wasn't going to let you, or me, anywhere near his truck, which leaves us without wheels."

"Damn, Mikie, I really screwed up." Richard started to run his hand through his hair but got caught up in all the tubing. "I couldn't sleep, and I didn't want to wake you, so I went for a drive. Is he dead?"

"What? Is who dead?"

"Bambi, you said I hit Bambi."

"No, I said I thought it was Bambi's brother who ran in front of the car. And no, he's not dead. You missed the deer but totaled your car."

"I needed to think, Mikie, I—"

"Richard, don't talk now. Don't think about anything. You need to rest and get well. Look, here's Marc."

"Well," Marc said, "you look a lot better than the last time I saw you. I talked to your mother this morning. She'll be here tomorrow. Richard, why didn't you tell her about David? Never mind, but you better rest because once she sees you're all right, she's probably going to kill you. Michael, Anna called, and they're going to take David to Pier 39 today. She said to tell you they would bring him home around four this afternoon. You're to get some rest. That's a direct order from Anna. So go home. Peter will take you; he's in the ER. Another false alarm, but he's already sent the mother home. He said he would finish his paperwork and wait for you there."

What did she do now? Michael wanted to kiss Richard good-bye, to tell him she loved him, but she couldn't. Should she squeeze his hand? Or say something funny? Maybe she should just bow and back out the door. Instead, she just said, "Try to sleep and don't give the nurses a miserable time. Try to be good, Richard. I don't know what we'll do with you if they throw you out of here." Then she left.

Peter walked with her into the quiet house. *Dear Peter*, she thought, *always there to pick up the pieces and hold me up until I can stand alone.*

220

Peter knew she needed a car, now more than ever. "Take my station wagon," he said.

Of course she refused. "No, Peter, I'm going to rent a car."

Peter was adamant. "It just sits in the garage, and it needs to be driven. You would be doing me an enormous favor, kitten, actually two. If you drive the rig, I wouldn't have to keep recharging the battery every other week, and I'd feel a lot better knowing you were driving it. It's built like a tank, so I won't worry as much about you getting hurt if some idiot hits you again."

She was so tired and not up to making a decision right now, but Peter was, and his request made sense. Both Peter and Allen said so. Michael told them what she knew about Richard's injuries and the accident, leaving out the part that he had left her bed and almost killed himself because he felt trapped and had gone searching for a way out of a relationship he never wanted in the first place.

Allen said he would go get the car with Peter, and as they left, Peter told her to go to bed. "Get some rest, kitten, before David comes home." His advice sounded good, but she doubted she could sleep.

Michael took the ER bag containing Richard's clothes into his room, immediately sensing his presence. She loved his room. It was large, two distinct areas. If it had a kitchen, he could rent it out as an apartment. The front half held his desk, computer, and file cabinet. A sofa and chair in shades of blue were placed facing a large entertainment center. Light filtered into the room from two large windows looking out toward the front lawn and French doors that led to the patio and pool. Richard's bed, a large closet with a dressing area, and the bathroom occupied the rest of the space. *Order and optimal flow—so typically Richard,* she thought. Each book and piece of paper on his desk sat neatly stacked, perfectly square. No throw pillows or frills covered his bed. The only items on the bathroom counter were a guest towel, folded in thirds, and a small tray holding a bar of soap and his tooth brush.

His tuxedo jacket from the night before lay carefully folded on the foot of the bed; his dress shoes and socks were on the floor under the edge of the spread. Each time she came into his room, to make the bed or clean the bathroom, she felt as if she had entered a model home by mistake. When she opened his drawers to put away his clean clothes, she

221

felt ashamed of the haphazard way she stuffed her own belongings into the dresser upstairs.

Richard took care of what belonged to him. Everything he owned had its place. How had she ever thought she could fit into his life? He was Mr. Perfect, had his life in order. She couldn't even find her shoes half the time. Michael had to face the truth. Last night would never have happened if he hadn't been drinking and let down his guard. When he did come to his senses, he hadn't been able to get away from her fast enough and had ended in a ditch, all broken to pieces. It had been a costly night.

Michael reached for a hanger in his closet to hang up his jacket. The scents of him rushed to her heart, traces of raw vanilla and musk mixed clean and crisp like a dense rainforest. Michael buried her face in the jacket and breathed deeply as she slid to the floor. Tears boiled in her eyes, and rushed down her face. Why had she come to Sausalito? Left alone, eventually, she would have gotten over Ryan and Andy and gone back to her work. Now, as she sat on the floor of his closet, unable to control the flood of tears, she just wanted to dissolve into the harsh reality that she had to leave, but where could she go? Even if she knew where to run, what difference would it make when she got there? Her problem was here, and she had to face it, now. God help her, she wanted to be part of his perfect life, and last night she thought he wanted this too, but she was wrong, so terribly wrong. No matter what Marc thought, she knew Richard did not love her.

She needed to get out of this house. Michael went upstairs and changed into her jogging clothes then took off for the hills. Even though she had walked, not run, she hurt like hell when she walked into the kitchen thirty minutes later to find Cassie and Allen waiting for her.

"We thought we'd lost you," Allen said. "Marc called from the hospital, said to tell you he was going home. Richard seems to be resting so Marc couldn't see any reason to stay. He'll call you later. Want something to eat?"

"You know, I do, but first, I want a shower."

"Dad? Michael? Wait till I show you what I got."

David rushed through the door in his usual way, words first. The food and the shower had helped, but even though she was full and clean, she still felt wrung out as David rushed into her arms.

"Well, I can't wait," she chuckled. He smelled like sunshine and hugged like a bear. Michael wasn't ready to tell David his dad was in the hospital. She just wanted to hold him as he rocked her back and forth.

"Would you like some coffee?" she asked Anna. "I know Cassie just made a fresh pot."

"We better go, unless you need us to stay. We thought we would go by you-know-where on our way home."

"That's a good idea. Anna thanks for last night, and for today."

Anna ruffled David's hair and kissed his cheek. "Our pleasure. I'd almost forgotten what it's like to keep up with him, but we survived." She kissed Michael. "Call me if you need anything. I can take him wherever he needs to go—, Scouts, swimming. Just let me know."

"David, why don't you go and find Bo? He's been looking for you all day. I'm going to walk Martin and Anna to their car, and then we have to talk."

He ran toward the kitchen, shouting for Bo before the words were out of her mouth. At the car, Michael asked, "Anna, will I be okay with Mrs. Hampton? She'll be here tomorrow. Marc called her."

"Lord, I haven't thought about Caroline." Anna took her hands and squeezed lightly. "But it will be okay. Caroline loves anyone who loves her men. She's sharp, sharp enough to know the genuine article and toss out the fakes. Just be you, Michael. You'll see what I mean."

"David, if we look hard enough, we can usually find a bright side to almost everything that's kind of sad or that makes us unhappy. Your grandma is coming to visit. She'll be here tomorrow. That's a good thing—and your dad is going to be just fine. Now, I want you do go to sleep, and in the morning, I'll take you to see your dad, okay?"

"Michael?"

"Yes, David?"

"Do you think I can be first to write my name on his cast? Do you think he's already let people sign his cast? I'd sure like to be first."

Michael kissed him again. It was going to be okay. Before dinner, she'd taken David out to the gazebo. She told him about the accident. She told him the facts, all she knew, then waited for him to ask his questions. Michael had held David and waited, watched as different emotions crossed his small face as he asked his questions: surprise, fear, confusion, anxiety, and finally after she had answered them all, acceptance.

The next morning, Cassie poured steaming coffee into her cup. "Dr. Singer's office called. David has an appointment on Wednesday to have X-rays taken of his arm. Ten o'clock. I've marked it on the calendar."

She needed to take care of so many things today, starting with offering Cassie a full-time position. Michael finally had to admit that the reason she had never hired new help was because she liked being in charge, and her subconscious dream of one day being Richard's wife and David's mother. But that was a fool's dream. She needed to wake up and face reality.

Cassie had saved the day, and her sanity, and Michael wanted her to stay, but she had to ask Richard first. She would do it today. She also needed to talk to him about moving back to the cottage, but decided she'd wait on that one, at least until he came home.

"Cassie, what did we ever do without you?"

"I'll second that." Allen walked through the back door, and his face lit up the minute he saw Cassie, although his words were directed toward Michael. "I checked out the car, and we lucked out. It's a lot better than anything you could have rented. Peter said we could keep it as long as we needed it."

"Allen, Marc called. He said Mrs. Hampton has arranged for a limo. We could have picked her up."

"Michael, you don't know Richard's mom. You don't do anything for Caroline unless she asks. Is she coming here first?"

"No, Marc said she would go straight to the hospital. I promised David I'd take him there this morning. I guess I'll meet her then and bring her back with us."

Electricity filled the car as she drove with extreme care to the hospital, charging David to the limit. He was eager to see his grandmother but apprehensive about his dad. Was he afraid? Did he think she hadn't told him the truth? Michael tousled his hair and turned the radio to a rock and roll station, trying to keep his mind off his dad.

"Usually children under twelve are not allowed on the surgical floor, but since his dad is chief of the medical staff, I'm sure, if David is reasonably quiet, we won't have any complaints." Dr. Singer smiled at David and then continued. "I have to warn you, Michael, Richard's not in an agreeable mood. I told you he would be an uncooperative patient, but that was an understatement. A nurse on the night shift has already threatened to quit. He had a terrible night and took it out on everyone. I knew this would happen. The damn fool won't take the pain medication as I prescribed. That's the trouble with treating a doctor; they always know better and try to second-guess everyone."

Dr. Singer had met them in the hall outside Richard's room, and after checking David's cast for swelling, they moved a few steps away from the boy so they could talk. "Richard's mother just went in. Maybe she can calm him down before one of the nurses tosses him out the window."

Michael opened the door and arrows of light shot into the darkened room. The blinds were closed, masking the room in an ominous atmosphere that immediately frightened David as shadows from the machines and the traction danced on the walls behind the bed. "This is ridiculous," she said. It was time Richard realized he wasn't the only one who could get mad.

"Really, Richard, this is no way to greet your mother, or your son. You can sleep later. Did you eat any breakfast?" By the time she finished opening the blinds, filling the room with light and warmth from the morning sun, she knew she had his attention. Good, she was through playing games with him. She wasn't going to allow him to call the shots, at least not as long as he was hooked to the bed and couldn't chase her out of the room. *Let him fire me*, she though. That would solve many of their problems, but she wasn't leaving before she got her licks in. Michael cocked her head and led with her chin.

"You must be Mrs. Hampton. I'm Michael McCall. I just spoke to Dr. Singer and he's confident Richard will have a complete recovery, if he can behave himself." Michael offered her hand to Richard's mother, who accepted it with a smile. Caroline Hampton was beautiful. Her

225

high cheekbones and elegant features were highlighted by short, silver-white hair. She looked like she'd just stepped off a fashion page from Vogue instead of an airplane from Los Angeles. Her smart, red Chanel suit brightened the room and displayed the fact that, even though she was in her late sixties, she was still fit and trim. David might favor his mother, but he definitely had his grandmother's blue eyes and devilish smile. As she watched the two, hugging and chatting away, Michael could easily understand why David had sought refuge with the gracious woman.

"I'm so glad to meet you. David has told me all about you, and I have never seen him so happy." Caroline Hampton looked over at her son, and her eyes said it all. She turned back to Michael and whispered, "Thank you."

As David talked to his grandmother, Michael moved to the side of the bed. Richard closed his eyes against the light. Or was it to shut her out? "Why can't you just do as Dr. Singer wants?" she asked him softly. Her fingers trembled slightly as she brushed a lock of hair as dark as midnight, still matted with flakes of dried blood, off his pale face. Her heart cried out to him. Even with his mother watching her every move, she would have kissed him. That is, she would have, except detours were not allowed, not part of her plan, so Michael just pulled back, grasping her throat with an unsteady hand that longed to touch him again.

She spun around. "David, come talk to your dad. We shouldn't stay too long, and I know you have loads to tell him. I'll wait outside."

"Don't go," Richard whispered, trying to find her hand. "I promise to be good. Please stay."

"Richard, visit with your mother and David. I'll be right outside. I'll see you again before we leave."

Michael left the room, almost running. How could she get through this? Miles said Richard would stay in the hospital at least five to seven days, or until the open incision healed enough to put him in a full leg cast. The biggest problem Miles faced wasn't Richard's leg, but the man himself, who thought he could jump up in a few days, slap on a walking cast, and do business as usual. She didn't understand all the medical jargon, but Marc seemed to. The break was serious enough; the rehabilitation was going to be near impossible. Terms like swelling, edema of soft tissue, contracture of ligaments, and muscle atrophy all raced through her head. Miles had told Marc earlier that he intended to introduce electrical stimulation along with an intense regimen of exercise and physical therapy. He wanted to keep Richard so busy he wouldn't have time to harass the help. Maybe if he did what he was told, he might be able to go home sooner.

"Michael, Dad wants to say good-bye. We already said good-bye. We can come every day to see him. Did you see how that machine works? Dad showed me. It shoots this stuff into his vein so he doesn't have to have a shot in the butt all the time and another spigot shoots sugar and water, so he doesn't have to drink from a glass. I'd rather drink from a glass. How about you, Grandma? I bet you want a glass too, huh?"

Caroline smiled over David's head. "Does he ever stop?"

"Oh yes, when he's asleep, he hardly talks at all. I'll only be a minute. I know Richard is tired. The best thing he can do is sleep."

"Mikie, is that you?"

"Yes, Richard, it's me." His left arm was bandaged from his shoulder to the elbow. At the top of his right hand, a needle was taped into a vein, just waiting for someone to pump something into it, just as David had said. A couple of plastic bags, suspended by a pole attached to the bed, steadily dripped sugar water—or some kind of magical stuff. A bandage rested above his left eye and another type of monitor gloved his left index finger.

"Have you taken anything for pain this morning? I thought not. Richard, let me call the nurse. You are allowed to admit you hurt, and you have to take something for relief." Michael pressed the call button when he didn't move to stop her. "I've called the nurse. I'll stay with you until you go to sleep." She closed the blinds and turned on the small light in the bathroom.

The door opened, and Michael thought it was the nurse, but it was Amy. Michael motioned for her not to come in. Outside in the hall, she said, "Amy, would you please take David and Mrs. Hampton home? I've finally convinced Richard to take a shot for the pain, but I promised him I'd stay until he goes to sleep." Michael rubbed her tired eyes. "I don't know how he made it through the night without taking anything for the pain."

Amy gave her a tight hug. "He's stubborn, for one thing, and a know-it-all to boot, and obstinate, and uncompromising, and incorrigible, and we all love him to pieces. Stay as long as you like. I can visit with Caroline until you get home."

Michael told David and Caroline good-bye and returned to the room. She stood in the corner as the nurse checked his vital signs and noted the chart, but as soon as the nurse walked out of the room, he held out his hand, knowing Michael was there.

She went to him just as a moth seeks a flame. Michael held his hand. She wanted to hold it against her tender breast, but she didn't.

"Are you still mad at me?"

"Oh, Richard, I'm not mad at you. I just want you to be as comfortable as they can make you. Take the shots. Let them help you get through these first days."

"I hurt like hell, Mikie."

"Of course you do. Richard, Allen says your car looks worse than the bathtub. I didn't want to see it. He took care of all that."

"May I have some water?"

Michael held his head and maneuvered the flexed straw between his dry lips. "Thanks, I'm so dry."

As if she'd been doing it forever, Michael reached for a washcloth and moistened it with warm water. She gently washed his face and neck, moving across his forehead carefully, but still he winced.

"I'm sorry, do you want me to stop?"

"No, it feels fantastic. I would kill for a shower right now, only you'd have to prop me up."

She found a bottle of lotion and warmed it in her hands before rubbing it on his parched lips and over his face. Michael slowly massaged the tightened cords in his neck, felt his rapid pulse as it danced under her long fingers. As she continued to administer a gentle kneading to his strained muscles, Michael felt him relax.

"Oh, Mikie, do you know what you do to me?"

"Sh-sh. Just relax." She straightened the pillow and the top of the sheet under his bare shoulders. Had he refused to wear one of the hospital's silly gowns? Maybe he'd hurt too much for them to put him in a gown?

"Mikie, I need to tell you." *What do I want to tell her?* He felt funny, like he was on a small boat, drifting aimlessly on a rippling pond. "Mikie, I left you. You were asleep, but I left. I had to, but I want—"

"Don't try to talk Richard. Go to sleep. I'll stay with you, just sleep. We can talk later."

Michael stood by his bed, holding his hand, and knew he had spoken the truth. Was being under the influence of a narcotic the same as being injected with truth serum? Does the truth always surface? It had with Richard. Michael didn't think he was capable of telling a lie, even in a drugged state. She gave him comfort, release. What did it matter if it was two nights ago, when they'd shared a passion almost too intense to be satisfied, or now, as he drifted away into a deep and much needed sleep. Richard had not told her he loved her, not that night, not now; he'd only told her he had to leave her. And just because he felt secure with her, let her persuade him into doing things others couldn't, let her see him as he would not let others see, well, it didn't mean a thing. She was still just the hired help.

CHAPTER TWENTY-FOUR

ICHAEL PULLED TO A STOP beside Allen's truck and took a deep breath. She turned off the key and saw Cassie standing by the back door.

"You have company," she said.

Michael didn't want company. She didn't have enough energy to smile and be personable. She needed sleep. She needed time alone, time to find a way to dig herself out of a quagmire sucking her deeper each day.

"It didn't start out to be a crowd, but that's what we've got. Don't take offense, slick, but you look like hell. Why don't you slip up the back way and I'll just tell them you've gone to bed?"

Michael leaned on the hood of the 4x4. Sure, she could do that, but they meant well. "Thanks, but I better go in. I'm sure Richard's mother will want a report on how he's doing. And I want to see how David's holding up."

"It's your call, but you don't have to worry about David. He's giving an in-depth overview to anyone who'll listen about all the machinery hooked to his dad and how it works. What's downright frightening is he sounds so credible."

Michael walked into the kitchen with Cassie and greeted Richard's mother and his closest friends. The long table held food and drink, but it was also the focal point of love and concern, and not just for Richard, but also for her. Michael expected questions about Richard; instead, his friends welcomed her with warmth and sincerity, stripping away her need for solitude.

Richard's mother fixed her a small plate of food, disregarding Michael's response that she wasn't hungry. Gill and Holly had come to hear the latest about Richard and to visit with Caroline. Amy called Marc and said Caroline wanted to see the girls. Sarah and Tom came to see her, and Anna and Martin were there to help any way they could.

Before everyone left, Marc and Caroline set up a tentative plan for visiting Richard. They agreed that scheduled visitations would break the monotony for him and go a long way toward saving the sanity of the nursing staff.

After telling everyone good-bye, Michael excused herself and sought her room and a long, relaxing soak in a hot tub.

As long as Caroline was here, Michael decided to keep her visits to a minimum. That way David could spend as much time as possible with his grandmother. Without going into details, Michael told Sarah of her plans to move back to the cottage. As usual, Sarah hadn't pushed for an explanation, although she had extracted a promise for a powwow before the end of the week.

Their routine settled in place overnight. Michael got permission from Dr. Singer to take David into the pool each day as long as his cast didn't get wet. Every day after lunch, Caroline brought David to the hospital to see Richard, and each night, she went alone to visit with her son. Michael decided not to worry Richard with any of the household problems. If he didn't like what she had done, he could do differently after she left. Michael talked to Allen about her idea of asking Cassie to stay on full-time.

"It works for me," he said. "Why don't you ask her?"

So she did, and Cassie accepted.

"But Michael, I want you to take me to the doctor." Michael helped David out of the pool and dried his hair with the towel. The sun played peek-a-boo with the spotty morning fog that had yet to move out of the valley and over the crest of Mt. Tamalpais. She wrapped the towel around his shivering shoulders and said, "David, your grandma is taking you, and when you're through, you'll go to see your dad. You'll probably be there in time to have lunch with him."

"Are you mad at my dad?" His brows drew together, and she could see he was bothered and deadly serious.

"No, of course I'm not mad at your dad. Why would you think that?"

"You haven't been to see him since Grandma got here. He thinks you're mad at him. He told me so."

"Well, I'm sure he was just kidding with you. Why would I be mad at him? It's just that he's had so much company. I don't want to tire him."

"That's not a good excuse."

"David, I'm not trying to make an excuse. I simply decided not to go to the hospital. Now I think we'd better go inside and get you dressed."

He wrapped his arms around her. "I'm sorry. Please don't be mad at me. It's just that Dad wants to see you; he said so. Don't be mad."

Michael held him to her as her fingers combed through his wet hair. "It's all right, David, and I'm not mad at you. I know all this has been tremendously hard on you. It's hard on your dad. Please don't cry. All right, I'll go with you and your grandma today. We'll all go to the doctor's and the hospital, and then we'll have a special lunch."

"Great, we can have lunch with Dad. Come on, let's get dressed."

It didn't take her long to realize he had just manipulated her—again. Forget the research; genes were hereditary. Just like his father, David had a way of getting her to do things she clearly had not planned to do.

As they walked from the professional tower of the medical center to the hospital unit, Michael felt ambivalent. It seemed the entire Hampton family conspired against her. When David rushed into the house to tell Caroline that Michael was going with them to see his dad, Caroline suddenly decided today would be an excellent time to have her hair done. "Is that all right with you?" she had asked? What was Michael supposed to say? *No, you can't have your hair done because I don't want to be alone with your son.*

David bounced before her, a veteran of the hallways. He knew everyone and said hello to both patients and staff. No one questioned his presence on the surgical floor as he raced on like he worked there, lacking only a white jacket and a stethoscope.

"Dad, look who's here. I got my arm checked, and it's great." David stopped halfway through the door. "Who are you? And why are you kissing my dad?"

Michael wanted to know the same thing. An attractive woman with short brown hair and big brown eyes sat on the edge of the bed, wrapped in Richard's arms. It was obvious they hadn't expected David to come charging into the room with Michael in tow, and their embarrassment showed. Richard pulled back, donning a rather silly smile.

"David, you're early. Where's your grandmother?"

Michael wanted to leave the room. He hadn't even looked at her, much less said hello. The woman had no such problem.

"Hi, I'm Sue Kingsley. I'm a nurse. I work with Richard at the Medical Center in San Francisco. He certainly did a job on himself, huh?"

Michael didn't answer. She felt as if someone had poured water on her emotional circuit board, sending sparks crashing inside her head like fireworks, causing an overload. You didn't have to read tea leaves to see that Sue Kingsley did more than just work with Richard. Her hand still rested on Richard, only now her fingers just twisted the edge of the blanket instead of the hair on his bare chest.

"Grandma's getting her hair washed. You said you wanted to see Michael, so I made her come with me today."

"David, I'll wait for you in the hall. Take your time and visit with your dad." Michael quickly left the room, even as Richard called out, telling her to stay.

"Well, that settles that," she muttered to the back of the door she'd just slammed too hard. *"Hi, I'm a nurse,"* Michael mimicked sarcastically as she slumped into a chair in the hall. What kind of game was he playing? Sure, they were early today. Okay... Maybe they shouldn't have barged in like that. Bullshit! If he wanted privacy, why didn't he hang out a damn sign? He probably had nurses lined up for visits every hour on the hour. After all, this was his back yard. The bastard! She was furious! *"Oh, McCall,"* she mimicked again, *"I can't get involved."* Hell no, he couldn't get involved, not with her. He was no dummy. Why buy another cow when you already owned a frickin' damn dairy? Well, he could go to hell on a trolley car for all she cared. She would tell him today that she was moving out. No. She would write him a formal letter informing him of her intentions because she never wanted to speak to him again. Period!

Michael bit at her fingernail as Sue Kingsley walked out of the room with a big smile and waved. "Hey, it was nice meeting you. He wants you to come in now. Bye-bye."

She continued to gnaw at her nail but flipped her head to one side and plastered a nasty smirk on her face in reply. *No way, José,* she said to herself. This was it. The game was over. It was over.

"Dad says he needs to talk to you. Please, Michael. I'm supposed to wait here for you. He says it will only take a minute."

David had left his dad's room and sat in the chair next to her, pleading his case with his eyes. She knew he didn't understand. *Damn you to hell, Richard, why do you have to involve David in this?*

"Okay Sport. I'll only be a minute and then I vote for pizza. How about you?"

His smile was his answer. She ruffled his hair and headed toward the door.

"What was so important you had to send David after me?" Her words were loaded, just begging for a fight, but he didn't pick up the gauntlet.

"You look beautiful. Is that suit from your new wardrobe?"

She had wanted to look especially nice today and worn a lightweight, watermelon-colored gabardine suit, with white tuxedo collar and French cuffs. She did look elegant, she knew she did, but why had she bothered?

He grinned at her as if nothing had happened. *What a fool I am. Of course he can look that way because to him, nothing has happened. Wake up, stupid,* she shouted to herself as she glared at him.

She was only last week's play toy. Had he even once led her to believe otherwise? No. Oh sure, he wanted to make love to her, but she had been more than willing. *Let's call a spade a spade, toots. You're just a hot little number living upstairs. Let it go and move on.* What had he said at the dance? You buys your ticket and takes your chance.

"Yes, Richard, it's new," she said, so composed she even surprised herself. "I'm pleased you like it. David said you wanted to talk to me. I've promised to take him to lunch, so tell me what it is you want."

"I'm sorry you left the room. I wanted to introduce you to Sue." His smile was not quite as big as before.

"Really, Richard, I'm just the nanny, remember? You certainly don't have to introduce me to your lady friends."

"My what? McCall, what's the matter with you?"

"With me? There's nothing the matter with me."

"Like hell there isn't. You're acting as if I've done something terrible to you. You've pouted all week. You've stayed away from here as if I had the plague. Now, are you going to tell me what's wrong or not?" His smile was now a frown.

The silence loomed between them like the morning fog. They regarded each other across the bed, two fiercely indomitable wills clashing in the hush of the room. His dark eyes measured her with a cool, appraising look as he waited for her to say something. "There is nothing wrong with me, Dr. Hampton, and I'd like you to stopped yelling at me. But while I'm here, I do have a few things I need to discuss with you. I had planned to wait until you were feeling better, but it appears you're doing just grand. I have asked Cassie to stay on full-time. She has accepted, but only if it's agreeable with you."

"Tell her that's okay with me. Next?"

"She knows of a cleaning company. I have spoken with them, and I think a schedule of heavy cleaning twice a month would be adequate. Cassie agrees."

"Fine, next?"

"I have placed an advertisement with an agency for a new nanny for David. I will set up the interviews for some time after you are released from the hospital."

"You did what?" His eyes narrowed, and he stared at her with a definite scowl.

"I said I placed a—"

"I heard what you said. What I want to know is why?"

"I only did what you were supposed to do over three weeks ago. Or am I wrong? Did you place the ad, Richard?"

"No, I—"

"Really Richard, I fail to see why you are so angry. I told you I was leaving. What had you planned to do, wait until my bags were packed, then decide you had to do something?"

"I thought you had changed your mind."

"And why would you think that?"

The silence again spread throughout the room. Michael wanted to end their conversation. His face was drawn; she knew his leg was killing him, and it was her doing. Her words had angered him so much he had all but jumped out of the bed, pulling against the traction. It had to be finished.

"There is just one more thing I need to say, and then I'll go. I know your leg is hurting you. As soon as you're home and able to cope, I'm moving back to the cottage. I will come to the house before David is out of bed, and I won't leave until he goes to bed at night. We seem to be constantly at odds with one another, and I don't think it's a fitting environment for David."

"Fine." This time his words were barely audible. He just raised his arm, then dropped it to the covers. He turned his head to the window, and she would have had to be an idiot not to realize she had just been dismissed.

Richard hurt like hell, and he wanted a shot, but it wasn't time yet. He longed to sink deep into that world where all problems and fear were left at the dock. Where he could slip away from life as he had always known it—float beyond reason and responsibility. He wanted to go where he found her waiting for him each time he traveled the calm lagoon… but she wouldn't be there anymore. She was leaving him. She'd given him everything he'd ever wanted or dreamed of. She'd held him against her love-spent body and told him she loved him. How could she leave?

Today had turned into a disaster. He hadn't expected Sue to appear for a visit. He planned to call Michael this afternoon and ask her to come to him tonight so they could talk. There was so much he wanted to explain to her, but he needed to do it when no one else was around. Richard wanted to tell her how happy she made him and how much he loved her. He wanted to ask her to marry him. Now she was leaving. Richard didn't want to believe she'd just been playing with him. Had she actually been using Peter all along, just to make him jealous? Richard clenched his eyes and fought the pain. He didn't want to believe she could be that brazen, that cruel, but what else could he think?

Two hours later, the nurse checked his vitals and gave him a shot. It pulsed through his system but hadn't pulled him away, not yet, but soon. There was no use denying the truth any longer. *She is just like Eve.* He had let down his guard, let her in through the front door, and he had no one to blame but himself. Old habits had kept Richard in line, at least at first. But then he had deceived himself, forgotten what had nearly cost him everything. All women were the same. Why had he let himself reach for something that didn't exist, at least not for him? Well, let her leave, if that's what she wanted. *I don't need her.* What he needed to do was make a phone call.

"Sue? Richard. Sorry to bother you, but I've changed my mind. If you have the time coming, I'd be happy to have you come to the house and be my nurse. Miles seems to think I can go home around the first of the week. That's great. I'll call you later. Just go ahead and make arrangements."

CHAPTER TWENTY-FIVE

T EN DAYS AFTER HIS ACCIDENT, Richard came home. He'd
pursued his therapy like a man possessed, working harder
than prescribed each day. Two days earlier, Richard forced the
decision regarding a cast. He wanted to go home, and Miles finally
determined that his incision had healed enough to have a cast applied.

All this Michael learned from Marc. He told her Miles was not at all
pleased when Richard chose to invoke the ancient saying, "Physician,
heal thy self." He didn't like to be pushed, but Miles finally agreed and
applied a long leg cast that reached from Richard's toes to the top of his
thigh.

A special hospital bed waited in the space where the sofa and chair
had previously stood in Richard's room. All of Richard's instructions
had been followed to the letter; everything was ready for him to come
home.

Two days ago, Richard had told his mother he had hired a full-
time nurse, leaving out the specifics. Five minutes before the ambulance
pulled into the drive, bringing the tenacious lord of the manor home,
his nurse arrived.

When the doorbell rang, David raced to the door, expecting to greet
his dad. "Michael, Grandma, come quick."

Michael stood behind Caroline, unable to hold back the flood of
uncharitable thoughts whirling through her head when she saw Sue
Kingsley standing on the front porch with her suitcase in hand. She
quickly replaced her startled, unbelieving look with a forced smile.

"Hello, may I help you?" Caroline addressed the woman in a
courteous manner, but her voice held an edge of annoyance. Her son
would be here any minute, and she didn't need or want any distractions.

"Hi, David, remember me? I'm Sue. I'm going to be your daddy's nurse for a few weeks. Is he here yet?"

Michael stood her ground. Not because she teetered on the verge of tossing Ms. Kingsley out on her duff, but because she couldn't believe he would bring this woman here, to his home, to flaunt her in Michael's face. *Yeah right, get real, McCall,* she told herself as she continued to wear her silly smile. *It's his house; he can do whatever he damn well wants to do. Can't you get it through your thick skull that Richard doesn't care what you like, or dislike?*

Caroline on the other hand, didn't have any such qualms and simply said, "His nurse?"

"Dad's home." The ambulance came to a stop at the front steps. David flew out the door and waited for the driver to open the rear doors and let him see his dad.

"Look, Michael, look who brought Dad home. It's Josh and Harry. Hi, you guys. That's my dad. Did you sign his cast? It's a lot bigger than mine, but look, mine's all full. Look, here's your name."

Michael walked past Caroline and Sue and said hello to Harry.

"You folks trying for some kind of record here?"

"Sure, Harry. Life is such a drag we thought we'd come up with a new sport. See how many cars we can total without killing ourselves. So far, we're up by two. Nice talking to you."

Michael stood by the side of the ambulance, hoping to catch a glimpse of Richard, but when Sue rounded the corner of the open door and climbed into the back of the ambulance, she turned and walked away. David called to her and so did Caroline. Michael didn't stop, just said over her shoulder, "Sorry, I have to make a telephone call."

The hardest part was telling David. He refused to understand why she was going back to the cottage. Michael told him he would see her as much as ever. She wouldn't leave until he was sound asleep and she would be there before he got out of bed.

"But what if I want you during the night? What if I get sick and you're not here?"

"Do you remember how it was with Anna? I've set up the intercom system she used. If you need anything during the night, all you have to do is call out and Cassie will hear you. It only takes me fifteen minutes to get here from the cottage. And you'll have my phone number so if you ever need me, all you have to do is call me yourself."

Michael helped Cassie with the dinner dishes and told her of her decision to go back to the cottage.

"I don't understand, but you're a big girl. I guess you know what you're doing. And don't worry about David. I'm a light sleeper. He'll be just fine."

Caroline, on the other hand, wasn't about to acquiesce. "Why are you running away? I don't like to pry—but I'm going to anyway. There's enough friction between you and Richard to create a forest fire. I know it has nothing to do with the way you manage David. So what gives?"

Michael and Caroline had spent the past weeks getting to know each other, and most of their conversations had nothing to do with the Hampton men. They had quickly established a bond based on respect and laughter.

"Please, Caroline. I'm not running away from anything. This is something I've planned to do for some time now. Richard and I discussed it weeks ago. If he hadn't hired a full-time nurse, I might have stayed to help you, but as you can see, I'm not needed." Michael knew Caroline didn't buy her explanation, but she didn't push it any further.

When it came time to tell Richard, she realized it wasn't going to be easy, but she couldn't put it off any longer. Michael knew Sue was in the kitchen when she knocked on his door. She knocked softly and then opened the door. The hospital bed seemed out of place, and although all the tubes and machines were gone, Richard looked miserable, like a prisoner in his own room.

The new lamp on his desk softened the light in the room and the semi-darkness raised her courage level. She didn't want to look him in the eyes. She didn't want to argue with him. She just needed to be gone.

"I'm moving back to the cottage tonight. I've spoken to David, and I think he understands. Everyone has my phone number in case I'm needed, and I'll be here early in the morning."

He wanted to throw something, but he couldn't reach anything heavy enough. *Why is she doing this?* Son of a bitch, he hadn't been in the house five hours and already she was leaving. "Well, I'm certainly pleased to hear that David understands all this—because I don't comprehend any of it."

"What don't you understand, Richard?"

"Why now, McCall? You said you would wait until I was able to manage before you left. I thought that meant you would wait until I was up and walking."

"That's going to take several months, and besides, you have plenty of help now that Ms. Kingsley has moved in. If you find yourself in need of additional help, I'm sure there are many more where she came from."

"Don't be a bitch, McCall. You don't do it very well, and it doesn't become you."

"Is that so? Well, I guess I'll just have to try harder." She had said what she'd come to say. Michael started toward the door.

"I don't want you to go to the cottage. I want you to stay here."

Michael turned back to face him. "Well, people in hell want ice water, Dr. Hampton, and it's time you learned you don't always get everything you want."

Even in the darkened room, she could see the cords in his neck tighten as an infuriated scowl settled over his face. His expression was unmistakably that of a man accustomed to exercising authority and of being obeyed, but not this time. If he'd called her Mikie, she might have given in, maybe..., but he didn't. She waited for his next words, but there weren't any. He had accepted her leaving. Oh, he'd said he wanted her to stay, but he just couldn't, or wouldn't, say the only words that mattered.

Michael hadn't been gone five minutes before all hell broke loose. Everyone in the house soon realized Richard's new nurse didn't have the sense God gave little children when it came to handling Richard and his out-of-control temper.

Caroline threatened to have Richard removed, back to the hospital or to the garage, whichever he preferred if he didn't settle down. Nothing suited him. He didn't like his food. The room was too hot. The bed was too short. He didn't want a bath. Only when David came into the room did Richard calm down and behave normally.

A week later, David poked his head in Richard's room. Before he went to bed, he wanted to read his dad a story about an Indian tribe he'd learned about in Scouts. Richard pretended to listen, but at night, when the house was still, his thoughts always turned to Michael. No matter how hard he tried to listen to David's story and to push her out of his thoughts, it didn't work. He closed his eyes and for the millionth time, damned her to hell.

Soon after David left, Richard asked for Allen. "I want you to bring me a glass of Scotch. No, bring the bottle."

"Are you out of your mind? With all the medication you're taking, I'm not giving you anything stronger than milk."

"Don't argue with me, Allen. Just get me the bottle. You're welcome to join me if you'd like. And I'm not taking any medication tonight."

"Holy blazes to hell, Richard, what's gotten into you tonight? That new nurse you hired is blubbering all over the kitchen. Your mother has disowned you and locked herself in her room. I don't understand why you're acting like a damn fool. I know you hurt, but we're all trying our best to help you out."

"Are you going to get me the Scotch or just yank at my ear?"

"You don't need to be drinking."

"Suit yourself. I can get it without your help."

"You really mean to do this, don't you?"

"You bet your balls I do."

"I'm going to call Michael. She'll…"

"Allen, I swear to God, do not mention her name to me, and if you call her, I'll break your damn neck in so many pieces you'll look like a jigsaw puzzle."

"Fine, Richard, whatever floats your boat. I'll get the bottle. Are you sure one will be enough?"

"One will do nicely, thank you."

"Ice?"

"No, neat."

Five minutes later, Richard broke the seal on the bottle of Scotch. He was glad his mother had gone to bed, deciding not to come in and fight with him. He was alone now. Sue had stormed out of the room in tears when he informed her he wasn't going to need his evening shot. Women! One was just as ineffectual as the next. Well, he didn't need or want her company. Holy blazes, he never realized she was so inclined to cry at the drop of a hat.

He poured a small amount of Scotch and stared at the amber liquid as he gently swirled the glass in his hand. This was going to be a long, arduous night, and he stacked all his chips on the hope that the alcohol would dull his senses and soothe the edge of his desire. The wind outside echoed his bristling mood. Richard could hear the tree branches scratching against the windows, a prelude to a storm. He raised the glass to his lips and let the soothing spirits roll down his throat. Richard closed his eyes and remembered another storm. He remembered how she had looked when he stepped into her room, when he took her into his arms.

Richard refilled the glass and rubbed the edge against his lips and damned her again, but at the same time, he wished it was her lips pressed against his mouth instead of the cut crystal. This time he drank the entire contents of the glass, then filled it again, even though his head began to spin from the alcohol. He could count on one hand the number of times he'd been drunk during the past twenty years, and have fingers left over, but he planned to add to the list tonight. A cynical smile covered his face as he welcomed the befuddled sensation surging through his body. He encouraged it as he yearned for a dreamless sleep and complete oblivion.

Sometime during the early hours of the morning, Richard swore under his breath, knowing he was the worst kind of a fool. His sleep had not been peaceful. He'd tossed and turned, turned as much as his cast allowed, and dreamed of Michael McCall. Now he tried not to move at all. His head pounded against his temples and above his eyes. His mouth was dry, and his leg throbbed so badly he wanted to scream. And he'd not solved a damn thing, except to reaffirm the fact that he loved her and had no more idea what he was going to do about it than he had before he dumped a half bottle of Scotch down his sorry throat.

"If you've come to say I told you so, you can save your breath." Richard shielded his eyes with his arm as Allen opened the drapes, allowing the morning light to filter into the room.

"Hey, kid, you're a big boy. You can do any stupid thing you want to do. You sure don't need any advice from an old goat like me. I'm only here because we drew straws, and I lost. So do you want breakfast, coffee, maybe another drink, anything?"

"I give up, Allen. Do you think Cassie would make me some coffee, something strong enough to strip the paper off the wall?"

"I think that can be arranged Anything else?"

"Maybe some dry toast."

"You got it."

"Is she here yet?"

"Who?"

"You're really pissed at me, aren't you?"

"Where did you ever get an idea like that? What makes you think I don't enjoy watching you play Russian roulette with your life? Like some green-assed kid instead of a forty-four-year-old man with a son, who, I might add, doesn't understand why his dad is acting so strangely. Pissed isn't the word, bucko. Try disgusted... Or how about disappointed? Want me to continue?"

"I get the picture, Allen, but you're too late, about three hours to be exact. I've already said the same words, and believe me they didn't fall on deaf ears. Is my mother still upset with me?"

"Yeah, I guess you could assume you're still on her hit list. She was up early checking the airline schedules."

"You didn't answer my first question. Is Michael here?"

"Of course she's here. She had the coffee on before anyone else was up. She's the thorn in your side, isn't she?"

"How did you guess?"

"I've got eyes, friend. So does everyone else who knows you. All it takes to send the temperature beyond boiling is the two of you to be in the same room. Why don't you just sit her down and have a good talk?"

"I can't talk to her... She's so bullheaded. Anyway, she's leaving."

"Stop her."

"I don't know how or even if I want to."

"Fine, then send her away and be done with it. Cassie and I can look after David until you find someone else to take her place. Do it, Richard. Settle it now. If you let this drag on, you're only going to prolong your misery."

His arm felt like a hundred pounds pressing against his eyes and his head throbbed from his hangover. Who was he trying to fool, Allen or himself?

"I don't want her to go, Allen." Richard spoke softly. "I usually don't have this problem, but I swear to God, I don't know what to do."

"Well, why don't we start with coffee and some breakfast? Take a little advice from a guy with gray hair and let it be for now. Let's get you up and on your feet first. And cheer up. My money says she isn't going anywhere until you're well enough for her to knock some sense into you." Allen reached the door before he turned around and asked, "Tell me one thing."

"What?"

"Why in the name of hell did you bring Miss Crybaby here?"

"Allen, she's just a nurse."

"Yeah, right. You ever heard of a male nurse?"

Michael turned off the shower. She longed for the big tub in her room at Richard's house, but that was part of the past, and she promised herself she would look forward, not back. Each day had ended a little better than the one before, and for a week and a half now; Richard had accepted the routine his mother had set in place without too much complaining. Caroline went home yesterday. She told Michael she had talked to Dr. Singer and felt confident Richard had finally decided to quit second-guessing his doctor and do as he was told.

Michael spent all of her time with David. They were in the pool each day, and when he went to his Scout meetings, she went with him. They went to the movies and to every museum within fifty miles. One day, Cassie packed a lunch, and the four of them went four-wheeling, with Allen doing the driving. She even made a pact with herself to be courteous to Sue.

Michael waited for Richard to request her appearance, but after a week, she finally decided she would still be waiting the day hell froze over, and even then, he probably wouldn't want to see her. Two nights ago, Sarah had appeared at the cottage with her nightgown and toothbrush, demanding to know what was going on.

This time, Michael told all—, every word, each caress, all the worry and confusion causing her mixed and muddled feelings. They never went to bed. When the sun rose over the bay, she still didn't have answers.

Sarah listened as she always did, holding Michael in her arms and mopping up the tears until there were no more to shed.

"I feel so damn guilty. Tom and I don't work that hard at our marriage, and it's almost perfect."

Sarah gripped Michael by the shoulders and looked her squarely in the eyes. "I want you to listen to me. I have all the faith in the world that you'll get through this, and you will. All you have to do is find out, once and for all, how he feels. Don't pull away from me. I'm not through yet."

"But I am. What do I do, Sarah? Do I barge into his room and ask him if he loves me? Huh? Or maybe I should settle for sex. I'll just tell him I'm happy to jump into his bed whenever he wants. Either way, it sounds pretty ridiculous, doesn't it?"

Patience plus controlling her temper, was Sarah's final advice before she left Michael the next morning. Sure, that was easy for her to say.

When the phone rang, Michael shot up in the bed. She glanced at the clock as she reached for the phone. It read midnight. "Hello?"

"Michael, you... you gotta come quick. Dad's really bad, and I... I don't..., I don't know what to do."

David was hysterical. His sobs reached across the line and pulled her fully awake. "David, it's all right. I'm here. Please don't cry. Where's Mrs. Kingsley? David, go get Mrs. Kingsley."

"She's gone."

"Where? What do you mean she's gone?"

"Michael, I don't know, but she's gone. Dad says she's gone for good."

"David, listen to me. I'm on my way. Go get Allen or Cassie. Tell them I'm coming right now."

His sobs increased. She could hardly make out his words through his tears. "They're gone, Michael. Allen took Cassie out to dinner, and they're not ba... back yet."

"Okay, David, it's all right, darling, just listen to me. Everything is going to be fine. Where are you? Are you in your dad's room? Let me talk to your dad."

"Michael, I'm in the kitchen. When I heard him moaning, I went into his room, but he just told me to go back to bed. He said he was all right, but I know better. He'll be mad at me if he knows I'm calling you. He said we shouldn't bother you. Come quick, please... Come quick."

In her desperation to get to David, Michael shaved five minutes off the usual time it took her to reach the house. She had barely taken the time to pull on her jeans and a shirt. David and Bo waited for her by the back door, and when he saw her roll to a stop, he ran to meet her.

"David, I'm here now. Please don't cry anymore. I'm going to take care of everything, I want you to take Bo and go upstairs to your room. I'm going to check on your dad, and then I'll come up and tell you how he is. Come on now. I need you to help me so I can help him. Just go upstairs. Okay?"

Michael watched the boy and his dog climb the stairs and then went into Richard's room. "David, is that you? Go to bed, son. I'm all right."

She hurried to the bed and reached for his hand. "I sent David upstairs Richard. He's so worried about you."

"Mikie, is that you? Did he call you? I told him not to bother you, I'll be all right." His words were strained.

"I know you will, but he did the right thing when he called me. Richard, where's Sue? Why isn't she here? Never mind, it doesn't matter." She held his wrist and tried to find his pulse. It raced wildly, and his breathing seemed labored.

"Richard, you're going to have to help me. Is it time for your shot? Where does she keep her notes?"

"I'm okay. The pain is just so intense tonight. I didn't mean to wake David. It will pass, it always does. I'm fine, really."

"Yeah right, and I'm Wonder Woman." Michael bit her lip. He didn't need a smart-ass; he needed help. His head felt hot and clammy. She picked up the phone and called Dr. Singer. He also made it to the house in record time.

"You're a damn fool, Richard. I told you that by over-exercising you would do more harm than good. I'm changing your therapist, and so help me God, if you try to manipulate this new group, you can find yourself another doctor. You've probably set yourself back a couple of weeks. Be still so I can give you this shot."

Michael stood away from the bed but heard everything Miles shouted at Richard, even the gentle way he told him to rest before saying good-bye. She walked with Miles to his car. "Thank you for coming. I didn't know what to do."

"It's okay. I told you to call any time you needed me. He will get well, you know. In spite of all his meddling, his leg is healing, but because he decided to double his routine today, his muscles shut down with spasms. You take a man like Richard, one who has always been physically active, and place him at bed rest, you end up with more than one problem. Muscles have to be re-educated. I know that sounds funny, but it's true. He knows that," he said emphatically. "Richard knows the theory, and he knows good and well what he should be doing. His therapy needs to be slow and gentle, just repeated minimal effort. Stay on top of this Michael. He's his own worst enemy."

"Is he gone?"

"Yes, Richard, he's gone. I thought you'd be asleep, so I've been with David. He needed to know you were all right. He's gone back to sleep."

"Are you leaving now?"

"No. I'm not going anywhere. I promised David I wouldn't leave if that's all right with you?"

Richard continued to fight the pull of the shot Miles had stabbed into his backside. He needed to stay awake as long as he could see her, but she said she was staying. She wasn't going back to the cottage. He inhaled the clean scent of her as she straightened his bed covers. Sue always drenched herself in some nauseating perfume that lingered even after she left the room, but Michael smelled fresh—fresh as a pine meadow in early spring.

She cradled his head in her hand as she removed his pillow and shook it to fluff up the down. Richard inched into her, drawn like a magnet to her ample breasts. "Ouch," he cried as she replaced the pillow and removed her hand. "Careful, Mikie," he whispered. "I'm fragile."

"I think, Dr. Hampton, that you're nothing but a fake." Michael tried to be funny, but as she retracted her hand, she bumped his leg in the process. This time, when he recoiled from the blow, she knew he wasn't faking.

"Richard, I'm sorry."

He pulled his fist to his mouth and closed his eyes. His face reflected the pain, but he tried to laugh it off. "I'll be good, just don't hit me again. Although I know I deserve it."

Michael began a slow massage of his forehead, her fingertips moving lightly over his dry skin—back and forth, up and down—, trying to relieve the tension on his face. As her fingers continued to stroke his forehead, she felt him relax. Michael moved her fingers to his temples and drew small circles, pressing a little harder now, then down his neck to the base of his skull. Both hands met and held Richard's neck as her fingers rubbed and pulled like a tiny vibrator. Her palms gripped his shoulder and kneaded the constricted muscles, and he worked with her, rolling his shoulders and head as her strong hands led the way.

Michael felt the warmth invade her body; currents of heat penetrated her skin and then gathered strength to join in force at the pulsing flesh between her legs. She shook and inhaled deeply, but her hands stayed calm and steady as they moved lower, beneath his arms, down both sides of his bare torso and under his back.

The anger she'd carried for the past two weeks melted away, as did her resolve never to touch him again. The room became a place of peace and harmony, and contentment replaced the cloak of misery she'd worn too long.

Soon, he slept. His face rolled to one side and his mouth opened slightly as his breathing settled into an even rhythm. She continued to knead the muscles in his lower back, and even though he slept, she saw evidence on his face that he still felt the workings of her hands.

Michael pulled the sheet up over his broad torso, but not before her fingers played lightly in the dark curls on his chest. He twitched but didn't wake. *Leave him alone,* an inner voice warned. *Let him sleep.* But she couldn't; the urge was too strong. Sometime during the past week, the bandage over his left eye had been removed and she studied the scar crowning his dark brow, a perfect arch as if drawn with a brush. The wound was still red but relatively smooth under her fingertips. Gently she kissed the scar and then his open mouth. The tip of her tongue roamed over his dry lips, devilishly coaxing his tongue to mate with hers. And it did, moving instinctively with a will of its own. Even in deep slumber, Richard answered her need as his mouth molded to hers and eagerly accepted the bounty of her love.

CHAPTER TWENTY-SIX

INSTEAD OF GOING UP TO her room, Michael fell asleep in Richard's big bed. Several times during the night she awoke to his muttering and went to him. She straightened his covers, rubbed his lower back, and although he never woke up, he seemed to feel her touch and would relax.

Early in the morning, nestled deep in the pillows, Michael heard him call her name. He sounded uncertain, as if he honestly didn't believe she was there. She rolled off the bed and stretched like a puppy.

"You're here. I thought I was dreaming."

She stretched again, this time with a yawn as her arms reached toward the ceiling, drawing her shirt tight, outlining her breasts. She moved close to his bed. "Of course I'm here. I told you I promised David I would stay. How are you feeling?"

"Now that you're here, I feel great. You look kind of rumpled." His eyes shot to the floor. "Like I thought—, no shoes."

"Do you remember anything that happened last night?"

"Sure"

"Good, then you remember what a panic David was in. I didn't take time to make myself presentable, including finding my shoes. I needed to get here and reassure your son you weren't going to die. Oh, I see you do remember."

"Honest, McCall, I—"

"What?"

"What did I say?"

"What did you call me?"

"McCall, but—what did I do?"

"Nothing, DOCTOR Hampton, absolutely nothing." Michael stormed out of the room, slamming the door with such force two pictures flew off the wall. She got as far as the staircase and changed her mind.

His mouth was still open, stunned by her tempestuous words and her violent exit, when the door flew open and crashed against the wall. He shut his mouth, hoping he could get out of her line of fire if she decided to throw something at him.

Michael charged into the room and then attacked the door, hurling it closed, sending more pictures crashing to the floor. "Explain to me, DOCTOR, why you call me Mikie when it's dark and you're so damn hot to touch me. Then tell me what it is I do that makes you feel the need to change your tune and call me McCall."

Why am I so upset? Really, what's in a name? This was crazy—but she was furious, even though she knew she was being totally irrational. Michael knew she should leave the room and cool down. No, damn it, that's what she had done before and the only thing running away had accomplished was to tie her in knots, like a twisted piece of yesterday's newspaper, waiting for a match. Well, calling her McCall had caused a bonfire she didn't want put out until he answered her.

"You don't have the slightest idea what I'm talking about, do you? Ten minutes ago, when I woke up, you called me Mikie, and now I'm McCall. Is it because I'm just the hired help after eight o'clock in the morning? Who am I, Richard? Do you know? Do you even care?"

Michael pivoted around and walked to the window, pacing like a caged cat. She swung around and returned to the bed, smacking his healthy leg with the flat of her hand. "I love you so much, but you're tearing me apart. I am not two people, Richard. I'm me... just plain me." She clenched her eyes shut and took a deep breath. "Would you please tell me why you have such a difficult time knowing who I am and what to call me? And while you're at it, let's get to the bottom line here. I want to know the truth. Dig a little deeper, Richard. Tell me what I mean to you... if anything?"

Michael stood by his bed, her hands clinched on her slender hips. Her uncombed hair fell in a shimmering mass of darkness and curled wildly about her angry face. Her flushed skin glowed, fresh like a child, and her green eyes blazed with fire. Richard's body responded with a need so primitive he all but cried out. He wanted her now—no caresses, no foreplay, just the feel of her wrapped tightly around him as he thrust to the very core of her.

But he didn't cry out. Richard pressed the power button and raised the head of the bed to a sitting position. He never lost eye contact as he absorbed all the delights of her fabulous pouting mouth, the lift of her chin, and the arch of her brow as she stared straight into his eyes and waited for an answer.

He sensed her impatience as she jammed her hands into tight fitting jeans. His blood surged through his veins to pound violently in his loins, quickened by Michael's look.

His hoarse whisper broke the silence. "My God, you are a witch."

"What?"

"Come here, witch." He offered his hand. When she didn't move, his eyes narrowed and his mood sobered. His voice was low and shaky, and the hand he held out to her trembled as he said. "Mikie, come here, come closer and I'll give you your answer."

Mesmerized by his look, and his words, she moved toward him. One last step and she was in his arms. He lifted her off the floor and onto the bed, pulling her roughly against his bare chest. The thin material of her T-shirt did nothing to hold back the warmth of him—the pounding of his heart as it beat against hers and Michael felt the heat passing between their bodies as his hands held her face.

"I'm several different kinds of a fool for not telling you sooner, but I thought you knew." He kissed her eyes, the tip of her nose; his teeth nipped at her ear. "Mikie, I adore you. You're an enchantress, and I'm lost to your magic."

Richard's mouth muffled any words she might have said as he pulled her even closer and rushed to seduce. His lips crushed against hers, reckless, starving for the taste of her as his hands slipped into her hair and locked at the back of her head. His tongue sought entrance beyond her lips, and he felt her open beneath him as he thrust into the warmth of her mouth. Richard's kiss was gentle and then harsh, his tongue a million places at once. He claimed her mouth, demanding then coaxing, lingering here and there, only long enough to delight in the sweet pleasure it gave him.

Curled against his chest, Michael moaned as his hand edged under her shirt and surrounded her breast, circling, kneading her smooth flesh with skilled fingers that manipulated her nipple until she no longer could endure the savage need, the tormenting pleasure.

Her nails bit into his chest as she moved closer to him. Then he slowed his pursuit. With a provoking but gentle lightness, he nipped at the fullness of her lower lip. His tongue danced over her open mouth, across her white teeth, rubbed against her tongue, then withdrew, lingering a breath away, only to attack again.

"Open your eyes, Mikie, and look at me," he softly demanded. "What do you see? Do you see a man totally consumed? Huh? A man humbled by your goodness, your beauty? A man who panics every time he knows you're more than a breath away?" He cradled her in one arm and stroked her face with his fingertips. "Because that's what I am, Mikie. I'm all that and more. I'm drawn to you as surely as the tide is drawn to the shore; I have no choice. And you're wrong, my little dove. Sometimes you are like a chameleon, and when I call you McCall, you're just as much under my skin. I get gooseflesh sparring with you, hoping to make you blush but yearning for your fabulous smile. Do you realize how totally you control me when you're McCall? You're a force that demands all my will and attention."

Richard kissed the tip of her nose as his finger played with dark curls, caressed her lower lip. "But you see, when you're McCall, you're not mine alone. You belong to David, to your friends and mine. But when you're Mikie, my witch, you're all mine. You drive me insane, and I'll admit, I've fought it, feeling this way. But I'm not going to fight it any longer because we belong together. When you're Mikie, you're mine, and I won't share you—not with anyone."

Richard finally lowered his mouth and kissed her, a kiss as tender and warm as a summer breeze, covering her in the most incredible mantle of joy she had ever known.

Michael lay in his arms, and he held her tightly, his head buried in her hair as their bodies cooled, racked with desire and frustration. Slowly they regained a sense of balance, pulled back from a whirlpool of impassioned emotions where moments ago they had come so close to recklessly abandoning all reason. Michael wasn't greedy. Well, yes, she was, but she could wait. His words had stripped away all the doubts and dispirited feelings that had all but driven her away from him. He loved her. He may not have said those exact words, but it didn't matter. She knew he loved her.

Richard heard Cassie moving in the kitchen and knew it was only a matter of time before someone knocked on his door. He hurt from wanting Michael, but now was not the time, and how the hell was he going to make love to her with this damn cast? It would be hard, but he'd find a way, just not now. The worst thing that could happen right now would be to have David barge in and embarrass her. Richard stroked the side of her face and shivered just from the thought of having her naked and trembling beneath him. He breathed deeply, resolved to wait; he only wished he could convince the rest of his body.

"Mikie, please don't leave me again. I can't function knowing you're not here. Just ask Allen. Oh Lord, just talk to my mother. I think they really wanted to kill me."

"You had Mrs. Kingsley."

"Ouch! Low blow. That was a terrible move, I admit it, but it was your fault. I only asked her to come here after you told me you were moving back to the cottage. I was mad; I wasn't thinking straight. But it was a major mistake, and I told her so last night. She quit before I could send her away."

"Dad?" True to form, David's words barreled through the house seconds before he rushed into the room with Bo at his side. Michael heard him coming and rolled out of Richard's arms and onto the floor, blushing as if she'd just been caught necking behind the barn.

David stood by the bed. "Gee, Dad, you look great. Looks like Michael fixed you up real good last night. I had to call her, Dad. She told me I could call her if I needed her."

"You did the right thing, David. I'm proud of you. You acted extremely responsibly, very grownup. And yes, Michael certainly fixed me up."

The next few weeks passed quickly. Richard hired a male nurse who came to the house each day. He also kept his promise to Miles and stuck to the prescribed regimen of physical therapy. Six weeks after the accident they celebrated when the medical supply company hauled the hospital bed away.

In reality, they were living together, just like any average American family, except for one small thing. They were not married. Michael tried to be patient, knowing, hoping that any day he would bring up the subject of marriage. After she'd forced him to tell her how he felt about her, their lives settled into a marvelous harmony. Each day after therapy, Richard worked on a medical paper he had started a year ago. Michael and David swam and worked in the garden. They went to the library, to Scouts, and drove all over the county in the 4x4 Michael had finally bought from Peter.

They only fought over one thing. Michael refused to move into Richard's room. She couldn't do that, not until they were married, although Michael had never mentioned the word marriage to Richard. She had pushed him enough, and she was determined not to bring up the subject. It was because of David, she'd told him. David wouldn't understand, and she finally convinced Richard she was right, even though he hated it when she left his bed each night and returned to her room.

Their nights started with his bath. His male nurse, Kenny, was great, but Richard wouldn't let Kenny give him a bath. So each night after David was in bed, Michael would help Richard bathe, which stimulated them both to the point of madness as she massaged the tightness he'd accumulated during the day.

Richard was a masterful lover. One night he would be tender and gentle, prolonging his release until he overwhelmed her with a sexual savoir-faire she never knew existed. He had all the time in the world, he would tell her with a kiss. When a man rushes to achieve pleasure, he runs the risk of never knowing it at all. The next night he would want her as soon as she walked through the door. His hands would snake into her hair along with muffled words, words meaning to hell with a bath or caresses. She soon learned to recognize the look—as his eyes told her of his need to bury himself deep within her velvety warmth, to watch her lips go dry—to hear her moan as he filled her with all the desire he'd held in check all day.

Michael learned so much about Richard during their nights together. He talked of his practice, of his years growing up. Some nights he would tell her erotic stories as he lay next to her with his hands crossed on his chest but seducing her with his tales of sexual fantasies until she begged him to touch her. One night he sent her into a fit of laughter over his plight of being dominated by a liberated woman who demanded to be on top, which was the only practical way they could complete their exchange of sexual talents.

Another thing Michael learned about Richard was how quickly he could pout when he didn't get his way. One night he refused to let her go upstairs, but instead of getting angry and losing her temper, she told him he was just experiencing PMS. When Richard raised his dark brow, she gave him a gigantic kiss and told him to relax; the "Piss and Moan Syndrome" never killed anyone, and she then walked out the door.

David blossomed in this new environment. He had grown almost two inches since June, and he matured. He was a smart kid, and when he showed his dad his certificate from the library, having read the most books in his age group, he wore his pride of accomplishment with a grown-up air that surprised them all. Then he caught the flu.

Michael answered the phone and immediately recognized the voice. Anxious Alice was still muddled and unsure why she hadn't given up the position of assistant den mother, but her distress seemed legitimate. A young cub of the den was throwing up all over and maybe it would be a smart idea for the other boys to go home. Four days later, David spent most of his time bent over the toilet in his bathroom while Michael held a damp cloth to his pale face. She kept him away from Richard and the rest of the household, except Bo, who stayed by David's bed as long as Michael would let him.

David had caught the big bug. His temperature rose and lingered, as did the horrible achy feeling that prevented him from getting much sleep. In an attempt to cool his restless and heated body, Michael had applied compresses dipped in water and rubbing alcohol. After twenty-four hours, Richard called Dr. Wooden, David's pediatrician, who consented to make a house call. It was the flu, all right, he'd told them. The next big news flash was that David would need an antibiotic, lots of liquids, and bed rest. Michael should continue with the hourly bathing until his fever broke. In a few days, Dr. Wooden predicted, David would feel better.

His prediction came true. David got well. But Michael took to her bed, or rather to her bathroom. Cassie offered to help, but Michael didn't want anyone else catching the bug. She'd refused to let Cassie or Allen help her with David, and she didn't want anyone in her room now. Richard called in a prescription, which might have helped had she been able to keep it down—a fact she was too sick to tell anyone. After the third day, Cassie refused to be turned away and found out Michael hadn't been able to keep anything in her stomach for days.

Richard panicked. He hobbled up the stairs with the help of his crutches and both Allen and Nurse Kenny. She screamed at Richard to get out of her room and just leave her alone. But he wouldn't listen, and she didn't have the strength to make him or do more than moan when he gave her an injection to help the nausea.

The bug finally left, exorcized from the house without touching any additional victims, and life returned to normal. David's cast came off, and he started school. Richard persuaded Dr. Singer to let him trade his long-leg cast for one just above his knee. He finished his paper and sent it to his publisher. It seemed as if everything was on track for the Hampton family, but that didn't include Michael.

A week later, Michael ran out of Dr. Singer's office in search of a restroom. She rushed into the stall and dropped to the tile floor. As usual, nothing came up, just the retching pain of dry-heaves. She pressed her head against the side of the wall dividing the stalls. When the dizziness passed, Michael dug in her purse for a tissue to blot her face. The small tissue did little to relieve the clammy feeling or soak up the dampness caused by the cold sweats that always followed the urge to throw up.

The flu had rendered her almost helpless, and she still suffered its lingering aftermath. Her temperature returned to normal, but the gagging and retching were still with her. She hadn't told Richard, although he remarked almost daily that she needed to eat more to get her strength back. What was the point in eating? Nothing stayed down.

Cassie knew she was still throwing up, but Michael had threatened her with dismemberment if she told anyone. It was just a reflux thing. She read about it in one of Richard's medical books. It would pass, she'd told Cassie. But it hadn't.

Michael got to her feet and left the stall. She washed her face in cold water and patted it dry. She had to get back to Dr. Singer's office. Richard's cast came off for good today.

Richard eased himself behind the wheel of his new car. Two weeks ago he had gone to San Francisco with Marc and Allen to pick up his new Mercedes. It was black, exactly like the one he'd rolled in the ditch, only a newer model. He pushed the seat back to give himself plenty of legroom and fastened his seat belt.

"I feel like a kid with a new driver's license."

"Do you think you should be driving? I mean, shouldn't you give it a day or two before jumping back in the saddle?"

His reckless smile sent shivers all over her body. He leaned across the center console and kissed the tip of her nose, then her lips. "Oh, princess, getting back into the saddle is all I've dreamed about for months. You're not going to be a party-pooper and deny a guy a few pleasures, are you?"

He took the long way home, enjoying his newfound freedom. When they finally stopped at the back of the house, Michael saw the tightness in his face as he got out of the car. "Use the cane, Richard, at least for a couple of days."

His sour expression said it all. "I don't want to use a cane."

"I know you don't, but that's not the point. Really, Richard, for someone who is supposed to be intelligent, you don't have a clue. You haven't put any weight on that leg in over three months. What makes you think you can bounce back the first day and just trot off unassisted. Use the damn cane."

She hadn't meant to be short, but she didn't feel well and couldn't help being irritable. Michael cocked her head. "Well?"

"Okay, I'll use the cane, but don't be mad at me," he said with a smile.

His attempt at humor lifted her gloom, and she smiled back. "Richard, I'm sorry I snapped at you. It's just that I have this terrible headache. Come on, let me help you into the house."

He knew she was tired and sent her off to take a nap after telling her he had planned a special night. She munched a few soda crackers followed by a sip of hot tea before stretching out on her bed, a practice that often helped calm her stomach and gave her some nourishment. Michael closed her eyes and immediately dropped off to sleep.

She woke feeling better. Michael filled the tub and stepped into a mass of bubbles. Easing her shoulders under the water, she reveled in the warmth that caressed and rejuvenated her body. It was wonderful to see Richard so happy. He'd been so secretive about tonight. Did he intend to ask her to marry him? Now, after shedding the last reminders of his accident and so close to returning to work, would he ask her to become a permanent part of his and David's life?

Dinner was simple, soup and salad and a hot fudge sundae, and as Richard watched Michael and David playing a game of tag as she ushered him up to bed, he realized how rich he was. During the past months, he had experienced a metamorphosis, a 180-degree turn. He was convinced if he hadn't told her how he felt two months ago, Michael would have left him for good. Richard knew he couldn't exist without her. But loving her, keeping her near, forced him to walk a tightrope with no safety net—where only her presence and love held him safely aloft.

Knowing this about himself, why couldn't he tell her he loved her? Because he did love her. If he turned in the night and couldn't find her, he panicked. If she didn't answer when he called to her, he broke out in a cold sweat until she came to him. Richard knew using words like adore, cherish, devoted only bought him some time. Last night she had sat up and given him the strangest look when he'd told her—what was the word he used? Prized, that was the word. He actually told her he prized her above all else. My God, it's a wonder she hadn't kicked him out of bed.

Michael spoke so freely of her feelings for him. Why couldn't he do the same? Why couldn't he just say, "I Love You Mikie?"

Richard stood by the French door in his room, staring out into the darkness. He knew the answer. He was afraid. Richard was one hundred percent sure he had no reason to feel as he did, but still, the doubt lingered. *What would I do if she changed, like Eve?* He couldn't go through that again.

But Michael wasn't Eve, and he knew that. So why did he continue to torture himself like this? *Damn it to hell Richard, get real. The woman loves you and loves your son. What more do you want?* He would tell her tonight. Tonight after a wonderful night of love, he would tell her he loved her. And this time, he got to be on top.

CHAPTER TWENTY-SEVEN

THINGS DIDN'T GO QUITE AS Richard had planned. The night turned cloudy and cold and he felt the change in his leg. As he waited for Michael, he lit a fire, pulled the spread off his bed and placed it before the hearth.

Everything was ready. Even Tchaikovsky's Violin Concerto in D Major, Michael's favorite, waited for only a flick of a switch before filling the room with the music she loved.

Michael came to him after David went to bed, radiant in a deep emerald chemise and robe of satin and lace. Richard slipped his fingers under the lacy edge of the robe, lifting it off her shoulders, and then gently eased the straps of her gown over smooth shoulders and down her arms until the gown lay at her feet.

The glow from the fire created a lustrous sheen across her body and danced in the rich darkness of her hair. Michael stood before him, naked like a mythical nymph. Her eyes sparkled like polished jade, eyes that promised delight—but radiated desire.

He lowered her to the waiting pallet in front of the fire, and his tongue became an enthusiastic pathfinder as he made precise but gentle love to every inch of his Mikie McCall. Later, much later, she snuggled into his side, purring against him like a contented kitten as he rubbed an ice cube over her parched lips. Her eyes were closed, and the fringe of her thick, dark lashes cast shadows on her pale cheeks. But he saw more. The delicate skin beneath her eyes was drawn, darkened by more than the shadows of her lashes. Rings of fatigue and weariness settled in the delicate lines surrounding her eyes, and he realized how fragile she looked. Although she returned his passion, touch for touch, tonight she'd lacked the fierce fire that had scorched them both from the very beginning each time they made love.

Michael smiled, her lashes fluttered, but her eyes remained closed as Richard's hand wandered over her body. When he questioned her about being too thin, Michael told him she had gained back some of her weight, but as his hand traveled over her arm, her ribs, down her leg, reality delivered a sharp blow to his gut. My God, how much weight had she lost? She was too thin. Suddenly Richard rose to his side and looked at her with the eyes of a physician. He viewed her hollow cheeks and the outline of her ribs as she rested on her back.

Richard damned himself for being the worst kind of a fool. He was a doctor, for God's sake; he should have seen what was happening to her. She spent every day with David and came to him each night. And each night she'd left him exhausted. God only knows how she managed to get through a twenty-four-hour day, let alone have the strength to keep up the same routine for over two months.

"Mikie, why didn't you tell me you felt so bad?"

Her eyes shot opened, and a look of panic covered her face. "I'm fine, Richard. I'm sorry I was short with you this afternoon. I didn't—"

Richard put his fingertip to her lips. "Little dove, I'm not talking about this afternoon. I was a jerk; you should have hit me over the head with the cane. No, I'm talking about the past two months. You've waited on David and me and look at you. You're skin and bones, beautiful skin and bones, but baby, you've lost way too much weight. I want you to see a doctor tomorrow. Do you have a regular GP?"

Her mouth was so dry her words barely escaped her lips. "Yes, I do," she lied. "I'll call in the morning and make an appointment, but it's nothing, really. In fact, I've already started to put on weight. And Cassie is all but force-feeding me every day," she lied again. "Please don't worry about me."

Richard dropped down beside her and drew her into the circle of his arms. He kissed the hollow of her neck, teasing with his teeth. His lips replaced his fingers tracing the contours of her breast as shivers like quicksilver pulsed through her. "At least you haven't lost any weight here. Quite the opposite. I do believe, my sweet, that we've stirred your hormones into working overtime."

263

An hour later, Richard wrapped Michael in his terry robe and walked with her to her room. He wanted to carry her, but she wouldn't let him. He found her football shirt and pulled it over her head, then put her into bed and sat beside her, tucking a wayward curl behind her ear. "Sleep well, Mikie. In the morning, but not too early, we'll get you to a doctor and start fattening you up." He kissed her and left the room.

Michael waited until she was sure Richard had gone to bed. She went into the closet and turned on the light. Her reflection from the full-length mirror on the back of the closet door stared back at her. Pulling the nightshirt over her head, Michael's eyes became fixed on her naked image.

How could she have been so stupid, so dense? Her hand lifted her breast, felt the fullness of the heavy globe. He was right; she was skin and bones and had boobs like a Vegas showgirl. Not in a million years would she have thought of the obvious. She was pregnant.

Michael crawled back into bed, but she didn't sleep. She was going to have a child, Richard's child. When had she conceived? When would the baby be born? When did she have her last period? Michael laughed. Even if she could remember, using the date of her last period to decide when the baby would be born was about as legitimate as trying to manufacture snowballs in hell.

Until she'd met Beth, what little she knew about the female reproduction system she could have stuff into a nutshell. She never knew that a woman was supposed to have a period each month. Her mother had never bothered to explain what happens to a young girl's body when she becomes a woman. When she started her period, the nurse at school had given her a general overview, along with some pads, and sent her back to class. She didn't have another period for eleven months.

Michael was a virgin when she married Ryan and about as dumb as they come. She wanted children but couldn't understand why it was taking so long. Her doctor gave her a thorough examination and found nothing to prevent her from having a baby, but as the years went by, she gave up hope of ever having a child of her own. The doctor said she was trying too hard. Relax, he told her, let nature take its course. After five years of marriage, she finally conceived.

Michael wanted another child after Andy was born, but she never got pregnant again, until now. After Ryan died, the only date she'd ever had came out of a cereal box. Richard was the only man she had known, in the biblical sense, besides Ryan. And now she was pregnant.

It had to be the night of the gala. The first time they made love, they conceived this child.

Shivers of delight coursed through her tired body. There were so many things to do. She had to see a doctor and start eating. She needed to be healthy to nourish the child she carried within her.

What would Richard think? Would he be glad? He had wanted David and fought Eve with a vengeance, had all but ruined himself financially to make sure he kept his son. Would he want this child as much?

Her breath caught and hung tight in her chest. What if he didn't want her baby, didn't want her? Richard had never said he loved her.

Stop it, Michael, she admonished herself. Her body grew instantly hot when she recalled how just a short time ago he'd brought her to a new height of arousal. His mouth and hands had played her body like a master plays his violin, to a score filled with hunger and a carnal need, gentled only by love. No, she would not torture herself with doubts because she knew, just as she knew almost to the hour when their union had created the child within her, that he loved her.

Michael surprised both Cassie and Richard the next morning. She had coffee ready when they ventured into the kitchen. Breakfast she left to Cassie, grabbing an apple and heading out of the kitchen before the aroma of bacon and eggs turn her stomach against her. Later, she fixed herself a bowl of oatmeal and dry toast, and although she ate only half of what she fixed, it was a start.

Thank you, Sarah, Michael said to herself when the receptionist told her she could come in on Friday. Last week Sarah had given her the name of her gynecologist and threatened to have her bodily carried into his office if Michael didn't make an appointment and have a checkup. She told Michael to use her name to get in if she needed to, and it worked.

Instead of having to wait three months to see Dr. Sweet, the leading OB-GYN specialist in San Francisco, she had an appointment two days from now.

Dr. Sweet confirmed what she already knew. When she explained her history, he just laughed and said they'd toss out all the standard charts used to determine the birth date and throw darts at the calendar. Which they did, figuratively, then circled a date around the middle of April. He needed to run some tests. His nurse drew blood and then gave her a tiny bottle and directions to the bathroom to supply the rest. He gave her a list of vitamins to take and the diet he wanted her to start immediately. Her morning sickness should ease, especially if she got plenty of rest and kept something on her stomach all the times. Dr. Sweet told her he would see her in a month. She was to go home and rest and gain ten pounds.

Instead of going directly home, Michael went to Union Square and wandered through Neiman Marcus. In the baby department, she touched the soft baby clothes and listened to the music of the hanging mobiles. She looked at furniture, the cribs and changing tables. Michael sat in a rocking chair and felt content, perfectly at home. Before she left the store, Michael stopped at the bookshop and bought a book about Africa for David and three clothbound nursery rhymes for the baby. For herself, she bought a copy of *Natural Childbirth*.

Michael knew she had to talk to Richard about the baby, and soon. Although she actually didn't show it, she was four months pregnant. The last month had slipped by quickly—for so many reasons. School, Scouts, the PTA, all had lessened their private time together, and she hadn't found the right time to talk about their future. Richard returned to work a week after his cast came off. He was allowed in the OR only if the case lasted two hours or less, but he was needed in the office and that he could do. Hal Green had held down the fort for the last four months, with only their rotating senior resident for help.

Yesterday she had seen Dr. Sweet for the second time and he scolded her like a father. She had gained only seven pounds. Plus, she was anemic. The first blood test showed low hemoglobin, which could be the result of being so ill. Later today, she had to call his office, and if the second test was still low, he said he would take a different approach to regulate her blood. He had also asked her about her husband's family history. Dr. Sweet waited for her answer, but she didn't have one, so she did the only thing she could think of and said she had to throw up, which wasn't too far from the truth.

Michael's hand shook as she checked her hair one last time before going downstairs. She was excited. Dan would be here any minute, and she wanted to look her best. Michael had called Dan McClaren at the university last week. It wasn't fair to hang on to her job any longer. When she told him she would not be coming back to Southern California, he quizzed her until she broke down and said she hoped to be married soon. He congratulated her and then said he was attending a conference at Berkeley and wanted to see her. They arranged for him to come to the house this morning at ten.

"My God, you're absolutely radiant. So tell me about your man." And she did.

"You're sure this is what you want to do? We still have time to wait to make a decision."

"Yes, do it now. You know how much I love teaching, and who knows, maybe I'll go back to it someday, but not now. I wish you could meet David. He is such a wondrous child and even if I didn't love his father I'd stay just for him. Dan, no one could ever replace Andy or Ryan, but through David, I've been able to find peace for that part of my life. Now, when I reflect on my life with Andy and Ryan, it's with a wonderful reminiscence and not the horrible anger that plagued me for so long. It's time to move on, and thanks to the love I've found here, I can do that."

Dan took her in his arms and hugged her. "If you're sure that's what you want, if you're sure you're ready to travel this road, then I'll make all the arrangements. You don't know how happy this makes me." He hugged her again and kissed her forehead. "I don't think you realize how seeing you like this affects me. I really doubt I could have stayed away much longer without seeing you."

Richard stood outside the door to the library listening to Dan McClaren's words and felt like he had just been kicked in the balls. The door was ajar, and even though he knew he was eavesdropping, he watched as Michael rested her head against the chest of the man who held her tightly in his arms, held her tight and kissed her. The scene rendered him unable to move. When he first heard their voices, he bristled, unable to identify the man's voice. Almost instantly, Richard felt ashamed of his violent jealousy until he walked toward the room and saw Michael wrapped in the arms of another man. Now he was livid. Racked with a sense of anguish and violation, he remembered another time of betrayal. He threw open the door, blinded by rage, refusing to be logical or believe there might be a reasonable explanation why Michael would be in the arms of another man.

"Richard?" Michael pulled out of Dan's arms and started toward him. "You're home. I didn't expect you, but this is great. I want to introduce you—"

"The fact that you didn't expect me seems obvious enough, but you can save your introductions. All I want to know is why?"

"Richard, what's wrong? This is—"

His retort made her jump. "No more, Michael, no more lies. But tell me..., tell me how you intended to pull it off. Were you just going to leave? Or maybe have Cassie tell me? What, Michael? I think I deserve some kind of explanation. But take your time. Maybe you and your lover would like to confer. Just make it good because it's the last time you'll have a chance."

Her knees buckled, and she would have fallen to the floor if Dan hadn't caught her. She felt sick. She shook, chilled to the bone as she fought off waves of hysteria that penetrated her body and knocked the breath out of her lungs. All she could do was to stare at him, her mouth open but void of words.

"Fine, I'd just as soon not listen to any more lies." Five minutes after Richard walked into the house intending to ask her to marry him, he stormed out the door and got back in his car and drove off.

Somehow, Michael managed to explain to Dan that what he'd just witnessed was not what it looked like. She told him there was no way he possibly could understand, and it would take too long to explain what had set Richard off. Michael knew. As much as she hated to admit the truth, she knew what he thought.

Dan finally left, walking to his car in a daze. He didn't understand, but he would trust her and leave, for now, and he would call her later. But he would not leave the Bay Area until she made him understand why the man she described to him earlier as almost perfect had acted like the biggest asshole he had ever met.

Dan drove toward Sausalito. How could she love a prick like that? Shit, the clown hadn't even given her a chance to explain. And whatever gave him the idea that Michael and he were lovers? Michael had turned so pale, and Dan thought she was going to pass out; she was still shaking when he left her. Dan ran his hand over his face and wondered where the bastard was now. He looked at his watch and made a decision.

Dan flipped a U-turn and headed toward the medical center. Michael didn't have a brother; she didn't have any relatives, no one to stand up for her, but he'd be damned if he'd let that bastard treat her that way.

It took him ten minutes to park his car and get to the office. "Lady, I want to know if the doctor is in, yes or no. It's that simple."

The receptionist gave him a quizzical look. "Dr. Hampton is in, but if you don't have an appointment, I'm afraid that… wait a minute, you can't go there."

The door was marked "Private." He knocked once, and then threw it open and marched in, confronting a stone-faced Richard.

"What the hell do you want?"

"What do I want? I want to beat the living shit out of you, but before I do, you're going to listen to what I have to say."

"Get out of my office before I call security."

"Just try it, you self-centered, sanctimonious son of a bitch. You might be able to intimidate Michael, but not me. I don't happen to be madly in love with you. In fact, I don't see what she possibly could love about you, but she does."

"You don't know what you're talking about. How could she be in love with me and about to run off with you?"

"I swear to God, you're not only a bastard, you're a stupid bastard to boot. What makes you think Michael is going to run off with me?"

"I heard the two of you talking. You said you would make all the arrangements for the trip."

"Trip? I don't know what you're talking about."

269

"You asked her if she was ready to travel—"

"Oh, well, that's what you get when you eavesdrop, only half of the story. If you'd come in sooner, you would have heard her telling me how much she loves you, about all the love you and David have given her. I've never questioned Michael's intelligence before, or her judgment of people, but I do now. You don't get it, do you? Let's back up a bit and I'll tell you who the hell I am."

After Dan had left the office, Richard's body shook with sheer panic. The good news was that Mikie did love him, and the man Richard had wanted to kill was an extraordinarily dear and protective friend. The bad news Richard had to deal with was insurmountable. What would he do if she wouldn't forgive him for doubting her? Dan had said it all. He was a self-centered asshole, worse than that. He had only thought about himself. He'd flown into a rage and assumed the worse, cutting her off, not letting her explain. To have humiliated her like that was bad enough, but his lack of trust, the fact that he had not even given her the benefit of the doubt, was worse than cruel. It was brutal. Richard sat at his desk and held his throbbing head in his hands, doubting there was enough love in the world for her to forgive him. But he had to try.

He called the house, but no one answered. Allen and Cassie had taken David with them to San Francisco today, and he doubted Mikie would answer the phone. He tried two more times as he drove to the house, still no answer. Richard had just entered the house when the phone rang.

"Hello."

"Mrs. McCall, please, Dr. Sweet's office calling."

"Who?" Richard only knew one Dr. Sweet, an excellent ob-gyn in San Francisco.

"This is Carla from Dr. Sweet's office. Mrs. McCall was supposed to call today for her lab results. Is she there? Is this Mr. McCall?"

Richard lied. "Yes, this is Mr. McCall. I think she's resting at the moment."

"Good, that's what she needs. If you would give her a message for me, I won't bother her."

"Certainly, what's the message?" He wondered why they were just now getting the results of tests done last month.

"The blood work from yesterday was not what the doctor hoped for. He's very concerned about this pregnancy, her low hemoglobin. She's very anemic, and the doctor feels she is going to need a more aggressive program than he usually prescribes. You see, we need to address several problems here. Mr. McCall? Are you still there?"

Richard slumped against the wall, still holding the phone as the room whirled around him. "Are you telling me that Mikie..., that Mrs. McCall is pregnant?"

"My goodness, of course she's pregnant. She's almost four months. Don't tell me I've let the cat out of the bag? But that's not possible. Surely she's told you, and if she hasn't, where have you been? A person would have to be blind not to realize how sick she's been." Realizing she had just stepped over the line regarding professional ethics, she changed the conversation.

"Will you tell Mrs. McCall I called?"

"Yes." Richard told the nurse he would deliver the message to his wife. Yes, they would call the office tomorrow or something to that effect. If he hadn't felt guilty enough about the way he'd treated her this morning, the information he just received delivered the final blow.

He went into the kitchen and got a glass of water, which he didn't drink. He didn't deserve to hold a degree in medicine. Any first-year medical student could have delivered an accurate diagnosis. It had never entered his mind that Mikie might be pregnant, even though he lived in the same house with her and made love to her almost every night. Even when Richard finally noticed how drawn and tired she was, he hadn't suspected she was so wretchedly sick because she was carrying his child.

He had to find her. My God, how she must hate him, more now than ever. Richard had felt sorry for himself for years, even though he tried to wear it well. But nothing he had suffered with Eve, not fighting for David, nothing compared to what he had done to Mikie. Goddamn him to hell, he had never once even told her how he really felt. He had never told her he loved her.

"Sarah, are you sure she hasn't called?"

"Yes Richard, I'm sure. Tom and I have been out of town for the past week. What's wrong?"

"Nothing's wrong, Sarah. Well, that's not actually true. I said some pretty terrible things to her this morning, and now I can't find her. I just thought... I hoped you might have talked to her today." Richard listened while Mikie's closest friend ripped him apart.

"You're not telling me anything I haven't already said to myself. Thank you, Sarah, I deserved that, but look, can we continue this later? No, I've been to the cottage; she's not there. Sarah, I'm so worried. I don't know where else to look. Okay, and if she calls you, please, please, Sarah, let me know."

It was unanimous. Richard was a bastard and needed a good thrashing. By whose hand, no one could decide. He called Marc after he'd talked to Sarah and asked if he or Amy had seen Michael. After explaining in general terms what had happened, Marc called him a few names Sarah was too much of a lady to use and Dan was too angry to think of. Marc came unglued, told Richard he needed professional help, but then backed off and offered to help in the search.

Richard called Anna and asked if she would keep David overnight. He told her he and Michael needed some time alone, and that seemed to be enough of a reason for his request. Martin was waiting when David returned from San Francisco.

"But where's Michael? I want to show her the book I got. I need to talk to her, Dad. When will she be back?"

Richard wished he knew. He had asked himself the same question over and over all day. What could he tell David?

Ten o'clock that night, Richard called the police. They appreciated his concern, but she had not been gone long enough for them to get involved. If she didn't show up by this time tomorrow night, he should give them a call. Richard went to her room. It didn't look as if she'd taken anything, but then her belongings were scattered between here and the cottage. The only items he knew were gone for sure were her old high-top black tennis shoes.

Richard shot out of the chair, and it took him a second to realize he was in his room. He must have fallen asleep in the chair by the phone, which continued to ring. "Hello, Mikie?"

"Richard, it's Sarah. She's back."

"Sarah, where, is she with you?"

"No, she's at the cottage. I called the old gent who lives next door to the cottage after I talked to you yesterday. I ask him to keep an eye out for her and to call me if he saw her. The old guy adores Michael. Anyway, he just called, said she pulled into the drive about ten minutes ago. I'm only calling you because you're closer. Go to her, Richard, but so help me God, if you hurt her any more I'll rip your balls off. You'll be singing soprano after I get through castrating you with a dull pair of cuticle scissors."

He got the picture. "Sarah, thanks."

Richard drove up the drive slowly and parked far enough away from the house so she couldn't see his car. He knocked on the door, praying she was all right.

Michael was so cold. She wanted a fire but was too tired to gather in wood from the back porch. Her trip up the coast was the most foolish thing she had ever done. After driving until she ran out of gas, she sat in the cold car until a highway patrolman pulled up in the wee hours of the morning and helped her get to a service station. With a full tank, she turned around and drove to the cottage.

The thermostat registered sixty degrees, but it felt colder than that. She turned up the heat and decided to get in bed until the small house warmed up. Then she heard the knock at the front door. It was probably Charles from next door. He watched the place like a hawk.

"Mikie, thank God you're all right."

Michael slammed the door in his face and started to cry. No, damn it, she would not let him make her cry, not now, not ever again. "Go away."

He beat against the door. "Mikie, let me in. Please, I need to talk to you. We need to talk. Open the door."

Michael went into the bedroom and crawled under the quilts, covering her ears with her hands, hoping to shut him out. Then she heard the door fly open and his footsteps on the floor as he searched the house. He came into the bedroom. He pulled the quilt down and reached for her, but she swung out the other side of the bed and ran for the kitchen. She almost made it to the back door when she felt his hands on her shoulders, pulling her back against him, foiling her escape.

She twisted out of his grip and shouted at him. "Don't touch me. Just go away. We have NOTHING to talk about, and if you don't leave, I'll call the police." Michael bit her lip, catching it between her teeth to keep from crying as she ran into the living room. He followed her, but this time he caught her hand and tried to pull her to him. "Richard, let go of me."

Richard drew back, slashed by the hatred in her eyes, but he didn't drop her hand. "My God, Mikie, you're freezing." He dropped her hand and tried a different strategy. "Okay, I won't touch you, but let me get you warm. Please?"

Michael didn't need to say a word; he read it in her eyes, which were cloudy now. They were also the window to her soul, and no matter how much she protested, her eyes asked for help. Richard rushed into the bedroom and grabbed the quilt. He wrapped it around her and led her to the sofa and then used the microwave to fix her a cup of tea. Nothing you'd serve to the queen, but at least it was hot.

Michael held the mug between her hands and relished the warmth. She sipped it slowly, careful not to burn her mouth and used the time to regain her composure. She didn't want to fight with Richard anymore, but she knew he would not leave until he had his say, and the sooner that happened, the sooner she could get packed and out of town.

"Thank you, Richard, for the tea. Now I want you to go. I don't want to argue with you. I'm too tired, and there's nothing left to say. You said it all yesterday." She put the mug on the table and found enough courage to look at him.

"I was wrong. Let me explain."

"Oh, yes, of course, just like you let me explain yesterday."

"I was caught off guard, Mikie— I..."

"Richard, please do not call me that. My name is Michael."

He started to sit beside her, but when she jumped, he moved to the mantel. "Well, I'm not going to call you Michael. I want—"

"Richard, do you know any other words besides 'I want?' Do you realize how selfish you are?"

"I don't mean to be selfish, but if loving you makes me selfish, then that's what I am."

Michael stared across the room in disbelief. "What did you say?"

"I said I love you."

"How nice, but why, Richard? What prompted this earthshaking announcement now?"

"I've loved you forever, since that first day when I stood in this very room and watched you throw out your chin—ready to take me on—to be the champion for a little boy you'd just met, to protect him against his neglectful father."

"That day was months ago... a lifetime ago. Why now?"

"I've wanted to tell you, I—"

"I know, Richard. You wanted to tell me, but you never got around to it, or you never found the right time. Or it was too cold or too hot, whatever. That's one of your problems, you know. You always think you can take the next train, but guess what, Richard. The last one left yesterday. I would have been the happiest woman alive to hear you say you loved me, even a day ago. Do you hear me, Richard? I would have."

Michael drew a pillow to her chest and closed her eyes. "I read once that you should never want something so badly that you can't live without it. Well, there it is. I wanted something I couldn't have." She opened her eyes and drew a deep breath. "But that's all in the past. It's too late. I'm going back where I belong, back to people who love me for who I am, people who don't drive me out of my mind with their emotional ups and downs."

"You can't go. I won't let you leave me. I won't let you do that to us."

"Richard, there is no 'us.' Can't you understand that? There's you and David, but no us."

"What about the baby? The baby is part of us."

Michael jumped to her feet only to fall back to the sofa. "How do you know about my baby?"

"It's our baby."

Michael grabbed her mug and hurled it across the room. She missed his head by an inch but knocked a picture off the mantel, sending it crashing to the floor. "This is my baby, damn you, not ours. Mine! You had better go. We have nothing more to discuss."

"I don't think so, Mikie. This is my child too, and I have a say about what happens to it."

"Like hell you do! Oh, now I see. How could I have been so stupid? Really Richard, you are so transparent." Sarcasm coated her words like concrete. "Here comes the doting father. Now he's ready to tell his pitiful little plaything for the past four months that he loves her—now that he's found out she's carrying his child. Well, welcome to the real world, Richard. I'm not Eve."

Michael gained a small sense of satisfaction seeing his face go pale. "That's right, Dr. Hampton, I know all about Eve. Marc cared enough about my feelings to tell me why you left our bed that night and almost killed yourself. You were afraid I was another Eve—another bitch of a woman who only wanted to make your life miserable. Well, you don't need any help from me, Richard; you make your own misery in this world."

"Will you listen to me? Please, listen to me. I came home yesterday morning to ask you to marry me, to tell you that I love you and want you to be my wife." He dug into his coat pocket and pulled out a small velvet box, which he held out to her. "I wanted to give you this. I didn't find out about the baby until late in the afternoon after you'd gone, when your doctor's office called." He started toward her, but she backed away.

"I love you Mikie. Please believe me. I've gone about this all wrong. I admit I've screwed everything up… but I do love you."

"Richard, it's too late. I'm sure, in your own mind, you think you love me, but don't you see? This goes way beyond love. It's about trust. I'm sorry for all the pain and the heartache you went through with Eve, but I can't fight it anymore. I thought I could. When Marc told me what happened, I actually believed that my love could make a difference. I told myself that if I didn't push you into any corners, if I showed you how much I loved you—day by day—, you would see that I wasn't like her. But I was wrong."

Michael stood and paced the room. She lowered her voice and continued. "You stood outside the library and heard what you wanted to hear. It never once occurred to you that there was an explanation. You simply knew I had betrayed you. Now you come here and beg me to let you explain, but did you offer me that chance? No. You just assumed I was like Eve."

Everything was so clear now, and for the first time Michael truly understood why he'd held back. "I don't blame you because I realize now why you never actually accepted my love. You never believed I could love you without any strings attached. How could you possibly love me when you could not trust me? You never trusted me enough to give me your love."

"That's not true. I trust—"

"No, no, you don't. When you really love someone, you make a commitment to reach beyond love. It's a giant step because you're saying you trust this person enough to care for your love, to nurture and protect this precious gift so it will be safe, so it can survive and continue to grow. But you can't do that. She hurt you so badly... you couldn't trust me. So how could you possibly love me?"

Richard turned to the mantel and wiped his tears from his cheeks. He searched for the right words. When he thought he could trust his voice, he said, "I know you're not like Eve, but I need you to believe me because I do love you. Please don't leave me. Please."

"I have to. I'm going home and having my baby. And, Richard, believe me when I tell you that I will take care of this baby. I meant it when I said I was not Eve. I want this baby, even more than you wanted David."

Michael turned away from him and faced the big window, totally drained. She threw open the glass and welcomed the morning mist as the ghostly sounds of the bay rose up into the hills. She listened to the clinking of the rigging—the rub and creaking of the fishing fleet that mingled with the shrilling staccato of seagulls and the bark of a seal. The dampness cleared her mind as surely as the mist chilled her soul.

"I might even get married. I had several offers after Ryan died. But then, maybe not. I don't really need anyone. But who knows. It's a wonderful feeling to know that you're wanted. You may not want me, but I'm sure I can find someone who—"

Richard pulled her into his arms and crushed her to his chest. "I'm never going to let you go, never. Marry me." He gripped her by her arms and demanded she look into his eyes.

"Marry me, Mikie. You can't marry anyone but me. You're hurt. I've hurt you, but I do love you. You're right, everything you said. I'm a selfish bastard, and I don't know much about trust, but I can learn. Give me a chance—let me take care of you, please. Look at me, Mikie. Please, just look at me. You know deep down in your heart that I love you. Help me, Mikie. I've lived so long with hate and bitterness, and I've worn that bitterness like a hair shirt, but I don't want to be like that anymore. Don't cry, Mikie. Oh, baby, please don't cry. Give me another chance. I swear to God, I won't blow it this time."

Richard gathered the quilt around her shoulders and lifted her in his arms. He held her against his chest as tears rolled from her eyes and cascaded down her pale cheeks, a lament so wretched Richard trembled with panic and he didn't know what to do, so he just held her tight.

He dropped into the chair and held her against his heart. He kissed her hair, her face, wiped at the tears until they were both covered with the dampness.

"Mikie, listen to me. We'll get married today. We'll go to Reno. It's only a few hours away. We'll put all this behind us, and we will create a new life."

"No." Her voice was so weak he barely heard her. "You only want my baby. No, I don't need—"

"Sh-sh, Mikie, it's okay. And that's not so. I do want you. You have to believe me. And I know you don't need me." Richard kissed the tip of her nose and felt Michael shudder against his chest. He wiped her tears with the back of his hand. "Look at me, baby. I know you don't need me, but I need you. I'm a fool, and I've treated you so badly, but I need you, and I love you, and you're going to marry me, and you're going to marry me today."

Richard lowered her onto the bed, tucking the quilt around her. "Rest, little one. Try and get some sleep while I make a few phone calls."

"I'm so tired."

"I know, my darling. Just try to rest."

In less than two hours, Richard had everything in place. Allen delivered Richard's bag with a few things for the short trip and a change of clothes for the wedding. Cassie and Allen would take care of David. While Michael slept, Allen took care of the car. Gas, oil, tires—, all checked and ready for the trip to Reno.

Richard quietly rummaged through the small closet in the bedroom. He found a stylish white crepe suit with gold buttons and put it in a garment bag. He took a change of underclothes and a silk nightgown from her dresser and put them in his bag.

"Mikie, it's time to go. Do you need to go to the bathroom before we leave?"

Michael tried to blink the sleep out of her eyes and listen to what he was saying, but she was so tired. Why was he waking her up? He'd just told her to go to sleep. She wished he'd make up his mind.

"Do you have to use the bathroom? Here, sit up, that's a good girl."

She was so dizzy. Oh God, she was going to throw up. Michael pushed him aside and ran for the bathroom. She lay on the bathroom floor with her head in the toilet as the retching spasms worked through her. Richard squatted next to her, holding a damp towel to her forehead.

"Go away. Richard, please, let me keep what little dignity I have left."

"No way. I'm here now, for the duration. You've dealt with this all by yourself for way too long, but not anymore. Is it over? Are you ready to get up?"

"The only thing I'm ready to do, Richard, is die. Just leave me alone." But he had no plans to leave her alone ever again.

Halfway to Reno, it started to snow. Inside, the car was warm and cozy. Richard played her music on the CD player, everything from U2 to Bach, hoping to make the trip more enjoyable for her, but down deep he knew she was too sick to care. He stopped three times during the first hour, holding her head as she bent over the side of the road and tried to empty an already empty stomach. He wanted to give her a shot to relieve the nausea, but she wouldn't let him give her anything because of the baby. Richard finally pulled off the freeway and found a grocery store. He bought a package of soda crackers and some ginger ale. After nibbling a cracker and keeping it down, she dozed off.

They were staying at the Plaza. Richard called ahead to make sure their rooms would be ready when they got to Reno. Marc had called a classmate of his who would marry them, a federal judge licensed by the state to perform marriages. Richard didn't mind a drive-through if he wanted a quick hamburger, but he wasn't about to get married that way. He still had the large diamond ring in his pocket. He'd bought the ring a month ago, right after he had demanded she see a doctor. Why hadn't he given her the ring and asked her to marry him then? He knew why. Because she hadn't pushed. He'd been so busy and worn out from work that she hadn't wanted to bother him, not even to tell him about the baby. A huge smile covered his face as he thought about their baby. Was it a boy or a girl? It really didn't matter, but he would like a daughter, a beautiful spitfire, just like her mother.

Their room was a large suite, filled with fresh flowers. The trip had taken more time because of the snow. Plus, getting their license took longer than he'd planned. He knew Michael was struggling, but she didn't complain; but then, she never complained. If they hurried and changed they could still be at Judge Baldwin's office before five. Richard decided to wait until they finished taking a shower and changed their clothes before he called the judge to confirm the time.

"Richard, I don't want to take a shower. I want to go to bed."

"I know, baby. We'll take it together. I'll help you."

Richard adjusted the water and let her lean against him as he tried to keep the water off her hair. After lathering them both, he held her while the warm water rinsed the soap away, then wrapped a warmed towel around her and dried himself.

Michael didn't offer any assistance. If he wanted her clean, he could do it himself. All she wanted to do was go to bed. What was the big hurry anyway? It wasn't as if he was being chased by a pissed-off father or a couple of rowdy brothers ready to shoot his lousy ass because he'd wronged their kin. Oh no, she was going to throw up again.

Before Richard could turn around, she was on the floor, her head against the side of the toilet. "Oh Lord, Mikie, here, let me help you. Better now? That's my girl." He led her out of the bathroom to the bed where he'd laid out her white suit.

"Can you get dressed by yourself? I have to run downstairs for a minute, but I can wait and help you."

Michael sat on the edge of the bed, still wrapped in the large towel. He was trying so hard, she thought as she forced a smile. Richard was trying to do the right thing, and she had to help him. She waved him off, "I'm fine now. You go on, I'll be okay. I'll be ready when you get back."

Twenty minutes later, Richard opened the door, and the first thing he heard was Michael sobbing. He dropped the nosegay of roses on the floor and ran into the bedroom.

Michael had gotten dressed. Well, she'd tried to. After he'd left the suite, she gathered all the conscious effort she could muster toward the task of making herself look like a bride. She found a bra and a pair of panties, but no stockings. She should have taken the time to pack her own things. Oh well, her legs were tanned enough; she would have to do without stockings.

She pulled on the straight skirt. The weight she'd gained had gone to all the wrong places. She'd started to spread across her middle, and she couldn't zip the back of the skirt all the way. *Don't panic,* she told herself. Maybe the jacket would cover the gap. Next, Michael decided she better do something with her hair and her face. *Surely a little makeup will help.* No makeup bag. *Okay, so makeup is not a man's thing. But he could have at least thought to throw in my hairbrush. Screw it; I can't worry about looking like a ghost having a bad hair day.* And besides, she had to throw up again.

Michael pressed the damp washcloth to her forehead. "I have to get dressed," she muttered to herself. Richard would be back, and she was only half-dressed. She fought with her bra, but unlike the skirt that might work half-zipped, there was no way she could fasten the bra without a six-inch safety pin. She threw the worthless bra across the bed and reached for the jacket.

If the skirt hadn't fit, why had she thought the jacket might? Even when she stood her tallest, sucking in her breath, she could only button two of the six buttons needed to cover her full breasts. *Okay, be cool, just think.* Maybe she could get him to buy a scarf, something to drape across her chest. Michael was out of breath, and she still had to find her shoes. That was where Richard found her.

"Richard, where are my shoes?" Michael was beyond holding back her tears. "I've looked everywhere, but I can't find my shoes." The look on his face answered her question. "I can't do this. I'm sorry... but I can't. Not today, tomorrow, not even a week from next Tuesday. Not like this."

Richard helped her out of the ridiculous suit and held her in his arms until she fell asleep. Then he put her in bed and went into the next room and poured himself a straight Scotch from the mini-bar. She'd called him selfish. If you added arrogant, stupid, self-serving, unreasonable, and naïve—, hell, he could go on all night. All he'd thought about was what he wanted. Not once had he realistically thought about what she wanted, or even worse, what she needed. He just wanted them married, before she could run away again.

She was so sick. He'd thrown her in the damned car, bought her a box of crackers, and driven her through a snowstorm, and then made her stand in line for their license. He'd hustled her into a shower she didn't want to take and then left her alone to get dressed for her wedding.

Richard drained the glass. He'd grabbed the first thing to touch his hand instead of looking through the closet for a dress that might be comfortable. And he forgot to pack a pair of dress shoes. Richard didn't blame her for crying or refusing to leave the room. He didn't blame her at all. The suit was bad enough, but no matter how much she loved them, he couldn't blame her for not wanting to get married wearing her black high-top tennis shoes.

CHAPTER TWENTY-EIGHT

"I JUST NEED SOMEONE WHO'S RELIABLE. I'll only be gone a few hours." Richard ended his call to the hotel's concierge and returned to the bedroom. He'd sat by the bed, watching, knowing she had finally given way to the primal need to sleep. But even in sleep her body twitched, her face taut and worrisome as the pillow absorbed her troubled murmurs. The sound of the doorbell sent him flying into the outer room before the noise could wake her.

"Good evening, I'm Mrs. Cook, the baby sitter."

The little lady smiled, and Richard relaxed his shoulders and knew she would do just fine.

"The concierge said you would fill me in on what I'm supposed to do."

"There's really not much for you to do. My wife is pregnant, and I'm afraid the trip was too much for her. She's asleep now, but I have to run some errands and I don't want her to be alone in case she should wake up and I'm not here. Oh, she's still experiencing some nausea from the baby, so if she does wake up you might have to help her to the bathroom if she has to, ah... if she feels the need to throw up."

"What a thoughtful man you are. Well, you run along. I'll take excellent care of her."

Richard rummaged through the room and found her purse. He searched inside until he found her wallet and flipped it opened. He studied the information on her driver's license. All he'd wanted to know was her height, weight—he knew the color of her eyes—, but he found more.

"Dr. Hampton?"

Richard turned to Mrs. Cook. "What? Did you say something?"

"Yes, sir. What is your wife's name, you know, in case she does wake up?"

"Her name is Michael. Everyone calls her Michael."

After writing the address of three stores on a slip of paper, Richard headed for his car. As he threaded into the traffic, he remembered the day she moved into his house. *"You can't begin to realize just how much you don't know about me."* That's what she said, and every day he realized how true her words had been. Two months ago, she had planned a big party to celebrate the removal of David's cast, or so she told him, and it was, in part, but it was also to celebrate Richard's birthday. His mother came from L.A. and Michael packed the house with his closest friends, even people from the hospital were there. Richard couldn't remember the last time he'd had such a birthday party.

He pulled into the parking lot and turned off the key. He wanted to buy her a dress, a special dress made of fairy dust and gossamer wings, and a pair of satin shoes fit for a queen. But he had to do more, because tomorrow was her birthday.

Feeling a little strange, Richard walked into the maternity shop. If he closed his eyes, he could see the dress he wanted, but as he wandered throughout the store, he realized he was in over his head and threw up his hands and started to leave.

"May I help you?"

Richard turned to the voice and looked down at a pudgy little woman, about fifty, with a lovely face and bright-red hair, just a shade lighter than the dress she wore. Her name was Mrs. Browning and she owned the shop. It said so on a heart-shaped pin attached to her chest.

"I sure hope so. I need to buy a dress, and a pair of shoes to go with it."

"I see. And this dress is for a special occasion?"

"A wedding, we have to attend a wedding. You see, I kind of screwed up. I mean, I brought the wrong bag. I left her things at home." Richard tried to laugh as he ran his hand through his thick hair, wishing she wouldn't look at him like his nose was growing, as if she already knew he was lying.

"Anyway, I need a dress, a special dress. Can you help me?"

"You bet your buttons, mister…?"

"Hampton, Dr. Hampton."

"Okay, Mr. Dr. Hampton, and how pregnant are we?"

"She's four."

Mrs. Browning threw up her hands, like a policeman directing traffic, only much more intimidating. "Stop. Wait, wait, wait."

Her words startled him. "What? What's the matter?"

"I can see you're new at this, so let's take it one step at a time. First of all, doctor, your wife is not the only one pregnant here. What's good for one is good for all. Remember the story about the gander? Right? Right. It's a common mistake, mostly made by men, but you look trainable. So, how pregnant are we?"

Richard felt like he was back in third grade. "We're four months."

"Good. Now then, is she to be in the wedding?"

"What?"

"Is she a member of the wedding party?"

Richard's eyes followed her well-manicured hands as they patiently tried to coax the words from him. "Yes. No, I mean."

"Well, okay, is there a special color you're looking for?"

"Yes, something for a wedding. I mean, just something soft."

"Okay, and what size? What size is your wife?"

"She's five-feet-five and weighs about one hundred and four pounds." Without realizing it, Richard placed his hand on his chest as he remembered where her head had rested when they'd danced.

"But she's been very sick, and she's so frail. I doubt she weighs more than a hundred pounds now." What was he doing? He wasn't even capable of a simple thing like buying a dress.

"Dr. Hampton? Are you all right? Do you need to sit down?" Mrs. Browning thought the man was going to pass out. The color drained out of his face as a film of perspiration covered his forehead and upper lip.

"No, thank you. I'm fine."

"Are you sure?"

"No, in fact, I'm not fine at all."

"Can I help?"

"Not unless you've got a few hours."

"Well, I think that can be arranged."

"She's not my wife. I mean, that's why we're here, to get married, but she's so sick." Richard paced back and forth and opened the top button of his shirt. *I fucked up,* he said to himself as he turned back to the owner of the shop. "Mrs. Browning, I've seriously fucked up."

"Oh... I see. Well, a, okay. Why don't you call me Marge?"

She ushered him into the back room, dug in the bottom drawer of a file cabinet, pulled out a bottle of brandy, and poured him a drink. He emptied the glass; she filled it again and then left the room. As it was almost closing time, she locked the front door and flipped the hanging sign over to read "closed."

"Here, eat." Marge placed a plate of cheese and crackers in front of him. "We have work to do, young man, and we don't need you shit-faced right now, and because I hate to see a grown man cry, especially such a good-looking one, I'm going to help you through this. Now, let's get down to business."

After Richard's third drink, Marge Browning realized she knew more about Richard and his feelings than he first intended to share. He started out with the truth that he had screwed up—royally—but at least he was trying to fix things and had enough guts to admit his mistakes and try to make amends. Plus, she hadn't had a good adventure in a long time, so she was going to help him get out of this mess.

She led him through the store by the hand, suggesting one dress and then another. Before the hour was up, he'd found everything, from underwear to Michael's wedding dress.

Richard smiled for the first time in days, delighted with their selections. The dress was an empire fashion, with a bodice of satin brocade, embroidered with tiny roses and scalloped at the neckline. The intricate needlework was a shade darker than the sheer long sleeves and the ankle-length chiffon skirt, the color of champagne. Satin shoes and a small clutch purse completed the outfit.

Richard gained a few points when he told Marge they would be married by a federal judge instead of one of Reno's neon-lit wedding chapels that offered to tie the knot in five minutes, including rice.

"What about the ring," she asked, "and the wedding dinner, the license, the photographer, the flowers, the bride's hair?" The list went on and on, but Marge had all the answers. She watched him squirm; then smiled and told him not to worry, she had it covered.

Two hours later, Richard took a deep breath and put the list Marge handed him safely in his wallet. She knew how to make a point, so Richard seriously considered her threats of severe injury if he didn't complete each and every item she had assigned to him.

Back at the hotel, Richard paid Mrs. Cook and thanked her as he saw her to the door. Mikie hadn't moved, although her face seemed less drawn, more at ease. Leaving the bedroom door ajar, he went to the bar in the living room and filled a large glass with club soda over ice.

Richard checked the next item off his list. He called Judge Baldwin, and they agreed on four o'clock tomorrow afternoon. Marge's list contained three restaurants she thought Michael might like, and Richard made a reservation for six o'clock at the Towers. His black suit went out to be pressed, his shoes shined, and he'd had his hair trimmed before returning to the suite. That was it. He folded the completed list and called Marc. After bringing his friend current on the situation in Reno, Richard asked another favor. Marc assured him, come hell or high water, Mikie's birthday present would be waiting for her when they returned to San Rio the next day.

Richard refilled his glass with the rest of the club soda and dropped into a chair. He pulled the three tiny boxes from his jacket pocket and opened each one. After leaving Marge, he met with a Mr. Penny. Twenty minutes later, Richard paid the jeweler as they shared a small shot of Jack Daniels and a verbal tribute to Mrs. Browning.

The first box held the four-carat emerald-cut diamond solitaire, set on a band of white gold that he had bought a month ago. When he showed her the ring, Marge had taken one look at it and told Richard that the ring was lovely, but...

He almost choked on his own spit. "Good God woman," he yelled at her. "Didn't she realize she was looking at a stone that had cost him a small fortune?"

"Bigger is not always better, Richard," she replied. "Any way, that is only an engagement ring. You still need a wedding ring. Trust me." So he had.

The second box contained two bands of channel-set diamonds that were delicate, but brilliant enough to guard the solitaire. Richard stared into the third box at the necklace and earrings. In the time it had taken him to drive to Mr. Penny's jewelry store, Marge had called and put in her two cents regarding the necklace to complement Mikie's new dress. Deep red, pear-shaped garnets set in gold would adorn her ears and a larger stone of the same design would hang about her lovely neck on its slender gold chain.

As Richard walked into the bedroom, he rolled his shoulders and neck. He sat on the bed, wondering if he should sleep on the sofa but then decided against it as he stripped out of his clothes. Michael still slept. Richard gently lifted the covers and edged in beside her, and as if drawn by an invisible magnet, she turned into his arms. It felt good to hold her like this—her head resting on his chest and moving only with the beat of his heart.

They slept until ten o'clock. Michael woke first and felt his arm across her waist. When she pushed back, just a fraction, she felt him molded against her like a second skin. How many times had she longed to wake this way and feel him next to her? Michael sorted through the last remnants of sleep and remembered that they hadn't gotten married after all. No, she had folded, wiped out by a flood of tears and repressed hysteria, and he had put her to bed. Would he still want to marry her today? *Of course, he wants the baby, and he knows he can't have my baby without taking me.* It was a package deal, but it worked both ways because beggars can't be choosers. What a sad saying, but it fit her perfectly. She loved Richard, and she wanted to be his wife. From the very first moment she realized how much she loved him, Michael knew she would have made a deal with the devil to be his wife. And even though she hadn't dealt with the devil, she'd sold out. If she had stuck to her original plan and moved away, would he have come after her? If he hadn't found out about the baby, would he have told her he did love her after all? There were too many ifs, and now she'd never know, but she would be his wife. Maybe today she would be Richard's wife.

Michael slipped out of bed without waking him. She picked up his discarded shirt and put it on. After calling room service for tea and oatmeal and a pot of coffee for Richard, Michael saw the stack of boxes and shopping bags by the sofa.

"Mikie, Mikie?" Richard ran into the living room and saw her sitting on the floor by the sofa, her hands holding her new clothes.

He smiled and drew in a breath, relieved she hadn't run away. "While you were asleep, I found this little shop and bought a few things." His answer to the questions in her green eyes didn't remove the quizzical look from her face.

"A few things? Richard, there are more clothes here than I have in San Rio."

He dropped to the floor beside her and kissed the tip of her nose, unable to resist a taste of her puckered mouth. His eyes sought the large box, thankful she hadn't gotten to it yet. He lifted her off the floor and made her close her eyes.

"Richard, what are you doing?"

"Humor me, Mikie. Just keep your eyes closed." He put the large box on the table. "Okay, open your eyes."

Michael fingered the gold mesh ribbon. "What have you done? What's in the box, Richard?"

"Why don't you open it and see?"

Michael smiled like a child at her first real Christmas and carefully untied the ribbon, then lifted the lid. The tissue paper was cool to her trembling fingers as she moved it back to reveal her dress.

"Oh, baby, don't cry. You'll spot the dress. Then Marge will kill me. Let me hold it up so you can see the whole dress." Richard held the dress in front of him, and her expression told him all he needed to know. She loved it.

By the time room service arrived, they had opened every box and bag, spreading clothes all over the furniture in the room. Richard opened the door as he fished in yesterday's pants for a tip. Along with the money, he found his to-do list. Closing the door, he reached for the telephone, muttering under his breath as he dialed her number.

"What's the matter? Richard, is something wrong?"

He held up his hand to her and said into the receiver. "Marge? We're up. Yeah, it felt great. I didn't think I'd sleep that long. Wait a minute." He handed the receiver to Michael. "I want you to talk to this lady."

Michael didn't know if she could handle another surprise. "Who is it? Richard, what are you up to now?"

"Here, just talk to her."

"Hello, I'm afraid Richard hasn't told me who this is."

"Sounds just like him, but don't worry. I plan to have him physically removed, very soon. You can call me Marge, better known as your fairy godmother. Hello? Are you still there?"

When Michael hung up the phone, it was to be the last independent act she would do that day, at least until she was ready to say "I do."

They dressed and finished breakfast and had just begun gathering up her new clothes when the doorbell rang. Marge entered the room with authority, followed by her helpers. Richard waited until his suit was delivered, and then Marge's husband, Glen, led him away, as promised. "Not to worry, dear," Marge told Michael, "he'll reappear at the appropriate time."

Marge ushered the bride-to-be into a tub of warm water sprinkled with fragrant oil. After a relaxing soak, Marge helped Michael wash her hair. With her wet hair wrapped in a towel, Michael was handed over to Lisa for a manicure; even her tootsies were trimmed and polished.

"I'd like to see your hair up, interwoven with flowers. What do you think, Lisa?" Michael listened to Marge and the hairdresser as they lifted and twisted her damp hair, realizing they had no intention of asking for her opinion. But she wasn't put out. In fact, she felt so calm, so relaxed, she didn't mind at all. The best part of the day still amazed her. She had not had the urge to throw up, not once.

"Who wouldn't need to throw up the way that jerk's treated you? But we'll keep the crackers handy, just in case." Marge delivered her words with a tone of conviction that led Michael to realize that this stranger, truly a newfound fairy godmother, knew more about their lives than just the fact they were in Reno to get married. Had she placed a spell on him? Had Marge transformed Richard from a toad into a loving prince, ready to jump through hoops or out the window if need be, to make her wedding a day she would never forget?

It was time to go. She'd had some lunch, which stayed put, and her hair was brushed and twisted with delicate strands of garnet-colored ribbon and petals of white pearl hyacinths. She stepped carefully into her new wedding dress. It fit like a dream.

"What? You expected something else? Hey, I'm a card-carrying member of the Magician's Guild. One last thing, then we're out of here." Marge reached into her bag and pulled out the velvet box. "Richard wanted to give this to you before he left, but I talked him out of it."

Michael took the box, overwhelmed by all the gifts and pampering she had received today, but when she opened the box, she simply couldn't speak.

"He picked them out after he bought your dress." Marge lifted the necklace from the box and hooked it around Michael's neck, then set the earrings. She held Michael by her shoulders and kissed the side of her cheek.

Michael's hand touched the garnet around her neck. "He's given me so much. I didn't need another gift."

"It's customary for the groom to give a gift to his bride and Richard wanted me to tell you that it comes with all his love. Now, let's go get married."

Richard paced the floor in the chambers of the honorable Judge Baldwin as the judge and Glen Browning enjoyed a sip of sherry before the ceremony. "Are you sure they knew the time?"

"Just relax. She'll get your lady to the judge on time, trust me."

When they walked through the door, Richard searched for words to describe how incredible his bride looked. Beautiful, elegant, enchanting, and bewitching were simply not enough, so he just gazed silently—spellbound.

Michael's cheeks glowed like spring rosebuds kissed by the sun. The dress flowed straight to her ankles. No one would ever guess that a tiny child lay snugly beneath the chiffon, silently, ready to witness their coming together as they pledged their love and promised to cherish one another for the rest of their lives.

"With this ring, I thee wed." Only an hour ago Richard had said those words to her. Michael gently touched the three rings he had placed on her finger. The first band of diamonds was for the baby, he said, the solitaire for him, and the last band was for David.

Glen stood and offered a toast. "To the happy couple— life, liberty and the pursuit of happiness."

"Damn, Glen, you've had too much bubbly. I better take him home before he starts reciting the Gettysburg Address."

Marge, Glen, Judge Baldwin, and his wife had joined them for a toast at the Towers. Marge lifted her glass one last time. "Take care of her, Ritchie boy. You've got a treasure there." She walked into his open arms and received more than a hug of thanks.

"You don't need to say a thing. I haven't had so much fun in years." She took Richard's face between her chunky hands. "Remember our talk? Good. Be happy, love. It's going to be okay."

She then pulled Michael into her arms and hugged her tightly. "Just because you live in another town, don't forget me. You know, I have broom, will travel."

And then, they were alone. Michael didn't remember much about their dinner except it'd been ordered for a woman with a delicate stomach and was certainly not your usual wedding fare. She didn't think Richard minded at all. Then they danced, or rather he held her close to him on the dance floor while others whirled around their slow pace.

When they returned to their suite, Richard helped her undress. He removed the flowers and brushed her hair, then carried her to bed.

"I promised to call home. David doesn't know what we've been up to, but Allen said he would keep him up until we called." He pulled the phone onto the bed and dialed the number. "David? Yes, it's Dad. Yes, Michael is here. We have some news for you." Richard looked into her face. "Well, David, if you could have anything in the world, what would it be?" Richard's grin turned into a full-blown smile. "Right on, buddy. No, I'm not kidding. Would I do that? Here, talk to Michael."

"David, are you okay? What? Yes, David, we were married a few hours ago. I love you too. What? Well, David, thank you, but how did you know it's my birthday?" Now it was her turn to look at Richard.

"I can't wait. Yes, we'll be home tomorrow." She raised an eyebrow to Richard and received an affirmative nod. "Yes, David, I'm listening. What? I think that would be the best present I've ever had. Yes, David, I'd like that more than anything in the whole world."

Michael had cried more during the past four months than she had in her entire life, and she decided it had to stop, but she could not stop the stream of tears rushing down her face when she hung up the phone.

Richard drew her into his arms. "Why are you crying? What did David say to make you cry?"

She wiped her face with the back of her hand. "He wished me happy birthday. How did you know it was my birthday?"

"Are you crying because he wished you a happy birthday?"

"No, of course not. I'm crying because he wanted to know if he could call me mom."

CHAPTER TWENTY-NINE

INFECTIOUS GIGGLES ROLLED TOWARD RICHARD as he walked through the back door. His smile broadened into a wide grin. It was a pleasure to walk into a house that had never been a home until Mikie. David and two of his friends crowded around the oak table in the kitchen playing a game as Bo gnawed at a big rawhide bone at their feet.

"Hi, Dad, I'm winning. You wanna play? You gotta practice if you gonna beat Mom. She's good."

"No thanks, son, maybe later. Where is Mom?"

"She's upstairs. Cassie told her to go rest. Wait a minute, you guys, I gotta talk to my Dad." David pulled Richard into the hallway. "Dad, we gotta talk. Cassie says it's not good for Mom to walk up and down the stairs. So why is Mom still sleeping in her old room?"

Richard unconsciously ran his hands through David's hair. He didn't have an answer to give his son. He offered to help Michael move her things into his room as soon as they returned home from Reno, but she gave one excuse after another why she wasn't ready yet. He could understand the first week. Marc and Amy hosted a reception for the newlyweds at the club. Friends came to call, offering their congratulations. All the celebrating had taken a toll on Michael, and then came Thanksgiving. Michael asked Caroline to stay over for the holiday and with his mother in the house, Richard thought surely she would share his room. Wrong, but she did make Thanksgiving day the best he and David had ever had.

That was two weeks ago. Michael had stepped into the role of his wife with grace and ease, except she would not move into his room. First she claimed she didn't want to disturb his sleep and that she still felt queasy at night. That was a lie. Then she was too tired to move everything; give her a few days. He had. He pressed; she volleyed. How could she share a room with him? He was neat, and she was a slob. He didn't care; he'd adjust. Had she moved? No.

Richard realized it could go on like this forever if he didn't take control. After all, he told himself as David waited for his answer, he was the dad here. Why should he be afraid of someone almost half his size?

"David, it's just that she's been so sick and wanted to wait until she felt better."

"I can help. We can all help, and she won't have to do anything. She can just be the leader."

"I'll tell her what you said."

Richard knocked, out of habit, before opening the door. Michael came out of the bathroom dressed in her oversized terry robe, drying her hair with a towel.

"I knocked."

"This is your house, Richard. You don't have to knock. Did you have a good day?"

"Yes, it was fine, no major problems. How are you feeling? David said Cassie told you to rest."

"I'm fine, really." Michael watched him pace back and forth in front of the bed. The CD player filled the room with Tchaikovsky's Concerto and Michael knew she should turn down the volume, but then maybe he didn't intend to stay long. "Did you want something?"

"Yes, we have to talk about you moving downstairs."

"Richard, I told you—"

"I know what you've told me, but it's been weeks. Even David wants to know what's holding up the move."

"Really, Richard, why are you dragging David into this?"

"Because he just asked me. He wants to know why you're still up here. I think you've exhausted every viable reason not to make the move. I know you're not sick anymore. You should be caught up on your sleep. David said you could be the leader, and we'd do all the moving. Sounds like a good plan. At least, it works for me."

"Well, it doesn't work for me."

"Why? Just give me one damn legitimate reason why."

"Stop pacing like a wounded elephant."

Richard took her by the hand and pulled her to the sofa. "Okay, you sit. I'll sit."

"Fine."

"Fine. Well? Do you have one, a good reason not to move?"

"Yes, I do. This is very difficult for me, I mean… but you're right. We have to talk. I can't back away from this any longer. I'm afraid. Yes I am; I'm afraid. Tell me, Richard, tell me where I go when I do something you don't like, and you know I will. What happens to me when you decide to draw your own conclusions about something I've done? Where do I go until you cool down enough for me to explain my actions? Would you rather I run away again? Or just go to my own room?"

Michael dropped her head to her chest, trying to find the right words. "Did we solve any of our problems when we got married? I don't think so; nothing has really changed. You went out of your way to make our wedding day so beautiful, and I'll always be grateful to you for that. But why did you do it? What heavenly sign turned you around? Or did you just feel guilty?"

"I love you. I'm trying to make you understand that. Okay, sure, I felt guilty, and maybe some of what I did was because of the despicable way I'd treated you, throwing you in the car and heading for Reno. When we started out, it wasn't my intention to make you more miserable than you already were, but that was only part of the reason. I love you and I wanted our wedding day to be special."

"I'm sure, in your own way, you do love me, but I waited four months for you to tell me. You waited until you found out about the baby, then decided things had to be your way. Then you wanted to marry me, just hours after you'd thought the worst about me—when you wouldn't even give me a chance to explain. You hurt me with the things you said. You hurt me very badly."

Now it was Michael's turn to pace. "Do you think this is easy for me? I'm trying to work this out, but I'm so confused. Maybe I'm being selfish. I mean, you did marry me, and I know you want the baby. So what more could I want?" Michael stopped pacing and sat on the coffee table in front of him.

"Richard, I love you so much, but you're like a virus, and I have no immunity. Ever since the night of the storm, since the first time you kissed me, it's like I'm tied up with a rope and every time you have doubts about me or you're confused about your own feelings, you toss me over a cliff where I hang by that rope. Oh, you pull me back—you've always pulled me back, but after months of chafing against the rocks, the rope is frayed and the next time, it might not hold. I just need time, and my own space."

Richard unclenched his hands and told himself to remain calm. How could he make her believe he wasn't going to act like that anymore? Why couldn't she just accept that he loved her? Why couldn't she trust him?

"How many times do I have to tell you I'm sorry? And do you have to play that damn music so loud? No, I take it back. That's not music. Tchaikovsky was a lunatic. What was he thinking when he composed that concerto? It doesn't compliment the violin, just beats it black and blue. And where is your diamond?"

Michael fingered the two circles of gold and diamonds on her hand. "I put it in the safe. It's so big. I thought I might damage it."

"Then I'll buy you another one."

Bristling but trying to stay calm, Michael broached another subject. "There's something else we need to discuss. The car, my birthday present, I can't accept it. Besides, I already have a car. You'll just have to take it back."

"Get real, McCall. No one returns a Porsche. I thought you liked it. You told David you loved it, that it looked like a new shiny red wagon. I'm sorry I couldn't find you another bathtub, but who in their right mind would want to return a new Turbo Carrera?"

Richard jumped up from the sofa. "This is bullshit, McCall. It has nothing to do with your not needing a new car, or damaging a ring. You just don't want them because I bought them, because I gave them to you."

Michael's laugh was not meant to be funny. "So, now I'm McCall again. I think it's time you left before you have a stroke. I have to dress for dinner."

"Fine." He walked to the door. "But know this, McCall, I'm not returning your car, and I want you to wear the damn ring. I'll see you at dinner."

By the time Michael changed the disc on the CD player and turned the volume up full blast, Richard was back. Michael cocked her head, threw out her chin, and stood her ground, ready for round two. "What?"

"I'm sorry." Richard wondered if he'd ever learn to keep his mouth shut about her music as he watched the pictures bounce on the wall while Tina Turner shouted out the lyrics of "Missing You." Michael's eyes blazed with fire as she clenched her fists and rammed them onto her hips. Richard walked to the CD player and lowered the volume. His eyes asked permission, and she answered with a shrug of her shoulder.

"I'm sorry I lost my temper, but I won't have angry words between us. Not even for a minute, not ever. Weeks ago I would have pouted for days, but not now. I'm trying, princess, I really am. I know I'm selfish, self-centered, blind to facts or simple reason, but for years I've lived in this neat little box, surrounded by my grandiose self-pity and paranoia. I've trusted no one—no one completely— except David, and I almost ruined him. But he fought back; he found you."

He stood close, but he didn't touch her. "You came into our house and made it a home. It was easy to save David; he didn't have a lot of bad habits. With me, well, that's the problem. You see, I am a lost cause. Even though you bewitched me from the start, old habits die hard. Your love saved David from being like me, but, being the stubborn bastard that I am, you're going to have to work harder with me. I need someone to exorcize my demons and you're it."

What he needed now was air. Richard opened the French doors and drew the dampness deep into his lungs. "You gave me your love, Mikie, and I'm not giving it back. It's the greatest gift I've ever had, and I'm not going to let anything or anyone destroy what we have. I am going to convince you that you're not wrong to love me. I'm going to show you there can be trust between us. To start with, I'm not going to return the Porsche, but you don't have to drive it. I would like you to wear your diamond, but I'll understand if you don't. I won't press you to share my bed, but I pray to God that you'll want to, and soon. I have all the time in the world—I can wait. What I can't do, what I won't do, is live without you."

Richard took her into his arms. His kiss was gentle when he kissed the corners of her mouth. He didn't hurry when he felt her shudder or when her tongue met his and invited him in. Inch by fascinating inch, he slowly rediscovered her face as he kissed her eyes, her slender neck, swallowed her moans as he again sought her lips. He teetered on the edge of sanity as his hands removed the towel and inched into her hair, when they cupped her face, even when she rocked gently against him as his desire and rampaging need for her pulsed between them, but then he lost it.

Michael felt a jolt of lightning rush through her at his touch, flashing and electrifying as it built into a violent storm. How long could she hold out? Even now, her ragged emotions threatened mutiny, weakened to the point of destroying her resolve not to be led by her heart, ready to surrender and cross over the battle field and join forces with him. When Richard cried out her name, crushing her to him, she didn't care anymore. It didn't matter who won or lost. He only asked her for the same thing she demanded of him: trust. He had stormed out of her room in anger but returned just as quickly, to make it right, just like their wedding day. He had made it right—he'd made it perfect.

"Was it Mikie or McCall I just kissed?" he whispered in her ear as he nuzzled her hair. "Do you know? I find it extremely hard to tell the difference. I better leave now so you can get dressed."

Michael opened her eyes and fought for balance when Richard moved to the door, and as she grabbed the back of the sofa for support, his face lit up with a mischievous smile that finished her off.

"You know, Mikie, when you listen to Tina Turner, I think it's written somewhere you have to have the volume turned all the way up. Go ahead and turn it up, darlin'. What do we care what the neighbors think? Don't be late for dinner."

CHAPTER THIRTY

"WAKE UP PRINCESS. IT'S A little drippy outside, but the weatherman promises we'll see the sun sometime today."

Michael raised her head off the pillow and peeked at Richard from half-closed eyes. "What time is it?"

"Six-thirty."

"It's still dark time. Go away." She pulled the covers over her head.

Richard pulled them down again. "It's not dark time; the sun is just hiding, like you are. Here, I brought you a cup of hot chocolate. Careful now, sit up."

Michael leaned forward as he fluffed the pillow behind her back. For a week now, ever since the night he promised she would never be sorry for loving him, Richard came to her each morning before he left for the office. He brought her hot chocolate or herbal tea and coffee for himself. The tray usually held a piece of fruit or something extremely sweet and sinfully good, guaranteed to fatten her up. One morning David wandered in, along with Bo, and they had a real party, but usually, it was just the two of them.

"I have to go. A friend of mine is bringing his daughter in today. He called me yesterday, seemed extremely upset. I haven't seen Jake Simpson in months. Seems his daughter is having some problems and her regular doctor hasn't been able to help her. I'd like you to meet him sometime."

When he bent to kiss her good-bye, Michael couldn't resist pulling him closer, seeking more this morning than his usual light and tender kiss. "Drive carefully," she whispered. "This mist makes a mess of the roads."

"I can probably reschedule today if you need me here."

"I'll be fine; I know you have to go. Good-bye, and Richard, wipe that silly grin off your face. Just be careful."

Later that night, David ran into the living room three seconds behind his voice. "Mom, it's the hospital on the phone."

Michael took the portable phone from him. "Hello. Yes, I see. Oh no, that's terrible. Please tell him not to worry about us. Thank you for calling."

David curled into her on the sofa. "Is my dad coming home?"

"Not for a while. He's had a problem at the hospital. It may be a few more hours before he's able to come home."

Michael and David spent the next hour in the spare room they were redoing for the new baby. David had been so excited when he found out they were married and that Michael would be his mom, but when they told him about the baby, the boy puffed up like a young rooster. He was going to be a big brother. He didn't care if it was a boy or a girl; he just couldn't wait. David marked the month of April on the new calendar he kept in his room with bold red letters. "BABY COMING."

Michael tucked David in for the night and opened a new book, but after reading the same page three times, she put it down. She knew Richard would be delayed. Ruthie called her about six to say Richard would not be home for dinner. She told Michael he'd scheduled an emergency surgery on a young woman, and he'd probably be home by eight. But Richard was still in the OR, literally fighting to save the girl's life. There was nothing Michael could do but wait. When he hadn't come home by eleven o'clock, she went to bed.

Richard turned off the engine and dropped his head to his arms folded against the steering wheel. He pressed his eyes, burning with weariness, against his arms and shivered with fatigue and failure. His whole body shook with tides of despair and unwanted memories that had followed him home. Finally, he opened the car door, stepped into the rain, and saw the light from the kitchen. Richard glanced at his watch. It was one-thirty in the morning.

Michael waited for Richard by the table. She started toward him, but a warning voice whispered in her head. *Give him time, Michael.* The look on his face overwhelmed her, so drawn, a look of raw, troubled grief. Richard tried to smile, tried to disguise the deep despair she had first seen when he'd entered the room. But for all his efforts, the sorrow and dejection lay naked in his eyes.

"Hi, Mikie. Isn't it awfully late for you to be having dinner?"

Michael had forgotten the sandwich she held in her hand. "Your daughter was hungry. She doesn't know how to tell time yet. Have you eaten anything tonight?"

"No, I wasn't hungry."

"Do you want me to fix you something, some soup or a sandwich?"

"Ah... that's fine. It doesn't matter, whatever you're having."

"Well, we're having peanut butter and lettuce. Is that okay?"

"What? Sure, that's fine. I'll go wash up."

Michael fixed the sandwich, but when Richard sat down, she knew he wouldn't eat. He looked drained, hollow, his thoughts a million miles away.

After one bite, which stuck in his throat, Richard dropped the sandwich to the plate. "I guess I'm not hungry after all."

"It's the sandwich, it's dry. Let me fix you something else."

"No, the sandwich is fine, really. I'm just tired. I think I'll just go to bed." He kissed her and left the room.

Michael put the dishes away and turned off the lights. When she reached the stairs, she knew she should go to him. She found him sitting on the edge of his bed, his head in his hands. He'd managed to take off his shoes and trousers and unbutton his shirt. Michael walked to the bed and pushed his legs open and stood between his thighs. She pulled him into her arms, and his silent tears covered her silken gown as she held him against her breasts.

"She's dead," he whispered. "She died in the operating room. Oh God, Mikie. She was so young, but no matter what I did, I couldn't save her. It didn't have to happen. If only she'd come to me sooner, maybe I... In the name of God, Mikie, why couldn't I save her? I tried...I tried so hard."

Michael stroked the side of his head, ran her fingertips along his temples, rubbed where his pulse thundered under her thumb. The smell of his body blended with hers, seeped into her skin as Michael pulled him closer and used her body to communicate. She wanted to remove the burden he carried. He needed to vent, to scream, do something... anything to release the despair and the anger. She needed to help him, force him to change this sense of failure into harsh need, to help him let go of the bad and give it to her. Michael let her gown slip to the floor. "Love me, Richard. Let me share this with you. Make love to me. Now, love me now."

Richard's fingers snaked into her hair, his hands clutching the silky strands as he pulled her head back, baring her slender neck. His tongue delivered an incredibly light massage, savored the smooth skin of her throat, found her ear, then her mouth, and thrust wildly into the warmth. His mouth devoured hers, sucking gently, then harder. Richard's teeth cut against her flesh as he drew her tighter into the folds of his arms. He pulled away, looked at her with eyes that questioned, dark and searching. He saw her response and moved on.

When his mouth found Michael's breast, her head reeled and fell back. Her breathing slowed, and then caught up with her racing heart when his hand slid down past the softness of her rounded belly to that tiny spot that screamed for his attention. Richard's fingers grazed over hot, sensitive flesh—slowly, back and forth, in frenzied circles, stroking, kneading, possessing, until her body went rigid, her back arched, and she cried out his name in jumbled whimpers. A jagged spear of orgasmic pleasure shot through her, a shuddering rhythmic explosion, causing her legs to buckle. But he held her tight.

Richard felt her release, held her close, feeling each tremor as it pulsed against his hand. She was so hot against his chest, twisting and molding, and as his tongue spread moisture across her parched lips, she begged him for more. He began again. Richard's skilled fingers tormented her—, accurate, adventurous, relentless—as his mouth moved between her swollen breasts, suckling, nipping, driven now by an inherent need of his own, until her body again shivered with taut spasms of elation.

They fell onto the bed, lips and bodies bonded together, slick, sweating, and dampened by frantic desire and longing. He felt wired, like the air before a storm. Feelings locked away for years stirred deep within him, the desire to give and take and please, so physically keen, rising to the surface as he slowly slipped into her. He kissed her blazing green eyes and parted lips, swallowing her beseeching whispers before he thrust deeply, rapidly, holding her hips with his hands, never taking his eyes off her face as repressed current gathered force and broke free, then gathered again.

Michael felt him tense, the sharp evidence of his orgasm beginning to build, as she held his gaze that spoke of urgency and need. A low moan escaped his closed lips and then he stopped. Richard took her face between his powerful hands. He kissed her eyes with the tip of his tongue as their breathing slowed. Every emotion pulsed strongly in unison. Michael watched his eyes narrow as he set a new rhythm. He began to move with a wicked slowness, in and out of her glistening body, increasing his desire, satisfying his hunger. Thrusting in, then drawing out, pulling her with him, faster now, wave after wave until she heard him scream her name through a haze that threatened to overshadow her consciousness. Then he fell limp against her.

His heart pounded radically within his chest, and Richard felt like he'd been tossed by a violent sea—forced to hold his breath to keep from drowning, pushed to the point of accepting death, flipped and twisted by tremulous waves, then carried to the safety of the shore. He waited, hands gripping her hair, waited as tremors and heat oscillated over and through his spent body, purging, washing him clean, like baptism, leaving him chaste, freed from the guilt and despair that had followed him home.

He felt her move beneath him and rolled to his side, freeing her from his weight. Richard lifted damp curls from her face and smiled as she purred against his hand. She lay still, her eyes closed, giving him time to sort through what had just happened to them. Richard had made love to his Mikie McCall almost every night for over four months, but never in his life had he felt such power, such humility.

But he had used her harshly. He came home completely shattered, like a puzzle with pieces missing, and found her waiting. He came to her a mass of emotions, like twisted threads with zero value—utterly useless, waiting to be discarded—, but he totally underestimated her love, again. Mikie had retrieved each thread, patiently working out the knots until all the strands—his anger and rage, his self-doubt and his pain—lay intertwined, woven together into a beautiful and cohesive garment of strength and love. She had fought his rage with a fire of her own, refusing to lose him, determined to make things right.

"Did I hurt you?" Richard turned on the light by the bed and winced when he saw her face glowing red from his day-old beard. He gently touched her crimson breasts, also victims of his beard, then moved to her stomach where their child rested. Richard cupped the small mound with his hand, felt the warmth, then bent and kissed her smooth skin.

Then he shot up and stared into her eyes. "Mikie, did you have an ultrasound?"

"Richard, what are you talking about?"

"Did you have an ultrasound and forget to tell me?"

"No. Of course not. Why would you think that I—"

"You said our daughter was hungry. You were up when I came home because she was hungry."

"So?"

"Well, if you haven't had ultrasound how do you know it's a girl?"

Michael couldn't help it; she laughed. Maybe more freely than was necessary, but after the past few hours, it just felt right to laugh.

"Mikie, stop laughing and answer me." Richard pulled her into his arms, her back against his chest. He tickled her naked ribs, which only released another squeal of laughter.

"I just know she's a girl. I don't need any medical screening to know. You'll just have to trust me on this." She waited for a moment, looked back at his face. "Will you be disappointed if our baby is a girl?"

He felt Michael relax into him as he pulled her close and spread his hands over her middle. "Of course I won't be disappointed. Why would you think that?"

"Most men want a son."

"I have a son... we have a son. I would love a daughter, just like her mother, beautiful and silly and strong, someone to take care of her dad when he's old and feeble."

Sometime later, well after he had loved her again, but this time with a gentleness guided by love, as the mist cleared and the morning birds cleaned their wings and sang their songs, they slept.

"Richard, I can't go to a concert tonight. I have a doctor's appointment today. How long have you known about this charity affair, and why didn't you tell me sooner? My appointment is at two. I won't have time to come home and change and be back in the city for a concert."

Richard watched as she paced about her room. He had brought her hot tea and a fresh biscuit with honey. In the middle of a step, he lifted her against his chest, rocking her back and forth as her feet sought the carpet. "Easy, princess, you'll blow a gasket." He kissed the tip of her nose and lowered her to the floor.

"I didn't tell you earlier because I didn't know if you'd feel like going, but I have it all worked out. Allen will drive you to San Francisco for your appointment. You can take your dress-up clothes with you, and after your appointment, he will deliver you to Holly. Now, wait a minute before you shoot holes in my plan. Wait, you have butter on your chin."

Richard licked the butter off her chin then ran his tongue over her half-opened mouth. "Hum, where was I? Mikie, I wouldn't even think about going to this affair, I could send a check, but this is Holly's baby, so to speak. It's the only charity she worked with this year, and she would be crushed if we didn't attend. She's the one who suggested that you come to their house to change and get ready. She's even allotted time for you to rest before I meet you at the concert hall."

Richard knew all the right buttons to push to get her to do what he wanted. Michael very dramatically threw up her hands in submission. "Well, why not, it will be fun. Are you going to feed me?"

Richard smiled. "Of course I'm going to feed you. Here, open wide." He shoved a piece of a biscuit, dripping with honey into her mouth.

"No," she mumbled around the piece of biscuit. "I mean tonight." She pushed him away as he tried to help with the dripping honey.

"Yes, my love. You'll have a snack with Holly, and I'll fill you up after the concert, I promise. Now, come give me a kiss. I've got to go."

Richard savored the taste of butter and honey as he took his time telling her good-bye. Finally, he pushed her to arms' length and licked his lips. When he found his breath, he said, "See you tonight."

As he pulled out of the driveway, Richard wished he'd enough courage to bring up the forbidden subject of her moving downstairs, but it could wait another day. Tonight had been planned since last summer, and even with all the detours, all the twists and turns that had crossed their paths since then, he felt lucky to be pulling this off. No, he'd waited this long; he could wait another few days. At least she was wearing his ring every day and driving the little red Porsche. That was something.

Michael checked her list one last time before starting the engine. "He'd forget his head if... Well, you know the rest of that story." Michael settled behind the wheel of the Porsche and adjusted her seat belt. "Come on, Allen, we're late."

"You're sure you don't want me to drive?"

"Get in and shut the door and don't bend that bag or his shirt will wrinkle."

"You want me to drive?"

"I heard you the first time. No, I'm driving; buckle up. He forgot his clothes on purpose; I know he did. I should have known he wouldn't let me drive my little car into the city. It's not fair, you know. He buys me a racy new car but won't let me take it over the bridge. Go figure."

Michael synchronized her reflexes with the fine-tuned sports car after the first turn, gearing down with a smile as Allen gripped the door panel with white knuckles. By the time she pulled into the doctors' parking lot, she felt great, but she had to hurry. Richard told Allen they had to swap cars, and this side trip would put them behind schedule but then he also had forgotten his tux and evening attire.

"Want me to take the clothes up to his office?"

"No, we're running out of time. You switch the cars, and I'll meet you at the front circle. Besides, I want him to know I'm really ticked off that we have to take the big car. Don't frown, Allen, I'm only kidding. See you in a few minutes."

Richard was with a patient when she reached the office, so she gave Ruthie his evening clothes. "Tell him he lucked out this time, but I'll get him later. Michael hurried out of the office and headed for the elevator."

"Michael?"

Hal Green walked toward her. "How you doing, gal? I was going to call you." He gave her an affectionate hug.

Michael checked her watch. She really needed to go, but he looked like he wanted to say something, also a bit embarrassed. "Hal, it's good to see you. Is anything wrong?"

"No. In fact, actually, everything is great. I just wanted to tell you, I mean... I wanted to say thank you. Did Richard ever tell you that we've known each other for years? He's not only my partner, he's my friend, so I know what Richard's like, how he's always dealt with tragedy by shutting himself off from those of us who love him. But a person can only handle so much internal anguish, and after a while, its starts to eat away at your soul.

"When his young patient died last week, Richard blamed himself, which is only natural. But it wasn't his fault; I told him so. I hated the thought of him being alone that night, trying to sort out this kind of guilt, but when I saw him the next day, well, he was still upset, but he didn't blame himself anymore, and he said it was because of you. He said that you had refused to let him carry his doubts and guilt alone and that you forced him see beyond the horror of losing a patient— that your strength and love opened the way for him to find the courage to accept the fact that it's a higher order that calls the shots. You made the difference, Michael. For the first time since I've known Richard, he allowed someone into that dark place he has always gone to hide. You helped him; you helped make it right. And I just wanted you to know and to thank you for showing him how to love again."

He walked her to the elevator. Hal hugged Michael again, then said good-bye. As she walked toward Allen waiting by the black car, she tried to comprehend all he'd said, when the impact of his words penetrated her soul. She knew that Richard had always kept his feeling locked away. That fact had almost ruined their chance to share a life together. But he had talked to Hal, had openly shared private thoughts and feelings about how she had helped him.

She really had made a difference. Hal Green would never know the gift he'd just given her. She tried that night to be Richard's beacon in the fog, guiding his anger and despair into a secure haven, to lay at a safe anchor until the haze lifted and he could see clearly that he wasn't to blame. He'd let her see him naked—raw and hurting. He let her lead him back to sanity. He loved her. He trusted her.

The trip to San Francisco went quickly as Michael continued to ponder not only Hal's words, but also the significance they held. Richard had trusted her that night. Instead of sending her away, he had accepted her offer to help him through a dark time, knowing she would ask no questions, give no false pity. That she offered her body to him with love, to vent his rage and to wipe away his doubts about himself, and it had worked.

Dr. Sweet sent her out the door with smashing news. She had gained some weight, her blood was behaving, and he would see her in a month. She was in and out on schedule and Allen got her to Holly's house on time.

Holly insisted she rest, and Michael couldn't convince her she felt fine. She didn't want to rest. She wanted to see Richard. It was time, time to put all this fuss about the bedroom behind them. Sure, he'd hurt her—but it was time she saw the truth. For weeks, she had told herself that given time, he would come to love her like she loved him. What a fool she'd been. He did love her. He had been telling her so, not only with his glorious words, but each day he was so attentive and every deed was a gesture of love. That thought removed her frown, replacing it with a devilish smile.

"What happy bee crawled under your bonnet?" Holly came into the study carrying a tray. "This is your snack," she announced. "Your husband called to make sure I didn't forget to feed you."

Michael paced like a caged cat. "I should have told you that I wanted to talk to him if he called." Michael reached for one of the tiny tea sandwiches, pacing the room as she ate. He told her he would be in the OR all afternoon. When had he found time to call just to make sure she had a snack? She wanted to whirl around the room and kick up her heels with delight. He loved her.

Michael took a cup of tea from Holly but still didn't sit down. She stopped by Holly's desk, a beautifully carved 18th century piece. Her eyes were not looking for anything special, but when she saw tonight's program on the desk, they doubled in size. "Holly, is this the program for tonight?" It was a stupid question because the date was printed right on the program.

"Yes, it's going to be marvelous. We sold out the first month. Sometimes it pays to go out on a limb and present something different. I owe Richard a big kiss."

"This is terrible. I have to call Richard. I'm sorry Holly, but we won't be able to attend."

"Michael, what are you talking about? Of course you're going to attend. You're already here, and Richard is going to join us."

"You don't understand. Richard doesn't like this music. No, that's too mild. I mean, the correct word here is HATE. I wish he had told me sooner so I could have checked with you regarding the program."

"Are we talking about the same Richard? Honey, stop pacing and look at me. Michael, your Richard requested this program. He badgered me for weeks to do this selection until I finally gave in."

Michael stood in the middle of the room, shaking her head in disbelief. "But he hates Tchaikovsky. I mean, he really hates heavy metal, but he would rather listen to that than this score by Tchaikovsky."

"I know that, he told me, but you see, it's your favorite. I tried to tell him it was getting harder and harder to fill the concert hall for a charity affair, much less with a choice not everyone is familiar with. I mean, everyone loves *Swan Lake* and *The Nutcracker,* but not his Violin Concerto. What can I say? He wore me down, and the surprise of it all is that we sold out the first month."

"When?"

"What, when what?"

"When did he ask you to do this, the selection?"

"Oh, let me think. It was the middle of the summer, right before David got his cast off. I remember…, it was the night of Richard's birthday party. At first, I thought he was joking, but he called me every day until I agreed to look into it. I mean, I had to check with the guest conductor and all, and when he agreed, I asked the committee, and they thought it was a fabulous idea. Michael? Are you all right?"

"Yes Holly, I'm fine. In fact, I'm better than I've ever been in my whole life."

"Well, you look like the cat that ate the queen's cookies or something like that. I was never very proficient with nursery rhymes."

Richard decided someone should color-code limousines. They all looked alike. He paced outside the concert hall, checking his watch every few seconds. He had made good time after leaving the office, but then the traffic had been in his favor. Where were they?

The limo stopped at the curb, and Gill jumped out of the back seat before the driver could open the door. "Richard, we made it. Traffic was terrible, but here's your princess." Gill handed Michael out of the back seat and into Richard's arms.

"Wow, you look beautiful. You are beautiful."

Michael did a small pirouette. "It's the dress. Who wouldn't look nice in this dress?" She wore one of the dresses he had bought for her in Reno. It was white on white, a brocade top, empire design that rose high on her neck with long, fitted sleeves. The chiffon skirt, like her wedding dress, fell softly to her ankles. Her hair was down, framing her face with a deep richness that shimmered from the lights overhead.

Richard shielded her from the crush of the crowd as he took her arm and headed for his box. As soon as they were seated, Michael turned and kissed him. When she finally lifted her lips, she watched and enjoyed the way he savored her touch and the tiny quivers that shook them both.

"Thank you," she whispered as she kissed him again.

"Did I do something special? That was some kiss."

"Yes, I mean, knowing how much you hate the music you'll be sitting through for the next few hours, I'd say that was pretty special."

"Holly told you. She wasn't supposed to say anything, and I don't hate the music. In fact, I'm actually learning to enjoy it."

She started to say more, but Holly and Gill entered the box just as the lights dimmed and the music began.

During the intermission, Michael stayed seated while the others stretched their legs. She needed time to plan how she was going to tell Richard that she wanted to share his room, his life, everything. He loved her. Michael knew it now; he really loved her. Richard had buried his past. He'd tried to tell her, but she'd been so blind, so hurt, refusing to believe that he trusted her without any reservations, forcing him to take the only avenue left opened to him.

Hal's words had opened the door, allowing her to see that Richard had needed her, was grateful to her, but actions speak louder than words sometimes, and even though he all but shouted his love from the rooftops, it had taken a simple gesture like tonight to make her finally understand the truth.

The second half of the program flew by. She enjoyed the concert, but she wanted to leave, to go home with Richard— to their home, to their son. She wanted to sink into his large bed, to have him hold her and love her all night long.

"This is the worst part," Holly said. "I would like to sneak away and go have a quiet dinner and some good wine, but we have to stay and thank all the nice people for parting with their money."

Richard hugged Holly. "Hey, we understand. Thanks for letting us share the evening with you."

After hugs and kisses, Michael watched as Holly and Gill left the box. Richard looked down at her and offered his hand for support.

"Are you ready to go?"

"Richard, I have a slight problem. No, don't be alarmed, it's nothing. Well, except I can't leave, not just yet."

"Mikie, what's the matter?"

"Well, see, it's just that I slipped off my shoes, and now I can't get them back on. I've tried but—"

Richard bent on one knee and checked her feet. "Baby, why didn't you tell me your feet were swelling?" He tried the shoes, but he didn't have any better success than she'd had during the last fifteen minutes of the program.

"Looks like my Cinderella has a problem."

"You mean I don't get the prince? Richard, I'm sorry but can we wait until the crowd thins out? Maybe I can sneak out without anyone noticing that I don't have my shoes on."

"Getting you out of here isn't the problem, but how I'm going to sneak you into one of San Francisco's finer restaurants with bare feet might be." He put her shoes in his pockets and lifted her into his arms. "Don't worry, we'll think of something in the car. Come on, Cinderella, your pumpkin awaits you."

Michael didn't pay any attention to the strange looks they got as he carried her through the corridor; she had more important things on her mind. "Richard, I don't want to go to a restaurant. I want to go home. I can make us something to eat."

"Are you sure? I don't know if Cassie has anything thawed. I mean, she didn't expect us for dinner."

"I'll fix us a peanut butter and lettuce sandwich; only this time I'll put sliced bananas and strawberry jam on it too." She couldn't help nibbling on the edge of his ear.

"Wow, my mouth's watering already. How can I resist an offer like that? Are you sure you want to go home?"

"Yes. You see, if we go home now, maybe I'd have enough time to move some of my things before it's time to go to bed."

Richard stopped in the middle of the lobby, causing the flow of people to detour around them. "What did you say?"

"I said I want to move my things into your room. It's time I stop being such a fool and started acting like a proper wife. Richard, please say something."

"You're going to move into my room?"

"Yes, well if..., that is... if you still want me to."

In the middle of the concert hall, with hundreds of people watching, Richard twirled her around and around in a circle as he shouted for the whole world to hear. "Want you to? Of course I want you to. I love you. Oh, how I love you. Of course I want you in my room, in my bed, all the time, forever and ever, and beyond that." Then he kissed her.

"Richard," she laughed, "people are watching."

"Let them watch. We brush our teeth and pay our taxes. We can do anything we want. I love you. Oh, my God, Mikie, what was that?"

Richard stopped spinning and didn't move. "Mikie, did you feel that?"

"Yes, Richard, she's been downright bad today. I don't think she liked Dr. Sweet poking around."

"That's the baby? The baby's kicking?"

Michael kissed his startled mouth. "Yes, my love, I think you're making her dizzy."

"There, she did it again. My God, she's strong."

"Richard, I think your daughter is trying to tell you she wants to go for a ride in my fancy new Porsche." The baby kicked him again. "I think she wants her daddy to take us home."

EPILOGUE

"M OM, GUESS WHAT?" DAVID AND his friend Joey stormed into the kitchen with Bo in hot pursuit. Michael waited for the timer to go off, deciding that this was the last baking she was going to do until the baby was born. She looked at her watch. It was only ten to three, but she wished it were later. If it were six, Richard would be here rubbing her feet and legs. Oh, he did have great hands.

"What am I supposed to guess, sweet one?"

"Well, see, I forgot to tell you when I came home, but I got kicked out of school today. I got in a fight, and they just kicked me out." David waited until he saw the look on her face then shouted. "April fool's! Gotcha! Huh, Mom?"

"Oh David, you're so funny. You better never come home and tell me you've been kicked out of school."

David hugged her and the baby. Dad called it a two for one, 'cause Mom was so big, but he liked it—liked to feel his sister kick. "What time is it? Joey has to be ready to go home at three. Is it three yet?"

"Almost. Maybe you guys better clean up and get ready for his ride and put Bo outside in his run"

The timer went off, but as Michael reached to take the cookies out of the oven, she felt a terrible pain. She'd had nagging little pains for the past two days, but she didn't think they were actually contractions so she hadn't said anything. Now that she thought about it, last night she hadn't slept well. Michael dropped the cookie sheet on the counter and grabbed her stomach just as the warm liquid ran down her leg.

"David, David, come quick."

315

David heard the car pull up in front of the house at the same time he heard his mother calling his name. He ran into the kitchen and saw her sitting on the floor. "Mama, are you okay. Oh, Mama, what's the matter?"

"David, listen to me. You have to help me. Come here." Michael took his shaking hand and kissed it. "It's okay. Don't be scared. It's just the baby. Now, I want you to call 9-1-1, just like we talked about. Just dial 9-1-1 and tell them to send an ambulance. Now sweetheart, do it now. Hurry."

Joey had stayed behind David like a second skin, but now he tore out of the kitchen and out the front door to get his cousin as David ran to the telephone.

David punched the autodial. "Ruthie? Tell my dad to hurry. We're having a baby, NOW! Tell him to come quick." Then he pressed the disconnect button and dialed 9-1-1. "Come quick, my mom's having our baby. Come quick. Yes ma'am. Yes, that's our address, but you gotta come quick, you gotta come NOW! Please." He hung up the phone and sat by Michael on the floor. She was just about to tell him it was going to be all right when the spitting image of Don Johnson dropped down beside them, a younger version to be sure, but with the same eyes and smile.

"Hi, I'm Tommy Walker."

Michael couldn't speak. She knew her mouth was open, but she just stared at this gorgeous young man who took her hands in his, rubbing them together. Could this be *the* Tommy Walker, the guy with all the answers to life's little problems? She knew Tommy Walker was Joey's cousin, knew he was older, but she'd always thought more like twelve or so, not this great-looking, young man.

"Ma'am? It looks like your water broke, is that correct? How far along are you?"

Michael came to her senses. "I'm due, well, almost, I think, but please don't call me ma'am."

"Her name's Michael. She's my mom, and we're having a baby. I called my dad and 9-1-1."

"Okay, Michael. Look, I'm a fourth-year medical student at Stanford. If you don't mind, I mean, I might be able to help. Would you mind if I examined you?"

"Oh my God, who would have thought it?"

"What?"

"Nothing—just a private thought. Sure, go ahead." Michael grabbed her stomach and moaned. After what seemed like forever, the contraction eased and she breathed normally. At least, she tried to.

"First of all, how long ago did your water break?"

She told him.

"Joey, I want you to get me some newspaper, all you can find. Go. David, go get some clean towels and some pillows. Hurry boys."

As Tommy helped her change positions, she told him Richard kept a case of medical supplies in the hall closet in case of emergencies. After holding her while she passed through another contraction, he ran to get the case.

"We're in fantastic shape. There's enough stuff here to do major surgery, not that we'll need to. Please try to relax." He uttered a little laugh and a wide grin covered his handsome face. He took the newspapers from Joey and spread them out on the floor, then covered the paper with towels. He lifted her to the makeshift bed and helped her lie down. Tommy told the pale-faced boys to stand by her head while he raised her legs to examine her.

Meanwhile, at Richard's office, all hell broke loose.

"Did she call 9-1-1?"

"David didn't say, so I called the ER and told them to send an ambulance to your house." Ruthie ran behind Richard as he circled his private office. "Hal's on his way to finish here. Just go."

"But she's not due for another two weeks."

"Damn it, Richard, get a grip. Hey, what's two weeks? And at this stage in the game, who cares? If this kid is anything like her mom, the show's going to be over with by the time you get to your damn car. Go."

Back at the house, everything was moving along like clockwork. After his first examination, Tommy told Michael he didn't think they had time for a trip to the hospital. He had the two boys kneel behind her head on their knees. Tommy placed a pillow against their legs and helped Michael lie back. The other pillow he placed under her hips.

When he had everyone in place, he pulled on a pair of sterile gloves and said. "Okay, here's the plan. Boys, I want you to try to keep the pillow in place. Your legs might get tired, but we're moving fast. I think this is going to be one quick delivery. David hold your mom's hand if she wants you to. Michael, I want you to start pushing when you feel a contraction. I'll tell you when, so don't worry. When I tell you, I want you to pant, just like a puppy dog, but again, I'll tell you when. You two can help her with that, just pant like a little puppy with her."

"Is there going to be blood?"

"Not that you'll see, Joey." He didn't want his younger cousin dropping over from the sight of blood. Tommy adjusted the top towel so the boys couldn't see the birth field.

"Hey, you're doing great. Now, Michael, push. Push hard. That's my girl. Great, now relax. I know your back is killing you, but it's going fast. The cervix is totally dilated. Now, push again."

It took just one more forceful push and a little panting, and the newest Hampton shot into the world. Michael was crying, David was crying, and Joey uttered a loud "yuck", but it was over, almost. When Tommy held Michael's daughter up for inspection, he was crying too.

Tommy put a clean towel on Michael's stomach and placed the baby there. He wiped the mucus from her face, but there was no need for a soft swat to her tiny bottom. Miss Hampton arrived with a scream guaranteed to wake the dead. She definitely wanted everyone within earshot to know she was home.

Out on the road, the emergency forces converged toward the Hampton house. Within moments of each other, the two ambulances tore up the driveway, with the black Mercedes in hot pursuit, followed closely by Peter's sports car. Bringing up the rear, Allen's truck threw gravel into the air as he roared up to the back door with Cassie jumping out before he came to a full stop.

"Mikie! Mikie, David, where are you?"

David met his dad and the group of white coats at the door to the kitchen. "Don't yell, Dad. You'll wake up my sister. You should see her,

Dad. She looks like an Indian. She's got lots of black hair and, boy, can she scream."

Richard gently pushed past his son but needed to hold on to David when he looked into the kitchen. Michael was still on the floor, propped up against a stack of pillows, holding the baby in her arms. Joey stuck to David's tail, telling anyone that he never, ever, wanted to go through this again. In the corner was a stack of bloody newspaper.

Richard dropped to his knees by Michael's side as she lifted the soft new receiving blanket covering his daughter's face. He sat back on his legs and closed his eyes with a simple thank you before he kissed the new mother and child. "How, how did you manage?"

"We helped, Joey and me helped get the baby here. 'Course, Tommy Walker did most of the work; he did all the bloody stuff. He did good, Dad."

Richard looked at Michael, questions rolling over his face, which had just turned a stark white. "Tommy Walker... Good God, Mikie—a bunch of kids delivered the baby?"

Michael couldn't help but laugh. She saw Tommy over Richard's shoulder, returning to the kitchen after washing his hands. "Richard, I want you to meet someone."

Richard stood up, but when he turned around, he came face to face with an exceptionally handsome young man. He stared at the man and then turned back to his wife with an arched eyebrow.

"Richard, say hello to Tommy Walker."

ABOUT THE AUTHOR

I am part Cherokee, part Seneca; a nomad and I yearn to be off as I seek the elusive shadow wind that calls my soul and carries me deep within the mystery of life. I have lived by the sea, high in the pine forest where I longed to soar with eagles; in a valley near the river's edge next to God's creatures, and now I live in the delicate land of the southwestern desert with my youngest son and two small dogs who remind me each day how blessed we are. Please visit my website at www.barbarajduell. com